RAISING SPARKS

RAISING SPARKS

By

Ariel Kahn

Bluemoose

First published in 2018 by
Bluemoose Books Ltd
25 Sackville Street
Hebden Bridge
West Yorkshire
HX7 7DJ

www.bluemoosebooks.com

British Library Cataloguing-in-Publication data
A catalogue record for this book is available from the British Library

Hardback ISBN 978-1-910422-40-3

Paperback 978-1-910422-41-0

Printed and bound in the UK by Short Run Press

From 'The Souls of Those I Love', in Selected Poems by Anna Akhmatova
(trans. D.M. Thomas), published by Vintage Classics. Reproduced by
permission of The Random House Group Ltd.

For Noga

Humanity is born for trouble
As the sparks fly upwards
Job 5.7

Contents

Part IV
From Jaffa to Jerusalem, Earth
Nitzotzot, **Sparks**

Part I
Jerusalem, Air
Tzimtzum, Contraction

Chapter 1
The Tree

Every Friday was a race against the light. It moved in a sharp-edged square from the frosted window above the sink, then edged across the table where Malka sat chopping onions. She was trying hard not to cry. The light kissed her fingertips, slipped under her board, and left it floating in a brilliant puddle. If she dived into it, what would she find? Where would it take her? She rubbed her eyes roughly with a forearm, and the dust motes blazed around her like fireflies. The light passed through her unmoved, a door into another dimension, the idea of a window come loose from itself. When it reached the wall behind her, it would blush and fade, another missed opportunity. The ebbing light marked the arrival of *Shabbes* and all work ceased.

She chopped furiously, half-listening to her older sister, Estie, who was telling their mother what she'd learned that week, instead of doing her share. Little Devvie stood intent, her spoon poised in mid-air. Cinnamon poured from the jar in her other hand over the braised carrots for the *Tzimmes*. Malka said nothing. Today Estie seemed charged by the light. Her face was animated, her dark eyes flashed.

'We thank God for creating both the sun and the moon. Why do we need both? To teach us how men and women should behave. Men are like the sun – shining brightly in the day – full of action; women are like the moon, softly illuminating the home, and giving way to the shining glory of their husbands.'

Malka rolled her eyes. Her mother nodded from the sink, wrist-deep in noodles for the kugel, her headscarf so askew it seemed to be fighting gravity to stay on her head. Most people ordered their kugel from the local bakery. Not her mother.

Surreptitiously, Malka tipped the cinnamon-covered carrots into the bin and replaced them with a new batch, which she seasoned carefully. She kept her eyes on her mother. Her one hope of escape from the inane conversation and the sweating brown tiles was if her mother forgot something and sent her out for it. This week the atmosphere in the kitchen was particularly tense, as Estie's fiancé, Zechariah Gruber, was coming the following night for *Seuda Shlishis*, the final Sabbath meal. No cooking could be done on the Sabbath; everything had to be completed beforehand. Her mother, a great, if haphazard, cook, had been preparing all week, determined to leave nothing to chance. She dictated endless to-do lists, but in the middle of a stream of ingredients she would realise something was missing and look at Malka with entreaty. 'Could you just pop out a minute, Malkele?' Malka tried to make the most of these shopping trips, taking new routes, ducking down unknown alleyways, daring herself to get lost. Anything to delay her return. The apartment always felt even smaller after one of her walks.

'*A broch!*' her mother exclaimed, right on cue. 'We've run out of eggs and onions for the salad! How is that possible?' She took down the shopping list from the fridge, with each item carefully ticked off, and realised that she had written on both sides. 'I can't believe it. We only bought half the things we need!'

'Don't worry, I'll get them!' Malka cried.

She sprang up and seized the list before either of her sisters could volunteer. Not that they ever did. Malka wondered if her mother was just trying to get rid of her, or sensed her restlessness and was giving her a chance to escape. She was too eager to wonder about it for long. She threw off her apron and crumpled the list and the shekels her mother gave her into her skirt pocket.

4

'Malka! Your coat!'

'I don't need it,' she called back over her shoulder. The front door slammed, and she was free.

Their apartment was on the third floor of a narrow block in the Jewish quarter of the old city. On Fridays, this meant dragging all the groceries up three flights of stairs which stank of boiled vegetables and burnt chicken. As if this wasn't bad enough, she had to do it in the dark. To save electricity, the hall light went on for just a few seconds after the switch was depressed, before plunging you into darkness. Her arms laden with shopping bags, Malka would jab at the ground floor switch with her elbow, then see how far she could get before the light clicked off.

Malka shot downstairs, holding her breath. She burst out into the sunlight like a swimmer emerging from under water, taking deep, gulping mouthfuls of fragrant air, inhaling pine, wet earth, and jasmine. She glanced at the list. Sadly, it wasn't very long. She didn't see why vegetables needed to be kosher. Rather than catch a bus to the market in Machane Yehuda, Malka headed towards the Christian quarter, a route her father had expressly forbidden her to take.

The street sloped steeply away beneath her feet, slippery with crushed fruit. The air thick with the sound of Arabic as the merchants vied with one another to sell their wares. She loved it here. No-one noticed her in her uniform of long sleeves, dark ankle-length skirt and thick seamed stockings, her red hair swinging over her shoulder in a tight braid. No one except for the coffee-merchant at the very edge of the Christian quarter. Her feet always slowed outside his stall. Perched on his stool at the door, he nodded cheerfully. With his thick beard and moustache, the merchant wouldn't have looked out of place in her father's synagogue.

Each week, he taught her an Arabic phrase. She practised them at night in bed, rolling the sounds around on her tongue like sweets. She ordered her usual shot glass of steaming Turkish

5

coffee, taking quick sips and inhaling the aroma of cardamom. The trouble she would be in, if she was ever caught here, only deepened her pleasure.

'*Salaam Aleikhum.*'

'*Aleikhum Salaam,*' Malka nodded in return.

With the caffeine buzzing through her, Malka wove through the throngs of tourists until she reached her favourite stall with colourful mounds of fruit and vegetables piled at its entrance. She read through her list and chose carefully, hefting stubby carrots still sprinkled with soil, stroking the onions' papery skins. When she went to pay, she found a young boy of around her own age at the till, a slight moustache blooming above his lip. He looked at her appraisingly.

'My father is sick,' he said in Arabic-accented Hebrew.

'Wish him a full recovery.'

He frowned, puzzled, and slid her change across the counter. She blushed at her list. In her confusion, she had answered in Yiddish. She was meant to keep any conversation with men to a minimum. Especially men her own age. No wonder she was making a mess of it.

She picked up her bags and turned to leave. Something brushed against her leg. She started back. It was only a cat. It was a beautiful smoky grey, sleek and well-fed, unlike the hordes of gaunt street-cats that haunted the overflowing municipal bins. She put down her shopping and bent down to stroke it, but it backed slowly away from her towards a nearby flight of stairs, keeping eye contact. Its eyes were pale emerald.

'You want me to follow you?'

Malka delighted in discovering new corners of the city. Who better to reveal these than a cat? Clutching her shopping, she crept towards it. The cat moved almost lazily up the first two steps, then turned to look at her again. She darted forward, but again the cat evaded her. The chase began in earnest.

The narrow stone steps were worn water-smooth from centuries of passage. They seemed to curve in on themselves, like an ear listening to her footfalls. As she climbed, unfamiliar cooking scents drifted past, reminding her that she should be heading home.

The stairs opened suddenly onto a sweeping promenade, which overlooked the Western Wall from an unfamiliar angle. From here she could see only a curved sliver of the wall, a crescent, which mirrored the symbol on the golden mosque just behind it. She would never dare admit this to anyone, not even Devvie who shared her room, but Malka loved the symbol of this other religion, and secretly called it the smiling moon.

She wanted to put her bags down for a moment and enjoy the view, but the cat was a blaze of silver in the sunlight, already twitching its tail at the far end of the promenade, urging her on. Just as she drew close, the cat darted down a narrow passageway. Malka had to turn sideways to pass through it.

She found herself in a small courtyard dominated by a wizened eucalyptus tree, which twisted and strained against the paving stones that held it prisoner. Malka spotted her quarry across the courtyard, scratching at a small wooden door. It could not escape her now. She tiptoed through the cool shadows, wobbling a little on the uneven stones. The door had once been sky blue, but the paint was chipped and faded. It was slightly ajar.

Just as she reached it, the cat sprang through the gap. Malka stood staring foolishly at the door. She suddenly realised how hot and tired she was. She dropped her bags, clenching and unclenching her hands to let the blood flow back through them. The cat's head peeked round the door frame. Daring her. She grabbed her shopping.

'You're not getting away.'

The door creaked open at her touch. More stairs. She groaned.

'Hello? Anyone home? I found your cat!' she called. Her words echoed around the high domed ceiling, but there was no sign of life other than the cat, which was doing a little dance of welcome at her feet. Malka knelt and stroked its head. It pushed against her hand, curling its tail into a question mark.

Malka stood and looked around her. This was the biggest house she'd ever been in. The domed ceiling was crowned by a circular skylight, and the stairs curved up the wall ahead of her and through an arched doorway. Curious, Malka headed up the stairs, with the cat keeping her company. She ducked through the doorway into a large circular room, with another skylight. Most of the space was taken up with books. They were crammed onto bookshelves, and teetered in piles on the floor. Every chair was filled with papers, many of which spilled or cascaded down in frozen waterfalls. For some reason, the room smelt of cinnamon. As if she was in a forest of spices.

Then she noticed that a young man with a hat was sprawled in a little clearing on the floor, a mug steaming beside him. Malka tried to leave before he could notice her, and fell over the cat. Her shopping tumbled away from her, and the onions rolled across the floor towards the seated figure. He leapt up as she scrabbled to retrieve them, and their heads almost collided. It was Moshe, one of her father's students.

'What are you doing here?' they both said at once.

'You first,' Malka insisted, straightening her skirt. Attack was her best form of defence. Besides, what could she say – she'd followed a cat? She felt ridiculous and panicky. Alone with a man. *Yichud.* She'd broken so many rules already today, she shouldn't care, but this was more than a rule. It was a distillation of the air of prohibition that she had breathed all her life. She felt angry with Moshe for putting her into this situation. It didn't help that she'd surprised him.

'I'm studying,' he said, staring at her curiously. He had high cheek bones, and very pale blue eyes. A scar twisted one eyebrow. She remembered hearing that he'd earned it beating up a group of boys.

'What's wrong with the books in the yeshiva?'

He blushed. 'Nothing. It's just that there are certain topics we are not allowed to...' he stammered. 'Not that I hold that against your father, of course. I came to feed the cat. Then I just lost track of time.'

'So it's your cat?' It was the simplest of all the questions she wanted to ask.

'Who, Reb Moshe?' He bent to stroke the cat, which purred in most un-rabbinic fashion.

'You named your cat after yourself?'

He laughed. 'He's not mine. He belongs to Reb Zushya.'

She recognised that name. Reb Zushya was a famous recluse. A Kabbalist. She looked at the piles of books Moshe was studying, taking in their titles. *Sefer Yetzirah. Sefer Habahir.* The *Zohar*, in several editions. All Kabbalistic books. Every single one. Her father did not allow such books into the house, or in his yeshiva. *Tiflus*, he called them. Foolishness. There was something dangerous in his voice when he used this word, and any visiting scholar whose thinking smelt of Kabbalah was not invited back.

'Reb Zushya? I thought he was dead?'

'Yes. Belonged, I should have said. It was the cat that brought me here. Reb Zushya said that it was a sign. He took me as his student.' His voice coloured with a pride she remembered from her own years of learning with her father. Until one day his study door closed in her face, never to reopen.

'Why do you need to feed his cat?'

He was gazing towards the window and seemed not to have heard her. 'He died last winter, the day it snowed. They never found a will. It would be hard to find anything here. They searched through every book, every drawer.'

'Who did?'

'Rabbinical schools, both Orthodox and non. The Hebrew University. Various interested individuals. They found nothing. And now his home and his famous collection of books are all disputed property. Luckily, I have a key, so Reb Moshe here doesn't go hungry.' His eyes narrowed. 'Hey, how did you get in?'

'You left the door open.' She could feel a breeze from the hallway on her neck. If she hadn't closed it, then technically, they were not alone. She was still safe.

'I must be getting careless.' Reb Moshe was nosing at the bags by her feet. 'Forgive me, can I get you a cold drink?'

Malka nodded. Sweat snaked down her back, curled the wisps of hair at her forehead into tendrils, which she smoothed down with a finger. She would just drink and go, hoping that no lightning would strike her down before she got home. She didn't dare think what the time was.

Moshe disappeared through a curtained archway, and she heard a fridge door open and close, the hiss of a kettle. In the yeshiva, they called him the Russian *Ilui*. A genius. The term was not used lightly. Her father often brought his best students home for dinner on Friday nights. They all clamoured for his attention, each trying to out-argue the other. Moshe was always there, but he rarely spoke. She had caught him looking at her across the table once or twice, in a way that sent her racing for the safety of the kitchen.

He returned with a glass beaded with tiny droplets. Rather than pass it to her directly, he put it on a low table so they would not have to touch. She gripped it tightly. A sliver of lemon bobbed on the surface. Tiny green flecks swirled through it. Mint, she realised as she sipped. How had he had time to make this? He was watching her closely, and she drank too fast. The cat cocked its head to one side, a welcome distraction.

'Why... why is he called Reb Moshe?' she coughed.

'Reb Zushya believed the cat was a *gilgul* of his teacher. A reincarnation.' He drank his cinnamon tea slowly. Steam arabesques curled in the air above him.

'I know what a gilgul is.'

'Of course you do. Sorry.' When he was embarrassed, his Russian accent thickened and vowels rolled in his mouth, refusing to leave. He pursed his lips. 'Remember the municipal cull last summer?'

Malka shuddered. In the hottest months, the council left out poison for the feral cats that had plagued the city since the time of the British; domestic cats often ate it too. The cats screamed all night, like children in pain. Although she put her pillow over her head, she had not slept. She'd held Devvie as they both cried angry, helpless tears. In the morning, when they went to school, they passed heaps of dead cats being loaded onto wheelbarrows, and carted away to be burned. Devvie, who usually skipped ahead, held her hand so tightly that she'd left indentations in Malka's palm.

'I remember.'

'The morning after, I was on the way to yeshiva, but instead Reb Moshe led me here. He seemed so alive in the face of all that death, like a blessing. Reb Zushya was so grateful, he actually hugged me. He said there was no such thing as coincidence. If Reb Moshe had brought me to his home, I was meant to be there.' He smiled at the memory, and for a moment his face was beautiful. Behind his curly beard, he was still a boy. 'We only had a few months together, but he taught me so much. I treasure every word.'

She sipped from her glass and found it was empty.

'Would you like another? It's no trouble. Reb Zushya loved it. I still keep a jug in the fridge.'

Of course she would. It was delicious. 'I'd better be going,' she said hastily. She set the glass down carefully on the little table. For a moment, they both stared at it. Moshe swallowed.

'Can I ask you a favour? Please don't tell your father I was here.'

She smiled at the very idea of telling her father about the events of this afternoon.

'Don't worry. Your secret is safe with me.'

Malka stopped at the head of the stairs. There was a tree growing inside the house. Why hadn't she noticed it before? It was huge, the branches reaching almost to the skylight.

'It's magnificent.'

'What?'

'The tree.'

'What tree?' He looked at her curiously, his head on one side, just like the cat.

She reached over the railing to show him. The tree had strange, crumpled leaves. She pulled one off, and smoothed it in her palm. It had writing on it. She knew what it was. A *kepitel*.

Growing up almost in its shadow, she went to the Western Wall almost every day. Jews travelled from all over the world to pray there, and so they wanted to leave something of themselves behind. They wrote out their most fervent hopes, things which they didn't dare say aloud, and slipped these paper prayers, or *kepitelech*, into the cracks between the ancient stones, pressing these furled buds of longing together so tightly the huge stones seemed held aloft by prayers alone. Perhaps they were. She had seen the *kepitelech* dusted with snow and dripping with rainwater, painted rose by the dawn, glowing and ghostly in the moonlight. Someone had been collecting them, bringing them here, and attaching them to this huge tree. But who? Why?

She stroked the *kepitel* flat, trying to see what was written there. But it clenched tight like a fist, then lifted from her palm, as if caught by the wind. A roaring filled Malka's ears, of many voices speaking at once. It was coming from the tree. The air around her grew thick, and warm as bathwater. She gasped. All the *kepitelech* on the tree had begun to open and close in unison, beating like tiny hearts. Each called aloud the prayer inscribed upon it, in languages familiar and unknown. As she watched, a clump of paper prayers tore themselves free, and circled above her like a huge bird. The beating grew fiercer, the crying louder. They were all chanting the same word now, over and over.

'Ayeka? Ayeka? A-ye—kaaaa?'

It was the first question in the Torah. The one God asked after Adam and Chava ate from the tree of knowledge. Where are you? Malka felt it was being asked of her. She didn't know how to answer. She bit her lip, and the taste of iron filled her mouth. The whirling prayers darted arrow-like towards her. Moshe made no move to help her. Malka screamed. She hurtled down the stairs, towards the door. She slammed it behind her. She heard a sound like hailstones hammering against the door. The prayers were trying to get out, trying to get to her.

She ran through the streets until she found one she recognised, and didn't stop running until she reached her own block. She hurtled up the stairs in the dark, navigating by touch and smell alone. After what she had just seen, she didn't know if she would ever trust her eyes again.

She was about to knock on the door, when she realised that she had left the shopping back at Zushya's. She couldn't go back, and it was too late to replace what she'd bought. What should she do? The hallway light blinked on, dazzling her. She heard footsteps on the stairs. She flattened herself against the wall so they could pass, but the steps slowed and then stopped. She looked up. It was Moshe.

'I think these are yours.' The light clicked off. There was a rustle as he put the bags down beside her. When she found the switch, he was gone.

'Thank you,' she whispered.

Devvie opened the door to her frantic pounding.

'Malka, what happened to you? Estie's going to kill you,' she said.

Malka hurried past her, trying to look suitably contrite. The kitchen was like a furnace.

'So you decided to pay us a visit?'

Her mother looked flustered, rather than angry, but Estie's face was pale. Now she really does look like the moon, Malka thought, and smiled. She couldn't help it.

Estie snapped, 'She just wants to ruin everything for me!'

'I ran all the way here.' Malka said. She tied on her apron with shaking fingers, then heaved the bags up onto the table.

Miraculously, the eggs were unbroken. She handed them to her mother, who slipped them gently into the bubbling pot. There was a twist of paper amongst the coins at the bottom of the bag. A receipt? She didn't remember getting one. Absently, she crumpled it into her apron pocket, pushed the change into the charity box. Her mother looked up at the sound.

'Sorry, Mamme, I got everything you need.'

'Except for the time to cook it in.' Her mother's pursed lips softened, like a *challah* crust dipped in milk. 'You'd better start chopping while there's still time.'

This meant that she was not in trouble, at least with her mother. Estie looked ready to spring at her. She focussed on the onions, which turned slippery and pungent once released from their delicate wrappers. Their pale rings brought back in a rush her glimpse of the mosque, the sliver of lemon in the drink Moshe had given her, his slender fingers as he put the glass down, the cat which was a reincarnated rabbi, and the demonic tree. She pressed her fingers against her eyelids, trying to stop what she was seeing. Somebody took her arm. Malka flinched. Their family never touched one another. Then the familiar smells of baking and lavender water lifted her head. Only one person smelled like that. Malka buried her face in her mother's shoulder for as long as she dared, and let her mother stroke her hair.

'Here,' her mother said at last, handing her a dish towel. 'You dry the dishes. I'll finish those.'

The egg salad was done with minutes to spare. Her mother clapped her hands, and straightened her headscarf.

'Come my *shaineh maidelech*. Let's light the candles.'

As Malka pulled off her apron, the receipt fell to the floor and unfurled. A single word glared up at her. *Ayeka*. One of the *kepitelech* had followed her from Reb Zushya's. She had to hide it. She scooped it up and pressed it surreptitiously into the slot of the charity box. As she covered her eyes and recited the Sabbath blessing with her sisters, the setting sun stained her fingers like blood.

Chapter 2
Holy Pizza

How she hated Zechariah Gruber. She hated the way he chewed with his mouth open, his coarse lips flecked with grease. She hated the way he held his knife upright in his fist, like a weapon. She hated his scab-coloured beard. Only his bulk distinguished him. He moved with lazy grace, as though he were saving his energy for something much more important. But what could be more important than her sister?

She took refuge in the kitchen as often as she could without attracting attention. It wasn't only Zechariah she was hiding from. She had to force herself not to look at the charity box. Touching it was forbidden on the Sabbath, otherwise she would have emptied it onto the table, to see if she had imagined that scrap of paper last night. Of course she had. Haunted by the memory of the prayer-bird, she jumped every time she felt a tremor in the air. Thank God we never have chicken, Malka thought. Luckily, Estie saw her attempt to re-arrange the food platters as an act of contrition.

'Thanks Malka. Sorry I shouted at you last night. I was just anxious. But it's going well, don't you think? Wasn't it thoughtful, the way he passed me the potatoes?'

'*I* passed you the potatoes,' Malka said.

But her sister's optimism was incurable. This was only the third time she had met Zechariah. The first had also been in their home, with her parents just out of earshot in the kitchen, so it didn't count as far as Malka was concerned. But he had impressed Estie by taking her out for pizza on their only date.

It seemed a bit juvenile to Malka as a setting to entertain the possibility of marriage, but Estie had never eaten pizza before. Neither had Malka, although she'd often pressed her face to the window of the supervised pizzeria. It had separate seating for men and women, of course, but a few stools near the counter allowed them to sit tantalisingly close to each other as they waited for their orders. For this reason, the place was off-limits, as it was 'a place of levity'. But a *shidduch* date was different. It was a vital step towards marriage, the only time the couple would see one another alone before they wed. 'He had to book our stools, just like in a real restaurant,' Estie reported with excitement. Malka had annoyed Estie intensely by asking more questions about the food at that momentous encounter than the conversation.

'Next time I'll bring some home for you,' she said.

'That would be great, Estie,' Malka grinned. 'If there is a next time. By the way, you still have some pizza sauce on your chin.'

'What!'

'Just kidding.'

Estie had chased her round the table.

Devvie popped in to see what she was missing. She joined the sisterly huddle by the counter.

'So when are you getting married, Estie?' she asked.

'Shh! He hasn't asked me yet. But it's only a matter of time, God willing.'

Devvie was only fourteen, but Malka knew she kept a wedding scrapbook hidden under her bed. Malka had woken once late at night, thinking she heard mice, and watched as bridal dresses, bouquets and sleek toasters floated past in the glow of her sister's torch. No magazines were allowed in the house, and Malka had wondered how her sister had smuggled them in. She kept her sister's secret, and had to bite back the urge to tease her about it now.

Of course, Zechariah wouldn't ask her sister directly. He'd go through her father. Already, there had been circumspect investigations on both sides, to unearth any family secrets, such as madness, disability, or genetic conditions that might preclude this match. That was why she hadn't breathed a word to her sisters about her own strange vision last night. She had managed to glean a few salient facts of her own about Zechariah. In Malka's community, scholarship was valued above all else. Traditionally, the man who married the Rosh Yeshiva's eldest daughter became his successor, and was supposed to be a great scholar.

'Zechariah isn't even in the top *shiur*,' Malka said, before she could stop herself.

'That just means he's normal,' Estie hissed back. 'Not that you'd know anything about it.'

'*Is* he?' This was as close as Malka dared come to asking why he was an only child, and Estie understood her. 'What if he's spoiled, like rotten fruit?'

'They couldn't have any more,' Estie whispered furiously. 'His mother nearly died. Happy now?'

Malka felt terrible. She'd had no idea the family bravado was concealing tragedy. That made it almost heroic. She tried to catch her sister's arm, but Estie shrugged her off. Why was she making things so difficult for Estie? She knew why. Tradition dictated that they had to be married in turn. After Estie, she was next. And she was never getting married. For Malka, marriage was a cage, a prison by another name. No matter how many pictures Devvie stuck in her album.

Back in the dining room, Zechariah's father was holding forth. A successful businessman, he sported a clipped goatee instead of the full beard men in their community usually wore. It bobbed when he spoke and made him look like a startled goat. He caught Malka staring, and her face burned. He tugged the clump of grass on his chin with one hand.

'Regrettably, one has to show a different face in our dealings with the *Chiloinim*,' he said. She tried to revise her opinion of him more favourably. He owed her no explanation.

'In the world, but not *of* it,' her father commented approvingly. His deep bass thrummed through the table top. Malka could feel it through her glass. Once he had spoken, there was no more to be said.

Malka hid her grimace behind her hand. She glanced at Mrs Gruber. She was little better. She had arrived swathed in sagging layers of purple fabric, like an expensive wedding cake which had been left out for too long in the sun. She pursed her lips each time her husband spoke, only resuming eating when he'd finished. It was as if her whole life took place in his silences. So far, there hadn't been many of those. She kept hoping Zechariah would say something stupid, but he was clearly under strict instructions. He barely said a word during the meal, opening his mouth only to cram another mouthful in. There were fragments of carrot decorating his beard. He nodded vigorously as her father spoke, and a brief orange shower pattered into his plate. Malka was used to hearing her father addressed in the third person by his students, but there was something ridiculous about it from a prospective son-in-law.

'Would the *Rebbe* like some more of these delicious carrots?'

This innocuous comment was enough to set Estie aglow.

'See,' she whispered when they were next in the kitchen. 'He knew I made the carrots. He wanted me to feel appreciated.'

Malka considered several responses to this. She rejected them all. Time was short, and there were more important things to say.

'Estie, what do you actually like about him?'

Her sister eyed her suspiciously. Malka kept her face carefully impassive.

'How does he make you *feel*?' she persisted. Her sister pursed her lips, and looked down at the bowl of sliced cucumbers in dill and vinegar she was holding.

'Safe,' she said at last.

Her mother nodded approvingly from the counter. But Malka needed more.

'What is it you like about *him*? What is it about him that makes you think he's the one?'

Estie gave her a long look. 'You just see someone and you know. You know they're for you. Every person is born with the image of their intended mate implanted in their brain. That image stays clear for those of us who haven't filled our heads with *forbidden* knowledge.'

This last was clearly a dig at Malka's long-abandoned learning sessions with their father. He had singled her out, and Estie was not going to let her forget it. Malka tried to visualise her sister as a young girl carrying the picture of Zechariah in her head. It would be like one of those Russian doll sets in reverse, with the biggest doll inside the smallest doll. But for Devvie, this image had a different resonance.

'Has he touched you?' she chimed in.

'Devvie! *Tsnius!*' their mother warned.

Estie arranged the pleats in her skirt carefully. *Tsnius* meant they were forbidden to reveal or even speak about anything that related to their bodies, which were to be treated as cumbersome sleeves for their souls. Devvie had clearly been spending too long with her wedding albums if she could break such a cardinal rule. Their mother interposed herself quickly between her daughters, and handed Devvie the fish platter with a meaningful look as she hurried past. Soon Malka was left alone in the kitchen. She hesitated, knowing she was missed. But Devvie's question had stirred something in her.

Touching between unmarried couples was *tayva*, and strictly forbidden. It was discouraged within families too. Malka realised she had never seen her parents touch one another, even slightly, and they only touched her or her sisters in an emergency. That was why her contact with her mother last night had been so precious, and so unsettling. Why had her mother done it? Did her parents love one another? Why did this suddenly matter to her? She hurried back out, in time to hear Estie giving Zechariah a shy compliment.

'You have a beautiful suit.'

He grinned like an idiot. Mr Gruber nodded affably at Estie and answered for his son, his goat-beard wagging.

'You and your sisters will become the moral foundations of your own families one day. In our community, appearances are everything.'

However it had been intended, this remark seemed like a coded criticism. In the ensuing silence, the room filled with the flutter of papery wings. Malka could feel them brush the back of her neck. It was all she could do not to turn around. There was a muffled clinking noise from the sideboard. From the corner of her eye, Malka watched as the charity box started to sway drunkenly from side to side, as though something were trapped inside and raging to be free. With a start, she remembered the *kepitelech* she had stuffed into it. Somehow, it was trying to get out. To get at her. The box lurched forwards. Now it was right at the edge of the sideboard. Why did no one notice? In a moment, unless she did something, it would fall. She scraped her chair back and stood up. To her relief, the box straightened too, and was still. She leaned against the sideboard, and pushed it back surreptitiously with her elbow. Her father looked at her sharply.

'Malka, is everything alright?'

'Please forgive me, but I'm not feeling very well. I think I just need some fresh air.'

No-one said anything as she walked across the dining room to the hall. She kept listening for the crash of the fallen charity box behind her. As she closed the door, Malka waited for the rustle of wings. For the first time, she was afraid of what might be lurking in the dark. It was still the Sabbath, so she couldn't switch on the light. She had never gone down the stairs so fast.

Outside it was freezing cold, and she had no coat. Idiot. A few stars were struggling to be noticed. She counted three easily. So the Sabbath was out. Now her father and Mr Gruber would be able to get down to the details of their proposed merger; sign documents, talk figures. Barter for her sister. Suddenly just being outside wasn't enough. She had to get as far away as possible.

She began to run, not caring where she was going. Her braid came undone and, as she raced across the empty road, the wind whipped her hair into her eyes. So she didn't notice someone rushing the other way until they had almost collided. They both tried to stop, but it was too late. Something hard struck her in the stomach, and she doubled over, gasping. Holy books spilled across the street beneath her feet. A pair of white running shoes pointed towards her.

'I'm so sorry. Are you OK?'

The accented Hebrew was strangely familiar. Malka looked up at her assailant. It was Moshe. What was he doing here? At least she had another chance to show that she wasn't an ungrateful idiot.

'Thanks for bringing my bags yesterday. I'm sorry I forgot them. You saved me.'

Malka helped him pick up his books, and dusted off a volume tenderly. It was an ancient volume of the Zohar. It must be one of Zushya's. Her resentment flared up again like toothache. Clearly no one told Moshe what *he* was allowed to study. She handed it to him angrily.

'Where were you running to?'

'I'm just popping out for some food. How about you?'

'Trying to get as far away from home as possible.'

He looked startled.

'I think I made a fool of myself at a meal with my future in-laws. I may even have ruined my sister's chances.'

'I find that hard to believe. Your in-laws? Of course. How could I have forgotten? I've been hearing about it all week. Zechariah is my room-mate. I can tell you, I'm not going to miss his snoring when he finally moves out.'

'He snores? Yet another reason for my sister not to marry him.'

'Just tell her to get some ear plugs.'

They both laughed. On this horrible evening it was like a sudden gap in the storm clouds that pursued her. Then they closed in again. What would people think if they saw her talking to a man in the street?

'If you left early, does that mean you haven't eaten?'

Malka nodded.

'Malka, could I... would you like to join me?'

It was the first time she had ever heard him say her name. She had always hated it, but Moshe made it sound like music. She blushed. Thank God it was night.

'Join you for what?'

'Pizza. Let me buy you a slice to say sorry, for bumping into you so literally, and for scaring you the other day.'

'You didn't... I wasn't...'

Malka felt torn. She was both shocked and secretly delighted. Perhaps, as an immigrant, he didn't fully grasp the rules. Asking her directly for a date was unheard of without due preparation, going through the proper channels. But she didn't want to go back home yet. She remembered Estie's taunt about forbidden knowledge. Pizza with Moshe was exactly the kind of forbidden knowledge she was interested in.

'Alright. But just a slice.'

'Sure. I can walk you back afterwards if you like.'

'Is it far?'

'Not really.'

'Then no thanks. Too many eyes, too many spies.'

He grimaced, then set off without looking back. She followed at a safe distance. His white feet floated through the half-darkness ahead of her. They walked in silence until he suddenly stopped.

'Here we are! Lazlo's. The best pizza in the city.'

She tried not to let her disappointment show. The exterior was nondescript, almost shabby. She told herself not to judge by appearances. She was proved wrong as soon as they stepped inside. The place was like a fairy-tale king disguised in beggar's robes. Each wall had been painted a different, jewel-bright colour. They were hung with gold-framed mirrors, and the table tops sparkled. The place was packed, mostly with secular people, who all seemed to be talking at the tops of their voices. Was it even kosher? If Moshe ate here, surely it must be. The smell of baking dough silenced her doubts. You didn't have to be religious to like pizza. Hopefully, this meant that no-one would recognise her. She looked for Moshe, and saw him leaning against the counter at the front. Why hadn't he waited for her? She struggled to get through without touching anyone. Finally, she made it to the counter. There were still a few empty stools, and she slid onto one, suddenly conscious of her long-sleeved green dress, and how much she stood out. Moshe didn't seem to care. He wiped off the counter with his forearm and carefully put down his books; then he pulled over a stool and sat right next to her. In public. She felt ridiculously excited.

'Lazlo!' he called.

'Moshe! What'll it be tonight?' came the cheery reply. The speaker was very tall, his straggling oak-pale hair and shirt dusted with flour, as were his arms. His rolling accent was similar to Moshe's.

'A slice of Margherita with extra cheese.' He turned to her. 'How about you Malka?'

'Ah, the same, please,' was all she could manage.

They sat quietly a moment and watched Lazlo spin the dough above his head, then lower it gracefully, spread tomato sauce with the back of a ladle and sprinkle it liberally with two kinds of cheese, all before it had stopped moving. He slid the pizzas into an oven on the kind of long-handled wooden shovels they used to bake *matzos*. She looked sideways at Moshe. What should she say? Her experience of talking to boys was a complete zero. Then she thought of a safe question she could ask, something she'd actually been curious about.

'Why do you never say anything when my father invites your *shiur* home for Friday night? Everyone else spends the evening trying to out-quote one another, but you just sit there.'

'Learning isn't really about scoring points, is it?'

'So why do you come if you don't want to take part?'

'I have my reasons.' He stroked the scar above his eyebrow.

'Did you really get that fighting?'

His hand dropped quickly into his lap. 'A gang of boys were throwing stones at someone driving on *Shabbes*. I made them stop. They told me they had gathered the stones earlier so they weren't breaking any laws. I said that only made it worse. They wouldn't listen, and started throwing them at me too. One caught me on the forehead.'

He stroked the cover of the uppermost book. It was such a familiar, intimate gesture, it was almost shocking. It was the book she'd picked up. The same dark green as her dress.

'Doesn't this belong to Reb Zushya?'

He nodded, blushing to the tips of his ears. His scar stood out, a white seam. 'I know I shouldn't take it out. It's an early edition of the Zohar, hundreds of years old. But then, so is everything in Reb Zushya's library. I'm sure he'd rather it was used than locked in some humidity-controlled vault.'

'I doubt he'd appreciate food stains though.'

'Well, I can't take this book to the yeshiva, or I'd get into trouble. To be honest, I love studying Kabbalah here. First, it means I look like a weirdo, so no-one bothers me. Second, I can't imagine a more mystical place.'

Malka looked around in case she was missing something. 'You must be joking.'

'Actually, one of my favourite ideas from the Safed Kabbalists,' he said, stroking the volume again, 'is that there is a spark hidden inside everything and everyone in the world – every encounter, every experience, and every sensation. If you can be really present in the moment, you can set a spark free and return it to its source.'

Holy pizza? The only sparks she saw were the ones dancing in the air around the oven. With a flourish, Lazlo placed two huge wheels spinning on the counter before them.

'I thought you said just one slice?' Malka suddenly remembered the stories about Moshe being a glutton, the bags of food he carried away from her house after the meal. It was Lazlo who answered her.

'Believe me, one slice is never enough. As it's your first time here, it's on the house.'

The pizza did smell heavenly. Malka was ravenous. She tore into it with her fingers, relieved that they no longer had to talk. It was so hot that she burned the roof of her mouth, and gulped from the glass of water Moshe handed her.

'Why are you always in such a hurry? Let it cool down first,' he laughed. Somehow, she didn't mind him laughing at her.

'Lazlo is right, this is my first time.' Eating pizza, and going on a date, she thought. This was a date, wasn't it?

'Well, if you eat it slowly, it'll last longer. Unless you need to get home?'

She shook her head, her mouth full, and watched his long fingers tear thin strips from his pizza, roll them up, and pop them into his mouth. Was that how you were supposed to do it? He had a splash of sauce on his cheek. She touched her own cheek and made a wiping gesture. He grabbed a handful of napkins from a metal dispenser, mopping roughly at the stain.

'Sorry, I'm not used to company. How is your pizza? Or should I say, how was it?'

'Delicious,' she said, her mouth still full. 'The dough is so crisp.'

'Hear that Lazlo? Another convert!'

Lazlo favoured them with a gold-toothed grin.

'He was an engineer back home,' Moshe said.

'Now I engineer excellent pizza!' Lazlo grinned again.

For the first time she could remember, Malka felt included in a conversation. Was there something wrong with her that she preferred the company of men? Why did she listen so hard when men spoke? Perhaps because they could travel freely in a world that was forbidden to her. Half-heartedly, she tried to rekindle her resentment. But she was having too much fun.

Moshe leaned forward. 'Now it's my turn to ask you some questions.'

'About what?'

'The tree that you saw at Reb Zushya's house.'

Malka took a deep breath. I will not run away, she told herself. Whatever she said would sound crazy. So she decided to trust him. As simply as possible, she described what she'd experienced in Reb Zushya's hallway, leaving out how terrified she'd felt, and the *kepitel* that had followed her home. She waited for him to tell her she'd imagined it.

Moshe looked at her strangely. 'You saw the heavenly tree?'

She laughed. 'There was nothing heavenly about it.'

Moshe opened the green volume carefully on the counter. 'This is by the great Lion of Safed, Isaac Luria. He was the last person to see the tree you are talking about. Here, let me show you.' She peered over his shoulder, their heads almost touching. There on the title page was a diagram of a tree, its shape familiar, its branches curved around empty spaces, with words scattered amongst the leaves.

'I recognise some of these.' She pointed. '*Chochma. Bina. Daat.* All words for wisdom.'

Moshe turned to her. The flecks in his eyes seemed to dance.

'We have as many words for wisdom as the Inuit do for snow. *Chochma* is rational knowledge, book-learning. But that is only part of the story for the Kabbalists. On the opposite branch is *Bina*, intuition, the knowledge you feel in your gut. Between them, fed by both, is *Daat*, true understanding.' There was a new energy in his voice.

'What does this have to do with my tree?'

'Many of the oldest Kabbalistic texts, like this one, draw the *Sefirot*, this map of our connection to the Divine, as a tree. See how each word is drawn on a leaf, just like your vision? I think that what you saw was a version of this frontispiece, of the great tree connecting heaven and earth.'

'But it felt so angry. Not divine at all.'

'Angry, you say?'

She let herself remember. 'Well... hurting, maybe. Broken.' She shuddered.

'Look here, at the bottom of the tree.'

She followed his pointing finger. Unlike the others, the sphere at the root of the tree was split in two, and each half had a different name, *Malkhut* and *Shekhina*.

'What do these mean?'

'In the Kabbalah, the tree is the point where our world and the Divine meet, or where they once met. As you can see, this connection is damaged. This break is symbolised by the missing Shekhina, the Divine Feminine. The Kabbalists seek to return Her to Her Beloved, and heal the cosmos.'

'So in the Kabbalah, God is female?'

He nodded. 'Of course. Our ideas of God reflect all that is human.'

'But then why are women forbidden from studying religious texts, as if our brains would burn up? Why are we shut out? It makes no sense.'

'You are asking the wrong person. I've never understood this about your community. Either we are all in God's image, or none of us are.'

He looked at her and pursed his lips. 'Maybe that's why they all failed. All those great Kabbalists. They were all men. Perhaps it takes a woman to find the Shekhina. The legends say that every day God's voice cries out, seeking his Beloved. Asking her...'

'*Ayeka.* Where are you. Are you saying that the voice I heard was God's voice?'

'You didn't just hear it. You saw it. Reb Zushya, who shaped his entire life around the quest for the Shekhina – he never saw it. But you have. That has to mean something.'

'But why me? I'm not a Kabbalist. I'm just a girl.'

He looked at her closely. 'Are you sure about that?'

'Of course. I know nothing about Kabbalah.'

He smiled. 'Remember the tree. *Chochma*, or book-knowledge, isn't everything. I've read as much as I can, and I had a great teacher in Reb Zushya. But for me it has always been just words on the page. Perhaps you are the real thing, and your gift waited quietly inside you, curled up like a cat, until the moment it could spring to life.'

'So that's why you wanted to see me? To let me know I'm a Kabbalist?' Malka tried to keep the disappointment out of her voice. 'That's like telling a lion at the Zoo about the plains of Africa. You can access all these books. I can't. My future is to get married, and have babies. As many as possible.'

Moshe's face was a sunset. After a moment, he spoke, so softly she had to lean close to catch his words.

'You could think about it another way. Maybe the Ayeka you heard was aimed not at the Shekhina, but at you. Maybe that's why it was so scary.' He looked down at his hands, and spread them on the counter until they were almost touching hers. She withdrew her hands quickly. Her voice was fierce.

'It wasn't just scary. It was terrifying.'

'The Baal Shem Tov, founder of the Hasidic movement, writes that when Moshe saw the burning bush, what he actually saw was the divine spirit, the '*chashmal*' that sustains all matter. He was terrified too.'

'*Chashmal*? Isn't that electricity?'

'Maybe in Modern Hebrew. But that's not its true, original meaning, is it?' His voice was a challenge.

Malka closed her eyes, and saw pages turn. It had been a long time. She waited till the words steadied and came into focus. Other books in her mental library opened, offering themselves to her in a competing array. Passages highlighted themselves helpfully. When she looked up, Moshe was smiling, expectant.

'You're right. *Chashmal* is actually two separate words, *Chash* and *Mal*. Speech and Silence. So literally it means the silent language, or maybe better the language of silence. It first appears in Ezekiel's vision as the energy that sustains the Universe. But no one knows what it really *is*. It is as if...' She broke off, and found herself whispering. 'The Babylonian Talmud warns that looking for its true meaning is dangerous.' She quoted from memory. 'In Chagigah, page 13a, it says that a child was contemplating this word, and suddenly understood it. Instantly, a fire came out of the word and burnt him up.'

Moshe grinned in delight. 'God, I love it when you talk Torah. That's exactly what makes me want to learn Kabbalah. The lure of the forbidden.'

'Why would you want to learn something so dangerous?'

'The hope that there might be something hidden beneath the surface of my life, like a secret map of dreams.' He closed the volume gently.

'The Zohar hints that the Shekhina gives voice to the silenced, the supressed. She brings world and word back together, as they were at the moment of creation. I had the good fortune to stumble into a teacher who taught me how to listen for that silence. I can't find it in the yeshiva, so I come here instead.' His fingers thrummed on the counter.

'To raise the sparks?' Despite her misgivings, Malka caught his excitement.

'Exactly. In the Torah, the world was spoken into existence. So for the Kabbalist, it is God's language we see when we look around, that we can still hear if we allow ourselves to listen.' He leaned towards her again, so that their shadows overlapped on the counter.

'Malka, please don't be offended. How do you know so much? I thought girls in your community are allowed only a very basic religious education?'

'It's your community too, no?' Her face darkened. 'My father used to learn with me.'

29

'Really? But I thought...'

'Don't say it.'

'Listen. My mother cleans floors here, but back home she was a translator. She speaks eight languages. I got my love of books and reading from her. So I'm the last person to think women are less intelligent than men. It's clearly nonsense. But that's what people in your community think. Or at least, how they act.'

'Moshe, what about your father? Where does he fit in?'

Moshe looked down at his empty plate, as if the answer lay there. He pushed some of the crumbs together, pinched them in his fingers and scattered them again.

'He doesn't. He stayed behind in Russia. My parents are not together. He abandoned us, really. So we needed your community, my mother and I. They offered us food and a place to stay, if I studied in your father's yeshiva. But however hard I try, it doesn't feel like home. I'm still shut out.'

Moshe was so close that she could see tiny flecks of green in his eyes, like the mint in the glass he'd given her at Zushya's. She understood the hurt in his voice. Shut out. That was exactly how she felt. With an effort, she looked down at the counter, only for it to become a door beneath her palms. She recognised the grain, the familiar whorls and knots. Her father had made her swear never to tell anyone about their learning together, but breaking that promise now felt good, it felt right.

'My father's study does not have a 'do not enter' sign on the door. It doesn't need to. The eleventh commandment when I was growing up was simple. His study was the Holy of Holies, and only he, the High Priest, was allowed inside. So as soon as I could walk, I used to stand outside, leaning my forehead against the wood, willing it to open. Imagining that if I concentrated enough, I could pass through. Then, one morning, the door suddenly swung away from me, and I fell across the threshold. When I looked up and saw my father, I was ready to run. But instead of shouting, as I expected, he invited me in.'

'How old were you?'

'I was five. I was shocked by what I saw. Hundreds of books lay in drifts across the floor, tumbled across every available surface. The room had been visited by its own private hurricane. The disarray was all the more shocking because my father looked as though he ironed his beard every day.'

'He still does,' Moshe laughed. 'But how can you remember all of this?'

'When your deepest desire comes true, you remember. He swept a big blue chair clear of papers with one arm. My feet didn't even reach the edge of the seat. At first I was disappointed that the room was not filled with the trees and magical fruit I'd imagined.'

'You thought there was a forest in your flat?'

She laughed. 'In a way, there was. When my father started opening books to read to me, I realised that the embossed covers of blue, red, and black were really doorways. They led to places of wonder and delight. That was why he couldn't bear to close any of them.'

Moshe looked down at his empty plate. 'Your father is a great teacher. But he's also very... traditional. He took a real risk studying with you. It makes me see him differently. Do you still learn together?'

Malka sighed. It still hurt even to think about it. 'For seven years, we studied every day, early in the morning before prayers, and last thing before I went to bed. At first, he read to me, but soon, we were having a conversation. As I grew taller, so did the pile of books between us. All day at school, I counted the moments until I could race home and be back in the study with him. I felt chosen, special. Apart from one locked cabinet, there was nothing he would not study with me. He did not learn with my sisters. Estie, my older sister, still hates me for it. But then, just before my twelfth birthday, it all stopped.'

'Just like that? Why?'

She shook her head. 'He never said. One morning I came down, and the door wouldn't open.'

'That must have really hurt.'

'It did. I knocked until my knuckles were raw.'

'That's not what I meant.'

'I know.' Malka struggled to hold back tears. It was painful, to be this open, this visible.

Moshe watched the weather of her face closely.

'Thank you for sharing this with me. It means a lot. Reb Zushya used to say, there are no accidents. We have run into each other twice in the last two days. I never take books from his home, but tonight I felt I had to bring this one to Lazlo's. Then you tell me about the tree, and I understand it for the first time. Malka, would you like to learn Kabbalah with me? We could meet here, so no-one would know about it.'

Malka's blood thundered. It was a long time since she'd let herself want something this much. Wanting anything meant you could be hurt. If anyone did find out, she'd never be allowed out again without being watched every moment. If at all. She would kiss her beloved walks goodbye. For the first time, Malka noticed how quiet it was. She looked around. They were the last customers in the place, and Lazlo was wiping the counter with a cloth. It must be very late. Her parents would be beside themselves. She slid off the stool and brushed the crumbs off her dress.

Moshe stood up too. 'You don't have to answer right away. Just promise me you will think about it.'

'I don't think it would be a good idea.' she said in a rush. 'I'm in enough trouble as it is. Thanks for the pizza.'

She carried his hurt smile home with her through the dark. It no longer mattered so much what her parents might say. At least, not until she got to the front door.

Chapter 3
Broken Vessels

An hour after Malka had walked out on him at the pizzeria, Moshe sat slumped at his desk in the yeshiva study hall, Reb Zushya's Zohar concealed inside an open Talmud. Although it was now around 1 a.m. on a Saturday night, several hundred boys sat, stood, or stooped over lecterns all around him, swaying back and forth in their black suits and white shirts, the air fierce with their words and gestures. From a Heavenly perspective, they must look like notes fallen from some vast musical score, now jumbled and discordant. 'Don't you have a life?' he wanted to shout. But like him, they were taking refuge from their hormones, from a world that frightened them. Perhaps that was why they were called *Charedim*. The trembling ones. The chair at the front where her father sat during the week was empty tonight. Probably finalising things with Zechariah's father. Soon, he'd have a room of his own. In the meantime, Moshe often stayed at his desk until the early hours. He preferred a sleeping Zechariah, even though he snored like a bear with a cold. When he was awake, Zechariah stared at Moshe as if he was an insect. When he spoke, it was only to make fun of Moshe's accent. He was not the only one, by any means, but at least in the lunch hall Moshe could stare at his plate and pretend not to hear. In their room, he could only turn his back and stare at the deep crack that ran like a scar down the wall, wishing it would widen and swallow him or, better yet, Zechariah.

Everyone in the study hall was learning in pairs, apart from him. The other boys claimed they couldn't understand him, and left him to his own devices. Usually, this suited him fine. But tonight he needed distraction, an escape from self-recrimination. So he had broken one of the yeshiva's cardinal rules. No Kabbalah. Never learn it, never talk about it. Never think about it. Yet the Zohar spoke to him more than any text he'd encountered. It was written like a novel, with flawed, failing characters, constantly surprised by epiphanies of the everyday. The Kabbalistic worldview made his blood sing, made every gesture, every moment, feel fraught with potential. He'd tried to explain this feeling to Malka, and only made a fool of himself. He'd felt it at the time, that his words were pushing her away from him, like a drowning man flailing at a raft. No wonder the Talmud cautioned that the silent are considered wise. So he re-read one of his favourite stories, about the four sages who entered Paradise while still alive, only to fail, flounder, or transform themselves through love.

Four men entered the Pardes — Ben Azzai, Ben Zoma, Acher, and Akiva. Ben Azzai looked and died; Ben Zoma looked and went mad; Acher destroyed the plants; Akiva entered in peace and departed in peace.

Reb Zushya had taught him that every story in the Zohar pointed beyond itself, into the reader, then back out into the world. On the Pardes story, Zushya was more specific. 'Each of these men represents a part of us we need to acknowledge. Each embodies one of the four elements. Ben Azzai is Air, Ben Zoma is Water, Acher is Fire, and Akiva is Earth.'

Moshe longed to be Akiva, staring truth in the face, yet emerging unharmed. Akiva had begun his journey as an illiterate shepherd and become the greatest sage of his era, driven by his love for Rachel, Kalba Savua's daughter. Moshe could relate to that. His first glimpse of Malka had opened something inside him he hadn't realised was closed. Every hour he put in, sweating over Aramaic and medieval commentaries, was driven by the desire to connect to her. For it had been clear from the first night at Reb Sabbatto's that this world of texts mattered to her, that it was part of the air she breathed, the way she thought. He wanted to share that language. But tonight, finally getting the chance to talk to her alone, he had blown it. He pondered Akiva's enigmatic final words to his fellow travellers, looking for clues to what he could have done differently.

'When you come to the place of pure marble stones, do not say, 'Water! Water!' for it is said, 'He who speaks untruths shall not stand before My eyes.'

Moshe recognised that Akiva was quoting from Psalms. But what did it mean? Why did the warning unsettle him?

A strange creaking sound made him look up, past the bookshelves with their battered, well-thumbed books, to the front of the study hall, where two floor-to-ceiling windows rose on either side of the ark like wings. At this time, they were usually spattered with stars. But, though it was a clear night, they seemed opaque. The room took on a shifting, underwater feel. Huge slabs of dark water were piling up against the windows, pressing against them. No one else seemed to have noticed. I'm seeing things, he told himself. It is just a trick of the light.

Then the windows shattered and the water rushed in with a roar. It swept everything before it. Shelves, books, gesticulating students, all pinwheeled past him amidst the foam. Moshe braced himself and held tight to his desk, the whorls in the wood whispering to his fingertips of their lost dreams of the forest. The tang of salt filled his nostrils. There is no sea in Jerusalem, he told himself. Not even a river. That was one of the reasons he'd agreed to come here. He never wanted to see the sea again. He chanted Akiva's warning like a mantra. *When you come to the place of pure marble stones, do not say, 'Water! Water!'* He kept it up until the water slowly receded. When he finally dared to look, the windows were whole again.

The last time he'd seen the sea, it blazed before him so vividly that he could not look away. His father had been given a rare break from his endless concert tours, so they celebrated with a beach holiday on the Amalfi coast. His parents were somewhere behind him, stunned by the heat, while he and Yulia dribbled wet sand through their fingers, making castles like fantastic melted candles. He had been six, and she was almost four. Yulia. He still couldn't say her name aloud. How old would she be now? Sixteen, the same age as Malka.

She had looked up at him, squinting in the sunlight, and begged for an ice-cream, so he asked his parents for some change. His father had pressed a handful of crumpled notes in his palm. When he returned with some sweaty change, strawberry gelato dripping down his arm, Yulia was nowhere to be seen, their castle abandoned to the tide. He raced along the beach, carrying the ice-cream aloft like a beacon.

'Have you seen Yulia?' he'd asked his parents, finally. His mother looked at him as though he'd slapped her.

'You were supposed to be keeping an eye on her,' his father said, already fighting to keep his voice even.

They combed the beach together. His parents' faces blurred in a kind of emotional time-lapse photography. As the shadows lengthened, the reality of his sister's disappearance grew sharper, and they were joined by strangers, lifeguards, and the police. Their family became a story in the past tense. There had been newspaper headlines, blurred images of Yulia taken on the same beach only days before, her arms red from sunburn. Her body was never found.

When they returned to the flat in Moscow, Moshe's parents moved to separate beds, then to separate rooms. He had taken to sleeping in Yulia's bed, where the enormity of his guilt burned through him with every inhalation, the smell of her sleeping self curdling inside him like spoilt milk. The piano stool still bore the indentation of the times she'd sat leaning against him as he practiced every day, never hard enough, according to his father. Yulia had said she could hear the music in his body, trying to get out. He shut the piano and hid his music. No one said a word to him. Then his mother had started talking about moving to Israel, bringing home leaflets. As he lay in the bed he had started wetting, Moshe knew that she was running away, and he was her willing accomplice. Surely anywhere is better than here, he'd thought.

His atheist father had maintained a furious silence. Only once, as she was filling in forms at breakfast, he leaned close and whispered, loud enough for Moshe to hear, 'I knew you were up to something when you gave him that Old Testament name.' Before he and his mother left for Israel, his father had warned him against catching religion, as if it were a disease.

'I've been there with the orchestra. It's a crazy place. There is even have a mental condition called Jerusalem Syndrome. At some stage, everyone who lives there thinks that they are the Messiah. If you feel it happening to you, I want you on the first flight home.'

His father's warning had come too late. Even back then, Moshe spoke to God all the time, skipping school and heading out into the woods. There was a place he loved, where old, twisted pines gathered, their black trunks brooding on ancient mysteries. It was cold there even in summer, and he had to stamp his feet to keep warm. In that clearing, Moshe had truly felt the beauty of solitude. When he'd cried out, his words rang out like the first ones ever spoken. In the forest, God had seemed like a giant stag snorting just beyond the clearing where he sat, waiting for the right word to bring Him close. But Moshe never found that word. So he gave up looking.

Tonight, listening to Malka, he had remembered his failed search for that missing word. She had offered him a clue: *Ayeka*. Where are you? He tried it out, but without conviction. He sensed that it was her word, not his. His thoughts circled Malka, returning to her like homing pigeons.

The years at the community high school in Mea Shearim had been the hardest. The move had signalled that they had given up on ever finding his sister. They were moving on, moving away. He was not ready, and woke each day filled with a rage he could barely contain. So he used his fists, choosing the biggest, toughest kids. At first, they felled him often. Then he learned to dance away, to anticipate, counter-attack. Often, when he got sent to the headmaster for fighting, and saw his mother's face when he came home with a black eye or split lip, Moshe asked himself if they had done the right thing coming here. Who was he punishing? His mother had suffered enough, hadn't she? Then, in his final term, when they had given up on him as a lost cause, his class was invited to attend a special prayer service at the yeshiva, here in the study hall, as a reward and incentive for further study. They had wanted to exclude him, due to his unpredictability, but his mother had insisted. It was his bar mitzvah year; something had to change. It had worked, beyond his teachers' wildest imaginings. It was then he saw Malka for the first time. It must be five years now, so she would have been eleven. A high window had been opened to try and let in some air, and her hair fluttered through the railings of the women's gallery like a flag, not yet bound in the tight braid that she wore now. It had been hard not to stare. She had appeared so utterly herself, yet so uncontained. A natural, in this unnatural world. When Moshe asked who she was, Zechariah, whose fists had often left their mark on his ribs, just snorted.

'That's the Rosh Yeshiva's favourite daughter. She's *soo* far out of your league.'

Moshe relished a challenge. So he applied himself, and discovered he shared his mother's flair for languages. Now the initially forbidding snakelike twists of Rashi's commentary were as familiar as the lines on his palms. When he entered the yeshiva at fifteen, he went straight into the top class, Rav Sabbatto's elite group of rabbinical students, something that usually took years. It still eluded Zechariah, despite his best efforts. But Moshe felt no sense of triumph. What he cherished about his Friday night visits to Reb Sabbatto's home was catching a glimpse of the fine blue vein, shaped like the Hebrew letter *Shin*, that beat at Malka's temple. The other students prepared for these monthly invitations as though they were military combat, and vied to out-do one another with quotation and counter quotation, fighting for Reb Sabbatto's attention like children. But they could never prepare enough to outwit her. 'It's unnatural, that a girl should know so much. No good will come of it,' they would console each other on the way back to the dorms. It was all Moshe could do not to grin at her triumphs.

She was not allowed to sit with them, of course. But she didn't have to. Each time she came in from the kitchen with some carefully seasoned dish, whoever was speaking would lick his lips nervously, waiting for her to strike. She listened a moment, and always spoke with her eyes cast down. 'May I venture a word,' she would say, before skewering their arguments and methodically tearing them to shreds. Only then would she glance up, always at her father. Until tonight, he'd never understood the complex emotions that played out over Reb Sabbatto's face on these occasions. Pride, certainly, but also fear, even dread. Yet he never moved to silence her. What had it taken for him to go against centuries of prejudice, and study with his daughter? If he had already broken with tradition so radically, why had he stopped?

In the barren days between these monthly sightings, Reb Zushya had been his saviour. In their short time together, Zushya had opened up the world of the Kabbalah for him, a mystical dimension hidden behind the mask of the everyday, a world in which no gesture was without meaning, no act too small to raise the sparks. Everything either brought God closer, or drove Him and his beloved Shekhina further apart. What fascinated him was Zushya's confidence that even he, a Russian immigrant who no one else would talk to, could have an impact, make a difference. He remembered their last conversation, Zushya's voice as strong and steady as always.

'The Kabbalist, through his mindful practice, must seek to create *Tikkun*, cosmic harmony, and heal the wounds of history.'

'But surely, some wounds cannot be healed,' Moshe had insisted.

Zushya shook his head. 'Our challenge is to be present to presence, in each and every moment. When it expresses your own experience, your faith becomes living poetry. Of course, that means you have to enter the world in all its fullness, not shut yourself away from it like me.'

How he missed the old man and his gentle teasing, the threads of loneliness that had woven them together. He would have loved Malka, and welcomed her, Moshe felt sure. He might even have given Moshe advice, which he desperately needed.

But despite Zushya's best efforts, until Malka had spoken about her experience of the tree tonight, the idea of the Shekhina had been just that for Moshe, an idea. If only he could have asked her what the tree meant to her, instead of trying to impress her with his own learning. He must have seemed just like all the other boys she had derided for trying too hard. How could he prove to her that he was different?

There had been one other revelation tonight. He'd never seen Malka eat before. On those Friday night battles, when they weren't serving, she and her sisters stayed in the kitchen with their mother. She ate the way she spoke, with passion. He had to see her again, make her laugh with her mouth full of food.

'Just tell her how you feel,' Lazlo had urged as they'd swept up together.

How could he? How could he risk the life he and his mother had built here? Everything depended on him toeing the line, not offending the powers that be. But right now, all he cared about was her stricken face when he asked if he could see her again. He pounded the desk with his fist, and several students looked up and shook their heads.

He was always driving away the people he cared about most. His father had made good his threats and refused to come with them, or go along with his mother's 'mad plan' to find her roots. One night, from his refuge in his sister's room, Moshe had heard them arguing.

'Running away won't make it any better. She's gone. Just deal with it.'

'Deal with it? I'm looking after the child we have left. I'm focussing on the living, not wallowing in the past.'

'I'm the first violinist. People depend on me. How could I leave?' His father's voice was low, urgent. His mother's was not, as if meant for other ears.

'I have a job too, but some things are more important. They have orchestras in Israel too, full of Russians. The real question is, how do you want your son to grow up?'

'Every time I look at him, I remember.'

After that, Moshe had pressed the pillow over his head. They had divorced shortly afterwards. In his lowest moments, Moshe felt sure that this was his fault too. He reminded his father of all they had lost. Not just his sister, but the people they had been before. But in his more rational moments, he reminded himself that his parents had been living separate lives for years. Growing up, he hardly ever saw his father. For all Moshe knew, he had a mistress, maybe even another family. His father's absence when they made *Aliyah* had made their absorption here easier. It meant that his mother could use her Jewish maiden name, Mandelbaum, on all the forms when they arrived. So why did he miss him so much?

Things were good for him and his mother now, or at least, better than when they'd arrived. What a shock that had been. As the wind whistled through the peeling walls of the prefab the absorption centre had provided, a single bulb creating more darkness than light, he'd wondered if they had entered Circe's cave.

Back home, before catching the 'Israel bug', she'd been translating Homer's *Odyssey* 'for the modern Russian reader', surrounded by piles of Greek and Russian dictionaries. She'd make him listen to passages from Vasily Zhukovsky's celebrated version while he ate his breakfast, followed by her own efforts, not minding when he stained her manuscript with jam and hot chocolate. Our private odyssey, she'd called it. She had brought it with them to Israel but, as far as he knew, it was still at the bottom of her suitcase, tied with string.

His mother's gift for languages had served her well, even then. Within a startlingly short time of their arrival, spending time with the other immigrants and refugees, she'd learned Amharic, Arabic, and Hebrew, and frequently used them all at once in her conversation, together with English and her native Russian, sewing them into sprawling, magic-carpet sentences that put you down in a completely different place from where you started.

'Mama,' he'd say at the supermarket checkout, as the cashier stared at her dumbfounded. 'Here people want to keep things simple. They fear the unexpected. They don't want it in their conversations.'

Their own experience of the unexpected had been the flock of black-suited men who descended on the absorption centre. Moshe remembered thinking that it must take a powerful faith to wear black in such heat. Now he knew that the *Charedi* community believed they were still living in the Europe of centuries past, and this modern state was simply a mirage. Maybe that's what Jerusalem syndrome really meant – that you were shaken out of time by the trauma of the past. He certainly understood that feeling. He suspected that that was also why his mother had been so eager to take up their offer to 'reconnect with the true faith of your ancestors.'

True, they had told her what she wanted to hear. In broken Russian, one spoke about the work opportunities she would have in their community, the private apartment they'd have, the yeshiva-run primary school Moshe would study in, with all meals provided – followed by yeshiva itself, if he was good enough. The speaker had not looked at her directly, even once. At the time Moshe had thought this a sign of dishonesty. Now he knew that he was simply forbidden to meet the gaze of a strange woman.

Of course, they'd leapt at the chance. But the studio flat in Mea Shearim was even smaller than the portacabin: once he was old enough to have his own room, he was expected to sleep in the dormitory at the yeshiva. His proud, witty, excitable, gifted mother worked as a cleaner, washing houses for women in the community all day for a pittance. When he took her hands in his and felt the calluses on her palms, he wanted to cry, to ask her if it was worth it, this crazy dream of belonging that they were chasing. But they never spoke of such things. Most days she was so exhausted she hardly spoke at all. He brought her food from the yeshiva whenever he could, telling anyone who asked that he wanted to eat dinner in his room, knowing that he was reinforcing his reputation as a loner, a misfit. Best of all was when he could hop on the bus, cradling paper plates and plastic cartons of soup from Reb Sabbatto's. It wasn't enough, but it was something. He would watch her eat, hoping for a word, a smile. Sometimes he was lucky, and she'd look at him as she used to, and stroke his hair.

With a shock Moshe realised that he hadn't brought her any food all weekend. He hadn't eaten at all on Friday night, too excited by his meeting with Malka. After returning her shopping he had gone straight back to Zushya's, looking for clues to the tree she had mentioned. Tonight he'd been so upset he'd come straight back to the yeshiva. He looked at his watch. It was almost time for morning prayers. He could have saved her something from Lazlo's, but he hadn't wanted Malka to think him any more freakish than she did already. His mother didn't like pizza anyway, her only flaw as far as he was concerned. He would bring her something more substantial later.

He remembered the first time he'd walked past the unassuming shopfront of the Pizzeria. The hint of baking dough, oregano and tomato sauce, had reeled him in. When he'd stepped inside, the place was a revelation, a Fabergé-like confection of carmine reds and duck-egg blues. There were gilt framed mirrors; babushka dolls lined up on the shelves behind the counter. Back home he would have dismissed it as tourist kitsch; here it made him smile. As a child, he'd always enjoyed going to the bakery. He'd loved the dark, thick-crusted loaves they made in winter, which could break your teeth if you weren't careful.

Lazlo marinated chillies on the windowsills and, in the summer, grew tomatoes in rich profusion. Moshe appreciated such attention to detail. Each time he came back, Lazlo's smile grew broader. When Moshe had no money, he just sat near the counter with a book. He tried to pick up words of Modern Hebrew, but it was often hard to make them out through the chewing. After Zushya died, he started studying at Lazlo's instead, especially subjects that were frowned on in the yeshiva. The voices of the rabbis from the distant past seemed more at home there. After all, many of them had been blacksmiths, tailors, and gardeners. They learned while making a living, not as a substitute for it.

When he started helping out with the cleaning, Lazlo stopped charging him for pizza. While they swept up, Moshe poured out his feelings for Malka, scrutinised that month's sightings. Lazlo listened in silence. Moshe wondered if Lazlo had left any family back home, but he didn't ask. Not that it was easy to upset Lazlo. Once, when Moshe dropped a whole crate of glasses, Lazlo just laughed.

'I'll take it out of your wages,' was all he said.

Moshe's father used to say the same thing whenever he broke something as a child, which was often. Trying to be helpful, he dropped plates, cutlery, and his father's favourite mug. That had been the winter after they got back from Italy. Yulia had loved playing with it for her tea parties. He had spent hours gluing it back together. When he'd got back from school, his father had waved it in his face, laughing and angry all at once.

'It looks like it should be at the Hermitage,' he'd said, and kept it displayed on the top of the piano.

Moshe had thought the cup was even better than before; he liked the way the cracks let the light in, and often took it down to peer through it. Then one day he'd held it to his ear, and the world had suddenly grown bigger. He'd felt the same way when Malka surprised him at Zushya's. The power of that feeling had finally given him the courage to ask her out.

Coming through the door with her, Lazlo's had felt different. There was so much fire about her, the place seemed to glow. Her light touched everything. When she was excited, the scattering of freckles at the bridge of her nose darkened, tiny splashes of colour that leapt out of her pale skin. He remembered a line from a Yevtushenko poem. *Love's slipshod watchman, fear hems me in.* It was true. He was a coward. What else was stopping him going to Rav Sabbatto right now and asking if he could date his daughter? After what she'd told him, he knew Malka would hate him forever if he did. He stood up and paced all the way to the windows, which were touched now by dawn's rosy fingertips.

Gradually, the creaking desks around him stilled. More people bustled in for morning prayers. A few glanced his way. He felt jagged with lack of sleep, a thing of shards and fragments like his father's cup. As prayers began and he put on his *tefillin*, he concentrated on the cup and heard again the terrifying sound of the sea. He closed his eyes and disappeared through a crack, into the gathering light. Then someone grabbed his arm. Moshe reacted instinctively, slamming his elbow into his assailant before he stepped back and finished his prayer.

'I'm sorry. You caught me by surprise.'

It was one of the other rabbinical students, rubbing his chin in pain, but managing to grin nonetheless.

'Prayers finished ages ago. The Rosh Yeshiva wants to see you immediately.'

Reb Sabbatto must have somehow found out that he and Malka had been seen together. Apologising again to his victim, Moshe hurried downstairs to Reb Sabbatto's office. He felt both scared, and excited. Perhaps this was his chance to finally declare himself. If he could just explain how he felt about Malka, surely his teacher would understand? He might even be pleased.

45

After all, Moshe was one of the best students he had. That had to count for something. He took a deep breath, then knocked at the door, which was slightly ajar.

'Enter.'

Reb Sabbatto sat behind his desk. The tiny room was as austere as the man himself, a world away from the private chaos that Malka had described in his study at home. A couple of long shelves of books. The only other furniture was a desk, and two plastic chairs.

'Moshe Mandelbaum. Please sit down.' He motioned with one hand. His face was unusually pale.

Only then did Moshe notice that Reb Sabbatto's hand was resting gingerly on the cover of a familiar volume. Reb Zushya's Zohar. He felt a moment of icy confusion. He'd left the book open inside his Talmud during prayers. Someone must have noticed, and brought it to the Rosh Yeshiva. Why had he taken such a risk? How would he explain the presence of this book without breaking his promise to Reb Zushya?

For Reb Zushya had sworn him to secrecy on his deathbed.

'I was put in *cherem*, Moshe. If you tell anyone of our acquaintance, your own life will be ruined.'

'Excommunicated? Who did that to you, and why?' Moshe had asked. But there had been no answer. The old man had turned his head towards the window of his little room, and had reached out towards it with one trembling hand. Moshe had caught it gently and lowered it to the blanket. Slowly, Zushya's fingers had unclenched like a fading flower. 'Find her,' he had breathed. Then his eyes had closed.

If you were in Cherem, no one could talk to you, pray with you, do business with you. You were shipwrecked, islanded. Until the day you died. Zushya was such a gentle, holy soul. Whom could he have offended? It would take someone who hated the ideas Reb Zushya stood for. Moshe looked at Rav Sabbatto with sudden suspicion.

'Moshe, are you listening to me? I asked you to sit down. Perhaps I should not be surprised at your inability to follow the most basic instruction. I've called you here for reasons of gross misconduct. Not only have you brought expressly forbidden material to my yeshiva. You have stolen an extremely valuable book.'

Moshe remained standing. 'Rebbe, I'm sorry. Please. Let me explain.' Surely this great scholar would listen to reason. Moshe knew that it was forbidden even to mention the word Kabbalah within these walls, though he'd never understood why. As far as Moshe had discerned in his studies, most of the great lawmakers, such as Joseph Caro, author of the legal classic the *Shulkan Aruch*, which he glimpsed over Reb Sabbatto's shoulder had been mystics too. They hadn't separated reason and insight, law and emotion, the way Reb Sabbatto did.

'I'm afraid it is too late for that. Rather than call the police and jeopardise the life you and your poor mother have created, I have chosen to look after this matter myself. You have half an hour to collect your things. I do not want to see you in my yeshiva again.'

'You are throwing me out, just like that?'

Reb Sabbatto rose from his chair. He strode to the door and opened it. 'Your blatant disregard for the rules and values of this yeshiva leaves me no choice. It's a shame, you were such a promising student, but I suppose the apple never falls far from the tree. I tried to ignore the rumours that your father was a *goy* and now I am punished for my foolishness.'

Moshe felt his fists clench at his sides. He stared at his former mentor, his hoped-for father in law. The so-called scholar. He felt a familiar fire in the pit of his stomach. He was going to say something he would regret.

'You racist pig. Call yourself a Rosh Yeshiva? You are a disgrace to your religion.'

Reb Sabbatto restrained himself with a visible effort.

'With your invocation of that *treif* animal, you prove my point. Your reckless study of these texts has already led you astray.'

Moshe stood in the doorway, determined to have the last word.

'You think you are protecting the flame, keeping the light. But you are just extinguishing it. You worship the walls and fences you've built to keep God out.'

Moshe slammed the door behind him and walked away, trying to ignore the sound of his dreams burning.

Chapter 4
Into the Blue

M alka had been grounded for running out on the Grubers. Even her Friday shopping excursions had been stopped. She comforted herself that although Estie wasn't talking to her, at least she hadn't sabotaged her sister's chances. The cloud of silence that followed her around actually came as a relief. To her surprise, the only thing that really hurt was that she couldn't see Moshe. When he didn't appear at the usual Friday night gathering, she realised how much she'd been looking forward to seeing him. She'd asked to be excused, gone to her room, and spent the rest of the evening staring at the wall.

It was already a week since she'd run out of Lazlo's. She had to see Moshe again or she would explode. So she made a plan. A stupid one, but still a Plan. So after the Sabbath, she lay in bed fully dressed, pretending she was still unwell, and waited for Devvie's breathing to slow and deepen. She heard the key turn in the lock on the bedroom door. They were taking no chances. What if I need the bathroom, she thought. Am I just supposed to hold it till morning? It was a challenge. So she climbed out of the window onto the balcony of the apartment, which ran along the whole side of their flat. She crouched there, peering through the glass until the lights went out. Her parents were finally going to bed. Earlier, she had left the living room window open, just a crack. Now she prised it up and sneaked back into her own home. She took off her shoes and carried them through the apartment to the front door. She left it on the latch so she could get in again, and put on her shoes in the dark. Still without switching on the light, she crept downstairs, praying no-one would hear her.

Only when she stood blinking in the moonlight did she realise just how flawed her plan was. There were two places she knew of where Moshe might be. Reb Zushya's, or Lazlo's. But really, he could be anywhere. She willed him to be somewhere she could find him. She had to show him she was not the frightened girl she had seemed. She needed to prove it to herself, too. The thought of going to Reb Zushya's was the scarier option, so she would go there first, while her courage held.

She steeled herself as she climbed the steps towards the courtyard. She was taking a huge risk, openly defying her parents, but it was worth it if there was even a small chance that Moshe might be there. At the same time, she prayed that the house would be empty, and she could go back home and start to forget about someone who had so casually rearranged all the furniture of her life. Yet she also hoped he was a creature of habit, that he'd be there. She wanted to apologise for leaving so suddenly, to explain that it hadn't been his fault. If he wasn't around, she would leave him a note before she set off for Lazlo's. She had brought a pad and pen with her specially.

The walls of the old city were bone white in the moonlight. Her footsteps rang on the cobbles like an accusation. A group of soldiers on night patrol loomed suddenly out of the darkness.

'Where are you going, young lady?' the leader asked.

'Dawn prayers at the Kotel.'

He nodded and signalled for the group to move on, and she congratulated herself on her quick thinking. Dawn prayers were an established custom at the Wall. It used to be her favourite time to visit. She and her father would go there regularly after their late night study sessions. Until one night, a man standing next to them had started shaking, his whole body jerking, tugged by invisible strings, his shadow stretching out towards hers, impossibly long. Terrified, she had pressed against her father's coat.

'Don't be afraid Malkale,' he murmured. 'He's just a dancer, a dancer for God.'

But the man and his shadow had haunted her dreams for weeks. She clasped her arms tightly around her chest. Come on, she told herself as she entered the courtyard. You are not a little girl any more. Once again, she stood before Zushya's faded blue door. This time, it was closed. She knocked quickly, before her courage could fail her. As she did so, paws scrabbled against the wood on the other side. A key turned in the lock. She tried to prepare her face to greet Moshe calmly, tried to think what she would say. Her mouth was dry. As soon as the door opened, the cat streaked out over her feet like quicksilver. When Malka looked up, her father's face was suspended between door and frame. Malka wasn't sure who was more shocked. She looked past him into the house. No tree in sight. So he was real.

'Tateh?'

'Come inside. Quickly.' His breath was ragged, as though he'd been running.

'What are you doing here?' she whispered as he hurried up the stairs ahead of her. She felt dizzy, and she held on tightly to the banister as she climbed. It was as though two separate worlds had collapsed into one another. Her father stopped in mid-stride, as though her question had only just reached him.

'I came to return something. How do you know about this place? What are you doing here in the middle of the night? I was sure I locked your door.' It was strange. He didn't seem angry. If she didn't know him better, she would have sworn he was afraid.

'What are you returning?'

He started. 'A book.'

They reached the narrow upper landing.

'Why would you take one of Reb Zushya's books? Aren't they all about the Kabbalah?'

He gaped at her, then grabbed her fiercely by her upper arms and shook her, as if she was a doll.

'How. Do. You. Know. That?'

Her teeth rattled together. 'Tateh! You are hurting me!'

He collected himself with an effort, and let go of her. They stood looking at one another as she rubbed her arms.

'Don't you know the meaning of the word grounded?' he said at last. He sighed. 'Of course not.'

They climbed the last three steps to Zushya's study. Apart from a single low lamp burning on a table, the room was dark. He pulled a heavy armchair into the lamp-light, and motioned for her to do the same. The familiarity of the gesture was comforting, but the context made it somehow ominous. She stayed stubbornly on her feet, trying to gauge how much trouble she was in. He had never hurt her before. Never. What did it mean?

'Nu, are you going to stand there all night?'

She perched on the edge of her chair, ready to run if he moved again. He sighed and reached back, switching on another lamp. He looked old, faded.

'Malka, forgive me. Seeing you here, in this house, it was too much. I haven't been back here myself for many years. Since before you were born.'

Had he just apologised to her? This also was unprecedented. He looked down at the floor. 'Has it ever struck you that our family is – well – *small*, by the standards of the community?'

Of course it had. She'd been teased for it throughout her childhood. 'They are afraid to have another one like you,' Yael, the class bully had hissed at her once. It was true that her classmates were often one of ten, eleven, or even more children, and usually took care of their younger siblings, like mothers-in-waiting. But Malka had always thought of her own family as the normal one, and all the others as aberrations, part of the desperate drive to 'replenish the lost souls of the Holocaust', as she'd once heard her father say.

'I think it is time you knew why.' He stared past her, out of the cone of light, up towards the domed ceiling, veined with shadows. 'Your mother and I had great difficulties having children.'

Malka leapt up, her ears burning. For years she had hoped her father would talk to her again. But this was not what she wanted to hear. He never spoke about anything personal, never. This was more difficult than his silence, his violence.

'Sit down. Please. You need to hear this. You are old enough, and you are here. I owe it to you.' His voice was raw, pleading. Her father was behaving like a stranger. Or perhaps she only thought she knew him? This idea was so unsettling that she sank back into her seat. 'We tried everything, saw every doctor. Nothing worked. So we tried something else. Something dangerous. I felt we had no choice.'

'Dangerous?' The word echoed in the room, seeking a home. Finding none. Her father was the most cautious person she knew. Or thought she knew.

'We wanted a child more than anything. Children, if possible. But we'd exhausted every conventional treatment. We were desperate. Who ever heard of a Rosh Yeshiva without children? Your mother cried every day, .'

Suddenly, Malka knew.

'You came to Reb Zushya, didn't you?'

He nodded. 'There is a certain ritual. A Kabbalistic ritual.'

'I thought you hated Kabbalah?'

'That came... later. Please, let me finish. This is very hard for me. The ritual is very dangerous if performed incorrectly. There was only one person I knew of who I could trust to perform it.' He indicated the serried rows of books behind him. 'He didn't agree at first, but I insisted. So Reb Zushya performed it, and your mother bore your older sister a year later.'

Malka tried to imagine her father in the same room as a Kabbalist, but couldn't.

'What did this ritual consist of? Why was it so dangerous?' She remembered the bird made of prayers that had attacked her, chased her out of the door. 'Did he use birds as part of it, by any chance?'

Her father exhaled like a punctured bicycle tyre. 'Yes. How did you...? He brought in a large cage full of birds, and put it on this table. Your mother hates animals, and it was all I could do to keep her here. The birds are said to absorb the shadow of the *Other Side* which hangs over the... afflicted couple. The *kapparot* ceremony is a degraded version of the same thing.'

Malka had often seen people in the neighbourhood performing *kapparot* on the eve of Yom Kippur, waving chickens over their heads to absorb their sins, then slaughtering them to avert misfortune. It had always seemed to her a cruel, superstitious act, and her father had expressly forbidden anyone in the family to participate in it. Yet here he was, calmly describing how he had broken his own rules. Surely that made him a hypocrite?

'The birds were wild, and kept hurling themselves against the bars. The noise was awful. But Reb Zushya was almost dreamlike in his calm. He soothed your mother, got her to lie down on his tallit, which had a map of the Sefirot drawn on it.'

Malka remembered Moshe showing her the Sefirot in Reb Zushya's book. There was a connection here, but she didn't know what it was.

'Then, at a certain stage in the ritual, Reb Zushya opened the window. Most of the birds streamed off into the night. Only three remained.'

'And there are three of us.' Malka had not meant to speak her thought aloud. Her father started at her words. It was as if he had been speaking to himself, and had forgotten she was there. He rubbed a hand over his face, and ruffled his beard. Malka didn't know why, but this gesture unsettled her even more.

'I'll never forget the terror on your mother's face. She looked just as you do now. You see why I banned the study of Kabbalah in my yeshiva? It is unreason, madness.' The image of the puppet man and his broken dance came back to her.

'I've not spoken of this to anyone. I know I have been unfair to you. I hope that now my actions will make more sense.' He looked down at his hands, and up at her for a moment, then away.

'Please, continue,' she said. It was the phrase he had used each time she had sat in his study, as he smoothed out the page with his forefinger and pointed to where she had left off the day before. The effect on him was instantaneous. His head jerked upright, and he spoke in a rush.

'The three birds flew straight towards your mother. I moved to shoo them away, but Zushya stopped me with a look. They settled on her body. One perched by your mother's head, another at her feet. But the third bird wouldn't keep still.' He looked at her again. 'It swooped towards her stomach, then flew around the room in widening circles. The window was open, but it just flung itself against the wall, again and again. I tried to help it find the way out, but it fell into my hands. Dead.'

'The birds stand for us, right?'

He nodded wordlessly.

'If only two of the birds survived, then why are there three of us?' Malka felt that everything depended on his answer, that when he spoke he would finally unlock the meaning of all those years of silence.

He sighed. 'I still do not understand that. Reb Zushya said it meant that we would have three children. The birds were all female, so they would be girls. The one at the head would be the oldest, and the one at the feet the youngest. The middle one... the middle one would not live long.' He splayed his fingers on his thighs. He was sweating.

Malka trembled. All the anger, all the hurt she'd felt at those years of rejection burned through her.

'Do you have any idea what it felt like, all these years of silence? To show me a whole world, then snatch it away? Why?' Why did you do it?'

He glanced towards the window. It was slightly open. 'I thought perhaps, if we learned together, maybe we could find an answer. But as I watched you grow, each day it hurt more and more to say goodbye. What if this was the last page we studied together? I couldn't let myself get too attached. So I took the coward's way. I shut the books, I closed the door. I tried to leave you, before you left me.'

The shadows that the lamp cast seemed to slip and slide. Malka felt she was going to be sick. Everything she thought she knew, everything she believed, was wrong. She lurched out of the room, and fled down the stairs, just as she had the last time she was here. Her father called after her.

'Malka! Come back here this minute!'

He had no power over her. Not any more. She ran through the night as though someone were after her. Mercifully, the front door was still unlatched. She pushed her bedroom door open with her fingertips, and stood over Devvie, catching her breath. Her sister's rumpled face was so open. She felt she was peering back in time, at a girl she would never be. She lay down in bed and closed her eyes, then jerked them open. She could hear the flutter of birds' wings above her. 'Please,' she prayed. 'I don't want to die. Not yet.'

When she heard Devvie getting up for school, Malka turned her face to the wall and ignored the hand Devvie laid on her shoulder. She couldn't bear to look her sister in the eyes.

She felt Devvie hesitate in the doorway, reluctant to leave without her. Then she was gone. Estie was at the seminary having marriage classes. Her father had already left, thank God, and her mother was at the insurance firm where she had worked every morning for as long as Malka could remember. She sat up and looked around the room. This was not her home, not any more. If she stayed here, her fate would find her. Already the walls seemed to be closing in. What would Moshe do? Leap out of bed like a lion, like the Talmud said.

She approached her father's study. She didn't know how, but she knew it would be unlocked. Perhaps because her father had no secrets left to hide. As the door swung open, she saw what a shabby place it really was. A place for hiding from the world. Well, she was done with that. She glanced at the forbidden book-case, and shuddered. Her fear made her just like her father. At this moment, that felt like the worst thing in the world. He claimed to hate Kabbalah. If what he had said last night was true, then she owed her very being to it. So did that mean he hated her too? Then she noticed that the key to the glass cabinet was still in the lock.

She swung the door open, and ran her finger across the books trapped inside. One volume looked much older than the rest. It was dark green, the same colour as the one Moshe had brought to the Pizzeria. She took it down and opened it to the title page. It was the same book. There, in front of her, was the tree. As she watched, the branches started to writhe and dance, reaching up off the page towards her. She closed it quickly, and pressed the book shut with all her strength, fearful that if she let go the tree would force its way out. How had it followed her here? Then she knew. Her father had said he'd meant to return something. Instead, he'd locked it away. Shut it out, just as he'd done to her.

'No,' she said aloud. She opened the book again, slowly, until the tree was fully revealed. She dared it to move again, but it remained still. Dormant, she told herself. The title was caught in its roots. *A Tree of Life: The Writings of Rabbi Isaac Luria, the Holy Ari of Safed, collected by his student Chaim Vital.* The Lion of Safed. Of course. Moshe had said he was the last person to see the tree. It was the sign she'd been looking for. Luria had gone on a journey, found a new name, a new identity. What did the Talmud say? Change your name, change your fate.

She would leave a message for Moshe. One that only he would understand. She had no idea how she would get it to him, but she'd figure that out later. She traced the tree with her finger. If she was to understand it, she had to know it intimately. A piece of paper slipped out of the back of the book. It was flimsy, almost transparent. One side was covered in crabbed handwriting, columns of Hebrew letters in seemingly random groupings that made no sense to her. The other side was blank. She placed it over the frontispiece, and started to draw the branches. She had not drawn since she was a child. As she lost herself in the vein-like traceries of the roots, she realised why her father had really stopped studying with her. Not because she might die, but because she had stubbornly refused to. As long as she was a doomed girl, what harm was there in filling her head with wisdom she would never use? Every day she lived was not a victory, but a threat. She compared her copy of the tree with the original. Not bad. If she was to change her fate, first she had to understand it. To do that, she must go to the home of the secrets he had kept from her. Safed was a whole city of Kabbalists. Surely someone there would be able to help her. She would leap like a lion into her future. Every moment she spent in this apartment, in this city, was a moment wasted. And who knew if it might be her last?

She replaced the book, locked the cabinet, then slipped her drawing into an envelope she found lying on the desk. She wrote Moshe's name on the front. Even if someone else opened it, they would not know what her tree meant. She went to her room and hid the envelope under Devvie's pillow, then packed her schoolbag with clothes. She would need money. She went to the charity box which had tried to leap off the sideboard. Maybe it had been trying to tell her the same thing? She needed to leave. She stuffed the box into her bag too. They did say charity begins at home. Twenty minutes later, she was heading for the central bus station.

On her way, she realized she would have to get rid of most of what she'd packed. She couldn't run the risk of people in the station recognizing her description later, so she stopped in a charity shop on the way, painfully counting out the change from the charity box. The elderly cashier stared.

'Don't forget your receipt!'

'*Todah*,' Malka smiled. In Hebrew, a receipt was a kabbalah. Something you were given, bestowed. Like the blessing of a new life. As soon as she got to the central bus station, she ducked into a reeking toilet cubicle and slipped off her skirt. She pushed the hated, coarse fabric deep into the bin. Quickly, she changed into the jeans and torn sweater she'd bought, piled her hair up on her head and crammed a woolly hat over it. She walked out as casually as possible. She had to force herself not to look down at her legs. It was strange not hearing the static whisper of her skirt against her stockings.

Wearing men's clothing, such as trousers, was strictly prohibited in her community. A clear sign that she was off The Path. Once you left, she had always been told, there was no way back. She told herself she didn't care. She had hoped to feel free, unbound, but the jeans clung damply to her legs as she jostled in line for her bus ticket. At least they were not itchy like the skirt. This was not her only disappointment. She discovered for the first time what it was like not to be invisible. Without her religious uniform, she was a sitting target. Men, young and old, kept trying to get her attention. 'Hey cutie!' splashed over her like dirty water. She stared fixedly ahead. At last she reached the ticket office. A woman with dyed blonde hair sat behind the window, chewing gum.

'A student ticket to Safed please.'

'ID?'

Malka fumbled in her pocket and proffered her crumpled ID card.

'Sixteen! Shouldn't you be in school?'

'I'm going on a field trip.'

'On your own?'

Malka stared her down.

'You need a *Rav Kav*. For a semester or a year?'

'A semester.' That would be cheaper, she thought. She handed over most of the remaining contents of the charity box. Hurriedly, she filled in the form and attached a crumpled photo from school, which she carried in her purse. It was one of the few in which she was smiling. The cashier handed it to her with a flourish.

'You need the 982, from platform 18,' the woman said. 'If you run, you'll just catch it. The next one leaves in two hours. Next!'

Malka grabbed her card with a hurried thanks, and sprinted in the direction of the woman's pointing finger. Now she understood the benefit of trousers. They allowed her to leap over the swinging rifles and heavy duffle bags of soldiers, mounds of shopping, and buggies crammed with stupefied, snivelling children. She reached the bus just as it was pulling away. She raced alongside and hammered on the door. The doors opened with a hiss. The driver glared at her.

'Are you crazy? I nearly spilled my coffee. Well? Get in!'

The bus lurched forward as soon as she boarded, and she hurtled down the aisle towards the back. There were a couple of empty seats. Malka slid to the fogged window and leaned her bag next to her as a barrier. A fan above her head puffed out heat and diesel fumes. Just in front of her, a black hat swayed back and forth, and Malka could hear the familiar sing-song chant of Talmud study. She resisted the urge to hunch down in her seat. No-one would recognize her in her new garb, and anyway, no one would be looking for her yet.

She felt a brief pang. This was the last thing her mother needed before the wedding next week. Would they cancel it? Of course not. So many eyes would be on her family, they would probably have to keep her absence quiet to avoid the scandal spoiling the *simcha*. She couldn't imagine how, but she hoped Estie would forgive her one day. They would probably be glad she was gone. After all, what was she to them but an embarrassment, a burden? Anyway, if her father was to be believed, each day might be her last. You couldn't judge a dying person by the standards of a healthy one. Stop it, you're not dying, she told herself, you are just starting to live. Leave those lies behind you in Jerusalem.

She wiped the window with her sleeve and stared out, fighting her panic. The bus was winding its way down the steep hill that sloped away from the city she'd lived in all her life. A light rain slanted down. She watched the beads of water trickle down the glass. A line from Psalms rose to her lips: 'Those who sow with tears will reap with joy.' She slumped back in her seat. She hoped that was true. The energy she'd used to break away from Jerusalem's gravity had exhausted her.

Malka was jolted awake. She hadn't been aware of falling asleep. The bus had pulled in to a huge, sprawling indoor station, like a giant shopping mall. There were more people passing the window than she'd ever seen, even at the Western Wall on the High Holy Days. Even through the glass, the noise was extraordinary. This must be Tel Aviv. To her father and her teachers, it was the embodiment of hell on earth, a place of godless immorality. She imagined rushing out of the bus and losing herself in the crowd, but stayed firmly in her seat, the enormity of what she was doing finally sinking in.

Bags and boxes swung past her head as people hurried on or off the bus. It reminded her of Yaakov's vision of angels ascending and descending when he had fled home and his brother's curse. She was also in flight from dark forces that sought to confine and even kill her. But the people around her, sweaty and crumpled from the first leg of the journey, seemed far from angelic. Moshe had said there was a spark hidden inside everything and everyone, so perhaps she shouldn't be so quick to judge. After all, hadn't a cat brought her to Zushya's house that first time? Messengers could come in curious guises.

'Excuse me, is this seat taken?'

A girl with long, knotted hair leaned over her and smiled. Malka nodded, then realized too late that it was a man. Before she had the chance to refuse, he'd already lifted her bag up to the overhead rack and hunched down beside her. For the first time in her life, she was sitting next to a strange man. You can do this, she told herself, and turned deliberately to look at him.

'Hi, I'm Avshalom.'

What were his parents thinking? Why would you call your child after King David's rebellious, arrogant son? He had met a horrible end, killed in battle when his long hair caught in the branches of an oak tree. She shrank back. Trees. Death. The curse was following her. It felt as if the whole world had become a private language addressed to her. Malka couldn't trust herself to say anything, so she closed her eyes and pretended to sleep. Then she stopped pretending.

When she next woke, the bus had almost reached Safed. It had stopped in Tiberias, right opposite a sign for The Sea of Galilee. She knew it was just a lake with delusions of grandeur, But she wanted to see it. Until now, the largest body of water she'd encountered was the *mikveh*. She'd always thought that Jerusalem was missing a body of water. The Sultan's Pool outside the old city was a pool in name only. Her family must have realised she had gone by now. She forced herself not to think about them, and stepped off the bus. 'Twenty minute break! I'm not waiting for anyone!' the driver called after her. From the wan light, it must be late afternoon.

The lake was huge. She slipped eagerly out of her sweaty, scuffed shoes and stepped onto the cool pebbles that edged the water. At the same moment, the clouds shifted, bathing the lake in sunlight: streaks of blue and gold moved across the surface like a rippling carpet. The movement reminded her of Lazlo, whirling dough above his head into a perfect circle. He'd managed to make something new of himself, as had Moshe, both so far from home. They had seemed so happy, so complete. Now it was her turn.

She swept her arms above her head and opened her palms, casting her old self like bread upon the waters. She gave a cry of joy. If this was how she felt now, what would it be like when she reached Safed?

Then, far out over the lake, she saw the tree again. This time, it was hanging upside down like a thick frayed rope, its branches spreading right across the lake, their tips kissing the water. Its roots disappeared into the clouds. This time, Malka was determined not to run from it. She rolled up her trousers and waded into the icy water up to her knees. Pebbles gave way to thick mud underfoot. But as she drew close, the tree shimmered and faded. It was a blessing, a sign she was doing the right thing. She reached down and scooped up a pebble, a shimmering white that was almost blue. She rubbed it against her shirt and saw there was a cloudy swirl of grey on one side, like a question mark. She slipped it into her pocket. Shivering now, she unrolled her jeans over her legs and skipped back to the bus to warm up, carrying her scuffed shoes still covered with Jerusalem dirt.

The bus ground its gears as it struggled upwards. The light began to ebb. The stony hillsides turned yolk yellow, then orange. Right now, back in Jerusalem, the same light would be lingering at the edge of the table in the kitchen, before slowly climbing up the wall. Although it was Sunday, her relief that she was not there to see it was overwhelming.

A rustle of anticipation swept through the other passengers. Malka pressed her nose to the glass, not wanting to miss her first glimpse of the mystical city. She still had absolutely no idea what to do when she arrived, but her vision by the lake gave her courage.

When the bus finally arrived at the tiny, ramshackle station, Malka saw knots of people gathered at the stop, waiting for relatives and friends. She had no-one, of course. She decided to wait until all the other passengers had got off. When everyone had gone, she stood up to get her bag. It wasn't there. She scanned the rack opposite, bent down and looked under her seat. She was sure she'd put it in the rack. Or rather, that young man had. She turned and studied the crowd outside frantically. He was nowhere to be seen. Everything she owned was in that bag. Perhaps someone had taken it by mistake?

The driver made impatient noises from the front. 'Last on, last off! Some of us have homes to go to.'

'I think someone took my bag.' She tried hard not to cry.

'You should have kept an eye on it. Ask in the Left Luggage office – maybe someone handed it in there.'

Malka knew this was simply a ruse to get her off the bus, but it worked. When she got to the tin shack bearing a dented 'Left Luggage' sign, it was closed, the metal grille covered with posters and graffiti. She sat down on the kerb and tried to think. She was in a strange city, with no money or possessions, nothing except the clothes she wore and the pebble in her pocket. The flakes of dry mud inside her shoes chafed her feet as she made her way up the steep road from the station into the city of Safed itself. She was freezing. Why did she never remember to take a coat? Maybe she was being tested, like the prophets of old who wandered like beggars from one city to the next, with only the word of God to keep them warm. She would not be found wanting. She would keep moving, treat it like one of her Friday walks.

Her first impression was one of neglect. Refuse swirled around her feet as she turned out of the station and into the wind. But there was beauty too. The pale stone from which the city was built, so different from the reddish warmth of Jerusalem stone, framed the deep blue of the evening sky, which was answered from each doorway, each window frame. These were painted in blues of all shades, like fallen pieces of heaven. Was that why Zushya's door was blue? I've come to the right place, she thought.

She glimpsed families eating together through the windows she passed. A comforting murmur spilled out of the open doorways of synagogues. But despite the familiar domesticity, she felt the city resisting her. Steps led off in every direction, but gave no clue as to their destination. A promising path she'd been following suddenly ended in a ruined courtyard with wild, straggling plants and cats engaged in mortal combat. So she tried another, and another. Where was she going? What was she looking for? She would know when she saw it.

It grew darker and colder. What had she done? She put her hand in her pocket and found her travel card. She could get the next bus home. Was there another bus tonight? She clasped her lucky pebble. No. She would not give up. Not yet.

Just ahead of her, the houses on either side leaned so far over towards each other that they were almost touching. She turned sideways to slip through, just like when she'd followed Reb Zushya's cat. As she did so, she glimpsed an alcove at shoulder height, where a recessed window had been bricked up. Scraping her hands on the rough edges, she hefted herself up onto the narrow ledge. No one could see her from the street. She should be safe here. She struggled to find a comfortable position, curling and uncurling round an empty space that rose in her chest until she felt it would choke her. She was too exhausted to cry, and hoped that sleep would silence her aching stomach and throbbing feet. The unhoused air swirled with the snarls of fighting cats. Above her head, a light clicked off and a window banged shut. Malka pretended that it was her sister finally putting away her wedding magazines and switching off her torch.

'Good night, Devvie,' she whispered.

She strained for an answer, but there was none. Then, as she closed her eyes, every stone she'd stepped on seemed to gain a voice, until they swept over her like the roar of the sea.

Part II
Safed,
Fire
Shevirah,
Shattering

Chapter 5
Sabbath Bride

The morning light pressed against her lids, and Malka reached for her blanket so she could turn over and sleep on. When her hand encountered only air, the shock woke her. Then it all came back. Her bag had been stolen, she had no money and no clue what she was supposed to do next. Just at that moment, a tour group passed beneath the alcove. The words of the guide drifted up to her on the morning breeze.

'The two great scholars who lived in these houses, Joseph Caro and Solomon Alkabetz, were close friends. Alkabetz was a disciple of the great Isaac Luria, also known as the Ari, the Lion of Safed. He inspired Caro, a great legal scholar, to turn deeply towards mysticism. Caro kept a dream diary of his angelic visitations, and claimed that his legal rulings were dictated to him by the female spirit of the Mishna. The mystical path is always a dangerous one, perilously close to madness and unreason. Alkabetz was a poet. He composed the *Lecha Dodi*, the beautiful, Kabbalistic song of longing for the 'Sabbath Bride', which is still sung every Friday night in synagogues around the world. Look up a moment, and see how their houses lean into one another, almost kissing. After the two men died, their houses began to lean towards each other, as if their love had seeped into the very stones. Times have changed, of course. Caro's house on the right has become office space, with a laundry on the ground floor. The one on our left has stayed true to the spirit of Alkabetz. It is a new age Kabbalah centre, with a great bakery,

Dream Bread. The courtyard just ahead of us is a good place to take pictures. We'll have our sandwiches there.'

The three words that leapt out at Malka were Kabbalah, bakery, and sandwiches. She'd eaten nothing since the previous morning. She waited until the group had passed, then eased herself down, grazing one knee, and limped off to find the bakery.

The front windows of the whitewashed building bore a large sign in English, *Mystical Encounters,* in blue letters. When she'd asked for a sign, she hadn't expected to be taken so literally. Clearly, in Safed you had to be careful what you asked for. She read the sign again, slowly. The name could have been created just for her. It recast the moments of her life when she had felt most confused, most terrified, and most in need of guidance. Most of them had been in the last few weeks. Rather than moments of madness, as the guide had suggested, wasn't it better to think of them as encounters with another world, a mystical one? What better place to help her make sense of these experiences, and of herself?

Right now, she'd settle for a shower and a piece of toast. Moshe would probably have told her that these could be mystical encounters too. The thought of him gave her the courage she needed to push through the glass doors. She entered a narrow lobby with neon strip-lighting. Before she could take in any more, a high-pitched voice addressed her in English.

'Mystical Encounters, how may I help you?'

The voice came from beneath a mound of tightly-braided hair piled up behind a narrow desk. Underneath it sat a youth so slightly built she was amazed he didn't topple over. He reminded her a little of Avshalom, the man who had taken her bag. But that didn't mean all men with long hair couldn't be trusted.

'Are you new?' he asked, switching to Hebrew, peering up at her with watery eyes.

'I'd like to be,' she replied, also in Hebrew.

'Welcome. You look hungry. I think they are still having breakfast. Don't worry, we can sort out the practical stuff later. Do you want a hand with your bags?'

'No thank you. I don't have any.'

He stood up and peered over the counter. He gave a whistle of respect.

'Right then, I won't keep you. What's your old name?'

'Excuse me?'

'Avner will give you a new one when you are initiated, but I still need to put something down now.

'I'm Malka Sabbatto.'

Why did she say that? She could have told him anything. She was not the Rosh Yeshiva's daughter any more, or the naughtiest girl in class. This was her chance to be a new person, the person she had always wanted to be. It also made her easier to find. She had to be more careful.

'Great to meet you Malka. Just sign here please. Today is...'

'It's the eighteenth of *Kislev*.'

He looked at her strangely.

'You know, you're right, we should use the Jewish calendar here. I still can't quite get my head around it. Let's stick with the seventeenth of December.'

Malka tried out this strange new word. Dissemble. Did they use another calendar outside Jerusalem? Did time run differently here? She had so much to learn. Her stomach grumbled, embarrassingly loud.

'Sorry, I talk too much.' The shaggy head inclined sideways. 'Breakfast is straight down the corridor, and through the doors at the end. Come and get your key when you're done. There's plenty of time. It's nine now, and classes don't start for another hour.'

The smell of warm bread reeled her in. White tiles squeaked under her feet. A rush of saliva filled her mouth. Open doors with beds behind them beckoned tantalisingly on either side. First food, then sleep.

When she pushed through the swing doors at the other end of the corridor, she found herself in a low, crowded room. A counter down one side was laden with steel trays of food under heat lamps. Long, Formica-topped tables were jammed end-on against the opposite wall.

No one seemed to notice her arrival. She scanned the tables frantically for an empty seat. Then someone touched her shoulder. The shock of it made her teeth rattle.

'You can come sit with us, if you like,' a low male voice murmured.

Malka had never been touched by a strange man. Never. Well, her father had shaken her at Zushya's house. In that moment, he'd seemed like a stranger too. This is how people do things here, she told herself. They are not afraid to be in their bodies, to make contact through them, not just through words. Breathe. Concentrate. The man was still talking to her, but she was too busy staring at him to hear a word he was saying. He didn't look like any religious man she'd seen before. He was clean-shaven and very tall, with the closely cropped hair of a soldier, over which he wore an enormous white tasselled skullcap. She realised she was staring, so she slipped into the seat he'd pulled out for her. Sitting opposite was a woman with a mane of tangled blonde hair that floated around a broad, moonlike face. It made her look like a lion. Malka glanced again to make sure. Definitely a woman. Her face creased into a frown.

'What is it? Have I got food on my face?' She spoke with the soft rolling vowels that Malka recognised as American from the Kotel tourists.

Malka shook her head and smiled.

'Would you like some breakfast?'

Malka nodded vigorously. Now she was sitting, she had no energy left to get up again. The woman returned moments later with scrambled eggs, butter, hard cheese, strawberry jam and a huge hunk of soft, warm bread. The tall man and the moon-faced girl watched her eat in silence, until she'd cleaned out the jam ramekin and licked the last crumbs from her fingers.

'Like the bread? I baked it early this morning.' The tall man was American too, she realised, but he spoke Hebrew like a native.

'It was delicious. I didn't know men could bake.'

He grinned like a child. 'Where are you from? Or should I say *when*?'

Now she was full, she found it easier to talk. 'I got here last night from Yerushalayim, but my bag was stolen on the bus.'

'So you do talk! I was beginning to think you were mute.'

'Shira, give her a break! That's awful, about your bag,' he said. 'You can't trust anyone these days.'

All at once Malka burst into tears. Shira patted her shoulder. 'Everything's OK now,' she murmured. 'You're safe here.'

Malka wiped her face with the back of her arm.

'Hi, I'm Shira, this is Evven. And you are?'

'She's Malka,' someone said from behind her.

'Oh hey Avner,' her two guardian angels chorussed.

Malka twisted in her seat. So this was the leader of this place. He looked very young. Then she realised it was because he was beardless, like Evven. It made his face look oddly naked.

'Your name suits you. You look just like a queen,' Avner said. Malka reddened under his scrutiny. She stared him down. He was older than she'd first thought. He was deeply tanned, with laughter-lines radiating from his eyes and mouth, reaching right to his thick, curly hair.

'Malka, welcome to ME. Let's meet at reception after you're done, get the formalities out of the way.' He reached out and seized her hand. When she tried to withdraw, his fingers tightened. Then finally he let go, and the next moment he was gone. Shira looked after him with open admiration.

'He does that,' Shira said. 'It's like he can look into you, and see who you really are. I used to be Shirley.'

'Change your name, change your fate,' Evven quoted. 'I was Steve.'

'Now he's Evven, because his bread is hard as stone.'

'Thanks a lot, Shira. I noticed you took two portions.' He leaned across the table. 'Seriously, Malka, just think about it. The names we are given at birth aren't true to who we are. By renaming us, Avner helps set us free from our past, from everything that stops us fulfilling our potential. That's why we're encouraged not to be in contact with our families in any way once we join ME. This is our family now.'

'That's fine by me. My family won't want to hear from me anyway.'

There was a moment's silence. 'Well, their loss is our gain, for sure,' Shira said brightly.

'So is Avner his real name then, or did he change it?' Malka asked. 'If so, it's a strange choice. In the Torah, Avner was murdered for his treachery.'

Shira whistled. 'So you are a scholar, mystery girl. He says he's reclaiming it. It has a beautiful meaning. Father of light.'

'Shira has a crush on him,' Evven said.

Malka didn't know this word, but she sensed the feeling it described. 'But I thought you two were married?'

'Why would you think that?' Shira laughed, punching Evven softly on the shoulder.

'Sorry, I just thought... You seem so close to one another.'

'We're just good friends. Though as you see, he can be a pain in the neck sometimes.'

Malka blushed. She'd arrived in a different country. She had no experience of friendships between the sexes. Either you had nothing to do with boys, or you were married to one. There was no middle ground. Here, it seemed everything was middle ground. She had better change the subject before she made a bigger fool of herself.

'Why did he call this place ME?'

'ME, the place to be. The place to be me,' Shira chanted in English.

She sounded so much like a parrot from the Jerusalem zoo that Malka burst out laughing.

'That's more like it,' Shira said. She stood up. 'Come on, Malka, let's get you sorted.'

Evven rose too. 'I better get back to the bakery. See you later.'

Malka stood with Shira by the front desk holding a pile of blankets while Avner explained that 'as a guest of reduced circumstances' she would work in the bakery in exchange for bed and board. Once she had 'proved herself' (like dough, Shira giggled), she would be able to attend the beginners' classes when she was not preparing food or cleaning, 'So your body and soul can begin to find their true balance.'

Her heart sank. She didn't mind doing chores. But why the Beginners class? Wait, she wanted to say. There must be some mistake. I know more than my father's top students put together! She took a deep breath and held it. Be patient, she told herself, you are being tested. Remember, only last night you had no home, no clear purpose. Look at you today. This is mystical training, not a yeshiva where you learn things by rote. You need to make yourself ready to receive.

In fact, there were so many new things to learn that her first week passed by in a blur. She got used to sleeping in the dorm with the other women, who seemed to treat her like their kid sister. Her days were long, and by evening her whole body ached. She sank into her bed face-first every night, and only woke when Shira shook her for morning service, which was led by Avner and conducted on the flat roof, overlooking the sweep of the hills. Malka felt her prayers and hopes soar aloft, into the blue. It was the highlight of her day.

Her first Shabbat at ME was also the first night of Hanukkah, one of her favourite festivals. Friday afternoon before the festival, everyone changed into white. The other girls had picked flowers that morning, and Shira threaded jasmine through Malka's hair. Evven greeted her and Shira as they all headed to the dining hall for lighting. He had slaved in the Dream Bakery since dawn, and still smelled strongly of oil. The miracle of holy oil in the Temple had somehow been translated into a compulsion to eat doughnuts. Lots of them. Doughnuts with jam, chocolate, or her favourite, cinnamon. Evven's were marvellous, dusted with sugar, piping hot, crisp on the outside and pillow soft inside. People queued in the street for them all day, and Malka was drafted to help out. She had been surprised to see a cluster of young *Charedi* boys by the bakery entrance, their wispy *payot* tucked behind their ears. They hovered in the doorway, but didn't come in. Was the bakery kosher enough for them? She saw the way their eyes shone as they watched the other customers. So she took out a tray of damaged doughnuts and held it out to them. Still they hesitated, their longing on a leash she knew well. She bent down until her head almost touched that of the tallest one. '*Ess, ess,*' she whispered in Yiddish. This injunction to eat, which she had grown up with, worked like a spell. The boys fell on the doughnuts, and in moments only crumbs were left.

Evven shook his head at her. 'Those kids are like stray cats. Don't encourage them or they will never leave you alone.' But for Malka the boys had been a link to all she had left behind, and giving them the discards was a kind of peace offering. Those who leave can never return, she had been warned since childhood. Now, on her way to light candles with her new friends, Malka found that she didn't care. She realised that her Friday walks had been rehearsals, pushing against the gravity of her old world until she'd been strong enough to break free. Like the rest of the group, she was dressed in white as if it were Yom Kippur, the day on which all sins were forgiven.

Avner, also in white, recited the blessings and lit a giant branched *Hannukia* in the dining hall. His shirt was open at the neck, and an enormous, bowl-like white kippa encircled his head. All of the tables had clusters of candles for the Sabbath. In Jerusalem, her father would be lighting the silver *Hannukia*, which she had always been allowed to carry carefully down the stairs, without spilling a drop, to put outside their apartment block with those from the other households in lockable glass cases, shining for all to see. Her chest tightened at the thought of home. Avner's voice brought her back just in time.

'When Hannukah falls on Shabbat, there is a scholarly debate about which to light first – the miracle of creation we celebrate with the Shabbat candles we light every week, or the miracle of re-creation, of discovering one unspoilt cruse of oil in the ruins of the Temple. Finding hope in the darkness. I can understand how the Maccabees felt when they discovered that lost oil, every time I look at your shining faces. Today, we light and are lit. For the mitzvah, the commandment of Hannukah is only fulfilled when our lights are seen by others. This is the heart of our purpose at ME: to kindle one another and raise the sparks within us. Let's prepare ourselves. Look deeply into the eyes of the person next to you, and think about some part of you which you'd like to bring into the light.'

At the mention of sparks, Malka could see Moshe in the Pizzeria, his face stained with sauce. Shira squeezed her hand. As they stared at one another, Malka found it hard not to laugh. Then Shira leaned so close that her face filled Malka's field of vision, and her eyes blurred into one.

'Happy Christmas babe,' Shira whispered in English.

'Miss who?'

'It's a festival they have back home this time of year. Not that you'd know it in this country, outside of Bethlehem. Didn't they have Christmas in Jerusalem?'

'I don't know. We never celebrated it.'

'It's not a Jewish festival, though I suppose it remembers a Jewish guy. That's what I love about you, Malka. You are so... untouched.'

'Is that a good thing?'

Before Shira could reply, Avner spoke again.

'Now light the two candles for Shabbat with your partner, one each. Repeat after me. One for Adam and *Gevurah*, strength, one for Eve and *Chesed*, gentleness. Let us channel the divine light as it streams into our world to achieve balance, and create *Tiferet*, true spiritual beauty and harmony.'

Malka missed the silence that usually surrounded this ritual. She lit her tea-light and placed it next to Shira's. When she covered her eyes to recite the blessing, Malka saw her mother bending over the thin white candles, one for each member of the family. Would there still be one for her? She thought of the silver candlesticks she had so often rubbed free from tarnish. She prayed for her mother's understanding, her forgiveness. She didn't dare think of her sisters or her father. Shira seemed to pick up on how she was feeling, and hugged her. Malka leaned her head on her friend's shoulder for a moment.

Then, at some unseen signal, the entire ME community turned and filed out into the street. It was cold, but clear and bright.

'Come on,' Shira said. 'Let's dance.' They clasped hands, and danced together down the steep steps leading out of the city, singing the *Lecha Dodi* to greet the Sabbath Bride, just as the Ari had once done with his disciples. Families on their way to *shul* stopped and stared. Let them. This was the birthplace of this song, the cradle of Kabbalah. This was where Malka was meant to be.

As they wound through the streets, the women around Malka bombarded her with questions.

'Hey, Jerusalem girl! What's your deal? Where have you been all week?'

'Give her a break – she's been busting her ass with me all week.' Shira moved ahead to put some space between them and the rest of the group. 'None of them have your background,' Shira whispered. 'They see you as the real deal, and I think they are a little jealous. It doesn't help that you are the youngest here. Most of us are in our twenties.'

Yes, Malka wanted to say, so you know who you are, you've lived a little. You are women, I'm just a girl. Why would you be jealous of me?

At the city limits, Avner halted them with a wave of his hand. Sweat beaded his forehead like a private rainstorm.

'As we leave the city, let us join our song with that of the trees and flowers.'

He led them over a fence into an olive grove.

'Who do these fields belong to?' Malka asked.

'The Earth is the Lord's,' Avner replied, 'but we are its guardians. To serve and protect it.'

Malka knew the verse, but wondered if the owner of the ground they were tramping through would feel the same way. She tried to silence her doubts. Be in the moment, she told herself. For surely, this was a moment worth being in.

The setting sun softened the twisted forms of the olive trees, and touched their silvery leaves with fire. Then she saw it, framed between two trees. A square of light, just like the one that had haunted her in the apartment in Jerusalem. Finally, she had walked through it, leapt into another life as she'd always dreamed. She took Shira's hand, and Shira looked at her and grinned. There was a gap between her two top teeth, which always made her look mischievous. Her hair was bound up and entwined with jasmine. She'd wanted to do the same for Malka, but these days Malka preferred her own hair loose.

They circled breathlessly in a muddy clearing. As Malka swung her arms in time to the beat of their feet, a sense of exultation swept through her. Together with the other women, she reached up to draw down God's blessing, then whirled again, her white dress billowing like a flower in the wind.

They kept singing all the way back to the city. The kiosks and cafes were now all closed for *Shabbes*. It's Shabbat, she corrected herself. No more Yiddish. I speak Hebrew now.

They reached the Ashkenazi synagogue, the younger of the two which claimed the Ari's name. The sign outside said 'closed for repairs,' but they swept gaily past it, towards a white stone building surrounded by an arched wall. As they entered the synagogue, the separate lines of men and women threaded through each other, and then formed a circle around the sky-blue dais on which Avner stood.

Why did this place remind her of Zushya's house? It must be the domed ceiling. As she looked up, the painted trees that adorned the ceiling seemed to turn on their heads, their roots twisting, until they resembled the one she'd seen over the lake. When they righted themselves, she realised they looked exactly like the one she'd traced in her father's study, the tree that had so terrified her at Zushya's house. The tree changes as I change, she realised. I felt trapped in Jerusalem, so the tree burst out of the house. I felt rootless in Tiberias, so the tree was overturned. Now I'm here, the trees are dancing in welcome.

Familiar Shabbat melodies filled the synagogue, but they were sung by men and women together, which made them doubly strange. Clearly Avner rejected the principle of *Kol Isha Erva*, that the raised voice of a woman leads to sin. In the brief pause before the evening prayers began, Avner turned to his flock.

'We stand together in the synagogue of the Lion of Safed. Like Jews all over the world, we give thanks for the six days of creation. But at ME, we take it further. We look at creation as Kabbalists. Luria was the greatest Kabbalist of them all. One of his most powerful teachings is about the nature of creation. It is a teaching that speaks to the heart of my vision when I set up our community. It is a celebration of failure.' His voice grew stronger, and he seemed to gaze down directly at Malka.

'Luria explained that there were four stages of creation. The first he called *Tzimtzum*, or withdrawal. God stepped back to make room for the Universe. As all of you have stepped away from the lives you knew, to make space for transformation. Then divine light poured into creation. But the vessels of this world could not hold God's light, and they shattered. This was the next stage, of *Shevirah*, broken-ness and despair, where all seemed lost. But Luria leads us through the darkness and out the other side. For those sparks of light were scattered everywhere, waiting for us to find them, both within and around us. Luria suggests that if we fully inhabit our own broken-ness, we can find the sparks of light hidden there. If we find and liberate them, we can help repair the cosmos, bring them back to the shining, radiant state of their original form. This is the final stage, of *Tikkun*, or cosmic healing. For in healing ourselves we repair the broken connection between the world and the word, between the Divine and the human. We reunite God with His missing female face – the Shekhina.'

Avner nodded meaningfully, looking around at each member of the group in turn.

'In the Zohar, the Shekhina is known by another, older name. She is called the Sabbath Queen, whom we welcomed in the *Lecha Dodi* we sang earlier tonight. Someone with this very name joined our community earlier this week: Malka Sabbatto. The *Baal Shem Tov*, the Master of the Good Name who founded Hasidism, said there was no such thing as an accident. I agree. That's why I'm going to break with precedent and let her hold on to her birth-name. Our challenge will be to get her to connect to it differently, to purge it of dross and darkness. Malka, come here please.'

She felt her face grow hot. Shira pushed her gently forward until she stood at the foot of the dais. Avner beckoned. Slowly, she climbed the four steps. He did not look at her as she stood beside him.

'I ask you all to join with me in praying that just as we welcome her human namesake, through our actions and energies we can re-unite the Shekhina with her divine betrothed.'

He gestured upward. 'That's the essence of our challenge, our purpose at ME. To draw down the Shekhina, and reconnect her to her divine lover. In the *Lecha Dodi* prayer we just recited, the

Ari's great disciple Rabbi Shlomo Alkabetz described the union of God and his people as that between a groom and his bride on their wedding night. The Kabbalah constantly hints that the erotic and the sacred are one. That is why its teachings are secret, and so often forbidden. What is it that links our prayers in the synagogue to the holy dance between lovers? If we can open ourselves as vessels to receive God's light, may He fill the hollow spaces inside us so that all distinction between us and Him is obliterated, as it is between lovers in the moment of sexual ecstasy.'

Avner's words spoke to no experience in her, yet Malka felt them tingling in her body. No wonder her father banned the study of Kabbalah.

'Once, these truths were kept hidden, but our generation thirsts for them, as a deer thirsts for living water. We are a generation of seekers, and we are ready, I believe, to have the full meaning of these sources opened for us. So many leave our faith for the pleasures of the flesh, then flee what they think of as the sins of their body, using their faith to punish their flesh, in an endless, futile cycle. This is not our way. Here, we aim to make the meeting of body and spirit a Mystical Encounter.'

His voice took on the singsong quality of her father's Friday night discourses. Malka imagined her father's face if he could hear Avner's teaching. She suppressed a smile and straightened her shoulders. Avner was speaking to her like a grownup, while her father had wanted to keep her a child. When Avner's gaze swept over her, she boldly returned his stare, wanting him to see that she understood. He held his closed hand out towards her, then opened it slowly. There was something nestling in his palm.

'Malka, I ask you to wear this simple red band as a sign of our holy fellowship. It is woven from four separate strands, one for each of Luria's stages, then bound into a circle for, like our close-knit community, it will not easily be parted.'

Avner held it out to her, and Malka took another step towards him. She could smell his sweat. As he tied it on her wrist, his fingers lightly brushed her skin. Malka noticed that they trembled. He spoke again, so close now that his words thrilled right through her.

'Malka, look into my eyes, and recite after me. I bind myself to You forever, I bind myself to You with kindness and judgement, I bind myself to You in faith, so I may know You.'

She echoed him obediently. Though she knew that 'You' was meant to refer to God, she found Avner's proximity distracting. It was the blessing her father said when he wound the *tefillin* strap around his arm. It was so familiar, she'd never stopped to think about it, but Avner charged it with new meaning. In her community, girls were forbidden to wear tefillin, but here everyone wore the red thread, even Avner. Here they were all equal before God, just as she'd always dreamed. Someone clapped, and soon the synagogue rang with applause.

Dazed, Malka stumbled back down to the group. She looked for Shira, but couldn't find her. It was quiet for a moment. Then a woman began to sing The Song of Songs, her voice sweet with yearning and joy. 'May he kiss me with the kisses of his mouth.' Malka had never heard a woman lead a service. With delight, she realised it was Shira. She had been aptly renamed, for she seemed able to gather all the songs Malka wished that she had sung, all the hurts she carried inside her. Shira's voice touched them gently, and lifted them into itself. She was reciting the Song of Songs, dedicated to Solomon, *Shlomo*, whose name meant both peace and wholeness. For the first time she could remember, Malka felt that those words might apply to her too. At last, she was part of the Song of the King in whom all wholeness was found.

Chapter 6
Take This Longing

M oshe raced over the spring carpet of anemones and cyclamen, butterflies wheeling and arcing above him, as he threaded through the trees. He headed for the stream he'd found, and knelt, filling his palms with ice cold water, which he sipped slowly, like wine. He ran here every day, first thing in the morning; the ritual had taken the place of his morning prayers. At first he'd been slow, his joints stiff, his muscles cramped. Gradually, as the days went by, his body became more limber. His strides lengthened until he could feel the shock of each impact travel up his spine, and sweat poured from him in rivulets.

At Estie's wedding he had danced for Malka's eyes, imagining that she could see him through the separation barrier, the *mechitzah*. Only afterwards did he hear that she had been too ill to attend. When he asked why she was absent from the *sheva brachot*, the seven festive meals after the wedding, Zechariah finally told him that she was missing, had 'gone off the path' and was never to be spoken of again. So now he and Malka had even more in common. The community was still conducting its own search. They didn't want her back, they just wanted to know that she was safe. The family were reluctant to inform 'outsiders' like the police. Moshe had never understood this ghettoism, but now he was grateful for it. If he could be the one to find her, then perhaps he could make amends. He knew it was egotistical to think her disappearance had anything to do with him. After all, they had only spent a few hours together.

But so much had happened during that time, for him at least. He treasured every moment, replaying their conversation until its threads frayed and tangled. One question haunted him. How did you find someone who didn't want to be found? What if something happened to her? He had to try. Surely the police would get involved soon. He didn't have much time.

So each day, after his early run in the forest, Moshe conducted his own search. On the days when Lazlo gave him the morning shift off, he consulted maps and searched methodically through cafés, parks, and bookstores. All the places he imagined Malka taking refuge in. By subterfuge, he'd got Zechariah to obtain a picture of her, which he showed to the proprietors and staff of the places he visited every day, until they had only to see him enter to shake their heads and send him on his way again.

Then, after night shift, no matter how tired he was, he roamed through parts of the city he'd never been to before Malka's disappearance, visiting bars, clubs, and more shadowy spaces. Through her, he discovered the hidden faces of the city. He peered into darkened doorways, slipped on garbage rotting in narrow alleyways. As night wore on his steps grew heavier; his legs would start to tremble. He willed himself on, through the green spaces where kids played football during the day. After dark they became the domain of clans of homeless children, who defended their territory fiercely. Gradually, he gained their trust and learned what it truly was to feel unwanted, unseen. In a way, they reminded him of Malka. He sensed that this was how she thought of herself, when the very opposite was true.

The agony of it was, he saw her everywhere. He was sure he'd found her when a woman tossed her red scarf over her shoulder as she turned a corner, leaving the suggestion of a braid curving through the air. He would race to catch up, already knowing he would be disappointed. He heard Malka's laugh in the dark corners of bars and smoky cafés. The city became a map of his longing. After a couple of months of this, he knew she had left

Jerusalem. But then why could he still feel her in the very stones, burning up through his shoes until he wanted to cry out?

Once spring came, he fled his failure through the hills. He let his feet carry him where they would, and gave himself up to their rhythm, over rain-slicked rocks and snowy escarpments, liberating his body's music. In this way, he discovered the secret olive grove. It must once have belonged to an Arab farmer; now the forest had surrounded it. But the trees grew on, stubbornly. He loved the curling arabesques their branches made, and the music of their laughing silver leaves. Following a mysterious prompting, he brought a needle with him from his sewing kit, and over several weeks carefully traced words onto their leaves. Then he let the wind sift them at random, turn them into the poetry of chance, seeking clues in their combinations like a diviner. This morning, he was brought up short by a shimmering square of light caught between the trees ahead, like a window floating in space. It blazed through his leaf-poems, casting gilded Hebrew word-shapes in random combinations on the forest floor. *Stone. Song. Sleeping. Power. Fire.*

If only the invisible current that charged his leaf-words with meaning would carry them to Malka, whisper them against her skin, unbind her tightly wound hair and storm through its strands so they whipped against her face, caught between her lips. He stroked the rough bark and closed his eyes, abandoning himself to the sea music caught in the branches. Somehow, when he was here, reminders of the sea didn't scare him.

'Yulia.' For the first time in years he spoke her name aloud, and something broke inside him. He fell to his knees in the dirt. The hurt, the guilt, were undiminished. Whoever said time heals all wounds was a liar. Angry tears coursed down his cheeks. Who was he really crying for? He blinked up at the distant slivers of pale sky. His faith was in fragments too. He'd been rejected by the Orthodox world he'd tried so hard to belong to. But that same community that rejected him had also driven away the girl he loved. Here, he was returned to an older form of faith, something much more universal. Here, he could speak his mind without fear.

'I won't let you take her. Not again.'

He dried his face on his T-shirt and looked at his watch. Shit! He was late for his shift at Lazlo's. He set off at top speed, the trees a flickering blur on either side. He hoped Lazlo would be understanding. This job was now all that stood between him and his mother being out on the street. For the last few months Moshe had slept on the sofa, which was as soft and yielding as concrete. He waited tensely for the letter confirming that, as he was no longer at the yeshiva, he had broken the terms of their agreement, and they must therefore leave the apartment. But though he had been kicked out nearly three months ago, so far it had failed to arrive. Perhaps, in the furore surrounding Malka's disappearance, their situation had been overlooked. But it was only a matter of time.

He wove through sprawling heaps of rubbish, scattering hordes of mewling, scrawny cats. He hoped Reb Moshe was getting enough food. Since getting caught with his book, he hadn't dared visit Reb Zushya's. What was he afraid of? He had nothing more to lose. What was with all the bags? Then he remembered, the city was in the midst of yet another municipal strike that had been dragging on for weeks, and the stench around the mounds of plastic bags was almost visible. The mounds grew larger as he passed the central bus station, as all the bins had been removed because of the risk of bombs being planted in them. It would be simple enough to plant one inside these mounds, except that everyone gave them a wide berth. Taxi-drivers sitting in their cabs glanced up briefly from their tabloids as he passed. If only the trail she had left were visible, like smoke in the air, he would follow her anywhere.

When he reached the service entrance of the pizzeria, there was a scribbled note pinned to the door. The writing was vaguely familiar. His heart leapt when he saw his name on it, even though he knew it couldn't be from Malka. But what if it was something to do with her? He picked it up and smoothed the paper flat against the wall. There was no message, only a mobile phone number. He ducked into the pizzeria, which was already busy. He ignored Lazlo's raised eyebrow and pulled the phone on the counter towards him.

'Hi, it's Moshe. Who is this?'

'Moshe! It's Zechariah. Miss me?'

Moshe's mouth hung open. Sometimes the best response was silence.

'I need to keep the line free for orders,' Lazlo reminded him.

Moshe nodded and cupped the phone to his ear.

'I'm at the Pizzeria, so this has to be quick.'

'Sure. Do you have any plans for tonight?' Zechariah asked.

'Why?'

'I'd like to invite you for dinner.'

A feeling of unreality swept over Moshe, and he squeezed the handset tightly. He wanted to say that he'd rather have root canal. But his mother had been subsisting on pizza for weeks. She never complained, but she deserved better.

'Only if I can bring my mother along.'

'Sure, of course. The more the merrier.'

Moshe doubted that.

'So we'll see you both around five for lighting?'

'We'll be there. Should we bring anything?'

'Just yourselves.'

He took down Zechariah's address, in the fancy side of Rechavia. Then he changed quickly, tied on his apron and finally got to work. Usually he found it hard watching couples eating side by side, gazing raptly at their mobile phones. She's right next to you, just reach out and touch her, he wanted to shout at the guys. Just look up and see her. But today he just counted the minutes till closing time.

As soon as he got home, he ironed his good shirt, and cleaned his running shoes as best he could. He told his mother they were going out for dinner. She brightened, until he told her where.

'Zechariah, your nasty room-mate? Why did you agree?'

'It's complicated, mama. But won't it make a nice change?'

'No, it won't. You promised you would finally break away from this crazy community and apply for university.'

'I will, soon.'

'You've been saying that for months. What's stopping you?'

He hadn't told his mother about Malka. She'd only laugh at him, and he couldn't face that, not from her.

He heard her humming the refrain from Tchaikovsky's Violin Concerto in the shower, and he smiled. The truth was, they hadn't been out for a meal together since they'd arrived in Israel. When she emerged from the bathroom in her favourite blue dress, she too was smiling.

'May I have this dance?' she said, and offered him her arm.

They picked up flowers and some fresh strawberries on the way, then took the bus to Rechavia. His mother marvelled aloud at the sweep of manicured hedges, the Bauhaus buildings in their cladding of Jerusalem stone. Moshe caught her excitement, and felt his spirits lift. Maybe this was a good idea after all?

When they reached the apartment block, the sound of voices carried from the open window, but as soon as he buzzed it went quiet. At first, he didn't recognise Estie when she opened the door. She was wearing a bright kerchief over her head. Such colourful headscarves were forbidden in this community, which favoured sombre black. How had Zechariah allowed it? Had marriage mellowed him? Moshe hoped so. She stood looking at him closely, her expression unreadable. His mother broke the awkward silence.

'Are we too early? Should we come back later?' She waved the flowers like a peace offering.

Estie brightened. 'Not at all, come in, come in. These are lovely, thank you. Zechariah is still in *shul.*' She read the anxiety on Moshe's face and smiled. 'Don't worry, my father won't be joining us.'

With this gentle allusion to his fallen state, she ushered them in. His mother and Estie lit side by side, and the sight of the thin candle flames all reaching up together rekindled his hope. After the blessings, Estie ushered his mother into the kitchen, leaving Moshe alone on a long beige sofa in the lounge. He didn't stay there for long. He found his mother comfortably ensconced on a bar stool beside Malka's mother at an island in the gleaming white kitchen. Over by the sink, the two Sabbatto sisters chatted quietly as they washed and sliced the strawberries. They had their backs to him, so he stood for a moment unobserved. Devvie sucked her juice-stained fingers. She sensed him looking and turned. She was so much like Malka, it was painful. The same paint-fleck freckles, the same quizzical expression. Her hair was a paler shade of red, but otherwise they could have been twins.

Then Mrs Sabbatto noticed him too. The Rebbitzen. To his surprise, she ushered his mother back through the doorway into the living room, with a nod to her daughters. Moshe didn't have time to wonder what was going on. As soon as the older women were out of earshot, Estie drew out the stool his mother had so recently vacated. Even before he sat down, she began speaking in a low, urgent whisper.

'How well do you know my sister?'

It was the first time she had ever spoken to him, though he must have seen her hundreds of times. There was a toughness in her face and voice, only slightly undercut by the bright flag of her head-covering. He decided to state only the facts.

'We went for pizza, once. The night Zechariah's family came round, and Malka ran out the house.'

Estie's eyes narrowed. 'How did you arrange it?'

'It sounds ridiculous, but we literally bumped into each other.' Estie shook her head in disbelief.

'What did Malka say to you that night?' she asked.

Devvie burst in. 'Do you have any idea where she might be?'

'I wish I did. I keep worrying I offended her in some way.'

'Actually, I think she liked you,' Devvie broke in. 'Why else would she have left you a letter?'

Estie glared at Devvie. 'Let me go and fetch it.'

It was amazing. He'd never heard Devvie's voice before. She was clearly too excited to observe protocol. This whole situation was unprecedented. Perhaps it had been Estie who had invited him, rather than Zechariah? Maybe they knew something about Malka? His heart leapt at the mention of a letter. If Malka had written to him, surely he must mean something to her?

Estie returned with a crumpled envelope. She sat opposite him, holding on to it tightly. It was all he could do not to reach across the table and grab it.

'This was left under my younger sister's pillow. As you can see, it has your name on it. Our mother keeps pressuring my father to involve the police. But since my sister left, he's shut himself in his study and refuses to come out, or speak to anyone. So I've decided to take matters into my own hands. I'm sure the police will question you, if they find out about this, so it's best to be prepared.' Estie studied him closely.

So Reb Sabbatto had become a recluse, the fate he'd imposed on Reb Zushya as a punishment for helping him, Moshe thought. There was poetic justice in that. But he also felt a twinge of sympathy for this man who had driven his own daughter away. Seeing her sisters brought home to him how sheltered Malka was, how vulnerable, and he was filled with terror and outrage.

'But Malka's been missing for months! Why have you held on to this for so long?'

Estie tucked a stray hair under her headscarf, and was silent. The answer was obvious. Moshe was in *Cherem*, like Reb Zushya before him, and even to mention his name was forbidden. But surely her sister's fate was more important than her father's edict? When he looked at her pinched face, he sensed that this was precisely the conflict Estie had been struggling with.

'Once you were thrown out of the yeshiva, contacting you became... difficult. But I miss my sister too much not to try everything. I persuaded Zechariah to invite you tonight so I could give it to you myself.'

By now, Devvie was bouncing in her seat. '*Nu*, Estie! Let him open it!'

Moshe tore open the envelope, and a single sheet fluttered down to the table. He recognised the densely packed script.

'But this is Reb Zushya's writing! How did Malka get this?'

He ran a finger over the columns of his teacher's writing. It was written in columns, like a Torah scroll. But the words were gibberish, unless it was some sort of Kabbalistic code. Why had Malka taken this? What was she trying to tell him? He turned it over. On the other side was a crude, hand-drawn tree. Estie took it from him tenderly. She stroked the drawing, as if this contact might reveal its secret, then passed it back to Moshe, but Devvie intercepted it.

'Malka drew this tree. It must be a clue of some kind.' She held it out to him again, and Moshe looked more closely. The drawing reminded him of something.

'One moment.' Moshe rummaged through his backpack. He always brought a book with him. Now that he no longer had the key to Zushya's, he was gradually buying Cordovero's anthology of the Ari's writings from Ludwig Meyer with his tips, one volume at a time.

'Look at this.' He put the book down on the counter beside the postcard. On the cover was a stylised tree, which looked remarkably like the one Malka had drawn. He turned the book over. 'The picture credit says it's from the ceiling of the Ari's Synagogue in Safed.'

Estie looked shocked. 'But we've never been to Safed. How did Malka know to draw this?'

Moshe looked at the tree again, and his mouth went dry.

'That night in the Pizzeria, Malka said she had seen a tree like this the previous time we'd met, growing in Reb Zushya's house. It had terrified her. Then I showed her the same tree. Devvie is right, it's a clue of some kind.' It also felt incriminating, evidence of his guilt. For the frontispiece he had shown her was in Reb Zushya's book, the same book that had got him kicked out of yeshiva.

'I thought you said you only met her at the Pizzeria?' Devvie asked warily.

Moshe spoke in a rush. 'This was before that. We met briefly in Zushya's house. She ran away, saying something about a tree of prayers, and left when I asked her about it at the Pizzeria. I told her no one had seen the tree since Luria, in Safed. But that was hundreds of years ago. Oh God! What if she went to Safed to try and find out what it meant?' What if this is all my fault, he thought.

Estie's face was pale. 'You told my little sister she had a mystical vision. How could you do such a thing?'

'Because it was true. This is the tree of Knowledge from Eden. It is the link between heaven and earth, past and present. It is the core symbol of the Kabbalah. Until Malka told me what she'd seen, I thought it was just an idea. Not something... real.'

'You believed her?'

'You know your sister. She is incapable of lying. That night, she was terrified. She—'

He was about to say more, when they heard the door open. Moshe rose quickly and put the precious drawing in his pocket. Estie made as if to protest, then turned and busied herself opening the wine. 'It's Zechariah. Go out and greet him,' she whispered.

As he shook hands with his former room-mate, Moshe recognized an emotion he'd never seen on Zechariah's face before: anxiety, which swiftly shaded to relief. He pumped Moshe's hand vigorously.

'It's good to see you. How are you? This must be your mother. Delighted.'

Moshe's mother rose. She knew better than to offer her hand.

'Thank you both so much for coming. I'm sorry if I kept you waiting. Please, come to the table.'

The two mothers were seated next to one another. Rebbitzen Sabbatto looked as if she was holding herself upright through sheer force of will. Moshe noticed there was an extra place set next to Devvie. He didn't need to ask who it was for. Estie had lit a candle for Malka too. He thought about the drawing in his pocket. It was a message, a challenge. He promised himself he would not let her down. A circle of expectant faces peered at him. He looked at Zechariah, who was motioning for him to sit at the head of the table.

'Moshe, will you make Kiddush?'

'But I'm—'

'I insist.'

Was this the same man who had bullied him so relentlessly? Moshe had been excommunicated by his father-in-law. As such, he was forbidden to say any blessing in public, and certainly from doing so on their behalf. Asking him to do so was a direct contravention of Reb Sabatto's edict. Surely Zechariah knew that? Yet he seemed oblivious as he poured everyone wine, apart from Devvie, who had white grape juice.

His voice shaking, Moshe first counted the Omer. It was the Thirty-second day of the Omer, the precious days between Passover and Shavuot, exile and redemption. He recited the Blessing over Wine, looking at each person round the table. The Rebbitzen smiled with her lips, but her eyes were caught in nets of sad wrinkles. 'Amen' she said softly, and drank. 'Amen,' echoed the others round the table.

After they washed, Zechariah blessed the bread, and held out a piece to Moshe in his huge hand.

'You know, there is a precedent for relating to people who have been put in *cherem*.' He spoke with his mouth full, splattering crumbs. 'Rabbi Meir in the Talmud still met with his teacher, Elisha ben Abuya, even after he became a heretic and was renamed *Acher*, the Other.' He blushed and looked at

Rebbitzen Sabbatto, who had started back as if his words burned her.

'I'm sorry my husband is not here tonight.' She smiled at Moshe once more, and this time, a light danced for a moment in her eyes. 'He always spoke of you with such pride. But he blames himself for Malka's disappearance.' She sighed. 'Who knows, he may be right.'

'Mamme!' Estie's voice shook.

The Rebbitzen regarded her steadily. 'Your father was not always against the Kabbalah, as he is now. Before you were born, he and I visited the great Kabbalist, Reb Zushya, in secret.'

At the mention of Reb Zushya, Estie looked at Moshe. He shook his head, not wanting to interrupt. Devvie had no such qualms.

'But why did you visit Reb Zushya, Mamme?' Her voice was raw with shock. 'How did Tatte allow it?'

'For my sake, and for yours. Your father asked him to help us have children. At first he refused, but your father was unrelenting. I'm not sure I would have agreed if I'd known what was involved. I hate birds.'

Moshe spilled his wine and the red stain spread across the tablecloth. Welcoming distraction, he poured salt over the stain, and watched it turn pale pink. 'Reb Zushya performed the ritual of the birds? But that ritual is for—'

Thankfully, Estie interrupted him. 'Why did you never tell us about this before?' she asked.

'I couldn't. Your father swore me to secrecy. But now it seems relevant. I—'

'Wait,' Estie broke in again. 'Did our father put Reb Zushya in *Cherem* to keep this secret?'

Rebbitzen Sabbatto sighed deeply. 'That shames me most of all. Reb Zushya was so kind and gentle, though I could tell he was as scared as I was. But my husband was determined no one would learn of his use of Kabbalah, after all his public pronouncements against it. From that day, he forbade anyone in the community to speak with Reb Zushya, or have any dealings with him. He didn't relent, even when you were born. It weighs heavily on my conscience that the poor man died alone.'

'But that's terrible!' Devvie whispered.

'Never judge another until you have stood in their shoes,' Estie spoke with a touch of her old fire.

'But he wasn't alone at the end.' Everyone turned back to Moshe. 'I also visited Reb Zushya. I'd heard whispered talk of him as a legendary recluse. But I think there is a difference between loneliness and solitude. He welcomed me into his home and I spent every moment I could with him. Often, he insisted we study through the night. It was as if he'd hoarded all these words for years, and they just spilled out of him. As if he knew he didn't have much time. Those were his last few months. At the end of each evening, I would carry him to the sofa and spread blankets over him. He was as light as a bird.' Moshe's voice faltered at his clumsiness. 'I was with him the night he died. He asked me to open the window, though it was snowing. 'She's out there, somewhere,' he said. When I returned, he was reaching out with one hand, the other curled around his head. I thought he was sleeping.'

Rebbitzen Sabbatto looked up sharply. 'You knew Reb Zushya? You learned with him? Forgive me, but you are just a boy! He always refused to teach anyone. Why you?'

Moshe traced patterns in the pink salt, saw that he'd made a tree, and hastily erased it. 'I don't really know. He said it was the quality of my silence. He was a connoisseur of silences. The first day I met him, we sat and drank tea for hours, and watched the light steal the colours from the carpet as it faded. All without a word. For me, your husband's yeshiva was a kind of question-generation machine, always humming. But none of those questions touched me like Reb Zushya's silence. I learned that his whole life was curved like a bird's wing around that silence.' Moshe cursed himself for the clumsiness of his image, but the Rebbitzen just nodded, waiting for him to continue. 'He was waiting for the right pupil to come along. When they didn't, he made do with me.' Moshe smiled.

Devvie spoke suddenly. 'But what's the big deal about keeping quiet? What's the point of it?'

Moshe sighed. 'I asked Reb Zushya exactly that, when I got up the courage. He said that as a Kabbalist, he believed that if you listened to creation carefully enough, you could hear God's word still sighing through it, like the wind in the trees. If you were a really gifted listener, you might make out some of the words. If you were exceptional, you would find that language within yourself, and use it to help remake the world, heal what is broken. That's who Zushya was waiting for. You can see why he was disappointed. It might have been different if he'd met Malka.'

'My daughter? Why?'

'I think she's the real thing. A natural Kabbalist. She just needs the right teacher. I think she may have gone looking for one.'

Devvie cut in sharply. 'But isn't Kabbalah really dangerous? Malka used to tell me the story of Elisha Ben Abuya, one of the four sages who visit Paradise using the Kabbalah. Didn't he become a heretic? Didn't one of his friends die, and one go mad?'

'Elisha had already lost his faith before that,' Moshe said quietly, 'after he saw a child die while obeying his parent's command.' Both his mother and Rebbitzen Sabbatto flinched.

'That's what happened to one of the birds,' Malka's mother said at last. 'We had to burn the body. The smell from the feathers was terrible.' She shuddered, and Devvie passed her a glass of water.

'Is that why we never eat chicken, only fish?'

Her mother sipped, laughed, coughed, nodded. 'I couldn't bear to touch a bird again.'

Moshe was excited that Malka had learned his favourite text too. It brought them closer, somehow. He could see that the talk of birds was painful for Malka's mother. So he slipped into yeshiva mode, and turning to Devvie, completed the story of Elisha.

'The Talmud relates that Elisha Ben Abuya lost his faith when he saw a child who had been told to fetch some eggs from a nest by his mother, fall from the ladder and die. Others say the child was bitten by a snake, that symbol of doubt and despair in the Torah. The only two commandments which specifically mention the reward of long life for keeping them are honouring your parents, and protecting the feelings of the mother bird by shooing her away. The child should have been doubly safe. Remember, the stories in the Talmud, like those in the Torah, point beyond themselves, they are not meant to be taken literally. They tell us about events taking place inside us.'

Moshe felt his mother's shoulders shaking tearfully beside him. Rebbitzen Sabbatto handed her a napkin. 'I can see what my daughter saw in you, Moshe. You both speak your mind, regardless of the consequences. From what your mother has told me, your family has known loss too. You understand us, perhaps better than others might.' She squeezed his mother's hand.

Moshe was shocked his mother would speak of their secret sorrow to someone she had just met. But what right did he have to judge? Besides, Rebbitzen Sabbatto wasn't just anyone.

'I know your daughter is alright,' he said, then blushed at his clumsiness. He raised his glass. 'May she be found safe and well.'

Moshe realised that his glass was empty. Zechariah motioned for his wife to stay seated, and rose with surprising swiftness to refill their cups himself. Their glasses cast ruby stars across the white tablecloth. They all raised their glasses and drank. Zechariah actually smiled at him. I must finally be doing something right, Moshe thought. If only Malka could hear me. Thinking of her gave him the courage to share his own personal connection to the last of the four sages.

'Since I came across it, that story has always been my inspiration. Akiva, the last of the four who visited Paradise in the story you mention, grew up ignorant of the Torah, just as I did. Like me, he was drawn to learning out of love.' He looked at Rebbitzen Sabbatto. 'When I first saw Malka, I knew I had to see her again, even though she seemed impossibly out of reach, like Rachel, Kalba Savua's daughter, who chose Akiva. To prove himself worthy of her, he rose to become the greatest scholar of the age. While it would be arrogance to compare myself to him, I too poured my whole being into studying, with both Reb Zushya and Reb Sabbatto, and rose, much more humbly, to the top *shiur* in your husband's yeshiva. I know this means I am not a true scholar, for a true scholar learns Torah *lishmah*, for its own sake, with no thought of reward. The only reward I sought was the Shabbat visits to your home, for a glimpse of Malka, which I would treasure all week until my next sighting. I hardly knew her, but when we finally had the opportunity to speak, Malka made me see that the Kabbalah was more than just a cluster of symbols. She made me realise how unworkable your husband's ban on Kabbalah was. The Talmud itself entwines *Halachah* and *Aggadah*, rules and stories.' Like lovers, he thought, and blushed. 'Trying to separate the law from mysticism is like trying to draw a line in water. Akiva approached paradise knowing that our relationship with the Divine must be modelled on the love we have for one another. That's why, alone of the four scholars, Akiva enters whole and leaves whole. He emerged to champion the inclusion of the Song of Songs in the Bible, and he called that great love song, the only book in the bible narrated by a woman, 'the Holy of Holies'. For me, Akiva's story suggests that only if we risk ourselves in love, risk losing that love, can we experience the possibility of wholeness.'

It was probably the longest speech he'd ever made. Malka's family were used to him sitting at the fringes of the table, observing, unobtrusive. There was a moment of silence. Zechariah spoke first. His voice was hesitant, deferential, a world away from his former taunting bravado. 'I remember that story too, though I am not a scholar like you. Akiva picked straw out of his beloved's hair. Her wealthy father disowned her, sure she'd married beneath herself.' He gave a slow, amazed glance at Estie, who blushed the colour of her headscarf. Only then did Moshe realise that it was the exact shade of Malka's hair. That must mean something, surely?

Slowly, Rebbitzen Sabbatto stood, and they all rose with her. 'Please forgive me, I'm very tired.' She looked at Moshe for a long moment. 'I haven't slept well in many weeks, but I think perhaps I will tonight, knowing Malka has you as her champion. If anyone can find her, it's you, who so clearly love her.'

She walked towards the front door, leaning on her two daughters like an invalid. She turned in the doorway and looked back at Moshe again.

'Please. Find her, and bring her home. For all of us.'

'Tomorrow night is Lag Ba'Omer. Malka usually collected the wood for our little bonfire,' Estie said. 'I hadn't planned on making one this year, but Devvie will help me. We will make a beacon for you. May it be God's will that you return her to us, speedily and in our days.'

'Amen,' Devvie chimed.

Once the door closed, they looked at one another with the discomfort of those who had been surprised into intimacy. Moshe's mother stood. 'I think it is time we were going too.' Her voice shook. Zechariah moved to stand between them and the door.

'Before you go, could I just borrow Moshe for a moment?' Before she could reply, Zechariah pulled Moshe out onto the balcony and shut the door behind them. Despite himself, Moshe was curious. Zechariah spoke in an undertone.

'I went to the *yoetz* the day before the wedding of course, and I've read the manuals. I want to please my wife. It's a mitzvah. But I don't know how.' Zechariah spoke looking out over the railings.

'I don't understand. The wedding was months ago. Have you never...?'

Zechariah's face was a sunset. 'On the wedding night Estie said she had her period, though it was not her time, from nerves. I had prepared myself, but after the moment passed I didn't know how to approach her. I couldn't... That is, I want her to feel how special she is to me.'

Moshe looked at his hulking former tormentor. Whatever he had been expecting, it wasn't this.

'Why are you telling me?' Moshe said at last.

'You were not always like us. I know it's forbidden to ask a *baal teshuva* about his former life, but I thought you might have had – relations – with women before?'

Moshe nodded doubtfully. 'Just a few high school crushes, nothing serious.'

Zechariah looked at him with puppy-dog eyes.

'I knew I could ask you. What do you suggest?'

Moshe thought of the tough girl in the kitchen in her bright headscarf.

'Just listen to her.'

'That's it?'

'That's a lot. She needs to trust you. Show her what she means to you, and things will happen in their own time. Perhaps it is better this way, and you can get to know each other first?'

'Perhaps. Please, don't tell anyone about this.'

For the first time Moshe could remember, Zechariah hugged him. Who said the age of miracles is past? he thought.

On the way home, his mother walked fast, keeping ahead of him. He had to hurry to keep up. Words poured from her in an angry torrent.

'I gave up everything to get us here. Everything. I know this may not be the life you wanted. But please, don't throw it all away gallivanting after some girl you hardly know. So the yeshiva didn't work out. That just means it is time to leave that world behind. You should go to university, advance yourself. It's what your father would have wanted, too.' She spoke these last few words as though they were definitive.

This rare opening was just what Moshe needed. 'Mama, do you miss him?'

She sighed. 'All the time.'

'Well, that's how I feel about Malka.'

His mother stopped so abruptly that he almost crossed the road without her.

'How can you compare the two? Your father and I were married for years. You know this girl, what, five minutes?'

'Her name is Malka. We only spoke twice, it's true. But all those times I left you alone on Friday night to go to the Rabbi's house, it was to catch a glimpse of her.'

'Yes, I heard your swansong in there. Romantic claptrap. You went on one date. Now she's gone. So get over her. She obviously wasn't interested in you.'

Moshe said nothing. He knew why his mother was so insistent that he forget Malka. She had her own agenda of forgetting, which had brought them half-way round the world. For years it had been his too, the guilt like tar sticking to his feet. But he'd had enough. Once they had climbed the stairs to his mother's tiny apartment, he stopped on the landing outside her door.

'Ima, when I was with Malka, I felt at home. For the first time since we got here.'

His mother's hand shook on the keys, but otherwise she didn't respond.

'Ima, listen to me. We can never bring Yulia back. You are right, Malka is different. She is alive, and I think she needs me. Besides, I need her. You have to let me go. You have to let Yulia go.'

'Come sit with me a moment in the kitchen.'

They sat looking at one another across the tiny kitchen table. At length, his mother spoke.

'Moshe, you are all I have here. But if I was Malka, and wanted to be found, I'd want you to be the one who found me.' She gave a small smile. It was all the approval he could hope for.

Chapter 7
The Cave

Malka couldn't believe she had to work on a Saturday night. Worse still was knowing she'd be back in the kitchen again first thing tomorrow. She'd been at ME for three months now, and still hadn't been allowed to join a single class. Instead, she'd been stuck in the basement, buried alive. Was this what she had come to Safed for? The only thing that kept her going these days was Shira's smiling face and, right now, even that wasn't enough.

The bakery equipment took up the whole basement of Mystical Encounters. It supplied bread and cakes to many of the local hotels and cafés. It was *Purim* tomorrow, so they would be especially busy. She would probably be stuck here for most of the night. The basement already thrummed with the sound of extractors working at full power. Thick pipes ran above her head, and vents gaped on the walls like metal mouths. It was so hot that Malka began sweating as soon as she arrived. Shira was working a batch of dough, her frizzy mane hidden under a cap, thumping so hard that her powerful forearms quivered. So maybe she was 'pissed off' too. She had taught Malka this phrase and other useful expressions, during their shifts together. I came to Safed to become a Kabbalist, and instead I learned to swear, Malka thought. Evven had seasoned Shira's English expressions with some choice ones in Arabic.

'You took your time, sister.'

Yes, Malka thought. She's definitely pissed off. Or maybe even one of the other words she taught me, to be used only in emergencies. 'Sorry. I just... Well, everyone else has gone out, apart from us. Don't you think it's a bit unfair? Avner goes on about liberating the Divine Feminine, but we are stuck in the kitchen for weeks on end.'

Shira sighed and wiped her brow with a forearm, leaving a slick of flour across her face. 'Give it time, Malka. Trust the process. Your chance to shine will come. This is also a place of transformation, you know. It's a beautiful thing, watching the pale dough turn to gold. Come, you can help me prep these *Purim Challot*. We need to add raisins, and use hundreds and thousands instead of poppy seeds or sesame.'

She passed Malka her paper hat and apron. Malka coiled her hair on top of her head like the round *challah* Shira was shaping, and pressed the hat precariously onto this unwieldy mass. Then Malka reached over and wiped her friends' floury face with an oven glove.

'Too hot to handle, am I?'

They smiled at each other across the table. The last few days, she and Shira had worked late into the night. Even after resting over Shabbat, she still ached all over. Where did Shira get her energy from?

Malka started on a fresh batch of poppy-seed mixture for the *hamentashen*, the fragile triangular Purim biscuits she loved. She stirred in the milk, which turned a beautiful eggshell blue around the tiny seeds. She let it simmer gently, folding in honey, sugar, raisins, softened butter to bind it all, then lemon zest and juice for balance, tasting and adjusting until the flavours sang. It was her favourite festival food. She leaned over the pan and inhaled. When the mixture smelt ready, she spooned some into the centre of each small circle of dough on the trays Shira had prepared, and folded them into little triangular parcels of pastry, pinching the edges together. Malka also filled several trays with the less traditional, jam or chocolate, the best sellers at the ME bakery. She dusted them lightly with icing sugar, sifting the sugar through the air like snow. She had always loved this festival, when silliness was mandatory, even for adults. Her father would go so far as to put on a red tie instead of his usual grey-blue one.

She looked up to see Shira struggling with a loaded tray, and hurried to help lift the *challah* dough into a warm oven to rise.

'Thanks babe. Do me a favour, go get some of those rum-soaked raisins from the store room for the next batch.'

Alcohol was not a standard ingredient in Challah, but it was a mitzvah on Purim to get so drunk that you did not know the difference between the hero of the Purim story, Mordechai, and the villain, Haman, who had sought to annihilate the Jews of Persia. Of course the true heroine was Esther, whose name meant hidden – and she hid her Jewish identity until the last moment, then stepped up to save the day. Malka smiled as she stepped into her own favourite hiding space, the store room. She loved the quiet density of this place, with its tall glass jars filled with flour standing in rows, surrounded by shorter, stouter ones filled with olives, raisins, and dried fruit. There was a rainbow of different jams, green-gold olive oil, racks of spices and dried herbs hanging in bunches. It smelt fabulous, like the essence of every cake you could think of. It was also much cooler than the main kitchen, and Malka found herself here often, especially when she felt homesick, which she did with particular intensity during festivals. She closed her eyes and inhaled the aroma of cloves and allspice, the ingredients her mother mixed for *Havdalah*, the ritual of separation which concluded the Sabbath with a heady moment of sensory bliss. Sometimes Malka would sneak a furtive sniff during the week, whenever she felt low. With slow deliberation, she selected the jars she needed and rejoined Shira, who pointed to three large tubs.

'Great. My arms need a break, so let's swap. This dough has already been proving, and just needs to be pounded again, then shaped into *challot* with your secret ingredients.'

Malka buried her hands wrist-deep in one of the tubs of dough. She slid them out and studied the shape she left behind. She copied the way Shira shaped the ends of the loaves, rounding them gently, as if she was stroking someone's shoulder. She pummelled the fleshy dough, felt it warm sleepily beneath her fingers, turn supple and elastic. Malka found that if she leaned her upper thighs against the edge of table, rocking herself against it as she pounded the dough, that warmth spread through her legs, and fluttered up into her stomach. Shira was right. She had discovered something about herself here, a sense of her body as a living thing. It had been like diving to recover a sunken ship, and slowly lifting it, glistening, to the surface. Usually she only had one tub, but today she kept going through all three. The edges of her body became blurry and diffused, and the tingling spread down her legs, lifting her onto her toes. It felt really good. She folded in the raisins and kneaded again, the scent of rum filling her nostrils, together with a faint aroma of cut grass, which she realised was coming from herself.

'That's it, now you are really getting into it,' Shira commented approvingly.

I am, she thought, I am. Then suddenly everything around her seemed to disappear, and she clenched her hands convulsively in the dough as a sweet, sharp feeling flickered through her. Her nerves glowed so brightly she could see them singing inside her like the filaments in a light bulb. She closed her eyes for a moment. 'Moshe,' she said softly. 'Moshe.' When she opened them, she found Shira staring at her.

'Was that what I think it was?' Shira laughed. 'You're really something. Innocent Jerusalem girl my ass.'

Malka held on to the table. Her legs were still trembling. The sight of her fingers, pressed so hard against the wood that their tips were white, took her right back to the memory of her first period. She had been eleven, gutting a large salmon on the kitchen table that kept slipping away from her knife. As she slid out its guts with one hand, something twisted inside her and ran down her leg, reddening her skirt. Had she cut herself? Just like now, she held onto the table, unable to let go. Her mother had found her there, staring unseeing into the salmon's glazed eye, and somehow understood. She'd held Malka close for the first time in years, smelling comfortingly of baking. She had rested her chin on top of Malka's head, and whispered into her hair. 'Stop, Estie will do it. In a few days, when you stop being *niddah*, we'll visit the *mikveh* together, plunge into the water side by side. So you can start to learn what being a woman means.' That's what I'm doing now, Malka thought. Her mother had never told her she could feel like this. Being a woman had been all about being unclean, and the fear of arousing male desire. Nothing about her own longings, which were to be as hidden as her flesh. For a moment, it made her angry. A smell of burning wood made her turn, looking for the source. Then she saw there were charred dimples in the table where her fingers had been. Or were they already there before? Surreptitiously, she rubbed flour into them, until they were hidden. Then Shira touched her arm, and she jumped.

'Earth calling Malka!' Shira hugged her. 'First time, huh? It's great, isn't it? You know, that's kind of how I ended up here. Chasing that feeling. I always wanted to just disappear. Sex made it possible, even for just a few moments.'

'But I thought in Judaism, you can only have sex once you are married?'

Shira gave her a long look. 'You just found your own answer to that, didn't you? It's not something I can put into words without making it sound cheap. I guess for me, sex means loving your body, just as it is, then sharing it with someone else who does. My trouble was I shared mine with people who wanted me to be someone else. Some picture in their head they pasted on me, until it became unstuck and we drifted apart.'

'I was taught the body is just an envelope for the soul.'

'You know, you may be on to something there. I think of my body as a letter I was given, which I'm slowly learning to read.

The best bits are always between the lines, aren't they? From what you say, some people throw the letter away, unread.'

'Shira, can I ask you something?'

'Trying to change the subject?'

'You just reminded me of something that's been bothering me. Every day, we throw away bin bags full of food – broken biscuits and yesterday's bread and cake. So many local families are poor.'

'I know, but what can we do about it? They are proud, and won't take handouts.'

'Well, on Purim you are supposed to give charity as well as food. Why can't we give the broken pieces away?'

'No way. We'd just be asking for trouble. You've seen the way these *charedi* kids cluster around the bins at closing time. Some of them are feral. Sorry, no offence.'

'They are just hungry.' Malka was adamant. In the end, Shira agreed to go with her to Avner at the end of their shift. She clearly expected a resounding no from the community leader. But Avner surprised them both.

'I think Malka may be on to something. Charity is one of God's faces, an expression of the *Sefira* of *Chesed*,' he said, his face bathed in the blue glow of his computer screen. 'Let's give it a try tomorrow.'

The following day, as she fulfilled all the Purim orders for local businesses, Malka accumulated a big basket of broken *hamentashen*. Towards the end of the morning, as the commercial customers collected their boxes, she beckoned to the group of boys she had noticed, clearly brothers, who always came in together. They never bought anything, but stayed in the bakery for hours, their faces pinched, their eyes gleaming.

Since they heard her speak Yiddish, every time she appeared they inched towards her. She knelt down with the basket. At first they hung back against the wall.

'*Nu*? *Shoin*,' Malka said, pretending to turn away. Then she felt a tug at her sleeve. It was the oldest boy.

'Hi, I'm Chezki,' he said. He couldn't have been more than eight. He indicated an identical pair with long, wispy sideburns.

'The twins are Dovid and Yoinason. Next is Shmuli, and Yossi is the youngest.'

Yossi peeped at her from behind Shmuli with the bright eyes of a squirrel. He wiped his nose vigorously on his sleeve, then slipped his hand shyly into her own. This seemed to settle things for the group.

'One at a time,' Chezki instructed. 'And just one *hamentash* each.'

'*A gutten Purim*,' each child said as they reached her. They chose carefully, then lifted their prize aloft, and carried it out of the bakery. Malka stepped out after them into the sunshine to watch them eat. Their pale faces were already flecked with crumbs of amber and caramel, smears of jam and chocolate.

Each of them ate in their own way. Chezki turned around so she couldn't see his face. Dovid broke his biscuit into smaller and smaller pieces, then sucked them up from his palm. Yoinason closed his eyes, blocking out all else as he slowly chewed, his face a picture of rapture. Yossi put the whole *hamentash* into his mouth at once, just like Devvie. Malka rubbed at her eyes with her apron. She handed Chezki the basket to take home, and watched until they disappeared.

'Some of our customers could learn manners from them,' Shira observed wryly. 'But I think they will be hard to get rid of now.'

Malka did not want to get rid of them. These boys reminded her of Jerusalem, and gave her a chance to speak Yiddish, her *mameloshn*.

Avner came over to her table during the Purim *seuda*. 'Looks like you're onto a winner,' he said, his teeth full of poppy seeds. 'Our clients at the local hotels are impressed with our new charitable ethos. Your kids are good publicity.' He sucked his teeth and held up the remains of his *hamentash*. 'These are delicious, by the way.'

Malka's shoulders lifted, like wings.

'That's more like it! I think that's the first time I've seen you smile since you got here.'

'I'm sorry. I'm really grateful for everything you've done for me. I just... I'm waiting for the chance to study.'

'So? What would you like to learn?'

'The Zohar, of course.'

Avner's eyes widened. 'The hard stuff, huh? 'Tell me, why does a young girl from the Old City want to learn Kabbalah?'

'It's a long story.'

'One I'd like to hear. Take a break from the bakery tomorrow morning. You've earned it. Come and see me in my office at seven, before morning prayers.'

Malka woke early. Everyone else was still asleep. Shira's face on the next bed was soft and childlike. Malka tiptoed to the shower. Her freckles glowed like fresh breadcrumbs in the light filtering through the bathroom window.

She was nervous about her appointment with Avner. What should she wear? She chose a pale green long-sleeved top and a pair of Shira's jeans, with a thick belt so they'd fit. She knew Shira wouldn't mind. She pocketed her lucky stone with its swirled question mark: she would show it to Avner and explain about the tree she'd seen. She peered at Shira's watch on the bedside table. It was only six. She would go for a walk. It was time she rekindled her passion for wandering, and made friends with the city which had so confused and terrified her during that first terrible night, all those weeks ago. First she slipped into the library. She would borrow a few books, and find somewhere secret so she could prepare for her meeting with Avner, and show him that she knew what she was talking about. Along one wall there were multiple copies of the Zohar in different editions. She had no idea which one to take, so she grabbed a few volumes at random and hugged them to her chest.

Carrying her contraband, she headed up Hagdud Hashlishi, which rose steeply towards the top of the hill on which the city was built. She thought of Moshe carrying his books to Lazlo's. I must look just as silly as he did, she thought, smiling. There was a broad promenade ahead, just like the one above the *Kotel*. This one was surrounded by blue railings. The view was extraordinary: dark green hills shaded to blue and purple on the horizon; Mount Meron rose above them all, wearing a snow *kippah*. The legendary Kabbalist Shimon Bar Yochai was buried there. The Talmud told of the cave he and his son had hidden in to escape Roman persecution. They had stayed there for ten years, supposedly writing the Zohar in the process. When they finally came out, Bar Yochai had burned up everything he looked at, so God had sent them back to the cave to learn compassion. He became known as *Butzina de Kadisha*, the Holy Fire, and bonfires were lit across the country on the festival of *Lag Ba-Omer*, the anniversary of his death. She and her sisters would secretly gather wood and old boxes, hiding them from rival gangs of children, and watch the air shimmer above the fire. It was the only time Estie went against their father's instruction, which was to have nothing to do with such primitive customs. Even now she could smell wood-smoke. Malka breathed in the pine-scented air. She leaned over the railings. Flat turquoise slabs were laid into the hillside, like fallen doorways. Each marked the grave of a famous Kabbalist, and were usually crowded with visitors, all carrying stones to leave there, to mark their visit and weigh down the spirits of the deceased. Malka had avoided the graves so far. Death was the last thing she wanted to be reminded of. She inhaled deeply. Pine. Spread just below her was a young forest, which stretched away to the pale sharp edges of the newly built apartments for the Breslov Hasidic sect. The wind shook the branches, which waved at her encouragingly.

Malka made her way down the cobbled steps to the woodland. The earth was red and damp, slightly slippery, apart from under the trees where a carpet of needles made her steps soundless. She could understand Bar Yochai retreating from the world. She missed having somewhere she could be by herself. Everything at ME was so public. Malka raised her face towards the branches above, letting the wind stream through her hair. Suddenly a deafening shout echoed through the forest. A flock of birds rose startled into the air and wheeled towards her. Then the whole wood shook with voices. Malka flung herself to the ground.

'*Ribonoh Shel Olam!* Master of the Universe!'

Were the trees speaking? Was the forest haunted by the ghosts of ancient Kabbalists? Malka didn't stay to find out. She got up and ran. But the trees looked so alike, she had no idea which was the way out. She kept running, though the books she was carrying dug into her chest, and her side ached. At last, the voices grew fainter. She leaned against a tree trunk to catch her breath. Then she remembered something Shira had told her. The Breslov community had the custom to go out into the woods before morning prayers, just like the *Chasidim* in the Talmud, and pour out their hearts to God. That must be what she'd heard. They called it *Hisbodedut*, solitary communing with the Divine. But clearly, they did this in packs. Laughing with relief, Malka looked around to find her way back to ME. She was standing in a clearing spangled with coins of sunlight. At the far end of the clearing, someone had abandoned a pile of building materials. Typical. Then she looked closer, and her heart leapt. The slabbed cement blocks leaned against each other, leaving a hollow triangular space at their base. The blocks had clearly lain here for some time. The woodland was already reclaiming the rubble, entwining the outer blocks with ivy. The cracks were silted with moss.

She crawled inside and sat down. It was too low to stand up in, but it was warm and dry. This would be her cave, just like Bar Yochai's. She put down her pile of books with a sigh. She knew it took more than a cave to make you a Kabbalist. But she was determined to convince Avner that she was ready to attend classes. It was maddening to be so close to the knowledge she sought, only to be denied access to it. It was like being shut out of her father's study all over again. Malka stroked the cover of one of the books, and opened it. Perhaps, if he said no, she could become her own teacher.

The pages crackled as she riffled through them, mingling the scent of paper with pine and dry earth from the cave and woodland. The Zohar was nothing like any of the religious texts with which she was familiar. It was written in a hybrid language, flitting between Aramaic and Hebrew as if neither could fully contain its meaning. She smoothed it open on her lap. *The students of Rabbi Shimon sat together in silence, waiting for the master to begin.* She looked out of the cave, and saw the serried ranks of trees, waiting and still. *At length he spoke. 'As the rose amongst the thorns, so is my love amongst the maidens. The Rose is Knesset Yisrael, the community of Israel. For there is a rose above and a rose below. What of the rose amongst the thorns? It has red and white, just as Knesset Yisrael has Justice and Mercy... There are five strong petals on which the rose is set, and they are called salvations, and now they are known as the five gates. And this rose is called the cup of blessing, of which it is said: I will take up the cup of salvation, which must stand or repose on five fingers only.'*

Malka looked at her open hands, and stretched out her fingers. She recognised the quotations from Psalms and the Song of Songs. But the rest of it? She had no idea. She set the book down and curled her right hand slowly into a fist, until her nails pressed into her palm. Justice. When she released her fingers, there were white half-moons left by her nails, which slowly reddened and suffused with blood. Five petals, she thought. She opened her left hand and cupped the palm, trying to catch the light that pooled there. She took out her pebble. In this light, the question mark glittered like glass. The edges of her fingers grew transparent around it, and she could see the bones hidden inside them. Mercy. How could she become a cup of Blessing? What gates was Bar Yochai referring to? She skipped ahead, looking for answers.

'One of these words is Or, meaning light. This light was created and became enclosed as an embryo in the Brit, the covenant, and entering the rose as a principle of life, made it fruitful... and caused itself to be manifested in forty-two kinds of matter, which produced the Shem Hameforash, the great and secret name of God, which is composed of forty-two letters. This name was the basis for the creation of the world.'

She could make nothing of this paragraph either, so she began to chant it aloud, letting the sound wash over her, the cadences thrum through her, trying to feel the meaning, instead of think it. As she did so, a songbird with a blue body and black wings alighted on a slab of concrete just by her knee, pecked at the egg-like stone she held, and burst into song. Malka held her breath. Then softly, she began again, and joined her chanting with the birdsong. For a moment she felt that she and the bird, the stone and the book were all part of the same song, the song of creation itself. Then it was gone. She looked at her watch. Almost seven. She made a little nest of leaves for her pebble, dusted off the volume she had been studying and hid the rest of the volumes at the back of her cave. She found her way back easily.

Avner smiled broadly when he saw what she was holding. 'So what makes you think you are ready to study Kabbalah?' He sat on an office chair, behind a small desk that made him look like an overgrown schoolboy. He reached out and took the book from her. She noticed that his nails were manicured.

'You know, to feel the benefits of the Zohar, you don't actually need to read it. When they are troubled, which is often, I tell my students to just select a volume at random, let it fall open, like this, then run a finger down the page. Let the spirit of the Zohar guide them to the right word, and meditate on that word to release its energy and healing power. Of course, many of them can't read. Can you? Girls from your background are usually sheltered from the male world of words, aren't they?'

Malka seized the book and splayed it open on the desk between them. She jabbed her finger at a word in the middle of the page. '*Chashmal*,' she read, with a start. This was the word she'd discussed with Moshe at Lazlo's, all those months ago. Coincidence? Her voice shook slightly as she quoted from memory. 'Literally, it means the speaking silence. The Talmud says it is a word of great and dangerous power. It first appears in Ezekiel's vision of the divine chariot, and represents the energy that sustains the Universe. In Modern Hebrew, it is used to describe electricity.'

Avner looked at her, open-mouthed.

'Actually, I have been learning Talmud since I was five. My father is a Rosh Yeshiva, and we studied together every day for years.' Malka tried to keep her voice measured, but the frustration of the last few months burned in her throat and made it difficult to speak. She bit her lip. She didn't want to cry in front of him. When the silence grew uncomfortable, Avner motioned for her to sit down. Gently, he took the book from her.

'Malka, I had no idea. These last few months must have been hard for you. Don't think I haven't noticed. But we needed to thicken the vessel of your experience so that, when we reveal your hidden light, the vessel will not break. It seems that you carry a lot of fire within you, so it's a good thing we've made those walls nice and deep.'

Malka wanted to ask how he could be sure she wouldn't break when she felt that any moment she would shatter into pieces on his rug, but was distracted by a poster of a tree on the wall behind Avner. With a start, she recognized it as a giant version of the Sefirot from the frontispiece of the Zohar which Moshe had shown her, and which she had traced again as a message meant only for him. It was a diagram of the Kabbalistic relationship between spirit and matter, the heavenly connection she yearned for. She had come to Safed to look for a teacher.

Surely, this was a sign that Avner was the man she needed to unlock the mysterious threat that hung over her. She looked out of the window behind him. Beside it, instead of the conventional *East* sign you faced to pray, hung a scribal version of the *Shem Hamefurash*, God's unmentionable name. It was forbidden to even pronounce it. Hashem, 'The Name,' as it was referred to, was meant to suggest that it pointed to something outside language. According to what she'd read this morning in the cave, it also hinted that all matter, every living thing, was a form of God's language. The Zohar seemed to make no distinction between names and things. Names were things, and things were embodied names. She wanted to ask Avner about this, but didn't know how. Instead, Malka held up the volume of the Zohar. 'Well, I'm ready now. I want to study this. I want to know it intimately.' She blushed, and he looked at her with an amusement that stung her. She needed to show him why she was worthy. She pointed at the Tree.

'I recognize that poster. My first week here, during my initiation in the Ari Synagogue, I saw the trees on the ceiling move. Back in Jerusalem, I saw the same tree come to life when I entered the house of a famous Kabbalist.'

'Did he learn with you?'

'Reb Zushya? No, I never knew him. But I found out that my father, who claims to hate Kabbalah, visited him before I was born, together with my mother, and they conducted a secret Kabbalistic ritual together.'

Avner's eyes gleamed. 'What ritual was this?'

'It's why I ran. I mean, why I came here. When my father told me about it, he said that something went wrong with the ritual, which suggested my imminent death. That's what brought me here. I thought if I could understand it, I might prevent it, somehow. You know, change your place, change your fate...'

It sounded lame, even to her. But Avner was leaning so far over the desk towards her, she worried he would fall into her lap. It felt surprisingly good to have this kind of attention, to share the burden she'd been carrying. Only now did she realise how much it had weighed on her.

'Exactly what kind of ritual was this?' Avner asked again. She noticed his fingers were pressed into the tabletop, and that hers were, too. They were so close they were almost touching. She drew her hands back into her lap, and told him what she knew.

'So let me get this straight. Your father told you that this bird ritual was so your parents could have children?' His voice rose with excitement.

'Isn't it?'

Avner stroked his bare chin in a gesture that reminded her shockingly of her father when he was thinking.

'Malka, what do you remember of what I said at your initiation about the Shekhina?'

'Well, in the Torah and the Talmud it's the name for God's Presence. I know the Kabbalah gives the word a completely different meaning. You said it was the female face of God, and that the dance between lover and beloved in the Friday night *Lecha Dodi* prayer stands for our mission, to reunite God with Her.'

'Precisely. The ritual you describe... It is meant to bring down the Shekhina, to make her tangible. The bird died to bring her into this world in physical form.'

'So it doesn't mean I'm meant to die?'

Avner laughed. 'Everyone dies when their time comes. When they do, what do we say in our memorial prayer?'

'May their spirit be gathered under the wings of the Shekhina.'

'Exactly. Another Kabbalistic prayer, hiding in plain sight, just as you have been these last few months. Note the wings. The Shekhina is associated with birds, messengers between heaven and earth. That's the real reason birds were used in the ritual. '

'Why would my father lie to me? Was he just trying to scare me? Or do you think Reb Zushya lied to him?' Both seemed ridiculous.

118

'To be fair to your father, he may not have known the truth, as you suggest. Kabbalists are a secretive bunch. This Reb Zushya may have had his own reasons for keeping the true nature of this ritual from your father. The risks are great. But he left clues for the initiated to follow.' Avner was getting more and more excited. He was starting to frighten her.

'What clues?'

'You say your mother was there too. The ritual does not usually require the presence of a woman. Many, many Kabbalists, have tried to raise the Shekhina, to bring about the redemption. Perhaps... perhaps they failed because they were all...'

'All what?'

'All men.' He sat back in his chair and steepled his hands together. Hadn't Moshe suggested the same thing? Avner's next words shocked her out of her reverie. 'Malka, I'm afraid you are not suitable for my Kabbalah class.'

Malka's shoulders slumped. 'Why not?' After everything he'd just said, this made no sense. She gripped the Zohar tightly, ready to argue.

'I think you are too advanced, even for the top class. So I'd like to study with you myself. A *Chavrutah*, just the two of us. I believe you may be a true mystic. You've no idea how rare that is. Only a very few could have understood you, could have appreciated your gift. That's why you were sent to me. I knew there was something special about you, but I didn't know how special. I'm looking forward to finding out.'

Chapter 8
A Dangerous Garden

'Tell me again about the tree, Avner. If it is a symbol of healing and connection, why was it so terrifying? Why did I feel it was trying to destroy me the first time I saw it?'

They sat sprawled on a pile of cushions on the floor of Avner's office. These days Malka barely ate, barely slept. She didn't care. The only thing she was hungry for was this new world of secrets, hints, clues. Nothing else existed. Learning with Avner was completely different from her studies with her father. She felt she was entering a truer world, one hidden beneath the everyday, in which, as Moshe had suggested, every moment, every gesture, every action, was freighted with meaning, with the possibility of raising sparks.

Avner opened one of the volumes of the Zohar he'd taken down from the shelf behind his desk and riffled through the pages until he found what he was looking for. 'That first tree you saw was meant to scare you. It was a test, to see if you were ready. Here, listen to this.' He propped himself on his elbow, and read aloud.

'*The highest place… is the source of all light, and ignites all other lamps… from this place emerges a tree for quenching thirst and creating matter. This unique higher tree stands above all trees… But God set another tree below it… so that whoever wants to reach the higher tree can only enter with permission. Whoever wants to reach it, encounters the lower tree and is afraid to continue unless they are worthy. This lower tree is the guardian… so that the inhabitants of the earth will fear it and will not draw near, except for those who are worthy to draw near – and no-one else!* He looked up at her expectantly. 'Those who are worthy, see? It was meant to terrify you, and it succeeded at first. But you didn't let your fear stop you from leaping into the unknown. That's why the next time you saw the tree, over the Sea of Galilee, you went towards it.'

'But that wasn't the same tree. It was upside down, like the one in the Ari's synagogue.'

'You are right. One tree conceals the other. The first was the tree of terror, of knowledge of Good and Evil, of rules and regulations, the tree of the Law. This is the tree of *Gevurah* – the *Sefira* of barriers and boundaries. It guards the way to the true tree, the Tree of Life. This second tree is the one you saw once you responded to the call. This tree has its roots in Heaven for it represents the *Sefira* of *Chesed*, of mystical possibility, which only the true Kabbalist has access to. Those who reach this higher tree can gain access to special powers.'

Malka thought of the scorch-marks on the bakery table. 'What kind of powers? What am I?'

'That depends. I think the question is, what *could* you be? I have an idea, but at this stage it's just that.'

'Please. Tell me.'

'The Torah says that God spoke the world into existence. Kabbalists believe that speech still resonates through the cosmos, sustaining the Universe. We live in a time when words and their meanings are ruptured, torn from each other, like God and the Shekhina.' His voice lingered caressingly on the 'na', as if unwilling to let the word go. 'The Shekhina represents the healing power of God's original language. The language of creation. Why did the dove that Noah sent from the ark become a symbol of peace? In the Kabbalah, that bird is the symbol of the Shekhina, because it bridges the seen and unseen worlds – it brings back a branch from the heavenly tree in its beak. So it suggests her role of *Tikkun*, repair. Like Noah, we float in a closed little box of our perceptions, on top of a great sea of meaning, and sometimes the Shekhina flutters her wings and brings us an olive branch from the world of the spirit. If we could reach out and take that branch, touch the tree, we could bridge the gap between our own speech and God's, release the creative energy buried within all speech. Malka, I believe you are my olive branch.'

Malka shook her head in confusion.

'Sorry, I'm getting ahead of myself. Wait. I know how I can explain it. Tonight is *Rosh Chodesh Nissan*, right? We say the *Kiddush Levanah* prayer to welcome the new month, the new moon of Nissan.'

Malka quoted from memory. 'May the light of the moon be like the light of the sun, like the light of the seven days of creation, as it was before it was diminished.'

Malka remembered her sister Estie holding forth on the status of men and women to their mother. 'Isn't this prayer based on a children's story, where the moon complains about not being equal to the sun, and God lessens its light as a punishment? I learned that *midrash* in nursery. Women always have to hide their light, so men can shine.'

'The whole Bible is just a children's story, if we read it like children. The word Midrash comes from the root *darash*, which means to seek, to search for. Look deeper. Women are associated with the moon. You were taught this story so you would know your place. But that's a corruption of the original story, which is about the possibility of change. The crucial point is that in the *midrash*, the moon is exiled. You see? It's our job to try to raise her up, rekindle her light, which is the original light of creation, of harmony. Sound familiar?'

'So the moon is the Shekhina too?'

'I think the Shekhina is a kind of code word for the divine energy which hides in plain sight, waiting to be released. The face of the Shekhina is everywhere, if you know where to look for her. Kabbalah teaches us that art of seeing.'

The hours sped by, and it was late before Malka finally crawled into bed, exhausted but happy. At last, Avner had let her back into the world of learning that had been closed to her for so long. Even better, he had taken the terror from her visions of the tree and her father's experience of the birds, and filled them with possibility and wonder. Just as she was drifting off, Shira prodded her shoulder.

'Hey sister, I hardly see you these days. Where have you been hiding?'

'I've been learning with Avner.'

'What, just the two of you?' Shira's eyes widened. 'I mean, that's great, it's just what you wanted.'

'You don't sound very convinced.'

'Maybe I'm a little envious. You know I carry a torch for him, and he's never singled out one student before. I'm glad it's you, sweetie. But I'm worried about you. Look how pale you are. Just like those yeshiva boys in Jerusalem you told me about, who stay indoors all day studying, never seeing the light of the sun. Is that what you want to become?'

'So what do you suggest? It's night now. Should I moonbathe?'

'You need to get out more. A bunch of us girls are going out clubbing, to celebrate the new moon. Come and join us!'

'Clubbing?' Shira had taught her a lot of English words, but knowing their meaning didn't always help. Malka had a visual image of people hitting one another. She looked warily at Shira's biceps.

'It means dancing, silly. You ever been dancing?'

'Only at weddings. Enough to know I can't dance.' She thought with a pang of Estie's wedding, which she had missed. Now her older sister was married to a monster, and the same fate awaited Devvie. But there was nothing she could do for her little sister, unless Devvie was brave enough to escape the clutches of that world, as she had done. Perhaps when she was ready, she could invite Devvie to join her?

Shira pulled her covers off.

'Hey! I'm tired. And I've got nothing to wear.'

'So that's your excuse? I've been dying to give you a makeover for weeks. Cinderella, you shall go to the ball!'

She dragged a large blue holdall from under her bed, and emptied its contents on top of Malka.

'Hey!' Malka rolled over and lifted a bra off her face. It was covered in lilac lace so delicate she feared it might flutter apart in her hands. She put it down quickly. 'You actually wear these?'

Shira grinned wickedly.

'Excellent start. Good underwear is a girl's secret weapon. Like in life, you just need the right support.' She pulled the neck of her white top to reveal a bright blue strap. 'But they need to fit you properly, you can't wear any of mine. Don't worry, we'll shop, sweetheart. In the meantime, let's see what works.'

Malka felt slightly dazed. It wasn't just fatigue. She had never been the focus of this kind of attention, and usually preferred not to think about how she looked. That was why she always got undressed in the dark, under her covers.

'Would you mind turning around?' she asked Shira.

'Sure thing.'

The air felt strange against her skin. She had never felt excitement at the thought of getting dressed before. She was fascinated by the visible shape of her stomach under a clingy vest. She liked the little buttons it had down the front. The only comments she'd had about her body growing up were from Estie, and she'd simply assumed that her sister was right and she was overweight. What if her sister was wrong, and every girl was simply a different shape?

'Your breasts are like apples,' Shira quoted to her teasingly from the Song of Songs.

Malka crossed her arms over her chest. 'Hey, I said turn around!'

'I'm just jealous. These always pull guys' eyes away from my face.' Shira lifted her own breasts and let them fall. 'I guess that's not such a bad thing.'

Malka blushed. 'What do you mean?'

'Well, my face is a bit lived in.' She stroked her slightly crooked lower jaw. 'Colourful, my last boyfriend called my face. Well, it was by the time he finished with me...'

'You mean he hit you? But that's terrible!' Surely this must be the case, even in the real world? Once, she would have thought it was terrible that Shira had let a boy touch her.

'I always go for the bad ones, that's my problem. But tonight is about you.' Shira began selecting items and throwing them at Malka.

'Here, try this skirt. This top might look good on you too.'

Malka picked up the skirt and stroked the fabric. It was crushed purple velvet, and felt like the skin of a peach. She put it down reluctantly. She'd promised herself when she left Jerusalem that she would never wear a skirt again.

'No? So try these, they have always been too small for me. Wishful thinking, that purchase.'

She handed Malka a tight pair of jeans, very different from the baggy ones she'd bought in the Jerusalem charity shop, which she had worn until they were frayed. She had grown used to the feeling of cloth hugging her body, instead of flapping against her legs and letting in draughts like the skirts she'd worn in her previous life. But these didn't just sit on her body, they clung to her.

'Great! Now go take a walk in your new skin.'

Malka twirled around. 'I really feel like a girl in these,' she said.

'You finally look like one,' Shira snorted, and put more and more clothes on Malka, until the two of them collapsed on the bed laughing, swathed in layers of clashing colours and strange fabrics like creatures from a fairy tale.

'What's your story, Malka? When will you tell me what brought you here?'

'You first. Where did you learn to sing like that? I love your voice.'

'Thanks honey. Truth is, I adored soul music. Probably because there was no soul in my home. Lots of rooms, but all empty. The people too. So I used to listen to the wind in the trees at night and imagine it was swaying to the sound of Ella Fitzgerald.'

'El-lah who? Is she Jewish?'

'Are you serious? Now you're dressed for the part, we need to get started on your musical education, girl. Let's go bring down the moon!'

As they boarded the bus to Tiberias, Malka glanced at the other girls. Floating in her little Avner-Evven-Shira bubble, she still hadn't been to a class. Apart from Shira, the ones she recognised were Negina, Rina, and Tzlil from the dorm. Avner gives all the women at ME musical names, except for me, she thought with a wry smile. The others thought she was smiling at them, and smiled back warily. They still didn't know what to make of her. They accepted her because of Shira. These last few weeks she'd been pushing even Shira away, losing herself in her studies with Avner. Perhaps this was her chance to join in, to finally feel part of the group. But when Shira led her down a side-street behind the bus-station, she began to have misgivings. The club, Lilith, was little more than a hole in the wall, a dark maw that swallowed the people waiting in line ahead of her. With mounting terror, Malka saw that there were many men jostling in the line, smoking, laughing, punching one another's shoulders. Their voices were loud, meant for other ears than those they spoke to.

'Wait. You didn't tell me there would be boys!'

Shira laughed and took her hand. 'Don't you worry, girl. Stick with me and you will be fine.'

'What kind of music do they play here?' Malka tried to be casual and belie the tremor in her voice.

'The best! Eighties anthems.' Shira looked at Malka's blank face. 'It's the rhythm that matters, not the words. Trust me, you'll love it.'

To her surprise, she did. The space inside was dark, but this was strangely comforting. In the flicker of strobe lights, even Shira was barely visible. No one could stare at Malka, even if they'd wanted to. But the music noticed her. As she moved away from the wall and into a space, her arms and legs moved of their own accord, lifted on the waves of sound. She felt the thrum of it in her toes, her fingers, thrilling right up her spine, just like when she had rocked herself against the edge of the bakery table. As she spun faster, she felt herself expand until she became one with the other dancers, merging with them into a single gigantic body filled with starlight and the heartbeat of the earth itself, amplified by the flickering light. So that's why they call it *chashmal*, she thought. What had Avner said about the upper tree? Tonight, she felt she was climbing its branches. She hadn't felt this way since she'd met Moshe at Lazlo's. She blinked away a sweat droplet and saw him perched on a red stool, smiling at her, his lips stained with tomato sauce. His image merged into the rising storm of music that whipped through her. She climbed higher. She glimpsed Moshe again through the branches. Words danced in the leaves. Then he was gone. She'd lost him. She would never see him again. All at once, she was falling. The lights flickered and went out, and the music stopped.

Malka peered through the blackness. 'What happened?'

Shira's voice sounded reassuringly at her side. 'Must be a power cut. It happens all the time. I guess that's our cue.' Shira led her back outside, and hugged her sweatily. 'O. My. God. I thought you said you couldn't dance? I will never believe anything you say again. You were amazing!'

'I was? I thought no-one could see me?' Malka shivered in the night air. The memory of Moshe had jolted her. He probably had no clue where she was. He must think that drawing was a

127

joke. What about her family? They would be horrified if they had seen her cavorting in such an immodest place. She felt suddenly nauseous. Her stomach spasmed, and Shira held back her hair as she threw up on the pavement, just missing their shoes.

'Best keep you off the booze, though,' Shira joked. She didn't let go of Malka's hand until they got back to ME. She didn't stop talking about Malka's dancing the whole way, but Malka welcomed the respite from her own thoughts. She feared the moment when she would have to close her eyes and be alone with them.

Malka was too tired to undress. Every part of her ached. Lying in bed, she found that the music still vibrated through her, lifting her towards the ceiling, refusing to let her go. It had somehow become bound up with Moshe's image. Now he was trying to tell her something, but the music drowned him out. She remembered the way he had stroked the volume of the Zohar on the pizzeria counter. She knew how that felt now. To desire knowledge. What would his long fingers feel like if they touched her that way? Once she'd thought it, no matter how many times she rolled over, the thought refused to go away.

She was woken by Shira shaking her shoulder.

'Come on, Sleeping Beauty, it's nine already. Class already started!'

'Shit!'

'Wash your mouth first, girl!'

She was finally being allowed to join a class, and she was late. What would Avner say? At least she was already dressed. She leapt out of bed and they raced down the corridor to the classroom. It was a room Malka hadn't seen before. They slid onto rubber mats at the back. Luckily, the room was dark, except for a spotlight at the front, where Avner stood in a red tracksuit.

'What kind of class is this?' she whispered to Shira. 'Where are the desks, the books?'

'This used to be the gym. Now it's a place for spiritual workouts,' Shira replied. 'Watch and learn!'

'I'm glad you girls could join us,' Avner smiled briefly and turned back to the class. 'In a couple of weeks, it will be *Pesach*, Passover, the festival of freedom. Who can set you free from your inner slavery?' His voice was low, urgent.

'M.E.! Me!' The room chorused. It was infectious. Malka found herself chanting along with the rest.

'To taste the true freedom that is the gift of *Pesach*, we need to leave our slave mentality behind us. The Hebrew word for Egypt, *Mitzrayim*, is recast by the Zohar as *Meytzarim*, narrowness, constriction. This teaches us that to be truly free, we must first become aware of the shackles we've created to prevent us reaching our potential, what the poet William Blake called our 'mind forged manacles'. To help you with this, I'm going to tie you up.'

Malka's eyes widened in alarm.

'What the fuck?' Shira whispered. 'He's never done anything like this before.'

'I thought you said that word was only for emergencies?' Malka whispered back. Her friend's unease made her even more anxious.

'Quiet at the back please. Listen carefully. The *Haggadah* we recite on *Seder* night says in every generation we must consider ourselves slaves. So I want to actualise that, make it concrete. I'm going to enable you to confront your inner slavery. If anyone feels uncomfortable, at any time, let me know and I will release you at once. For this to work, I need you to trust, to let go. This is a potentially transformative exercise. So, get comfortable on your mats, close your eyes, and clasp your hands together on your chest, like you are praying. I will come round with some rope, and bind your hands and feet together, as Isaac was bound by his father on the altar. This turned him into a *Korban*, a sacrifice. The root of this word, this state, is *Karov*, meaning closer. Being bound helps with what the Kabbalists called *Bittul*

Hayesh, the subjugation or annihilation of our ego. That ego, that 'Me' voice, is the last barrier between us and truly being close to God. That's why, when God finally spoke to the liberated Israelites at Sinai, the Talmud says he held the mountain over them until they agreed to accept his law. Obedience requires obliterating the ego. We must let go of our narrow sense of self, to embrace who we really are.'

As he spoke, he moved round the room with strands of white rope. He was getting closer. Malka willed herself to lie down on her mat. Taking comfort from the presence of Shira right beside her, Malka closed her eyes and clasped her hands together. She felt Avner's warm breath on her face and the rope tighten around her hands and feet. She strained a moment against the cord and felt it bite into her flesh. She was completely immobilised.

'I hope that's not too tight Malka,' he whispered in her ear, then straightened and spoke loudly to the class.

'Now you are all bound and ready, I want you to do a visualisation exercise. Choose one of the ten plagues with which God afflicted the Egyptians. Each of them was meant to raise awareness, to break the Egyptians from their restricted thinking. But each was ignored. Choose the one which resonates with you the most. That's the one which symbolises your own inner condition. Really go into it, let yourself feel it. Enter your slave state fully, and once you come through it, you will have released yourself. I will guide you through this process. Finally, when you are ready, open your eyes. Then I will come round and untie you, and those who wish to can share their experiences.'

'That's the part I hate most,' Shira muttered.

Malka tried to do as she was told. At first, all she could see was the blood beating in her lids in alternating flashes of purple and green. It was hard not to fight the ropes. She tried to remember the way she had felt the night before in the club, to feel the light surging through her. But instead, she saw herself from above, climbing the stairs to the flat in Jerusalem. She was carrying heavy bags in the dark. When she pressed the light switch, nothing happened. Then Malka found herself pulled down into the body she was observing. She stood outside the family front door and hammered against it until her fists were sore. There was no answer. Then something rustled in the darkness, and brushed against her face. A cobweb? She tried to wave it away and found her hand was full of feathers. Birds collided in the air around her. They struck her with the edges of their wings, again and again. Soon the space was so thick with them she could not move. Some were dying under the weight of the birds above them. In the thicket of wings, it was impossible to tell the living from the dead. More and more birds pressed down on top of her. Feathers filled her nose and mouth, caught in her hair. Sharp beaks scratched at her arms. In another moment, she would be theirs. She opened her eyes with a gasp. Avner's face floated serenely against the far wall, glowing in the huge mirror like a moon. He nodded to her and smiled. He came over quietly, untied her arms and legs, and then went around the room releasing the other students.

'Now gently come back to your body, and slowly open your eyes. When you are ready, sit up. That was intense, right? Time to share. Malka, would you like to go first?'

A room full of people swivelled towards her.

'Sorry, I'm not feeling well, will you excuse me?' It was just what she'd said to her family the night Zechariah's family visited. But this time she really meant it. Before anyone could stop her, she rose and fled the room.

An hour later, just before her shift with Shira in the bakery, Malka stood outside Avner's office. Yesterday she would have rushed straight in. Now she had to steel herself just to knock on the door.

'Come in.'

Avner looked up from behind his desk as she stepped across the threshold. He was still wearing his red tracksuit.

'Ah, Malka, it's you. No need to knock. I'm sorry if I put you on the spot this morning. How did you find the class? I know my unorthodox approach can be a little unsettling. How are you feeling?' He was looking at her strangely.

Maybe it was because she was still wearing the tight vest and jeans from last night instead of her usual baggy charity clothes. She tugged the vest away from herself. Why hadn't she changed? She felt ridiculous.

'Come, sit down.' He motioned to the cushions on the floor.

'I'd rather stand. Can I ask you something?'

'Sure.'

'Tell me the truth. Why have you given everyone else a new name, except for me? Is there something wrong with me?'

'Quite the opposite. Why, does it bother you?'

'The Talmud says if you change your name, you change your luck, your destiny. As you know, more than anything I came here to change my fate.'

'I don't think any of us can avoid our fate. As I've said before, Malka, your name expresses both who you are and who you might become. In fact, I think it might be the very weapon you need to defeat the forces that assail you. The Zohar suggests that the brightest sparks are often concealed in the thickest darkness.'

Malka started. She hadn't told him what she'd seen in the morning class. So how did he know?

'This morning you confronted your fear, the darkness that pursues you. That's the first step towards liberation. That's why Moshe goes into "the thick darkness" on Sinai. For that, the Torah says, is where God is.'

Her legs collapsed and she found herself sprawled amongst the cushions before she realised he was talking about the biblical Moshe. Why was she always making a fool of herself around Avner? He came round from behind the desk and sat beside her, as he did when they studied together. But he was closer this time. He smelt slightly acrid, of sweat. He patted her shoulder.

'You know Malka, I also ran away from my family. Before he could become Abraham, Abram was told *Lech Lecha*, meaning go to yourself. He had to leave everything he knew- his land, the place of his birth, his father's house, and go to the place that was God. For remember, in the Torah, Makom, the word for place, is also one of God's names. For God is above all a place inside us. Tell me, what did you see in the visualisation this morning?'

Malka shook her head. She didn't want to think about it.

'That's OK, share it when you are ready. I'm trying to say that like you, like Abram, I once thought I'd lost everything. But sometimes I think you have to let go of everything that made you, to find yourself. That's what I was aiming at with the exercise this morning. When I came to this country, after some unpleasantness in the States, I had a vision, in the middle of a field in Kibbutz Beit Sha'an, just like you did with your tree. For one ecstatic moment, the sun pressed down on my back like God's thumb, pushing me into the earth. It was beautiful, terrifying. When I came back to myself, sweating and trembling, muddy and laughing all at once, I left the tractor I was working on standing in the field, the engine still running. I knew I'd been called.'

'But didn't you miss your family?'

'Malka, if you are to fulfil your potential, you have to let go of the guilt you feel about those you left behind. They were not on your level, Malka, they didn't understand you and would have only held you back. This is where you are meant to be. But sometimes the darkness of the past yields unexpected gifts. I think that's what your experience this morning was trying to tell you.'

He smiled at her, and she glowed.

'I have an idea for something we could try, to help you let go of the past. But we need to go somewhere where we won't be disturbed.'

'I might know of a place.' Malka hadn't told anyone about her 'cave,' but she was eager to please him, to make up for disappointing him in class. So she told him of her place in the woods.

'You know, God works in mysterious ways. I was just exploring the possibility of creating a retreat for the advanced students, somewhere they can work on meditation and visualization. Your cave sounds perfect!'

Malka didn't want to share it with anyone else. 'It's very small. More of a hole than a cave.'

'Let's go check it out.' Avner stood up.

'What, now?'

'Sure. Now is a gift. That's why it's called the present.'

Chapter 9
Into Darkness

L ast night, talking with his mother, Moshe finally understood something which had always puzzled him. A year after Yulia had gone missing, his parents had conducted a ceremony on the beach. There had been a little shrine to her by then, with cuddly toys, flowers and candles left by locals. Moshe brought her favourite bear, ragged and chewed, and while his father spoke of the light Yulia had brought to their lives, he threw it into the water. He'd hoped it would reach her, that wherever she was she would not be alone. His mother had waded into the sea to get the bear back. He watched her fruitlessly fighting the waves, terrified that she would drown and he would lose her too.

Looking at his mother across the table, he'd suddenly understood the madness of plunging into the sea, and why she was fighting with him to stay. For her, every scrap of his sister had been precious. Though she had eventually returned empty-handed, dripping and furious, part of her never made it back to dry land. Yet she still came to see him off. She had looked haggard, but he could feel the fierce strength of her arms encircling him. He knew that each time she said goodbye she feared it might be the last time they would ever see each other. He could only imagine how much it cost her to let him go. He tried hard to reassure her. I will be back soon, I promise. But this was his version of leaping into the sea. He had no idea when he would return. Only that he couldn't give up.

The bus stopped in Tiberias, right by the Kinneret, a lake so big that Christians called it the Sea of Galilee. It was the largest body of water he'd seen in years. If he was to pour himself into finding the lost girl in his present, he must first make peace with the one from his past.

'We leave in twenty minutes!' the driver shouted after him.

When he crossed the road, Moshe narrowly missed being hit by a motorbike driving along the pavement. He stepped aside quickly, catching a glimpse of a mane of shaggy hair, then was nearly blinded by a flash of light, a spinning halo that sped past him towards the lake. He traced it back to its source, a spinning bicycle wheel held in a metal frame. An older man in mechanics' overalls stood with a young boy, guiding him as he worked the spokes to an equal tension, and as Moshe watched, the lopsided wheel slowly centred itself. The boy spun the wheel slowly, testing its trueness with a cupped palm. Circles of light haloed the pair as the sun burnished the wheel. The same fire touched the lake behind them. Moshe felt he'd been granted a private epiphany, and let the sense of grace carry him towards the rocky shore.

The water was so clear, he could see the stones at the bottom. He knelt and plunged his head beneath the surface. He noticed how each stone rested on those around it. The whole lake floor was one interlocking mosaic. He picked out a handful of flat white stones, and watched others roll in to take their place. He rose and shook his head, sending droplets dancing. The water from the lake was sweet in his mouth, with a mineral taste as refreshing as the resinous tang of his beloved stream in the Jerusalem hills. The stones nestled in his palm. He skimmed them one by one across the lake's surface. The first sank, but the second kept going. He still had two stones, so he must have picked up four. Like the four who entered the Pardes. He hoped it was a good sign. The late afternoon sun blurred the boundary between the water's edge and the shore into a single wash of pale gold. He had not prayed in many months but the space felt charged, numinous. He spoke aloud, his voice carrying across the water.

'Please, God. If I'm not meant to find her, keep her safe. You haven't done a very good job with the people I care about up till now. So make an effort. Start with her.'

Around him, all was quiet. From where he stood, the hum of traffic mingled with the sound of the waves lapping at his feet. The bus honked, and Moshe headed back aboard. Next stop Safed.

Late last night, after helping to clean and lock up the pizzeria, he'd asked Lazlo to come from a walk. Though he had been on his feet all day, Lazlo agreed without a murmur. They found a bench in Liberty Bell Park and watched illicit lovers creep past into the bushes. Although the woody scent of bonfires was all around them, Lazlo lit a cigarette, and smoke curlicued between his fingers. 'Happy Lag Ba'Omer. Don't fancy yourself as a fire-starter?'

Moshe shook his head. 'I'm going after her, Lazlo.'

Lazlo inhaled deeply, and looked at Moshe through veils of smoke.

'About time. What did your mother say when you told her?'

'That I'm pursuing a foolish fantasy.'

'She's right, of course.'

'Is that what you think?'

'Sometimes you have to know when to let go.'

'Do you mean me, or my mum?'

Lazlo leaned back and exhaled towards the sky. 'I married too young. We were still in school, and I thought we were just messing around. Then she became pregnant and her father made sure we married. For me, it was like a prison sentence. I left soon after the baby was born.'

'So you have a child back in Russia?'

'A son, yes. He'd be about your age now.'

'What's his name?'

'She called him Yuri. I write, and send money. I don't know if the letters reach him, but she cashes my checks.'

'You've never mentioned him before.'

'Why do you never speak of your father?'

'It hurts too much.'

'Exactly.'

'Why not bring him here, or go and meet him?'

'That's up to him. If he wants to, he knows where to find me. Though I'm just a name to him. If that. For all I know, he may think I'm dead. Perhaps he's right, in a way.' He threw the glowing butt into the fountain. He stood, and Moshe rose too. To his surprise, Lazlo enfolded him in an awkward, bearlike hug.

'Don't let her get away. She's special, that one.'

'I know. Just promise me you'll look after yourself, and keep an eye on my mother.'

'She's a grown woman.'

'Lazlo...'

'You have my word.'

He walked off without looking back. Moshe had watched him thread along the necklace of streetlights, until he disappeared into the darkness. The next morning, Moshe caught the bus to Safed.

The first thing that hit him as he got off the bus was the smell. It reminded him of Zechariah, on those days when he seemed to be conserving water with particular zeal. The bus depot was in a little depression, and he waded uphill through drifts of rubbish. The streets were littered with cans, broken bottles, empty shopping bags that wheeled drunkenly in the wind. Moshe consulted his map of Safed for suitably mystical names. There were so many. He decided to follow instinct, and headed for 'Messiah alley'.

The alley was so narrow, he had to turn sideways to pass through. Perhaps it was an allusion. *All of this world is a corridor en route to the world to come*. He'd marked several spots on the map that seemed like possibilities, and began climbing the steep, broken-slabbed steps toward the Ancient Synagogues. Perhaps if he showed Malka's photo to the attendants, they might recognize her. The older, Sephardi Ari Synagogue was closed for repairs, its gate locked. Damn. This was the one with the painted trees which adorned his copy of the Zohar, which Malka had drawn for him. He peered through the bars at the tantalizing blue door, remembering the creak of Reb Zushya's as he'd closed it carefully behind him earlier that morning. He'd left Reb Moshe some food, but the cat hadn't come when he called. He shook them again, but the gates remained resolutely shut. 'Malka, where are you?' he whispered. The wind whipped his words away.

He refused to give up so easily. He headed for the newer, *Ashkenazi* Ari Synagogue, which competed with the *Sephardi* one over the claim that the great mystic had prayed inside it. Since the Ari's family had arrived from Spain with the other Sephardim in the wake of the great expulsions of 1492, Moshe thought it unlikely. He could see from down the street that the front door of the pseudo-Ari synagogue was open. He quickened his step. As he approached, a wave of disinfectant stung his nostrils. The air was thick with it. He peered in to the dark, ornate room. A lone woman was mopping the floor vigorously. When she saw him peering in, she shook her head.

'We are closed for cleaning,' she said in Russian-accented Hebrew.

Moshe answered her in Russian. 'Little mother, Passover is long gone.' He held out Malka's picture. 'Can you help? I am looking for a lost girl.'

'Sorry. Only old men come here. Old men and tourists. Tell me, does it smell clean to you? They like it to smell clean.'

'Yes,' said Moshe. 'Like a hospital.'

She took this as a compliment, and smiled. 'Try the hostels on Bar Yochai Street.'

There were fifteen hostels, each one shabbier than the last. None of them had seen a girl with red hair. He felt a wave of despair engulf him. What if she'd changed her appearance, cut her hair, dyed it, covered it? A young woman hurried past pushing a double buggy with a gaggle of small children in tow. Perhaps she was their sister, rather than their mother. He headed after her, hoping to find someone else to ask. She entered a supermarket. Gazing at the shop-front, he realized that he was starving. He hadn't eaten anything all day. Inside, many of the shelves were bare. Those that still had stock were full of huge economy packs of toilet paper, cereal, beans. Nothing remotely tempting. He went to the cashiers and showed them Malka's picture. They looked at him blankly.

'Do you sell any sandwiches here?' Moshe asked. He rummaged in his pocket and drew out a battered note, the cashier shook her head.

'Sorry, we only take food coupons.'

Of course. In the more run-down areas of Jerusalem, they ran similar places, with state-subsidised food vouchers for the many impoverished ultra-orthodox families where the husbands studied but didn't work. Lazlo often grumbled about them. 'Show me where it is written that you are meant to sit all day and learn. All the Rabbis you tell me about in the Talmud had jobs, didn't they?' It was true. Maimonides in his code of Jewish Law, the *Mishneh Torah*, carefully codified how many days you should devote to Torah study based on your profession. Maimonides himself had been the Sultan's physician in the twelfth century, another gifted Spanish Jew. Borrowing freely from Arabic and Greek philosophy, he'd crafted a coherent philosophy of Judaism, interweaving lore and law. This syncretic vision was what Moshe himself had aspired to, when he'd first joined the yeshiva. Maimonides had also been called Moshe. 'From Moses in the Bible, until Moses Maimonides, there was no one like Moses,' the saying went. It hadn't been enough to stop his books being burned as heresy. Now the radical rabbi was part of the establishment, his books covered in the dust of reverence.

Luria had blazed a trail across the Middle East to Safed. His Kabbalah teacher, Joseph Caro, soon became his disciple. Yet the Ashkenazi community he had joined here scorned him and his Sephardi brethren. Some things hadn't changed in four hundred years. Perhaps everyone needed someone to look down on. Any Jew who spoke Arabic as a first language was somehow suspect to the European elite who ran the country. Yet once he was safely dead, the Ashkenazi community built a synagogue in his name.

Someone rammed a trolley into Moshe from behind, and he turned. A line of trolleys stretched behind him. The cashier stared at him pointedly.

'Sorry. Is there another supermarket near here?'

'There was, but it closed down.'

Moshe trudged to the top of the hill on which the city was built. He looked longingly at Mount Meron in the distance. The mountain wore its aura of mystery with studied nonchalance. What would its most famous resident, Shimon Bar Yochai, have done in his situation? He certainly wouldn't stop until he found what he was seeking. Moshe leaned out so far over the railings that he nearly fell into the trees below. That's what he needed. A walk in the woods to clear his head.

There was a network of pathways worn through the woodland. Moshe had read that the local *Breslovers* used them for *Hisbodedus*, their therapy time with God, so he kept a careful lookout. He didn't want to intrude on anyone. Prayer was not a spectator sport. That was why he hated the Western Wall. Too much symbolism, not enough silence.

The scent of the pine needles underfoot took him back to the forests of his childhood. But these trees were young. He followed the sound of birdsong and found himself in a little clearing. Someone had dumped a load of industrial rubbish there. Typical.

Then something caught his eye, and he went closer. There was a row of books tucked away in a low, precarious space between two concrete slabs. He bent down and slipped inside. He held his breath, waiting for the walls to fall on him. Nothing happened. He looked up and laughed at himself. The slabs were covered with ivy. They were not about to fall any time soon. The books inside were familiar – mostly volumes from the Zohar. They looked well used. Someone clearly fancied themselves as another Bar Yochai. A few were scattered at the back of the cave, as though a private storm had raged here. On the ground in the middle of the cave was a pile of ash. An odd place for a bonfire. When he waved his palm over the embers, they were still warm. A hole, no bigger than his fist, had been made in the concrete roof, presumably to let the smoke out, as it was blackened at the edges. Then, plastered against one slab, he noticed a strange mark. Graffiti? No, it was a sooty handprint, like a brand. I'm procrastinating again, he thought. A white glimmer caught his eye. A stone, very similar to the ones he had seen at the Sea of Galilee, nestled amongst the ashes, like a phoenix egg. It had a curlicue etched into it, like a closed eye. He took it as a souvenir. It was still warm from the fire. He crawled out of the cave, clutching the stone, and continued his search.

He caught the scent of wood smoke. Maybe it was the cave dweller at work again Moshe followed the drifting smoke towards a sign saying 'Park.' He knew by now not to get his hopes up.

The 'park' turned out to be a bare patch of scuffed earth, with shards of coloured glass scattered across it from a shattered map of the city. In one corner, a group of boys huddled round a fire. He'd found the source.

'What are you burning? Lag Ba'Omer was yesterday.'

They didn't look up.

'Tell me, have you seen this woman?' he asked out of habit.

'It's *ossur* to look at pictures of women,' one said. He couldn't have been more than seven.

'This is different. Her life might be in danger, so that ruling doesn't apply,' Moshe replied.

This piqued their interest, and they invited him to join them. His time in the yeshiva had been useful after all.

'Hi, I'm Chezki,' said the oldest. 'We found a dead bird, so we are giving it a funeral. Do you want to come and see?'

Moshe introduced himself, and sat down with them. He could see no evidence of a bird in the feeble fire. The circle of young Orthodox boys, their *payot* straggling in the wind, was strangely comforting. Chezki fed the fire with the innards of a newspaper, holding it between his knees. The paper flapped in the wind and seemed about to fly away, so Moshe caught it, and handed it back to him. The boy looked up at him.

'We haven't really found a bird, that's just what I tell any grownups who ask. I read to my brothers from this *chiloni* newspaper. We are strictly forbidden to read it. So after we read it, we burn it, because it's an unclean thing.'

Out of habit, Moshe scanned the page in his hand. The image of a clean-shaven man holding a police sign stared back at him. *Is missing cult leader dangerous sex offender?* He skimmed the first paragraph, as the boys watched.

Detectives are combing through the remains of Mystical Encounters, a cult organisation run by Abraham Markovich, a.k.a. Avner Marcus, an alleged sex offender, for any clues as to his whereabouts. The building was completely destroyed in last night's fire. Police are treating the fire as suspicious. Markovich himself may have set the building on fire for insurance purposes. The cult members were on a Lag Ba'Omer trip to Meron, so the building was empty, and no fatalities were reported. Cult members are being treated for shock. It has emerged that Markovich fled the States for Israel in the wake of a scandal at the all-girls high school where he taught. The incident was hushed up, and it seems that members of Mystical Encounters may have paid the price. The investigation is ongoing. Anyone with information about his whereabouts is asked to—'

One of the boys tugged at his sleeve, interrupting his reading. 'Can we see her? The lady in the picture?'

Moshe held out the photo, and the boy touched it gently with his ragged fingers.

'We know her!' he said. 'She's the biscuit lady.'

'Let me see, let me see.' The others crowded round Moshe, all talking at once. Two were identical twins. They were all siblings, he realized.

'Shah,' said Chezki. 'Let me tell him. There was a bakery. Run by the bad man in the newspaper, the American. But it was kosher. Whenever we went to pick up our *challos*, if she was there, she always gave me a biscuit.'

'Me too, me too!' The others chimed.

'She kept the broken ones in her pockets. She always saved them for us.'

'The cinnamon ones were my favourite,' whispered one of the twins, touching his lips. Moshe rose to his feet, his stomach churning, and they fell silent. He waved the newspaper at them.

'The girl in the picture, she stayed in this place?' He tried to keep his voice even.

They nodded enthusiastically. For them this was just a game. The smallest boy stood on tiptoe and whispered in Chezki's ear.

'Yossi wants to tell you something,' Chezki said. He pushed the little boy forward, who swallowed shyly, then spoke in a rush.

'I saw her. We stayed up really late because of Lag Ba'Omer. We went to Meron on the bus. When we came back, I was sleeping on my *tateh*'s shoulder.'

Chezki laughed. 'How could you see her if you were sleeping, you *baal chaloimos*?

'Wait, I'm not finished! A loud noise woke me. Someone ran past, and jumped in front of a bus. It was her for sure. I saw her in the headlights.'

In the silence, Moshe could hear the crackling flames. 'What happened?'

'It stopped just in time. She got on.'

'This was last night?' He couldn't believe he'd just missed her. Could it be true? 'Did you happen to see which bus it was?'

'I think it was going to Tel Aviv.'

The others looked at Yossi, shocked.

'She never would,' one of the twins said hotly.

'I would go there if I had to run away. No one would look for you in Hell. Besides, I've never seen the sea.'

'Yossi, I'm telling on you,' said Chezki.

'Then I will tell that you read newspapers.'

Moshe crouched down beside the boys. He'd been looking for a sign. Heavenly messengers came in strange guises. 'Chezki, don't tell on him. He just did a mitzvah. You should be proud of him.'

'I did?' Yossi smiled.

'Today, you've been God's hand in the world. All because you read those *treif* newspapers.' Moshe hugged him. The boy's head was hot against his own, and smelled of smoke. You've seen her, you've spoken to her, he thought. She'd been in danger of becoming just an idea for him, but these young boys had brought her back to life. This was the only lead he had, and despite his enduring terror of the sea, or perhaps because of it, he decided to trust this child's nocturnal vision. It was just like the Malka he knew, to make him confront his deepest fears. He tried not to think what might have happened to her if she'd been part of this awful man's cult.

He set off at a run for the bus station, not giving himself a chance to stop or think. If he did, he knew his courage would falter, and doubts would set in. He glanced back over his shoulder, and the little group were still standing there, watching and waving. He waved back. The bus to Tel Aviv was just loading. As they pulled away, Moshe leaned his forehead against the glass, and wondered what he would possibly do when he got there. In Safed, he'd had a chance of tracking her down. But Tel Aviv? Have faith, he told himself. You will need it.

Chapter 10
Strange Fire

Malka led Avner through the woodland to the abandoned building site. As they approached the clearing, she felt a twinge, the same cramps in her stomach she'd felt the night before. Was it her period? It was very early.

'I'm sorry, I'm not feeling so great. Maybe it was something I ate. I'd like to go back and just sleep it off. Maybe we can do this another time?'

Avner turned to her in the clearing. He was breathing fast.

'On the contrary. I think what you are suffering from is a kind of spiritual sea-sickness. I saw it in your face this morning, after the meditation class. You've swum away from the shore of your familiar self for the first time, and are tossing about in the deep water of true knowledge. I know what that's like, believe me. Hey, would you look at that! What a find!'

She wanted to stop him, to disagree, but he had already ducked inside the cave, and she had no choice but to crawl in after him. There was barely space for the two of them. She tried to see it through his eyes. One of the supports had fallen since she'd last been, and rainwater had dripped through as a result, creating a muddy pool in one corner. The books were still dry, luckily. She hoped he didn't think she had stolen them.

'I like your library.' When he turned to her, she could see pale bristles on his chin. If he had a beard, it would already be touched with white. Like her father's. He was older than he looked.

'This is perfect,' he said. He moved the volumes of the Zohar carefully to one side, further out of reach of the water. 'Which of these have you read?'

'All of them.' It was the truth.

He gave a low whistle. Her father had never looked this proud of her.

Looking steadily into her eyes, Avner slipped the red bracelet off her wrist, then removed his own. He had not touched her since her initiation, and it felt different this time, more lingering. Avner touched her as if he meant it, as if she was grown up, an equal. He stood, so she did too, and their heads almost touched in the narrow space. He placed the two bands on the floor, slightly overlapping one another.

'You are a trainee no more. It's time to step forward and fulfil your destiny. Come, let us draw down the moon.' Taking her hand, he knelt on the floor, holding her gaze, bringing her slowly down with him. He was making her nervous. She tried not to laugh.

'Malka, remember what we were saying about the two trees the other day? Let me tell you a secret. They also correspond to the two women created to be Adam's partners in Eden.'

'Two women? I thought there was only Eve.'

'That's because the rabbis demonised the first one, Lilith.'

Malka started. That was the name of the club from last night. Could it be a coincidence?

'Why do they have such a problem with her? Simple. The first time round, God created Man and Woman as equals. Like Adam, Lilith knew the power of God's name. But he couldn't handle her. He wanted someone subservient. So he banished her, and Eve took her place. She was more pliant, more suggestible. That's why Eve listened to the voice of the snake. I'm sure Lilith would have resisted.'

'Why are you telling me this?'

'After our conversation about your tree visions, I started thinking. The Zohar says that the Tree of Good and Evil was

Eve's tree, but the Tree of Life belongs to Lilith. The Zohar claims that Lilith is the Shekhina's opposite, that she is demonic, but I think that's just rabbis being scared of female power, as Adam was. I think the patriarchy has been keeping the Shekhina in chains. Think about a tree. It eats light, and embraces the sky, as the Shekhina longs to do with her Beloved. But its roots... They drink from the moist darkness, like Lilith. Malka, do you trust me?' His voice was unsteady, and there was a pleading expression on his face, something vulnerable. This really mattered to him.

She nodded, uncertain. 'What do you want me to do?'

'I believe we can only liberate the Shekhina by re-connecting her to her dark twin, to Lilith. Reconnecting the tree to its roots. Lie down, just like in class this morning.'

Malka lay on her back on the gritty floor of her cave, and looked up at him expectantly. His breath was shockingly loud in the enclosed space.

'Now remember, the birth of Solomon, the ancestor of the Messiah, came about when David lay with Batsheva. He sent her husband Uriah off to die on the front line, for he knew his desire was holy. Like them, we must enact the mingling of male and female realms. Close your eyes, and empty your mind of all thoughts of self.'

Malka had not been taught the story of David's adultery in school, of course, or of his execution of his mistress' husband by sending him into harms' way, but the Talmud discussed it at length, concocting myriad excuses for David's actions. So she'd gone back to the source in the Bible and seen that none of these excuses actually fitted the crime. She seized the opportunity to argue and sat up.

'But surely David sinned with Batsheva? Even the prophet Nathan who comes to him says so. He murdered her husband so he could possess her, and suffered for it the rest of his life.'

'Some holy actions may seem sinful to the uninitiated. I believe David knew what he was about. After all, he was a warrior for God, ready to pay a personal price for the greater good.'

Without breaking eye contact, he sat down beside her on the floor. She noticed that in his left eye, the pupil had a broken edge, and blackness leaked into the surrounding green, like in a child's painting.

'You sound like something from the *Sitra Achra*, the dark side.' She tried to turn her head, and he cupped her chin, forcing her to meet his gaze.

'You have to embrace the darkness to find the light. Every Kabbalist knows that. So did King David. Now, no more talking, Malka. I need you to concentrate. Remember the opening of the Zohar, of the Rose that is both white and red? White in her virginal state, the rose flushes red with desire for her Beloved, opening her petals to the dew, preparing herself for the light to be planted within her.' His voice softened to a whisper as he knelt beside her. 'Now, lie back down, close your eyes, and imagine I am the Sefira of Yesod, and you are Malkhut, your namesake. For that Sefira has a double life. It is the place where the Divine and the human mingle, the gateway to the Shekhina, both male and female. Together, let us become the point of light where God enters the world.'

Even with her eyes closed, Malka sensed Avner bending over her in the narrow space. His breath smelt of stale coffee. He stroked her arm, and she opened her eyes in alarm. His face was now so close to hers that his eyes had become one giant eye, the broken pupil like a hole in his face. His breath whistled in her ear. Then he lay down on top of her, pinning her arms with his hands. She felt the bones in her wrists grate together.

'Ow! What are you...?'

'Shh, don't speak. Hold still, concentrate. Let us make whole what was broken.'

He began to move his lower body against hers, supporting his torso so he could look down into her eyes. Pebbles and grit grated against her back.

149

'That's right. Rub out that ego, rub it out.'

He tugged at the waistband of her jeans, and she felt the button tear loose. For just a moment, one of her hands was free. She saw her chance, and raked her nails across his face. He arched back, cradling his face, and she rolled out from under him.

'Wait!' he cried. 'Don't stop now! We are so close, I can hear the footsteps of the Messiah.' The red marks she had made branded his cheek like scratches from a cat.

She hugged her knees to her chest, and drew as far away from him as she could, banging her head on the cave wall. One button had come away from her vest, and there was a spattering of earth at her throat. She lifted her eyes to his, and forced herself to hold his gaze and keep her voice steady, though every muscle screamed at her to get as far away from him as possible.

'Now is not the right time. I have my period. For a ritual like this, timing is everything. The Zohar suggests that the optimal time to summon the Shekhina is dawn on *Lag Ba'Omer*, the thirty-third day after Passover, when the barriers between heaven and earth are at their thinnest, for it is the anniversary of Bar Yochai's death. On his deathbed, the Zohar quotes him as saying "Now it is my desire to reveal secrets... This day will not go to its place like any other, for this entire day stands within my domain..." If we wait until then, his spirit will assist us. Let us journey to freedom through Passover first, as you suggested this morning, liberate ourselves from our past so we can create a better future. In the meantime, I can study and prepare myself to be a vessel. Then, at the appointed time, we can meet here.'

Something in what she said, or how she said it, must have been convincing. Avner stood up abruptly, brushing dirt from his knees.

'So be it,' he said huskily. 'Don't worry about my face, it's nothing. You are right, the date has a certain symmetry. Perhaps Bar Yochai's Holy Fire will fuel our quest, as you suggest. The other students at ME will be visiting Bar Yochai's tomb on mount

Meron for the traditional bonfire celebrations that evening, so we can be undisturbed. Let's meet back here at midnight on *Lag Ba'Omer*. You have a few weeks to make yourself ready.'

Malka got unsteadily to her feet. He stood blocking the exit from the cave. She tensed, ready to spring and knock him to the ground if she had to.

'I had better get back to the kitchen, or I will be missed.' She tugged her jeans back up with her free hand, a sweaty handprint soaking into the fabric. He touched a finger to her lips.

'Remember Malka, if it is to work, this ritual demands total secrecy. Not a word to anyone. Wait here for a few moments, before you leave. From now on, we shouldn't be seen together.'

Then, finally, he was gone. Malka ran out of the cave, and up the rocky scree behind it. She had to put as much distance as possible between them. She could see him standing in the clearing below her, adjusting his trousers for a moment. Then he strode downhill without looking back. She rubbed her bruised wrists. She had trusted him, opened up to him. And he had betrayed her.

'You bastard!'

Her voice echoed through the trees. She touched the tender side of her head. A thin trickle of blood was slowly matting her hair. The sight of the blood horrified her, and she scrambled down the slope and ducked back into the cave. Her knees gave way, and she sat in the dirt and rocked back and forth, hugging herself. She wept until her face was red and wet with tears and snot. She wanted her mother more than anything, even if only to hear that it was all her own fault. She needed to be home. But she had no home, not any more. Not in Jerusalem, and not here.

Had he raped her? How the idea had terrified her as a child, when she'd learnt about it with her father. 'It means violated,' he'd explained, stroking his beard. When she'd asked what that meant, he had said 'Ruined, destroyed like the Holy Temple had been. That's what your body is Malka, a Holy Temple. Keep it that way.' He explained that if she called attention to herself in any way, the men around her would not be liable for their actions. She had been six at the time. What did he think he was doing? The lesson had sunk in, deep into her very bones. Was this really her fault? A book lay splayed open on the floor, its pages torn. She picked it up and kissed it. When Avner had pressed down on top of her, she had reached out for it. The Zohar, where she had hoped to find God, or at least some answers. Her meditation stone, which might have served her as a weapon. She'd lost it now, the nest she'd made for it obliterated by their struggle.

'You did nothing,' she shouted, 'Nothing!'

She hurled the book towards the back of the cave, where it exploded in a shower of pages. She rushed and gathered them, smoothing their ruffled edges, murmuring to them softly. The book cover was light in her hands, an empty husk. Malka let it fall.

She glimpsed a flash of red against the dirt floor; the two bracelets, Avner's and her own, still touching one another. She stamped them into the mud until they were out of sight. Lies that needed burying. The promise of wholeness and safety that bracelet had offered her. The lie on which Mystical Encounters was built. She looked at the ragged mouth of the cave entrance. It no longer belonged to her. But she could not return to ME either. So where could she go? She stepped outside, gasping for air. It was so silent in the woods that the roaring of her blood sounded like a conflagration.

Then, in the clearing where she stood, a huge tree formed, with leaves of flame. It was like the tree she'd seen at Zushya's. No, not like it: it was the same tree. The Tree of Good and Evil, Avner had said. The Guardian, like the angel with the fiery sword at the entrance to Eden. Had it come to punish her, to burn her up? She breathed in, and felt her body ignite with warmth. The tree dissolved a little with each breath, and slowly streamed into her. She realised with a start that this was where the tree had always been. What she had feared, what she had run away from, was something inside her. Painfully, she held herself upright. She would protect it. She would not be broken.

Shira sensed that something was wrong. But when she asked Malka if everything was OK, Malka just nodded. What could she say? She didn't know which would be worse: Shira calling her a liar, or believing her. If she didn't talk about it, she could pretend it hadn't happened. She couldn't bear to shatter Shira's illusions, as he had shattered hers. She wished that, like Shira, she could still believe in something, but Avner had taken all that away. Malka had never felt so alone.

Since that afternoon in the cave, Avner avoided looking at her. She stopped attending classes, and took refuge in the kitchen. She made it her job to keep it spotless, scrubbing and scouring until her hands were raw. Pesach was the perfect excuse for her cleaning frenzy: everyone was doing it, so her particular madness was concealed in the universal drive to purge the puffed up pride symbolised by *chametz*, anything containing yeast, from every space before Pesach. The bakery would be shut for the festival. Shira smiled at her gratefully, but she knew that no matter how hard they worked, ME would never be clean. It was rotten with *chametz*. It always had been. So was she, letting Avner flatter her, lead her on with his ridiculous stories. She scrubbed herself red every night in the shower, and surrounded herself with an unbreakable wall of silence.

Seder night passed in a blur. She wouldn't let herself think of her family without her, it hurt too much. *Lag Ba'Omer* loomed ever closer, like a bus hurtling towards her. Maybe that's what she should do. Just step in front of a bus, and welcome the darkness. But she didn't have the courage.

Then all too soon it was here. Everyone else was so excited about their late-night trip to Meron. Malka didn't have to feign sickness. Shira offered to stay behind and miss the trip, but Malka shook her head and turned her face to the wall until her beloved room-mate had gone. She sensed that somewhere in the belly of the building, Avner still lurked. She concentrated all her energy on listening and, an hour later, she heard the door slam. That was him, heading for the cave. She was supposed to meet him there at midnight. She didn't have much time.

She leapt out of bed, grabbed a bag of clothes she'd prepared and ran down the corridor. The place seemed huge when it was empty. She'd meant to head straight out the door towards the bus station, still unsure if she'd jump in front of the bus or get on it, but her feet led her straight to Avner's office. The door was open, as though he had nothing to hide. Another lie. She sat in Avner's chair in the dark, and imagined him sitting here, looking up when she had knocked on the door. She pushed herself away from the desk, and a chair-wheel snagged in the mess of wiring that snaked behind the bookshelf. She pushed harder.

As she did so, a deeply buried memory surfaced. It had been the night before her seventh birthday, and she'd been too excited to sleep. So she had gone downstairs for some milk, and seeing a light, crept into her father's study. He was asleep at his desk, face-down on top of the book he'd been reading, his glasses clasped in one hand. She'd peered over his shoulder on tiptoe at the book he embraced like a pillow, catching glimpses of the words between his fingers. It was the first time she'd seen the word. How had she forgotten?

'*Chashmal*? But they didn't have electricity when the Talmud was written,' she'd murmured. Just as she'd asked Moshe, years later.

Her father started awake, closing the volume with a snap. She saw that it was not the Talmud that they usually studied together, but the Zohar. A book from the locked cupboard. He rolled his chair between her and the desk, blocking her view.

'It's not for you, Malkele,' he said through his matted beard, stroking her cheek to take the sting out of his words. 'I'm not even sure it is for me.' He stood, stretched, and placed it back in the cabinet, turning the key twice.

'Why are you reading about electricity?'

He had smiled. 'Chashmal is a stolen word, Malka. The secular country we live in is a *ganef*, it steals holy words and then empties them of meaning. Like chashmal. In Ezekiel's vision, it suggests some secret. We still don't know what it means, and are forbidden to try. The Gemara warns that just reading about it could be enough to destroy you. Listen to this. He rolled over to his well-thumbed Babylonian Talmud, and took out *Masechet Chagigah*. He opened the volume and pointed with his finger. 'Read, please.'

Malka didn't have to. She'd read it before, and whatever she read stayed with her. The words floated up as though on a screen. 'A young child was learning that passage and, in his purity and innocence, momentarily got the insight and meaning of the word "chashmal", whereupon fire went forth from chashmal and consumed him.' She shuddered. 'So he died just from reading about it?'

'That's right. And now you can switch it off with a finger.' He had clicked off his desk-lamp, and they had sat there silently in the dark. She could tell he wanted to say something else, so she waited quietly. But he sighed, stood, and took her by the hand back upstairs. Now she understood what had driven him to study a book he so obviously feared. He had been breaking his own rules to try and find a way to save her. Maybe that was why he had learned with her in the first place. Perhaps he had hoped that together, they would find a way to prevent the death that threatened her? She had hated him so much for shutting her out. For years, she felt she had failed him. What if it was fear that made him close the door? What if Avner was right, and he'd been afraid of a lie? How could she believe anything Avner said? She no longer knew who to trust. She felt as if she'd been stamped into the mud, together with the red thread. The Zohar said that *Chash* was silence. *Mal* was speech. The speaking silence. What would her own silence say if it could speak? If I were a man, none of this would have happened, she thought bitterly. Women are made to be broken. In her mind's eye, the Hebrew word for woman, *Isha,* floated up. As she watched, it broke in two, and released two new words. Aish Hashem. God's fire. The Kabbalah said that the shattering came before the light. What was her vision trying to tell her? To keep silent no longer.

'Chashmal', she said, softly. Dancing at the disco, her body had revealed a happiness she hardly dared feel. It had felt... well, electric. Now that happiness had been shattered, the heavenly connection she had longed for trampled into the dirt.

'ChashMAL!' she cried out. 'ChashMAL!' Louder, and louder, until she could taste blood and iron on her tongue. Rage coursed through her, lifting her onto the tips of her toes. *Chashmal*, she whispered, at last. Her right hand itched. It was so tightly clenched that her knuckles where white. Cautiously, she opened her fingers. Something smudged and red lay there. Crumpled, like a butterfly. With each heartbeat, it seemed to grow stronger, and fluttered into life, its wings unfurling. Not wings: petals. It was a rose. Her hand burned. The petals were flames. She threw it away from her, towards the window. A hole the size of her fist appeared in the glass, which rippled and bulged, then ran down the wall like melting ice. She drew her fingers to her lips, and sucked them to soothe the hurt. Now her left hand throbbed. When she opened it, faint white letters danced on her palm. As she watched, they moved closer together, tighter and tighter, faster and faster, until they became a ball of white light. The rose had been weightless, but this ball was heavy. It grew heavier, the smaller it got. It was just a pinprick now, but so bright it was painful to look at. She could carry it no longer. It rolled off her palm, onto the floor, and disappeared into the nest of wiring there. Malka slumped into Avner's chair, drained.

All at once, she could smell burning plastic. The overloaded socket by her feet was smoking, and bluish sparks leapt from the snaking wires. She knew she should run, but it was so beautiful, she couldn't move. Tendrils of flame danced up the window frames like some exotic climbing plant. The paint blistered and flaked off, disturbingly like human skin. The fire raced hungrily across the shelves, which blackened, curled, and fell with a sigh. The poster of the Sefirot on the wall curled and shut in on itself like a fist. She stood. It was not she who needed to be destroyed. It was this place. It had fed and grown fat on her dreams, and those of her friends. Let it burn.

She stepped back quickly as the fire spread to the cushions by her feet, where she and Avner had learned together. Avner always talks so much, she thought. He hates silence, fears it. The cushions gave off acrid smoke which made her retch, and she grabbed her bag and stumbled towards the door. What about the dorms, and all her friend's huddled, innocent possessions? They were far down the main corridor, through two sets of fire doors. She hoped they would be safe until someone noticed the blaze. She remembered Rabbi Abba's words about Bar Yochai's death. '*The entire day the house was filled with fire, and nobody could get close due to the wall of fire and light.*' Holy Fire. That was why, on *Lag Ba'Omer*, the whole country was full of fires, and the fire brigade would be stretched to the limit. The smoke in the hall thickened. She crouched down near the floor, where there was still some air. Feeling the fire's breath on her face, she remembered Avner bending down over her, and jerked upright, coughing. In that moment, the memory of the tree she carried inside came back to her. Enough of being frightened. All she had done in Safed was try to become herself. That was not a sin. Her only regret was that she would not be able to see Avner's face when he saw what she'd done.

As she passed through the hallway, the burning lintel curled the hair on top of her head. She ran towards the entrance. There was no time. She had to get out, fast. But she paused for a moment at the top of the stairs, looking down towards the bakery, the one place here she'd really felt at home. Because of Shira. She had no time to explain, no way to leave a message. Would Shira understand that Malka was setting her free? She had been taken in by Avner, too. Malka realised in this moment that Shira was the first real friend she'd ever had, the first person she had really trusted. Now she was letting her down, leaving her without a word of explanation. Just as she'd done to her family, to Moshe, to anyone who had loved her. But what choice did she have? She heard jars cracking like grinding teeth, and the flame that billowed up the stairs towards her was thick with scent.

Tiles leapt off the walls in fragments. Crouching, she worked her way carefully along the floor towards the front door, keeping just ahead of the flames. It was growing harder to breathe. Now there was only the canteen between her and the main exit. The tables cracked loudly as she passed, and she jumped back as the layers of wood ply splayed apart like pages from a burning book.

The key Avner had left in the lock for her was hot now, and would not turn. It must have expanded in the lock. For the first time that night, she was afraid. She shook the door and hurled herself against it, turning the key as it burned her fingers. At last it gave. Coughing, she shot through the front doors, running down the steps into the crisp night air. She didn't stop until she reached the phone-box on the corner. She felt a whoosh of air on the back of her neck as she ran: the fire had reached the front of the building. The big panes shattered, spraying the pavement with shards. In the distance, a lone siren's wail split the night. She glanced at her watch. It was one in the morning.

She strode downhill towards the bus station, small bonfires laughing back at her from gardens and courtyards throughout the city, spurring her on. She had come here with nothing, and she was leaving with almost nothing. Yet she was practically dancing. She let the feeling of euphoria carry her, sweep away her fear, the taste of smoke in her mouth. She knew it would not last, so she began to run, blurring past shadowy knots of figures, families who had stayed out all night dancing and singing. Where could she go? She would let the world bring her an answer.

As she reached the station, a bus was just pulling out. She leapt in front of it, waving her arms. It bore down on her, lights and horn blaring, like Ezekiel's chariot, ready to carry her off to heaven. The brakes screamed. It filled her vision, then stopped, the grille a finger's breadth from her face. The doors sagged open like tired wings.

'You trying to give me a heart attack?' The driver's voice shook. He wore gold-framed sunglasses, even though it was dark outside. He peered at her over the top of them. 'Hey, aren't you the girl that lost your bag a few months back? Good thing I've still got my army reflexes, or you would be flat as a *matzah*. Where to?'

'Anywhere but here,' Malka said.

'My last stop is Tel Aviv.'

Her father used to say that this 'secular city' was *Gehinom*, the closest thing to hell on earth. Even though it was just an hour from Jerusalem, it was the furthest place imaginable from her family and their values, and according to her father, the furthest place from God. Just what she needed. She rummaged in her pocket, and found some crumpled notes. She thrust them at the driver. He took one, gave her a sheaf of tickets, and punched holes in the top one. He tried to hand them to her with her change, but she leaped back before his hand could touch hers, and the cards fluttered down into his tray like feathers.

Part III
Jaffa,
Water
Tikkun,
Healing

Chapter 11
New Heart, New Spirit

Malka's bus arrived in the Tel Aviv central bus station around 3 a.m. As she stepped off, her sense of release evaporated. Streets snaked away from her in all directions. What was she doing here? Where should she go? She looked at her ticket for clues. Today was the seventh of May. She'd got used to the secular calendar at ME, and lost track of the calendar she'd grown up with. It was *Iyyar* now. What had happened to all those months since she'd left home? They had been stolen from her. What else had she lost? In the silent back streets, she could still hear flames crackling. She walked more quickly, but the sound followed her. The tendrils of smoke thickened, tugged at her hair, her ankles. Faster.

She walked until she could barely stand. The air began to taste of tears. She touched her cheek, but it was dry. Then she saw it. Between two buildings up ahead shimmered a lozenge of turquoise so beautiful Malka had to bite her lip to stop herself crying out. The sea. She crossed the road in a daze, grateful for the lack of traffic, traversed a broad wooden promenade, and stumbled down some steps. She kicked off her sandals and buried her toes in the cool sand. It felt incredibly old, and brand new, all at once. Sparks of early morning sunlight danced on the waves. Flecked with a honeyed orange near the horizon, the surf turned to burnt molasses on the shore.

As she walked towards the water, the sand changed underfoot, became denser, colder. She looked back at the way she'd come, her tracks like fingerprints in dough. Would she ever see Shira again? She had been Malka's first true friend, and Malka felt her loss like a wound. Would Shira understand what she'd done? Would she forgive her? It was unbearable to think of that bruised, disappointed look, of the curve of her failed shoulders when she talked of those who had let her down. Malka didn't dare to think about her family. They would never take her back now. Avner had seen to that. She was ruined, damaged.

What about Moshe? She would have to stop thinking about him, too. She kicked the sand, slewing two footprints into one another. He was just a boy she'd met once for pizza. The rest was fantasy. Safed had shown her how dangerous fantasy could be, what happened if you trusted someone. She would leave all of it behind, and start again. She didn't know how. But she did know there was something she had to do first. Something from her old world, to help her find a new one.

She found a secluded corner behind a pile of rocks, and discarded everything she was wearing. Without giving herself time to think, she ran naked into the water, the shock of it stopping her breath. She felt a moment's panic when the current swept her off her feet, and she remembered that she couldn't swim. Then the sea bed rose up to meet her and launched her back towards the surface. She dived under again. The sea pressed against her eyelids, slipped between her splayed toes. Beneath the surface, she could hear the sea whisper over her skin, feel it scour away smoke, sloughing off sweat and grime. She kept bobbing up, then going down again. When she finally stepped out of the water, the sun burnished her body with soft red light. Back amongst the rocks, she left her old clothes where they had fallen. She didn't want to touch them. She rummaged in her bag, and changed into underwear and a loose, sky-blue dress which Shira had given her, that gathered at her waist. The material was soft and light and the skirt had little tassels that kissed the sand as she moved, leaving a trail like some mysterious sea-creature.

She had dressed just in time. She was not alone. People ran along the water's edge, wearing almost nothing. Women ran alone or in pairs, men ran together with friends, or dogs. A group of elderly men stationed themselves nearby. They huddled together, swaying, and she wondered if they were going to pray. She got up to move. Then at some invisible signal, they all undressed, and began to twist into strange postures, like trees in an invisible storm. She stayed to watch, transfixed. Many of the poses seemed to involve standing on their heads. Did secular people pray to the sea? She wouldn't be surprised. It certainly seemed worthy of worship. It was like some giant winged creature, endlessly striving to take flight, endlessly failing, then rising again, undaunted, undefeated. The air above it seethed with a longing for transformation. She decided she would stay right here, let herself just be.

Malka sat and watched the waves until she breathed in time with them. As the day grew, so did the number of worshippers and their beach rituals. People unfolded towels, sunshades, opened board games. Clinking bottles accompanied their conversations, which lapped over and around her without ever including her. Malka didn't mind. She felt safe, unseen. A squat, hairy man passed right by her, with an icebox strapped to his chest, singing about watermelons and cold ice-lollies. With the handful of change she had left, Malka bought a glowing coral-pink half-moon from him, and let the juice run down her arm. A young girl in a green bathing suit threw a rainbow ball up in the air, and it landed on Malka's backpack. She dug one foot into the sand shyly when Malka rolled it back. The girl's mother apologised and offered Malka a small bottle.

'Thank you, but I'm not thirsty.'

'No, it's for your skin. If you're not careful, you will turn the same colour as your melon.'

Malka spread the cream from the bottle liberally on her arms, legs and face, relishing its coolness against her skin. She nodded her thanks.

Throughout the afternoon, different groups staked their claim to patches of the beach with bright towels, sunshades, and music. The girls were so naked, it hurt Malka's eyes to look at them. Boys and young men buzzed around them constantly, walking past in groups and then returning singly or in pairs and sitting down without ceremony. Sometimes the girls ignored them, laughing behind their hands with their friends, sometimes they sat up smiling, thrusting their chests out. It was like watching another species. Malka was at first glad, then disconcerted that no-one approached her. She glance down at her long skirt and tomato-red, freckled skin. No wonder, she thought. But it was fine, it was right. If anyone male had spoken to her she had no idea what she would have done. Hit them, probably.

As the shadows lengthened, she grew tired. She stretched out in the sand as she saw others do, her head cushioned on her rucksack, and let the warmth seep into her bones until she was almost melting. A whole day doing nothing. She'd never felt so good. The next thing she knew, it was dark, and she was woken by the smell of food.

She sat up and rubbed her eyes, groggy from too much sun. Her hair was matted with sand. Rows of spot-lit plastic tables were lined up along the beach to her left, with lines of young people advancing towards them. Was it some kind of soup kitchen? Hunger jerked her upright. All she had eaten today – yesterday? – was that piece of watermelon. She stood in line with the others, hugging her sore arms to her chest. The air was thick with cigarette smoke, and tiny red beacons bobbed in the air around her. She bumped into the person in front.

'Watch it!' A shape turned to her in the darkness, cigarette glowing like an exclamation mark. Malka could just about make out that it was a girl.

'Sorry.'

'This is my fourth time this week. I've no chance really, but you just gotta keep trying. Tonight's the last night.'

Malka glanced at her watch. It was almost midnight. 'No chance of what?'

'Getting in. Isn't that why you are here?'

'I'm hungry.'

'This won't help you then, it's just a tasting. Unless you get a lucky break, become one of the trainees. Then you're made.' She peered at Malka, her eyes pools of shadow. 'You're not one of those city girls, are you?'

Malka shook her head. 'Which city do you mean?'

The girl laughed thinly, and spat into the sand. 'Some of the pushy parents from the suburbs in Ramat Aviv bring their kids here in brand new sleeping bags, stop them washing for a few days, to try and get them in. But you can always tell in someone's eyes if they have a place to go back to. Baraka spots them every time, I'll give him that much. Oh, here we go.'

A man with a blinking box on his shoulder was moving down the line towards them. Malka started backwards in terror.

'Relax, you are on camera.'

'Why are they filming us?'

'We make good PR. All this talk of employing homeless kids is probably just a gimmick, to make Baraka look good. What do I care? Food is food. Gotta take any chance you get, right?'

Malka could certainly agree with that. As they drew closer to the tables, she saw they were piled with tiny plates. Each one had at its centre a curved spoon, like a beckoning finger, with only a single mouthful of food on it.

'Is this a joke?'

'Not a funny one.' The girl ground out her cigarette stub under her heel. 'We're up next. Looks like you've got the big guy.'

They parted ways and headed to adjacent tables. Behind Malka's table, a tiny, dark-skinned man perched on a plastic stool. Was the girl being sarcastic?

'*Salaam*,' he said. His voice was certainly big. It seemed to come from beneath his feet.

'*Aleikum Salaam,*' Malka replied, remembering the friendly coffee-seller in the Arab market in Jerusalem, greeting a young girl with plaits and thick stockings. What would that girl say if she could see herself now?

He looked at her a moment, then pushed three plates towards her. Each morsel was a different colour; red, green, orange. Like a traffic light. Were they even kosher? She decided not to care. Those rules were part of the prison she had left behind.

'What are these?'

'You tell me.' His voice was like the throb of a drum. He smiled at her, still and quiet amidst the hubbub.

It was some kind of test. Malka chose the red one first, and closed her eyes; she hated it when people watched her eat. She tasted salt fish, blended with the earthy tang of beetroot. The taste of her childhood. As a girl, she had stood on an upturned bucket and helped her father's mother, Bubbe Beila, salt and boil a whole carp. When it cooled, they minced it, then kneaded it into little balls with onion, sugar and the blood-coloured beets which Estie had chopped, until the kitchen looked like a murder scene. Which it was. For she also helped Bubbe catch the fish, scooping it up in her bucket as it swam placidly around the bath. Bubbe killed it with one well-aimed blow of the cleaver. Estie always covered her eyes, but Malka forced herself to watch. Bubbe let Malka taste the raw mixture, handing her a little spoon, 'Is it sweet enough?' she would ask, a sticking plaster over the number on her arm Malka knew not to ask about. By the time Devvie was born, Bubbe Beila had gone. Malka had not been allowed to the funeral. She swallowed and, instead of sweetness, a fiery heat seared the back of her throat. Malka's eyes watered. The bird-man looked at her expectantly, but she didn't trust herself to speak. Quickly, she took the next plate.

The green spoonful dissolved on her tongue. It actually tasted green, floral. Every year on *Shavuos*, to celebrate the giving of the Torah on Sinai, the women in the Jewish Quarter decorated the separation barrier at the Wall with flowers. She and her sisters would stand on folding chairs, twining flowers together and tying them on with green string. They bloomed for just a few days before they wilted and shrivelled. We were just decorating the bars of our cage, Malka thought. One year, to make things more interesting, Malka had collected the bell-shaped purple flowers that grew in clumps by the roadside. Estie said they were inappropriate, so Malka had eaten most of them on the way, though Estie tried to make her spit them out, in case they were poisonous. The taste in her mouth took her back to that dusty roadside. When she opened her eyes, the tiny man leaned towards her across the table, his head on one side.

'Do you know what you are eating?' His eyes glittered in the torchlight.

'It reminds me of something I ate as a child. With crunchy seeds like little wheels. *Lechem Aravi*, we called it. But that can't be it.'

He grinned. 'It can, and it is. *Hubeza* in Arabic, from *Hubz*, the bread of the poor. "Mallow" is its name in English. Its proper name in Hebrew is *Halamit*, from *Halamot*. The food of dreams. So often we ignore the bright flowers pushing their way up through the pavement, let the colours of our dreams fade. That's why I send my trainees out foraging, so they learn to look, to pay attention. Even in the city there is so much growing under your feet that you can eat.' His Hebrew was poetic but precise, as though it was a second language for him, just as it was for her.

Malka's stomach growled.

'Are you alright?'

'I'm hungry.' She blushed, but he nodded, smiling.

'If you could eat anything, right now, what would it be?'

'Pizza,' Malka said without thinking, and blushed again.

He smiled. 'It's been a while since I had such an honest answer.'

Malka was sure he was humouring her. 'Thank you. Can I go now?'

His eyes didn't leave her face. 'Wait.' He held out the last spoon. 'There's still one more.'

It was a single delicate orange envelope of pasta, which opened on her tongue. It was made with butternut squash and was stuffed with finely shredded carrots, honey, cinnamon. All the flavours of her mother's *Tzimme*s. She saw again the kitchen on a Friday, the tiles sweating with steam, the curve of her mother's back, her shoulders rolling as she stirred, and inhaled. It tastes like home, Malka thought. The tenderness, and the hurt. She turned away so her face was in shadow.

'You taste with your whole self, don't you? So do I.' He stood up. 'I'm Rukh Baraka,' he said, in that oceanic voice. The girl in the queue had mentioned his name, but it meant nothing to Malka. Clearly, it did to those around him. When he made a slight gesture with one hand, all the people giving out the food cleared their tables in moments, overturning the torches in the sand with a hiss.

Rukh stood on his chair, his torch the only one still burning. 'Thank you for coming everyone, that will be all for tonight.'

Malka headed back towards the cove where she'd been sleeping. As she'd been warned, she was still hungry. Rukh's voice stopped her.

'Where are you going, young lady?'

'I'm sorry?'

'You just made it. Come this way.'

She was too tired to be surprised. She rescued her bag from its hiding place and joined a small group huddled around a flatbed truck with balloon tyres, which had been driven right up to the edge of the beach. Its side was flecked with foam and spray. She couldn't see the girl she had spoken to. Malka stood slightly apart, beside an old man. No, he was young, but his hair was silver. Had he been born like that, or had something terrible happened to him? He noticed her staring, and blew smoke in her face out of the side of his mouth. Malka coughed angrily and moved away. That was one person she would have nothing to do with. When her eyes stopped watering, Rukh was standing on the flatbed, his arms sweeping in expansive circles so he looked even more birdlike.

'Just down the beach, on the Jaffa wharf, we are renovating an old apartment block, transforming it into what I hope will be the one of the greatest fish restaurants in the country. The Leviathan. From now on, it will also be your school and your home. You will live, breathe and sleep cooking, working with the finest chefs. Why you? You may well ask. Right now you might feel like lumps of shit, but I believe that hidden inside all that crap is a diamond. Those who train you will help you to scrape it all off. Your job is simply to shine. If you do it well, we will get along. If I'm wrong, if under all that shit is just more shit, I will spit you out on your arses, like the whale did to Yunis. You may know him as Jonah. He fled from this very port, trying to run away from his fate, as you have. So, are you with me?'

Malka had never heard anyone talk like that. Certainly not an adult. Coming from Rukh, it sounded like the truth. The other trainees must have felt the same, as they headed for the waiting coach, talking excitedly. Malka trailed after them. By the time she got on, all the seats were taken except for one by the boy with silver hair. She sat on the edge of the seat, and he turned away and stared pointedly out of the window. Smoke haloed his head, swirling around the large No Smoking sign. Malka decided that in her new life, she would be someone who spoke to boys.

'Do you mind putting out your cigarette? I've had enough smoke the last few days to last me a lifetime.'

He turned so their faces were inches apart. Even his eyelashes were frosted with silver. Then he shook his snowy head and carried on smoking. A tiny girl in a long sweater leaned across the aisle.

'Don't bother. He never says a word, never listens to anyone. God knows how he thinks he's going to get on as a trainee.'

'Ignorant Arab. He probably can't even read the No Smoking sign,' someone shouted from the back.

He kept looking studiously out of the window, but Malka saw him flinch. It was her fault for opening her mouth. She didn't understand. Wasn't Rukh also an Arab? She held her breath for a moment, but before anything more ugly could happen the engine started, blasting them with cold air, and everyone peered eagerly out of the windows. As a schoolgirl, Malka had always been jealous of those groups of lucky kids in air-conditioned coaches, going somewhere interesting. Now she was one of them. The coach drew up beside some fluttering green awnings. The door opened and the smell of fresh bread lifted her out of her seat. A bakery. Abulafia's, the sign said.

'After Abraham Abulafia?' She was confused. This was meant to be a secular city. Yet here was a bakery named after one of the great Spanish Kabbalists of the thirteenth century.

Her neighbour's eyes narrowed. 'Hardly. They are Arabs. Although they pretend not to be. They are even closed on your Passover. Can't make up their minds if they are Arab or Israeli.' His voice was hoarse, scarred.

'So you do speak. Can't they be both?' Malka saw immediately that this was the wrong question. He actually took his cigarette out of his mouth and stared at her.

'What planet are you from?' He jabbed his cigarette towards the window. 'For thousands of years, this was Gaza Road. Now it's Yefet Street. After Noah's son. Name changed to protect the guilty. Trying to escape the ghosts of the people who used to live here. Nothing beautiful about that.'

'Yefet doesn't necessarily mean beautiful. Rashi says it comes from an Aramaic root-word, Peta, meaning may he extend.' Idiot. She bit her lip. Silence is wisdom, she reminded herself.

'Well, they got that right. Extending all over the place. Thanks for the sermon.'

Before she could reply, Rukh stepped back on the coach and handed out flatbread. It was fresh, warm, and crusty. Malka lifted it to her nose and inhaled deeply. She noticed that her neighbour did the same. Hyssop, olive oil. Eating something freshly baked was like being hugged. She chewed slowly, to make it last, then licked her fingers. It was possibly the best bread she had ever eaten. Even her neighbour's face softened as he ate, and she could see that he was around her age.

'I'm Malka,' she said, seizing the moment.

He nodded, still chewing, but did not reply. Something sparked, deep in his eyes. He leaned close, and spoke low.

'That's your real name, isn't it? Keep it to yourself. Keep it hidden. These kids, with all they have been through, are like a pack of dogs, looking for vulnerability. You need a nickname here.'

Malka nodded. 'What's yours?'

He ran a hand through his hair. 'Snowy, obviously. Sheleg. Like the princess, *Shilgiah* – you know, Snow White?'

Malka shook her head. 'Can I ask you what happened to you?'

'I was born this way. According to my father, it is a sign of Allah's displeasure. He used to say that Allah spits on the souls of sinners like me.' He swung away and faced resolutely forward, and they travelled the rest of the way in silence.

Malka was relieved when the coach drew up in front of a rough-edged, white three-storey building right on the quay. It was a triangle which someone had sat on, the pointy end facing the sea. Scaffolding and ladders obscured its face, which was full of windows. They were led up a creaking temporary staircase on one side. So far, the place didn't inspire confidence. The boys were ushered through a door on the first floor, while the girls kept on going to the top. The other girls had all paired up so, to Malka's delight, for the first time in her life she had her own room. She even had her own shower. The happiness of small things! Despite the thin mattress, the bed in the bare white room looked incredibly inviting. A pile of white clothing was folded neatly on top. She was just about to lie down, fully dressed, when Rukh knocked at the door.

'Welcome to the Leviathan. You are on the first shift. Change into your whites and meet me downstairs in the kitchen in fifteen minutes.'

Why was it that however far she travelled, she always ended up in the kitchen? 'What, now? What about some sleep first?'

Rukh stared at her, and she stared back. There were flecks of gold in his dark eyes.

'I don't know what you did before this, and I don't care. You need to start pushing yourself if you want to make it here. Work now, sleep later, that's how I live my life. That's how I got where I am.'

Then, to her surprise, he smiled.

'You have *chutzpah*, I'll give you that. You'll need it. Fifteen minutes.'

As soon as he'd gone, she showered. Hot water was another blessing she would try never to take for granted. Grains of sand rushed down the plughole, and with them some of the nameless dread she'd been carrying. Then she dressed, the clothes so new that they rustled. She still had five minutes, so she opened the shutters on the window and looked down through the softening dark at the undulating, silken sea. It was even more beautiful framed by a window, sitting on a real bed. In the gathering light, it grew translucent, reborn. Somehow, she had been given another chance. She would not waste it.

The kitchen was extraordinary. It glimmered like something from a dream, polished metal that threw her reflection back at her with a soft blue sheen. Five others from the coach, including the white haired boy, crowded in with her. She could see the same wonder on their faces, the same sense that in this space they really might become something else. Rukh waited for them by a long central table, also in white now, flanked by two assistants, but Malka had eyes only for him. He balanced a knife

174

on one fingertip, the point dimpling the tip of his index finger, the handle pointing towards the sky. The knife and handle were of a single piece of burnished steel. The handle was curved, inviting. He drew them closer, like a performer.

'Perfect balance. That's what your tools have, and what you will develop, what you will become. All eighteen of you working in harmony, with the same purpose.'

Malka started. Eighteen was a mystical number. It stood for life, for luck. Did he know?

'You have been organised into three shifts of six, one for each station. You lucky ones have the first shift, the first chance to impress me. In a moment, each of you will be taken to your station, prepping dishes for a lunch I'm catering later today. You will find a lockable drawer by your station, with a rack of knives like these. Treat them better than your children. If you want to have any.'

Surely it was madness to allow a bunch of wayward teenagers access to knives? But when Malka glanced at her fellow trainees, she saw the pride which she felt reflected in their faces. He was trusting them, treating them with respect. She'd almost forgotten what that felt like. One by one, Rukh called them out and each was led to their station by one of the assistants. First up was a girl with short black hair and powerful arms, a fanged cobra tattoo curving over one shoulder. She had a leather jacket slung over the other shoulder like a cloak. Her eyes were stony, distant.

'That's Snake,' someone beside her whispered. It was Sheleg. 'She was a cage fighter for a while. Don't mess with her.'

Snake was followed by a very tall, very dark boy, with hair longer than Malka's.

'That's Shoko. Rumour says he was a Somali prince. Long way to fall.'

'Why are you telling me all this?' Malka whispered.

He turned to face her. 'When you look at me, what do you see?'

She looked back at him. 'A person?'

'Well believe it or not, that isn't a given round here. You are a long way from home, right?'

'Is it that obvious?'

'Let's just say I've been around here for a while. Hey!'

The nervy girl with long sleeves who had bad-mouthed him on the bus brushed by, scowling. She barely came to Malka's shoulder.

'How old is that girl?' she asked.

'Nails? She looks about twelve, doesn't she? One of the best car thieves in the city, but she broke into the wrong guy's car and needs to lay low. It's all in the fingers. Probably serve her well in the kitchen.'

'She seemed to know you. On the coach, she said...'

'In a previous life, she used to score from me.'

'What—'

He held up a warning hand. 'Don't look now, but here comes trouble.'

A huge boy shouldered roughly past them. His head was shaved so close that the scalp showed raw and pink in places, like undercooked meat.

'Curly, for obvious reasons. He beat me up so badly last summer that I couldn't walk for days.'

'But why?'

'You'll have to ask him. Could be he was just trying to earn his gang stripes. For some reason, not everyone likes people of my persuasion.'

Malka held her breath and let it out slowly, trying to calm herself. The more she learned about her fellow trainees, the more she felt that maybe her father was right. Maybe this was hell. It was certainly hot enough. The kitchen was already alive with the clash of trays, the hiss of steam.

Now just the two of them were left.

Curly passed close by. 'Shilgiyah, you're up next.'

'Did he just call you a princess?'

'I've been called worse. Quite advanced, for him.'

Malka's stomach knotted as Sheleg walked away. She had no nickname like the others, no tough image to keep them at a distance. How would she survive? She looked up, and Rukh beckoned. At least there was no one watching her make a fool of herself. She turned over possible names as she walked towards him, but in the end he did the job for her.

'Come on, Pizza,' he said with a laugh. A flash of Moshe's face, stained with tomato sauce. Malka forced a smile. She had wanted something tougher, but it would have to do for now. The tall, thin man beside Rukh leaned down and introduced himself as Rukh's sous-chef. She didn't catch his name, but he was already hurrying away, so she couldn't ask him to repeat it. He led her to her 'station,' where a tray of silver salmon waited for her beside a large tub of marinade.

'These are for the donors' lunch. Treat them with care. God knows why, but he's trusting you with the most expensive ingredient of the meal.'

Briskly, wielding one of the breathtakingly sharp knives from her drawer, he explained what she needed to do, stabbing the air with a finger at each new instruction. First, she had to gut and trim the fish, thread sprigs of thyme through their gills, and make a lattice of deep cuts in their sides. Then she had to lay them in the marinade, which smelt of cumin and preserved lemon, and rub it into the slashes. Finally, she had to scrape the entrails into a bin, then hose the table down and start again. When she'd finished the whole tray, someone would take the salmon away, and she would have to fetch another tray of fish from the walk-in freezer at the back of the kitchen and start again. At the end of her shift, once her station was spotless, she would clean up and take a break before her next shift, in five hours. On a chopping board the size of her family kitchen table, the sous-chef showed her how to move her wrist in a fluid motion, so the knife bit cleanly and without effort. Then he was gone.

Malka stroked the edge of the blade with the flat of her thumb, and a single drop of blood flowered. She lowered the first fish gently to the board. It was pink and silver and beautiful. She stood over it, knife poised, when suddenly it twitched its tail. She'd heard of fresh, but this was ridiculous. Surely they were supposed to be dead by now? Should she call someone? Wait for it to stop moving? She remembered Bubbe's cleaver. She certainly didn't want to kill it herself. Then, as she watched, it peeled itself away from the board and leapt into the air. It was long and powerful, a curve of muscle and scales suspended in the air before her like a question mark. She reached out quickly, but it slipped through her fingers and dived into the tub of marinade with barely a splash. She grabbed its tail to pull it out, and was yanked off the floor.

Before she knew it, she was underwater. Not in the marinade, but in the sea. She was still holding on to the fish, which had grown hugely in size. She inched along its back until she could slip her knees around its sides. It sensed her weight, and turned in tight circles, creating a flurry of bubbles. A shoal of electric blue fish darted around them, nibbling at her fingers, trying to make her let go. To Malka's relief, her fish burst through the shoal into clear water. She glimpsed something in the distance: another fish coming towards them. It was even bigger than her fish, and moving fast. A shark? She crouched down, then saw as it drew closer that there was someone on its back too. A woman. Her red hair coiled around her like seaweed. As they drew closer, she reached one arm out towards Malka, who leaned forward to make contact. But the salmon sensed Malka's movement, and dived from under her. It swished its tail violently, and the water clouded. Suddenly she couldn't breathe. Her lungs were empty. Just as she started to sink, the other woman grabbed Malka's shoulder and pulled her towards the surface at dizzying speed. Someone shook her.

'Hey, no sleeping on the job!'

Malka found herself slumped over the table, one arm in the marinade.

'Are you OK?' It was Sheleg. He nodded towards the table. 'You can let go now. It's not going anywhere.'

Malka looked down. She was holding the salmon by the tail. Its head lolled out the other side of the marinade tub. Her whites were spattered with oil. She felt a moment of absolute terror. She had been so sure that the crazy visions would not dare follow her here.

'Quick. Get a clean tunic on before Rukh sees you. Take mine, I'm just on shift break.'

'Thanks. I'm just tired.' It was the only explanation she would admit.

'Sure. Do you smoke? Of course not, I forgot. Shame. It's even better than coffee.'

'Coffee. I could so do with one of those. Turkish, with cardamom like in the Shuk.' She smiled at the memory.

He narrowed his eyes, as if seeking insult, but apparently found none. For the first time, he smiled at her and she glimpsed the gentle boy he must once have been. She took the folded tunic from him, but he didn't let go straight away.

'Malka, right?'

'I thought we're not supposed to...'

'I'm Mahmoud,' he whispered. 'But keep it to yourself.'

Then the mask came back down, and he left her with his tunic in her hand. She shrugged off her own, threw it into the laundry bin, put his on and raced back to her station. Her fish was gutted and cleaned. He'd prepped it for her. If she could make this extraordinary, prickly boy like her, then maybe she would be ok.

Chapter 12
The Edge of the Sea

Moshe raced along the water's edge, weaving between sea and sand, daring himself to go closer each time to the seething backwash, leaping back as the spray hissed at his heels. The sky blushed at the sins of the night, staining the water crimson. The distant call of a muezzin reminded him that, back in the yeshiva, it was time for prayers for those who had studied through the night, or risen early. But he and God were no longer speaking. He'd grown tired of their one-way conversations, the busy signal he always sensed once his pleas shaded into silence. All his praying, all his learning, had come to nothing. So he'd decided to leave the pallid yeshiva boy in the dust where he belonged. Instead of morning blessings, when he reached the outdoor gym, he raised himself heavenward on the parallel bars fifty times. Instead of the *Shema*, sit-ups; instead of the *Amidah*, press-ups; free weights instead of the *Aleinu* prayer. A shower instead of the psalm of the day.

He passed the rainbow façade of the Dan Hotel, which mocked him like a broken promise. Never again will I destroy the world through water, God had sworn to Noah. Well Moshe thought, you destroyed mine once already. Wasn't that enough? The hungry sea challenged him, dared him to come close. The next tragedy was only a wave away.

When he'd first arrived in Tel Aviv in early May, he had slept on the benches that fringed the beach, or rocky inlets on the beach itself, forcing himself to face his fear. He'd be useless here otherwise. Every night, in the sound of the sea, he heard a wordless keening cry, like tearing metal. He woke exhausted, rimed in sweat and salt. The sea was a constant presence, a whispering reminder, unravelling his frail hopes.

He fought back the same way he had in the yeshiva: by focusing on the details. Consulting maps, he worked his way out from the bus station in widening concentric circles, as though Malka was a stone dropped into the heart of the city, and he was tracing the ripples. He traversed the checkerboard of different neighbourhoods, from G'lilot all the way down to Neve Tzedek, just short of Jaffa. He tried every bar, every restaurant, ignoring pitying looks, advice and insults, blind to everything but his quest. Women reacted angrily when he tapped them on the shoulder, furious that he'd dared mistake them for someone else. Often they threatened him with the police, until he actually began to feel like a criminal. He fought his own mounting frustration, his mother's unanswerable question. What the hell was he doing here, chasing after a girl he hardly knew, to whom he probably meant nothing? Even if he found her, what would he say? She'd have every right to laugh in his face.

In little over a week, his money ran out. He was too proud to call home. So he washed and shaved as best he could in the sinks of the beachside toilets, and asked for work as he showed Malka's increasingly tattered picture, with equally unsuccessful results. One evening, he tried to enter a bar, his hair still matted with sand. A huge security guard with a white-blonde crew-cut had bawled him out in Russian, calling his mother all kinds of names. He clearly hadn't expected Moshe to understand him. In an instant, Moshe was back in the playground, facing one of the bullies who had haunted his childhood. Rage swamped him, spoke through him. Before Moshe knew what he was doing, the guard lay sprawled at his feet. Moshe stood over him, breathing hard. His hand felt as if he'd punched a wall. He looked down, and saw a gold tooth on the pavement. What had he done? He was acting like the kind of hoodlum he'd always despised. Reb Sabbatto was right, he belonged in the gutter.

He helped the fallen security guard up slowly, bracing himself for a counter-attack.

'*Izvinite*,' Moshe said. Though sorry didn't really cover it.

The giant leaned forward and spat blood on the sidewalk, then turned to Moshe. Instead of the anger he expected, there was grudging respect on the man's blood-streaked face. He gave his handkerchief to Moshe, so he could wipe the blood off his knuckles, before cleaning his own face. By now they had attracted a crowd of onlookers, so the guard ushered him inside. Luckily, the bar's owner saw the funny side. She tilted her close-cropped crimson crest to one side, and trilled with laughter.

'That was some punch. How old are you, karate kid?'

'Eighteen.'

'You got ID?'

He handed her his tattered ID card. 'Please don't call the police. I don't know what came over me.'

Too late, he realised that out of habit he'd also given her Malka's picture. She held the photograph close in the light.

'This doesn't look like you. She's a cutie though.' She pinned his ID to the bar with a brightly-taloned finger, studied it for a moment, and handed it back with the photo. He pocketed them quickly. When he looked up, she held out her hand.

'I'm Anat. Moshe, is it? Your namesake started out as a violent character too, if I remember my bible correctly. They should have called you David. Vladek must be twice your size! You don't need to hit anyone else to get my attention. We were short-staffed anyway, and now Vlad will need a replacement. Get a bulletproof vest on, before I change my mind.'

'Wait. You're not suing me, you're employing me?' Moshe was so used to hostility, it was hard to believe she wasn't teasing him.

'I like your spirit, that's what I look for. You able to use a weapon?'

He shook his head.

'We'll get you trained up. You can use your wages to buy him some new teeth.'

'Gold ones,' Vlad whistled wetly.

Anat curled her lip. 'You should be so lucky Vladimir. Abusing a potential customer. What were you thinking? Give him your uniform and a warm welcome.'

Vlad lifted his orange vest over his head and handed it to Moshe. The word *Bitachon* was emblazoned there in bright blue letters. Security. In Jerusalem, it was pronounced *bitoch'n*. There it meant faith, trust in God. Here, it seemed to mean the opposite. There is no security in faith. Trust only yourself. Anat was staring at him.

'What are you waiting for?'

He held up the vest. 'You can have faith in me.'

Another burst of trilling laughter. 'A religious security guard.' She shook her head. 'I thought I'd seen it all.'

It turned out that Anat owned a whole chain of bars, all called *Mastool*, after the stoner boyfriend she'd had in her hippie days. Moshe was suddenly very busy. What he'd loved most at first was the opportunity to scrutinise every woman who approached him. He still couldn't let go of the hope that the next one might be Malka. He smiled apologetically as he checked their bags, trying to convey that he was just doing his job.

Between shifts, instead of continuing his fruitless search, Moshe spent his spare time on the beach, working out. He was just gathering his energies, he told himself. He wasn't giving up, he was toughening up. He no longer hated the weight of the pistol tucked into his waistband, which Vladimir had trained him to use. The women he admitted to the club must have sensed this new detachment, because they started to flirt with him. Perhaps it was his new look. He'd kept his beard at first, thinking it would help Malka recognise him. But it didn't fit here. So he shaved it off.

'You scrub up well,' Anat commented. 'Now you and Vladimir could play good cop/bad cop on some crappy TV show.'

At the end of his first month, Moshe moved in to a tiny room, an adapted storage shed on the roof of an apartment block near the seafront, its shutters stained with tears of rust. Malka's picture was the only decoration he allowed himself, tucked into the top of a small shaving mirror screwed into the naked plaster. He'd found an abandoned bedstead, and there was a single bulb swinging from the ceiling that worked sporadically, usually when it wasn't needed. Moshe didn't mind the sparseness. I'm just passing through, he told himself.

When he paid the first instalment on Vladimir's gold teeth, they drank a glass of vodka at the swanky 223 bar on Dizengoff to seal their friendship. Since then, Vladimir had left Anat's employ and moved on to other gigs, but they still met for a drink now and then. One such evening, Vlad had asked to see the girl in his wallet. 'Let's see what all the fuss is about.'

Vladek picked up Malka's photo. It was like a postage stamp in his palm. 'So it's her fault I look like this?' Vlad grinned, his new teeth glittering.

'I guess you could say that.'

'I won't hold it against her. Where is she now?'

'That's just it. I've no idea.'

'You are still looking for her?'

Moshe swirled the vodka in his shot glass. 'Not so much any more, if I'm honest.'

'So what keeps you in this shit-hole?' His arm swung round to include the well-dressed customers lounging at the bar. Several of them looked up sharply, but then their gaze slid somewhere safer.

'My debts, for one thing. I could probably have bought you a car for what your dentist charges.'

'A car? In Tel Aviv? To find a parking space would be a miracle. These teeth are much more useful for picking up the ladies. They see themselves when I smile, they think they are on to a good thing.'

'Dream on, loverboy,' Moshe laughed. 'You remind me of Lazlo, a friend of mine in Jerusalem. His golden smile didn't help with the ladies at all. Shame, he's a great guy.'

Vladimir's grin lit up the bar. 'That was in Jerusalem. Here, appearances are what really matters.'

In truth, Moshe couldn't imagine going back to his life in Jerusalem, which had always felt like a half-life, and now seemed to belong to someone else. He could be himself here. Was Malka now no more than an excuse to stay? He wasn't ready to admit that, even to himself.

That night, he pried apart his shutters with a screwdriver. He left them open whenever he was home, losing himself in the relentless rhythm that seemed to grow louder at night. The cries of the gulls became the soundtrack to his longing.

For the first couple of months, he'd called Jerusalem every Friday with an update. But by the end of July, the heat, and the repetitive conversations had begun to get him down. 'I will call you if I find anything,' he'd told Estie. 'When,' she'd corrected him. '*When* you do. And my sister is not a thing.' He hadn't told her about the dangerous cult in Safed. Why worry her without proof? He still had the drawing of the tree Malka had left him, and worried at its meaning like a loose tooth.

'If Tateh ever found out Malka was in Tel Aviv, he would sit shiva for her,' Estie had replied. 'Maybe it's better if you don't find her.'

'You can't mean that.'

'Can't I?'

The conversations with his mother were even worse.

'I'm fine, mama. Are you eating? Sure, pizza counts. I'm glad you and Lazlo are getting on. No, nothing yet. I won't give up hope.' If he kept saying it, he might believe it.

He bought a gas burner and learned to cook *shakshuka*: eggs with tomatoes, chilli, smoked paprika and coriander from the flea market, which he ate straight from the pan with pitta bread from Abulafia's. He always bought some sweet flaky pastries for Vladimir, who said that as someone else was looking after his teeth, he could eat what he liked. 'Now there's even more of me to love,' he said, patting his growing paunch.

Moshe drew himself skyward on the bars one more time. Then he dried his feet with his socks, put on his shoes, and leapt on his bike. As he rode, Moshe flexed his muscles. What had he become? He had changed so much since he and Malka had last met. As she must have, if she was here. He tried to imagine that ponytailed *Yerushalmi* girl in Tel Aviv, but couldn't. She had left everything she knew. For her, there was no going back. He understood that. So when would he admit, to himself and those in Jerusalem, that he had no reason to stay?

He was still early for work, so he took a detour through old Jaffa. The narrow cobbled streets commanded his full attention. He stopped for a moment beside an art installation he loved, an orange tree raised off the ground in a ceramic jar, held suspended by taut wires, forever prevented from taking root. You and me both, Moshe thought as he reached up to stroke the smooth, cool bark. If only he could stop trying to find Malka, he could allow himself to feel at home. He sent up a wordless prayer that she was all right.

With the early-morning sun burnishing his shoulders and sending blazing discs winging ahead of his wheels, he almost believed she was. He checked his watch. There was still time for a quick espresso at his favourite café. He drank it standing up at the counter. He glanced idly at the TV news overhead. A shaky hand-held camera careened down a line of gaunt children standing barefoot in the moonlit sand. It was like a scene from a nightmare. The camera panned slowly down the line, and the children had the same blank, glassy stares as the Jerusalem gangs he'd talked with.

'What's this?' he asked the barista.

'Some fancy new restaurant in Jaffa. Baraka's latest cash cow.'

'Who are all these kids?'

'Filmed a few months back, but just released as pre-opening publicity. Seems he's using street kids as cooks, with Arabs as chefs. Would you want to eat anything there, even if you could afford it?'

Moshe put down his coffee. 'How can you be a racist in Jaffa?'

The barista rubbed his chin. 'Not racist. Realistic. You think anyone cares about these homeless kids? They are just window-dressing.'

Moshe hated to see people exploited, even in a good cause. He'd heard of Rukh Baraka, a working class Arab from Jaffa who had made it big, leaping from one end of the scale to the other. No wonder the Ashkenazi café worker couldn't handle such a boundary breaker. Tel Aviv was just as divided as Jerusalem, its divisions all the more powerful for being invisible, unspoken. Moshe slapped his change down.

'You can keep your coffee. It's too bitter. It's Arabica, by the way. Probably why you can't do it justice.'

Last time I'm going there, he thought as he cycled away. As he passed Abulafia's bakery the shutters were just being raised, and taxi drivers, clubbers, and other post-night-denizens were already clustered eagerly outside. It reminded him of the Arab market in Jerusalem, the shutters scrolled up by bleary-eyed men scratching their bellies, erasing the failed hopes and soured dreams of the night before. Maybe the two cities were not so different after all. The green awnings fluttered their eyelashes at him, teasing him with hints of cinnamon and sesame. He would pick up a few *burekas*, surprise his colleagues. He leaned his bike by the service window.

'*Ahalan.* The usual?'

Moshe picked up his pastries, and cycled into the dense urban sprawl of Tel Aviv.

He had a rough day. He had to break up two fights with broken bottles, and he got spat on and called a stinking immigrant for his pains. It hadn't bothered him in the past. It was as if Malka had been a buffer between him and reality, and now the scales had fallen from his eyes. He decided to get drunk with Vladimir.

'What am I even doing here, Vlad? Chasing a woman I hardly know, who may not even be here, based on a pencil sketch and the words of a child who may have been dreaming. '

Vlad tapped Moshe's chest. 'Aren't you giving up a little too easily here?'

Moshe looked at him.

'I've chased a mirage half-way across the country, slept rough, nearly been arrested. I sleep in a freezing tin shack. All because of her. You call that easy?'

'Tell me the truth. Haven't you loved every minute? Hasn't it all made you feel alive? When you punched me, I thought, you won't let anyone stand in your way. Except yourself.'

Then something extraordinary happened. Vladek started to recite poetry.

'*Love's slipshod watchman, fear hems me in. I am conscious that these minutes are short...*'

'*And that the colours in my eyes will vanish when your face sets.*' Moshe completed the verse. 'I didn't know you were a poetry fan!'

Vladek grinned shyly at Moshe. 'I'm not just a pretty face. Yevtushenko is great, but I prefer Akhmatova. Her poems get me through my shifts. I say them in my head, over and over, like mantras.'

'This calls for another drink.' Moshe ordered more vodka. The clean, antiseptic taste had been cut with both chili and lime. Moshe wasn't sure it worked. Everything gets corrupted here, he thought. Then chided himself. Stop overthinking. Be in the moment.

Vlad grinned at him. 'Fancy a dip in the sea? Skinny dipping is best. A great way to get rid of the blues.'

Moshe looked at his empty glass 'I can't swim.'

Vladimir looked at him hard. 'Why not?'

'I never learned.' He lowered his voice. 'Something happened when I was a kid, and now I hate the sea.'

Vladek slid off his stool and slapped some notes on the bar. 'You're not a kid any more. Come on. Let me teach you. Before I was a bouncer, I was a lifeguard on the beach here.'

'What, now? It must be 2 a.m.' Reluctantly, Moshe stood up, and swayed on his feet. I'm drunk, he thought.

'All the better. No one will see us. Besides,' Vladek leaned close. 'I can show you a secret place, where you can be under the waves but still safe on dry land. It's the perfect place to make friends with the sea.'

'Why would I need to do that?'

'What colour are your girlfriend's eyes?

'She's not... Blue, I think. Green.' He reached for his pocket.

'You should remember. Deep, dark blue. Come on, we don't want you drowning.'

Chapter 13
The Language of Birds

I t was not yet dawn, but already the air was humid. Malka swam out as far as she could before the Muezzin's cry sounded from Jami' al-Bahr. Then she recited the first verse of the *Shema* and dived beneath the waves. Every morning, she set out as soon as she woke and threw herself into the sea. If she could become at home in this unfamiliar, unstable element, she might make this place her own. At first she had paddled around, terrified each time the sand slid away beneath her. She watched other swimmers closely, mimicking their movements, clumsily at first but soon with increasing ease. She learned to respond to the shifting rhythms of the current. She was still scared when it tugged her under, but now she had faith that she would float back up. She was rewarded with precious moments when she soared, weightless on the crest of a wave, smiling through the salt and foam.

Once she could stay afloat, she tried to get a little further out each day before the call to prayer reached her. She'd been at the Leviathan two months now, and when she turned and looked back she could barely make out the beach. It was the fifth of July, and also *Shiva Asar Be'Tammuz*, a fast day. She was not fasting. She was done with all that. But it was not done with her. It was also Ramadan, and so the end of the Jewish fast at sunset also signalled the end of the Muslim *Sawm*. Both faiths, both calendars, danced to the moon's call, just like the waves surrounding her. So tonight the trainees had to prepare a special meal of fish, cooked with the dates with which the Muslim fast was traditionally broken. It was for Rukh's entire staff, of all faiths and none, as he put it. It was going to be a busy day in the kitchen. Though Rukh was fasting, his energy and attention were undimmed. 'You may be used to abuse,' he told them. 'But here you will suffer beautifully. Here you will be transformed.'

Today was Malka's seventeenth birthday. She'd told no-one. She didn't want a fuss. Only now did she allow herself a moment of secret celebration. She dived, and let the sun-shadows stripe her skin, a shimmering net of light. She held her breath until it hurt, then rose slowly to the surface. She spread her arms and lay like a starfish, face down, eyes open behind her goggles, alert for any movement in the depths. She still hoped she might meet the dream-woman, riding her great fish, in the flesh. Out here, such an encounter felt within touching distance.

As she raised her head and took another breath, the call to *Fajr* reached her, the words wrapping her in their delicate tracery. Each day at this moment of her own prayer, she opened a window in her mind to let the sea-lady in. She felt a space open up inside her that was larger than the sea. She always returned to the beach charged with purpose and self-belief. Sometimes, when that belief wavered, she spoke to the sea lady at work. Her silently moving lips led to confusion in the kitchen, and someone would often shout at her, startling her out of her reverie.

'What did you say Pizza? Speak up!'

The other trainees sensed she was not one of them. They laughed behind their hands when she proved ignorant of some basic given of their secular lives. Only Mahmoud refused to laugh at her. This too became a mark against her. 'Arab-lover,' she often heard muttered as she went past, like a curse. Once she had arrived at her station to find it covered in dirt, the lock to her drawer jammed. Wordlessly, Mahmoud had taken her hairpin and opened it.

She tried to forgive their prejudice. She supposed that when you had nothing, or were afraid of losing what you had, you held on to your hatreds to give you strength. The only Arabs she'd known until now were the stallholders in Jerusalem. She had never expected one would become her friend. Mahmoud seemed even more an outsider, more of a loner, than she was. Was that why she felt so safe with him? Perhaps it was their shared passion for work. They were always the first trainees in the kitchen, something else that didn't endear them to their colleagues.

The skein of her thoughts frayed apart as someone grabbed her by the arm and lifted her roughly out of the water. She opened her mouth to cry out and swallowed a huge mouthful of salt water. Her eyes streamed. Before her vision could clear, she was laid down on a cold metal surface that pressed into her back. She sat up and blinked desperately, fighting to get her breath back. A man's face was inches from her own. She screamed.

'Well, you are definitely alive, and now I'm almost deaf.'

Malka drew breath to scream again, and he backed away. He wore a battered blue cap at a rakish angle; a prayer mat lay unrolled at his feet. She was aboard one of the patched fishing boats from Jaffa harbour. It was painted a pale blue, so its edges blurred into both sea and sky.

'I was just swimming. Why did you pull me out? Put me back this instant.'

She tried to project both the anger that she felt and the assurance that she didn't. It was hard. She was shivering, and her voice shook. She realised that she was wearing only her swimsuit. She blushed with her whole body, and tried to cover herself with her arms. Her would-be rescuer handed her a rough blanket and looked away while she covered herself. He waited until she was decent before speaking again.

'We can throw you back in if you like. It looked like you were in trouble, and there's a dangerous undertow here. You shouldn't swim so far out.'

'I swim here every day!'

'Then you are either foolish, or lucky, or both.' Greying stubble framed his grin.

'Enough, Shakir,' another voice called. 'You can see she's OK. Let's put her back, we've no time to mess around with silly girls.'

'Let her catch her breath first. Look at her Yusuf, she's shivering, in shock,' Shakir said. 'What if she was your daughter? Would you leave her to the mercy of the sea?'

Yusuf was tall and grizzled. It was hard to guess his age, but his gaze was steely. He deferred to Shakir with a nod. She pulled the blanket tighter around her shoulders. Sensing her advantage, Malka changed tack.

'Please. Can you take me back?'

'Back where?'

She nodded towards the distant harbour. Shakir was right. She had drifted far out into the open sea. She must be more careful.

Shakir motioned to his mat. 'Let us finish our prayers. When we're done, I promise we will drop you off with the rest of our catch.'

'What catch? We've caught almost nothing,' Yusuf muttered.

'*In'shallah*. Where is your faith? Maybe you keep the fish away with your bellyaching.'

'I have to get back soon, or I will be late for my shift at the Leviathan.'

She thought the power of this name would move them, but Shakir stiffened. Beside him Yusuf spat vigorously. 'She works for that snob!'

'Enough, Yusuf,' Shakir said.

Malka sensed a current beneath their words. A story, a secret.

'What do you mean? Isn't Rukh one of you?' This sounded clumsy even to her.

Yusuf grunted. 'Once, maybe. Now our catch isn't good enough for him. Baraka only takes fish from the Tel Avivians. As if their fish comes from a different sea.'

'Go into the cabin,' Shakir said gently. 'It is warmer there, and there are some spare overalls. I will radio the harbour master, tell him we've picked you up, and he'll get the message to Rukh, so you won't be in trouble. But perhaps you'd like to stay out with us first? It might do you good to see how the fish you work with reaches the kitchen.'

Without waiting for a response, they turned unceremoniously and prostrated themselves on their mats. Malka ducked through the narrow entrance to the cabin. Just as Shakir had said, she found coarse fisherman's overalls on a low bench. She thought longingly of her own clothes hidden on the beach. Rocked by the pitch and roll of the boat, she shut the door, hurriedly slipped out of her wet suit and dried herself with the blanket. The overalls were scratchy and much too large, so she roped them tight around her waist with some looped cord she found in one of the pockets. She wrung out her suit over a bucket, left it to dry on a hook, and combed the knots out of her hair with her fingers. She caught the murmur of the men's voices, and opened the door. Mahmoud was teaching her Arabic, and she recognised some of their words.

'We have awoken, and all Creation has awoken for Allah, Lord of all the Worlds.'

She mouthed the syllables, rolling them on her tongue. She felt a tingling of recognition in her stomach. This was exactly how she had felt in the water, part of a great song, tiny but still significant.

'I ask You for the best the day has to offer, victory, support, light, blessings and guidance; and I seek refuge in You from the evil in it, and the evil to come after it.'

She closed her eyes and whispered along with the fishermen. She tried to pick up the thread of her interrupted conversation with the sea lady.

'Grant us the fullness of our desires.' She repeated the phrase, wove her voice through those of the praying men. She felt a knot form and pull tight. She felt it give, and something new rushed in. There was a great shout from outside. She stood and looked out. The two men were rolling up their mats, which they stowed in a compartment in the bows. The air above them was alive with swooping gulls, billowing like pages come loose from a giant book. Yusuf turned to her as she stepped on deck.

'Look at that!' he exclaimed.

The noise of the gulls was incredible. Shakir ducked past her into the cabin and the boat roared to life. It swung in a wide circle around the gulls, who were diving into the sea, then rising slowly, their beaks full.

'It's a big shoal,' Yusuf said, a lift in his voice.

The boat moved in quickly, through the clustered birds. Soon the air about them was dense with their sharp cries. The boat turned in tighter and tighter circles. Yusuf threw nets overboard with a casual grace, his back curving and straightening like a bow, his surliness cast aside like a cloak as he hefted the giant bales of mesh. It was beautiful to watch, but she wished she could do something to help. As if on cue, Shakir shouted through the cabin window.

'Do you think you can take the wheel? Just hold her steady. Yusuf needs me.'

Malka wrestled with the wheel and felt blisters forming on her palms. The engine shrieked, and the metal hull groaned, straining against the growing weight of the nets. With practised speed, Shakir and Yusuf hauled in the nets and emptied them into tubs and buckets. Shakir motioned for her to cut the engine. She turned the key and it was suddenly quiet. He motioned again, beckoning her outside. She grabbed her sodden costume and stuffed it into a pocket.

The deck was covered with slippery, glittering scales that mirrored the light. She stepped carefully in her bare feet. Shakir held up a large fish, still wriggling, and grinned. It was speckled and lithe, with a silvered underbelly and dark stripes along its back.

'These are Barbuniya, Red-striped Mullet. Very valuable.' He lifted another, with a startled, wide-eyed expression. 'This is Locus, white grouper. I haven't seen any out here for a while. You know,' he continued, folding the nets, 'it's strange. We passed this way earlier and found nothing. Perhaps you brought us luck today after all.'

Malka nodded. Who was she to contradict him? As Shakir had said, out here you had to have faith.

'When we drop you back, I'll have Yusuf bring a crate over as a thank you. I'm sure these are better than the stuff Rukh usually buys.'

Shakir swung the boat around. It was now so full of fish that there was hardly room for them to stand. Malka sat on the prow, leaning out over the water. She smiled into the sun, her cheeks splashed with salt spray. Shakir radioed other boats, spreading the news about the large shoal, and soon the sea around them was busy with other small craft. As they passed, the fishermen waved and smiled, looking curiously at Malka. She waved back, caught up in the general euphoria. As they neared the jetty, a tall thin man caught the rope Yusuf threw him, and shouted across the narrowing gap.

'What took you so long, Shakir?' He whistled when he saw how full the boat was. Then he saw Malka and his face sobered. 'Who is the stowaway? Is she legal?'

Shakir rubbed his chin with a callused hand, and regarded Malka for a long moment. 'She's one of yours, Yunis. No time to talk. I've got to crate these up so we don't miss the market. She'll tell you herself.'

He winked at Malka, then lowered the gangplank, stepping back so she could be the first ashore.

'Come out with us again tomorrow?' Shakir called after her. 'Maybe you can suggest a field trip to Rukh?' Shakir laughed. 'I meant it about the fish. I will send Yusuf over.'

She watched Yunis help the fishermen pack the fish into familiar polystyrene crates on beds of ice. There was no time to go back for her clothes. The Leviathan was nearby, and she wandered over in a daze. Suddenly conscious of her ridiculous fisherman's overalls, and her bare, dirty feet, she tried to slip in unseen through the delivery entrance. Rukh was waiting for her, his arms folded.

'Do you have any idea how worried I was about you? We are way behind on preparations for this evening. This is the last thing I need. *Al-ḥamdulillāh*, those fishermen picked you up. Where are your shoes?' Rukh's face darkened further as Yusuf staggered up behind her with a crate. 'I told you already, your catches aren't reliable any more. You never have any...' His voice trailed away. He bent and stroked a grouper tenderly with a finger. 'Where did these come from?'

'Ask her,' Yusuf nodded at Malka, matching Rukh's gruff tone. 'Compliments of Shakir. Do you want them or not?'

'If you get more like these, please show them to me first. I will pay you more than you'd get in the market. *Ramadan Mubarak*.'

'*Ramadan Mubarak*.' Yusuf seemed ill at ease. He left hurriedly.

Rukh straightened from his inspection and turned to Malka. 'I will forgive your tardiness just this once. But you might want to change into more conventional attire.'

Malka blushed and headed for the changing room, where her whites were waiting patiently on their peg where she'd left them the night before. She slung her costume into her locker. She'd deal with it later. Thank God she had a spare pair of socks. Snake followed her in and Malka braced herself for ridicule. Instead, the girl held out a pair of scuffed sneakers.

'I think we're the same size.'

Malka took them. The giving meant more to her than the gift. Snake was the unspoken leader of the girls at the Leviathan. So although a few of the others stared at her outfit, for once they said nothing. Today, she didn't care. She changed quickly and slipped on the shoes. They were a good fit. She darted back to the kitchen, looking forward to Rukh's thanks. Nothing doing.

'As you were late, I had to put someone else on your station. You are on delivery duty. Working in a kitchen is all about teamwork. Don't let your colleagues down again.'

She'd been so looking forward to working on 'her' fish and telling Mahmoud about the fishermen. But there was no time for self-pity. People called her constantly from around the kitchen, clamouring for more ingredients. As she wove through the bustling kitchen with laden trays, she kept thinking about the graceful way Yusuf cast his nets, bending and straightening as he had done in prayer, his work and his faith woven of the same cloth. She tried to echo his movements, and found a rhythm that took her fluidly between the different stations. All of them were full. Under the mounting pressure, three of the original eighteen trainees had stopped showing up. None of them from her group. She wondered if they were back on the streets. True, it was punishing work. But how could they give up the comfort of their own bed? A month seemed an impossibly short time in which to transform the remaining raw recruits into cooks, never mind chefs. Just when she felt ready to drop, her shift finished and Malka slunk towards the showers. But Rukh's voice brought her up short.

'Where do you think you are going? You're not done yet. Put any left-over ingredients away, and then get the stations ready for the next shift.'

Why was he always so hard on her? He didn't seem to treat anyone else like this. Snake nodded at her in commiseration. It meant so much to be acknowledged that Malka had to bite her lip to keep back the tears. At last, she got to her final task, fetching fish from the walk-in freezer to distribute amongst the various marked tables for the next shift. She consoled herself that some would be from Shakir and Yusuf.

She swung the heavy steel door open, wheeled her trolley in, and stepped into the blue darkness. Her breath fluttered before her like a flag. She switched on the timed light, remembering the one in the Jerusalem hallway, a lifetime ago. The darkness there had a different quality. It felt pregnant with possibility.

Malka raced between the hanging fish which glittered in their dresses of pale coral pink and delicate bluish white. She ran her fingers along them and set them dancing, their scales a sunburst of silver. When she reached the back wall, furred with ice, on impulse she leaned forward and touched it with her tongue. It burned, and for a terrifying moment she was stuck, until her breath melted it. Water ran down her chin.

She tried to remember which fish she was supposed to be taking out. Where was her list? She rummaged in her pockets, then retraced her steps to the entrance, looking back down the rows as she had when she first entered, to see if that would jog her memory. Then she began loading the trolley at random with fish she recognised. The fish seemed much heavier now, with none of the leaping energy they had displayed in the boat that morning. How they had twisted and turned in the fishermen's hands, trying desperately to find their way back to the sea.

To arrest this train of thought, she picked up the nearest fish. It was the large grouper that Shakir had shown her with such pride. She cradled it in her arms as he had done, then swung it onto the trolley. As she did so, she caught sight of her reflection in the trolley's mirrored surface. Her arms were as pale as the fish's underbelly. It was hard to tell where she stopped and the fish started. Her hair was cobwebbed with strands of ice. How long had she been in here?

As if on cue, the light clicked off, and she fumbled for the switch. It took agonising moments until she found it. She scrabbled at the door, but her fingers were too frozen and stiff to work the handle. She beat against it with both hands, but the kitchen was empty: everyone had already gone to the big celebratory dinner in one of Rukh's other restaurants. She couldn't feel her lips any more. Would someone miss her and come back for her? Surely she was not meant to die surrounded by fish in a freezer? Malka had a sudden image of Moshe sitting on a red stool at Lazlo's, his hand raised in farewell. Her lips still burned with cold.

'Please,' she whispered. 'I don't want to die never having kissed anyone.'

She pounded on the door again. Nothing. She leaned her forehead against it and closed her eyes. It opened so abruptly that she fell forwards onto her knees.

'What the hell are you doing in here?'

Mahmoud peered down at her from the dimness, ghostly in his whites. He held out a hand and lifted her up. She held on, stamping until she could feel her legs. Mahmoud brushed strands of ice from her hair. 'No wonder they call you the Ice Queen. Just don't take it so literally next time.'

'Why do they call me that?' Her lips were numb, and it was hard to get the words out.

'Isn't it obvious? You scare them. You are so intense, so focussed. You always keep your distance. It can be a good thing, if you choose it. I should know. But to me it feels as if you are hiding.'

They sat swinging their legs on the delivery bay porch, their heads bent over cups of strong coffee. Malka knew where her new nickname came from. She'd tried to make friends. But whenever the others slapped hands, made plans, or shared a crafty cigarette, warmed by the camaraderie of shared experience, she stood awkwardly in the margins. She had grown up without a television, a computer or newspapers. Most of what they spoke about was lost on her. On a Saturday night, she usually retreated to her room and the comfort of a book. She needed to discover the shape and extent of her ignorance, map its contours and its continents. She haunted second hand bookstores, but the more she read, the more she realised she didn't know. It felt hopeless. She blew on the coffee, dispersing clouds of steam, and sipped in silence. Mahmoud lit a cigarette and inhaled deeply. He turned away from her to exhale, his head haloed with evanescent veils of silver.

'Why aren't you at the dinner?' she asked.

'I'm fasting, but I don't pray. I'm no longer one of the faithful, so it didn't feel right.'

'Thank God for the non-believers.'

'This is the second time I've saved your ass. You owe me big time.'

'How did you know I was there?'

'Everyone needs a *bab-al sirr*, and the freezer is yours. I've seen you go there after every shift.'

'*Bab al-sirr?*'

'I discovered ours by chance, playing hide and seek with my older sisters. We were not allowed in my father's study, so I was sure they wouldn't look for me there. But just in case they did, I climbed behind the desk, and knocked over a pile of books against the bookshelf, which slid back and revealed a secret room behind it. Many old Arab houses have such spaces in case of war. Like the Israeli *miklat* nowadays. I squeezed into the narrow space, and hugged my knees. They never found me. After that, I hid there often. When I was meant to go to the mosque, I'd sneak one of my father's cigarettes, creep in there, and puff until my eyes watered.'

It was the first time he'd spoken of his family. His voice was hoarse, like a charred photograph, something saved from the fire. She looked at him for a long moment, swirling the coffee in her mouth. She wanted to share something too. Should she tell him it was her birthday? She'd heard Muslims didn't celebrate them. But then, neither had her family. She suddenly remembered her thoughts of Moshe when she feared she might die cold and alone in the freezer. 'Mahmoud, have you ever been in love?'

'Have you?'

Malka touched a thumb to her lower lip, and felt it slowly flush with blood. 'I've no idea. I don't know what love feels like, what it tastes like. What colour it is.'

Mahmoud's face closed in on itself. 'Don't look at me. You have to find your own answers.' He stood abruptly and stalked off.

What was she thinking? She'd never spoken the word love aloud, never heard it either. Now in a moment of foolishness, she'd hurt the only friend she'd had. What could she do to win him back? Malka stared at the grounds in her cup but found no answers there. She set it down, its handle a tiny question mark in the blue dusk.

Chapter 14
Ayat al-Nur, The Light Verse

Malka staggered under the weight of a tyre, and nearly slipped in a pool of oil.

'Not like that!' Mahmoud called across the yard. 'Roll it. Let it carry itself. Check for bumps, cuts or scars.'

Malka looked down at her legs.

'Not on you, on the tyre! Here, take this one, too.'

Another huge tyre rolled towards her and it took all her strength to arrest it. The day after he'd rescued her from the freezer, Mahmoud asked for her help with a special project. How could she refuse? She hadn't expected to tramp across Jaffa with a wheelbarrow to a breaker's yard where machines were left to rust. Mahmoud strode straight towards the heaped mounds of metal. A coiled spring ensnared her as she tried to follow.

'What are we doing here?' she asked.

Mahmoud lowered his voice and jabbed his finger at her, his head cocked to one side in Rukh's characteristic birdlike posture. 'Look around. What do you see? Junk, right? Well that's what people see when they look at us. Go deeper. This is a treasure hunt.'

Malka wondered what Rukh would say if he saw them now. They had 'borrowed' the barrow from the kitchen garden – officially, they were on a foraging trip. Mahmoud lifted a thick, oily chain from a bucket and placed it delicately round her neck. He bowed ridiculously. 'Your majesty.'

The smell of petrol and stale oil clogged her throat. But she laughed and bent her head, so the chain slipped into the barrow with a clang. 'Mahmoud, be serious.'

He winked. 'I'm most serious when I'm joking.'

She tried to see the mountains of twisted metal and abandoned machines through his eyes. She tried not to resent the fact that she could be far out to sea, relishing the stillness waiting beneath the surface. Go deeper, he said. She shaded her eyes with one hand, the tyre resting against her hip. It all depends how you look at things. Pretend this is a sea of metal, and we are going fishing. Seek, and you shall find.

She laid the tyres down, and threw her gaze out over the hulking mass of metal as if she was casting a net. High up on a mound to her left, she noticed a breast-like curve of dirty red metal, obscured by a twisted exhaust pipe. A word winked at her from the shadows. 'Cat,' she read. With a wash of homesickness, Malka remembered chasing Reb Moshe through the old city, following the silvery cat to a door where something monstrous waited for her. But Moshe had been there too. She clambered up the teetering pile.

'What have you found?' Mahmoud scrambled after her.

The two of them lugged the exhaust to one side, and it rolled away with the sound of a thousand pots falling. Beneath lay the chassis of a huge motorbike, its forks crushed.

'Never mind,' Malka said, and turned away.

'Are you kidding?' Mahmoud whispered. 'She's an M900. Her engine looks fine. It's just the suspension and the forks, new wheels. Nothing we can't handle. Let's hope my street smarts are still intact, and Bilal doesn't realise what he's got.'

The yard seemed deserted. Malka wondered, if this was treasure, why it was unguarded. But as she and Mahmoud staggered down the incline towards the barrow, dragging the wounded machine, a gravelly voice greeted them.

'Well, if it isn't the Prophet. Salaam.' A hunched, potbellied figure emerged from a hut Malka hadn't noticed, nestling between two of the metal heaps. His arms were thicker than her legs, and his hands were scarred and deeply grained with oil. At his feet trotted the largest dog she had ever seen. It was black and sleek, with ragged jaws. She edged behind Mahmoud.

'Bilal. Aleikum Salaam. Is this Andromeda? My, she's grown.' The dog allowed Mahmoud to scratch her between the ears.

'Sure has. It must be, what, a couple of years? Haven't seen you since Faroukh copped it.'

Mahmoud concentrated all his attention on getting the bike upright.

'What have you dug up here?' Bilal lifted the hulk effortlessly, and set it down between them. He whistled. 'You always liked a challenge.' With a rag, he wiped the insignia, revealing the rest of the English word Malka had noticed. It wasn't Cat, but Ducati. 'She's wrecked. A serious accident. Look at the forks, bent out of alignment. Even if you could get her roadworthy, the metal might hide all kinds of stress and trouble. Remind you of anyone?'

Mahmoud was still silent, his body rigid.

Bilal's voice grew tender. 'What, you didn't know? Can't say I was surprised. You were the only thing that kept him the right side of sane. Faroukh was always looking for a bigger high. I guess he found it. Drove that hot-rod you built for him straight off the pier and into the sea. Waste of a good machine, if you ask me.'

Still Mahmoud said nothing. Bilal gave him an appraising glance. 'For old times' sake, I'll do you a deal. If you can get this into the barrow, I will let you have it for a couple of hundred. Dollars, that is.' He seemed to notice Malka for the first time. 'This your sidekick? Doesn't seem your type.' He looked at her appraisingly. 'Tell you what. I will throw in those tyres to sweeten the deal, if she carries them. The bike, you lift alone.'

The dog nosed her ankle and Malka stifled a cry.

'Andromeda, sit!'

The dog crouched. She still came up to Malka's chest. The dog and her owner watched impassively as Mahmoud bent and lifted the chassis, staggering to the barrow, his legs trembling. He dropped it into the barrow with a crash that echoed round the yard. Malka rolled her tyres over, and hoisted them awkwardly on top of the frame.

'Eighty is all I have.' Mahmoud took a wad of notes from his back pocket that looked like his entire earnings from the Leviathan to date. Bilal thumbed through it, then lifted the bike gently and turned it around to face the back of the barrow. 'You'll find it easier to transport like this.' He looped a tyre over each handlebar like giant ear-rings. 'You can pay me the rest next month. No interest.'

Malka and Mahmoud wheeled the barrow along the road, each with one hand on the bike handle, and one on the barrow. It was slow work. When they reached the flea market, they stopped to massage their hands, ignoring the hooting traffic piling up behind them. Mahmoud lit a cigarette. He was covered in rust and grime. Is that how I look? Rukh will kill us for sure, Malka thought. She was full of questions, but decided to go for the most obvious.

'How do you know that guy?

'Bilal? From a previous life.' He patted the motorbike, which started to topple. He righted her hastily.

'What are you going to do with this monster?'

'Restore her, of course. She's a hidden diamond, just like us. Good thing we noticed her.'

'I noticed her, you mean.'

Mahmoud was quiet the rest of the way. When they reached the delivery bay of the Leviathan, Rukh was waiting for them, his arms folded, his face like thunder. Smirking trainees peered from the doorway behind him. Malka waited for the explosion. But as always, Rukh's voice was even.

'Your shift starts in twenty minutes. The two of you had better be spotless. I will check you personally. Tell me, where are you planning to keep that thing?'

'Out here, if that's OK.'

Rukh gave a barely perceptible nod, then turned to the others. 'What are you doing out here? I'm not running a theatre!' They bolted back inside.

Over several weeks, Mahmoud took the bike apart in a corner of the delivery bay. He stripped and cleaned it, then roamed breakers' yards for spare parts on his days off. Malka accompanied him whenever she could. She loved to watch him work. She sensed that as he scrubbed away the rust, something inside him was healing. He was raising sparks, making the broken whole again, just like the mystics in the Zohar. Slowly, the bike took shape, raised on a stand Mahmoud had built from a broken stool. Rukh inspected Mahmoud's hands minutely before each shift, turning his long fingers and callused palms to the light. He never had cause for complaint. They were scrubbed raw.

Late one night, as she sat soaking the chain for the hundredth time in the bath of rust remover, a glimmer of silver finally emerged between her fingers. Malka looked over to where Mahmoud knelt over some salvaged forks. He glanced up at her and smiled, smearing oil across his forehead. Now, she decided, was the time to ask him.

'Who was Faroukh?'

He put down the forks slowly, and motioned for her to sit beside him. 'He was the reason I came out. Him, and a bowl of peas.'

'Came out of where?'

'Sometimes, Malka, I think you come from the moon.' He took the chain she held out, wiped it with a cloth, and set it to dry in the sun. 'I never told anyone this story.'

'I'm listening.'

'The morning of my fifteenth birthday Nur, my sister, sat on the steps outside our house, shelling peas into a blue bowl in her lap. She kept one eye on my older sister Fatima's children, who chased a football they had made from plastic bags, which gusted away from them every time they tried to kick it, to roars of laughter. When Fatima worked, and sometimes even when she didn't, Nur took care of them after school, just as she had mothered me, though she was only eighteen.'

'What about your mother?'

'She died giving birth to me.'

'I'm sorry.'

'Don't be. I never knew her. What does haunt me is that it may be my fault that Nur never married. Fatima got away as soon as she could, accepting the clumsy suit of Mahfouz, the mechanic. He's the one who taught me how to do this.' He motioned to the bike on its stand, and for the first time Malka noticed a faint white scar across the top of two fingers. 'But Nur stayed to look after me and Ab. It's hard to say which of us gave her the most trouble.'

'How did you hurt your hand? Was it in the kitchen?'

Mahmoud rubbed his scarred fingers with his thumb. 'I collect scars the way trees collect rings. This is from the first time I refused to go to the madrasah. Fatima locked me in the woodshed until I changed my mind. I was six years old. I found an axe, and tried to break the door down. The lock held, but I managed to prune my fingers. I'd never seen so much blood.'

'My God!'

'My howls brought my sisters running. Fatima grabbed the axe and held it above my head. I thought she was going to kill me. I hid behind Nur's skirts. She tried to staunch the flow of blood with her hem. Fatima shouted at her. "How can you stand the brat! Every time I look at him, I see Umm's killer!"

'I'd never seen Nur angry, but words boiled out of her like they had been simmering for years. "You know as well as I that the doctors said it was dangerous for her to become pregnant again. But Ab wanted a son. At any cost. If you ask Allah enough, he gives you what you want. How can you blame the child?"

"Insha'Allah," Fatima replied, stunned by our placid sister's outburst. But Nur wasn't done. "Now for God's sake, help me find the rest of his finger." Nur found the missing piece and kept it on ice till the ambulance came. They said I would be lucky to be able to move it, that if the axe had fallen a little lower I might have lost my hand, my life.' He laughed. 'After that, I could skip school whenever I liked?'

'What about the peas?'

'You are right. God is in the details. You remember a few weeks back, I rescued you from the freezer?'

'You never let me forget it.'

'You asked me then how love tasted, and what colour it was. Like I said, it was my birthday. Our kitchen was tiny, just an alcove off the *Liwan*, but Nur conjured amazing things there. My earliest memories are of being held in one arm as she stirred with the other, watching, stirring, tasting. It seemed like magic, taking the onions which made me cry, and turning them into something sweet and golden. I loved peas best. Nur taught me to split the pods open with my thumbnail, popping the fresh peas into my mouth like edible jewels. She would pinch and release the shell between her thumb and forefinger, fluttering it around my head like an emerald butterfly until we both collapsed in laughter. Then one day Ab strode in and pulled me out by my ear, shouting that the kitchen was no place for a man. I was eight.' He lifted one lobe and showed her a scar like a puckered mouth. 'He forbade me from ever setting foot in the kitchen again. But the very next day, Nur ushered me in without a word, her own quiet rebellion. He needed her too much to risk an argument, and she knew it.'

'So every birthday after that, Nur made peas for me, our own ritual commemoration of a battle won.'

'Make peas, not war,' Malka said in English.

'Terrible,' Mahmoud smiled. 'Better leave the jokes to me.'

They grinned at one another. Thank God for Mahmoud, Malka thought. Without him she would have died of loneliness. Listening to him, she realised that it was more than chance, more than the two of them being the rejects amongst a group of rejects, which brought them together. She knew what it was to be banished from a place where you had felt at home, to long for the approval of a parent which was endlessly withheld.

'My fifteenth was the same, except it wasn't. I decided I had to tell her. So I tried to summon the words I needed, as the bowl in her lap slowly filled. A fly settled on the rim, then took off. The silence grew teeth. Nur rose and carried the peas into the kitchen, and I followed, watching as she stirred them into the onions that simmered there, already translucent. Finally, she turned to me, wiping her hands on her apron. There were threads of grey in the hair under her hijab. When I saw them, something twisted inside me. She felt me looking, and tucked the stray hair back.

"What is it? Were you kicked out of the madrasah again, *habibi*?" Her voice was even, unruffled. We could hear Fatima's kids shouting in the street. I said nothing.

"Does Ab know yet? People look at him with pity because of you, even though he's the Muezzin." Her words stung, as they were meant to, and I found my voice.

"It's not the madrasah, it's something else. Well, someone else."

"Who?"

"Faroukh."

"Faroukh! Why would you want to get involved with him? All he does is ride around on that silly motorbike." She tasted, scattered salt over the peas, then banged the pot down on the wooden table. We heard a hiss, and she lifted it quickly. She'd forgotten to put down the mat, and burned a halo onto the table-top. "Besides, his uncle deals drugs to the Israelis."

"You don't know anything about him," I said. "So he rides a motorbike. He's not afraid to make some noise, to be noticed.

When I go out at night, I have to creep down the stairs like a thief." I realised I was shouting at her.

"That's how it should be."

"Maybe for you,' I said. 'But I like noise. And I like him. I mean, I really like him."

'She said nothing, but her fingertips were pressed so hard against the counter they were white.

"Is it my fault?" she said at last.

"What? Why would you say that?"

"You always loved dressing up in my clothes when you were little, and I let you. I kept you in the kitchen when other boys your age were playing outside."

'I took two white bowls from the cupboard. "Those were the only times I remember being happy. I didn't want to go out anyway. The older boys used to throw dirt at me. They called me Allah's orphan."

'My sister flinched, like I'd slapped her. "You never told me. That's what you may become if you go through with this, Heaven forbid.'"

Malka finally understood what he was telling her. He loved men. No wonder she felt safe with him. 'But isn't all true love from God?'

'My sister didn't see it that way. "I don't want to live my life denying my feelings. That kind of life is no life at all," I told her.

'She ladled the peas equally into the two bowls. I sat in my usual chair. Once my feet had swung in the air. Now I pressed them down, and leaned my chair far back, balancing on the two hind legs. I knew she hated me doing it.

'The peas were tender, perfect. She watched me clear my plate, then filled it again. "Happy birthday," she said quietly.' Mahmoud's eyes narrowed. 'Malka, you may not know but some Muslims don't celebrate birthdays. If it's not in the Koran, you don't do it. So I knew she was breaking the rules for me. But as I watched her swallow that first mouthful, I realised that my birthday was also the anniversary of our mother's death.

I imagined what it must cost her to celebrate with me. She waited until I finished my second bowl before she launched her next salvo.

"Have you two done anything together?"

"Faroukh won't even look at me. Don't you dare look so relieved!"

"Perhaps it is just a crush? You know, I had one for a girl in my class. So much heartache, and then you get over it a few weeks later."

'I did not think about what this revelation said about her own private life. I was far too preoccupied with my own story. I made sure she was looking me in the eye, and I spoke as calmly as I could. "I've felt this way before I even had a name for it. Even now, all I can think about is Faroukh astride his motorbike, his hair flying behind him like a flag."

Nur raised her hands to her ears. "Alright, so maybe it's not a crush. Is it really worth ruining your life for?"

"There are some things we have no choice over. For me, this is one of them."

'She pushed her peas into two mounds with her spoon, one on each side of the bowl. I watched the gap between the two widen. When she spoke next there were tears in her voice.

"Mahmoud, be careful. Please."

'I pushed my empty bowl away. She came round the table, and hugged me tightly from behind, resting her head on my shoulder. "I'm tired of being careful," I whispered into her ear.

'In the difficult months that followed, her warning about me becoming Allah's orphan seemed prophetic. I was caught kissing another boy. Not Faroukh of course. He was still as elusive as ever. I was kicked out of both school and home. Even Nur couldn't ignore my father's express edict that no one help me. Throughout my childhood, I fantasised about leaving, but the reality was sadder and dirtier. I found myself on the street.'

'How did you manage?'

'I took this knife with me.' He lifted his shirt, and Malka caught the flash of a metal handle against his dark skin. 'Though I've never used it in anger. It's a silver ceremonial dagger, part of my mother's dowry. It was a part of her, and I wanted it with me. Rukh keeps it under lock and key usually, but he let me have it for the ceremony.'

'What ceremony?' Malka looked at the gleaming machine. "Are you going to circumcise its tailpipe?'

Mahmoud laughed. 'That's your second joke today! I detect a thaw. Nothing like that. I just want my mother's blessing, want to feel she's a part of my new life here.'

'Do you remember her at all?'

'There was a single photograph of my mother in the house. It hung in the hallway, and I passed it every day. It was a blurred image of a young woman, sitting on the porch of our house, squinting at the sun. Her hair seemed uncovered in the picture, although Ab always insisted that this was just a trick of the light. Her lips were open, as if she was speaking. I couldn't bear to leave her behind. Many nights I used to wonder what she might say about the new company her image kept, the strange walls I tacked her to. I wanted one of Nur as well, but after my mother's death there were no more photographs. My father took refuge from her ghost in religion. But to me, it seemed that we were all ghosts, and only she was real.'

Malka wondered about the impact of her own flight on those she had left behind. 'Did no one help you?'

'In our community, my father's word was law. Even Nur couldn't ignore an express edict. Finally I went to Faroukh, with the desperate heroism of one who had no other choice. Sometimes, having your dreams come true is the worst thing that can happen to you. He agreed to give me a room, for a price. I became another petty dealer. Faroukh was so close yet so unattainable that every day my throat burned from holding back tears. I sold people an escape that poisoned them, and skulked in back alleys to make ends meet. I was too ashamed to see Nur, even if she'd agreed to meet me. Within a year, I dropped out of dealing too. I wasn't made to be anyone's lackey. When I finally said I'd had enough, Faroukh just nodded and turned back to the bag he was filling. He didn't even say goodbye.'

Mahmoud's voice caught, and Malka handed him the rag she was holding. He shook his head. 'Pass me that chain?'

He dipped it gently in the oil bath, then threaded it into place on the sprockets. He lifted the bike off the stand and leaned it against the wall. He lit a celebratory cigarette, cupping his hands around the flame. Words and smoke emerged from his mouth together in spurts.

'I thought I'd already reached the bottom, but I soon discovered that I still had a long way to fall. What made it worse was that every day, wherever I was, whatever I was doing, my father's amplified voice burst in on me, calling the chosen to prayer, creating a circle of comfort that forever excluded me.'

Malka started. Could it be his father's voice she waited for each morning before diving into the water? 'Why didn't you leave Jaffa?'

'Sometimes I was desperate to get away, but I could never stray too far. I'm a child of the sea, and she keeps me on a tight leash. For a thousand and one nights, I slept on her shore, breathing salt, scavenging from bins.'

'Thank God Rukh's crew showed up on the beach.'

'Two years later. But maybe you're right. Thanks to Nur, I knew how food should taste, and I've never learned the art of keeping my mouth shut. "Too much cumin, not enough cardamom," I sneered, but they took me anyway, away from the grubby alleys of Ajami, and the clutching hands of older men. I had forgotten what a bed felt like, the whisper of sheets against my legs. Rukh's kitchen glimmered like something from a dream, and my fingers itched to touch every surface.'

'So are you happy now?'

'I love that I am allowed to be angry here, to shout and swear, as long as none of it travels down through the handle of my knife. Rukh doesn't care where I came from, as long as I show up on time every day. For the first time in my life, I do.' He dropped the stub of his cigarette, stamped hastily on the embers. 'But no matter how early I arrive, you are always there first. Do you sleep in the kitchen?'

'No, the freezer. I'm the Ice Queen, remember?' She pushed his shoulder. 'I'm glad you are here,' she said.

'Of course you are. You'd be an ice-sculpture now if I wasn't. Don't mind the others. They're just jealous of your talent. Suspicious, too, of the time you spend getting dirty with a dirty Arab. Right, I think she's ready.' He knelt beside the bike. 'If she is going to be part of the Leviathan crew, she needs a name.'

He slid the dagger from its sheath and drew the point of the blade in swirling lines of Arabic script, under the Ducati insignia. Malka crouched beside him.

'What have you called her?'

'Al-Buraq. The name of the winged steed which belonged to my namesake, the Prophet. She helped him reach the heavens, attain his dreams. It means lightning, just like the Hebrew word chashmal.' Malka shrank back. 'What did I say?'

'Nothing. It's a great name. I think your mother would be proud of you.'

They stood a moment side by side, in a charged silence. Then Mahmoud broke the spell. 'Come, let's give them something to be jealous about.'

He wiped his hands carefully, and turned the key on the bike. Nothing. His face set, he tried again, and then a third time. The engine roared into life. The noise was so loud, Malka could feel it thrumming in her stomach. People came running from the kitchen. In the lead was Rukh. He was carrying two helmets. White, of course. She and Mahmoud gaped at him.

'Just protecting my investment,' he said gruffly, taking the dagger from Mahmoud and wrapping it an oilcloth. 'I don't want you two smeared down the sidewalk like tuna tartare, and waste all that precious training. Besides,' he nodded at Malka, 'she missed her own birthday party.'

'What do you mean?'

'Her birthday was on the seventeenth of Tammuz. We already had a big meal organised, to break the Jewish fast and the *sawm*. So I baked a cake. Didn't they save you any?'

Malka swallowed. 'I've never had a birthday cake.'

This was not the only surprise. Snake stepped forward, her precious leather jacket dangling from her index finger. 'You can borrow this. Scuff it and you're dead meat.'

Malka took it, her eyes wide. As she slipped it on, she felt some of Snake's boldness infuse her.

Mahmoud leaned his head close to hers. 'So snakes do shed their skin, eh? Malka, what's the deal? Here I was, going on about a silly bowl of peas, and you never told me it was your birthday.'

'It was the night I got locked in the freezer. I was too busy being grateful for you saving my life, remember?' She took one of the helmets, inhaling the smell of the soft leather lining.

'Come on,' he said. 'We can still celebrate. Let's take her for a ride.'

Chapter 15
Ghosts and Visions

T he 'completely dry' part proved a slight exaggeration. They took off their shoes and socks, rolled up their jeans and waded straight into the freezing surf. Moshe grimaced as the water crept up his thighs. He could just make out Vlad's shirt, white in the moonlight. They headed for a cluster of rocks at the centre of the bay. The waves burst over them with a seething roar, and Moshe ducked. He tried to still the trembling in his legs. You can do this, he told himself. Face your fear. Name it. Own it.

Vlad got down on all fours and crawled along the rock, hugging the rock face. Then he turned and lay on his back, face to the sky. Moshe copied him and turned over awkwardly, scraping his knees. When he looked up, a gleaming wall of water towered over him. We are going to drown, he thought. But the jutting wall of rock sent the water arcing over them, a cascading roof of roaring darkness. Just as Vladek had promised, they were inside the sea, but also on dry land. Was this how the Israelites felt when they left Egypt? It was amazing. He could taste the salt spray on his lips, but his clothes stayed dry. He turned to Vladek, silhouetted against the rock like a fallen statue.

'How did you find this place?'

'It's famous. Greek legend says this is where Andromeda was chained so she could be eaten by the dragon. A good place to break free from any fears that hold you back, don't you think? Here you can look your dragon in the face.'

Moshe's stomach tightened in dread.

'Stand up. Your feet will be safe on dry land, and only your head will be in the water. Get used to it. Stay there as long as you can. Duck down to breathe.'

Moshe reached up to touch the curving roof. Water ran down his arm and soaked his T-shirt. He shuddered. It was like lying in a trench with enemy fire streaming over your head. He was supposed to just stand up in the midst of the barrage?

'Your namesake didn't hesitate. He just walked straight into the sea and it split around him.'

Moshe closed his eyes and had a vision of Andromeda tied to her post, straining against the ropes that bound her. She waited. Nothing happened. No dragon appeared, but the water welled up against her ankles, then washed against her shins, her calves, her thighs. Still no one came. The water teased her, drawing back then coming in a rush, covered in glittering green scales. It reared up and swallowed her. When it withdrew, she was slumped against the post, her red hair covering her face. She was still. He glimpsed Perseus, hanging back on the beach. Arriving too late.

'What if the myths are a lie? Maybe Perseus never got there, and re-wrote the story to cover his failure.'

Vladek closed his eyes and recited:

'The souls of those I love are on high stars.
How good that there's no-one left to lose
And one can weep.'

Then he turned to Moshe, his great head marble in the moonlight. At this moment, he looked godlike. 'This is a place where myths can be made, or remade.'

The gentleness of these words, and the faith underlying them, gave Moshe the courage he needed. He stood up, faced the beach, and spread his feet apart, steadying himself as the water pounded against his back, buffeted his shoulders. Taking a deep breath, he thrust his head into the next wave. Instantly he was drenched, blinded. The current cuffed him, and he slipped and fell, cutting his feet. Then a huge wave knocked him right off the rocks and dragged him under. He flailed wildly, trying to reach the surface, but the current was too strong. He couldn't breathe. This is it, he thought, strangely calm. Is this how my sister felt, in her last moments? Life and death only a breath apart, so close that they seemed the same thing. Then he heard a voice in the water.

You wanted them to yourself again, didn't you? You only pretended to be sad when they couldn't find me. You used to wish that I'd never been born.

Moshe mouthed his response, precious bubbles slipping away from him. 'I was just a child. I didn't mean it, even then. You know that.' The voice ignored him, carrying on its litany of accusation.

Well, you got your wish. The sea scrubbed me out. Then, when our father left, you were glad. You pushed him away, too. So you could have her all to yourself. Our mother. But now you've turned your back even on her. One by one, you left us all. You failed us. Just as you will fail this girl.

Moshe was sinking. He clawed through the curtains of water that piled on top of him. Then he felt himself hooked under the armpit and lifted bodily to the surface. Vladek heaved him out, scraping his ribs on the rocks. Everything hurt. Moshe didn't care. He sucked in great lungfuls of blessed air, happy to be alive.

'So you don't like Akhmatova. There's no need to drown yourself!'

Vladek lowered him slowly onto the shelf, and then sat beside him. They rested their backs against the rock shelf, their knees against their chests, and faced the rising sun. Moshe thought of the voice in the water, waiting for him all these years. What if everything he'd heard was true?

Vlad rubbed his head with rough affection. 'For a moment there, I thought I'd lost you.'

'I heard my sister's voice in the water.'

Vlad eyed him curiously. 'You never told me you have a sister?'

'I had a sister.'

Slowly at first, then in spurts, Moshe told him the whole story. When he was finished, Vladek sat in silence until the entire disc of the sun made it over the horizon.

'Watch this,' he said.

The sun caught the bridge of water that streamed over them, and it glowed like molten glass, amber beads dropping on their heads like blessings.

'Maybe it's the power of suggestion,' Vladek said. 'Do you remember how the poem continues?' He raised his voice above the rush of water.

'*Rising from the past, my shadow is running in silence to meet me... And this shower, sun-drenched, rare, brings me consolation, good news.*

'Maybe your sister has been waiting all these years to meet you. To say goodbye. So you can let her go. Maybe she wants you to stop blaming yourself. You were just a kid. Stop carrying her and make space for new life.' He stood slowly. 'Come on, let's get back to shore and dry off. Ah. We might have a problem.' Moshe looked back the way they had come. The tide had come in. Dark water stretched away from them towards the distant beach.

'We've no choice now. We'll have to swim back.'

'Shit!'

'Don't panic. Sit and watch a minute.' Vladek lay full length on the ledge, and showed Moshe how to move his arms and legs, how to turn his head to breathe. He made Moshe lie down beside him, and copy his movements. Then he threw Moshe a pair of goggles and showed him how to tighten them. 'Always I carry some for sobering up.' They moved to a shallow pool at the edge of Andromeda's rock, and repeated the whole thing again, in the water. At first Moshe thrashed wildly, but soon he managed to paddle across the pool, scooping at the water and puffing like a long distance runner. Vladek nodded.

'I think you are ready. I will swim beside you. Don't fight it, the sea is not your enemy. And don't forget to breathe.' He slipped under the surface of the slate blue water. For a moment the sea was blank, and Moshe felt a lurch of horror. Then Vladek bobbed up a couple of metres away, grinning.

'Come on in, the water's lovely.'

Moshe jumped in with a great splash and held his breath. This time he bobbed to the surface, and Vlad swam over with a few graceful strokes.

'Let the waves carry you towards the shore. Use their momentum, work with the current.'

The beach seemed horribly far. He sensed the bottom dropping away beneath him, and the cold of it stilled his legs. He went under once more. This time he tried to stay calm, to take in his surroundings. For the first time, he noticed the curves and hollows dimpling the surface of the sand below, mirroring the movements of the sea above. He was caught in the middle of a great dance. Then he sensed movement ahead of him. He peered through the water. It looked like a giant fish. Was it a shark? He tried to get away, but it drew inexorably closer. He realised with relief that it was a huge salmon. It looked like there was something stuck on its back. Seaweed? It glowed red in the growing light, and spread its tendrils in the current. Not seaweed. Hair. Someone was riding its back, reaching one white arm towards him. He stretched out his hand, but grasped only a handful of sand. Sand! He'd made it to the beach. When he looked again, the fish was gone. He staggered ashore, the water streaming off him, and collapsed beside Vladek as though he'd swum for miles. When he finally sat up, Vladek pushed him back over again, laughing.

As the morning sun dried them, it left ghost-map traceries of salt on their skin. An ice-cream seller came towards them, and Moshe beckoned him over. Vladek shrank back.

'What is it?'

'The way you feel about the sea, I feel about ice-cream.'

Moshe looked at the giant beside him, incredulous. 'You're afraid of ice-cream?' He waved the seller on.

'Yes. I mean no. Not ice-cream exactly, but what it reminds me of. Something that happened in the army.'

'Tell me.'

'I was an officer in Lebanon. We were huddled together in a crater near the front line, sharing a quick cigarette. It was Purim, although I hadn't known it then. We heard the sound of an ice-cream truck. I thought I was hallucinating. Battle can do funny things to you, but I saw from their faces that the others heard it too. Then we saw the truck. It was dented and scraped and spattered with rubble. A jaunty tune came from a speaker on the roof. One wing mirror hung from a shred of metal. But it was real, and it came to a stop right beside us. I stood up, my weapon cocked, ready for a surprise attack. My men did likewise. As if waiting for this signal, men in white poured out the back of the truck, wearing big white *kippot* tufted like pineapples.' He gestured above his own crewcut as though plucking invisible hairs. 'They led my men in a whirling dance, handed out ice-creams, then piled back in the truck and moved off towards the front line.'

'That doesn't sound so terrible.'

'With the ice cream streaking their faces, my men looked like the children they still were. It made them vulnerable. It made them weak. They all died that day. All of them.'

'But not you.'

'I lived to tell the tale.'

'Vladek, you just said I shouldn't blame myself. You shouldn't either. As for those Hasidim, isn't there something glorious about driving an ice-cream truck into a war zone? I haven't been in the army yet. But from what I know, we die whether we are prepared or not. At least your men had a moment of joy – a moment of remembering who they really were, apart from the war.'

'You know Moshe, until I met you, I never understood those guys, dancing amidst the barbed wire. Now I see that faith can be a kind of love, and love a kind of faith. It can have strange consequences. If you hadn't been chasing your imaginary girlfriend, I'd never have met you.'

Moshe punched Vladek's shoulder. 'She's not imaginary. You're not going to believe this, but I just saw her.'

Vladek scanned the beach. 'Where?'

'When I was underwater. She was riding a giant fish. It's a sign of some kind. Malka's here in Jaffa. I know it.'

Vladek looked at him for a long moment. He didn't laugh. 'I believe the sea is a living thing, full of secrets, mysteries. She holds the traces of all who pass through her, dissolved in her currents like salt. It doesn't surprise me that she would speak to a sensitive soul like you.'

'Listen to the poet,' Moshe grinned. 'You are really something. I'm surprised no one has snapped you up.'

'I've never had a girlfriend.' Vladek lowered his voice. 'Not even an imaginary one. I just... I can't talk to women, not like this, like I'm talking to you. I'm too worried about being a – what do they call it in Ivrit? A *fryer*.'

Moshe thought about the word. He'd always hated it. It meant weak, someone who could be taken advantage of. It embodied the fear of vulnerability that haunted Israeli men. He'd always thought it was the army's fault, and it looked like maybe he was right.

'You could never be a *fryer*, Vladek.'

'I may have survived Lebanon, but I left part of myself behind. The part that feels. Just like your little sister took a part of you with her. But it seems like the sea just brought it back. So maybe there's still hope for me?'

Moshe looked at his friend. 'Of course there is. Today you helped me get over a fear that's haunted me for years. The least

I can do is help cure your fear of ice cream. The girlfriend bit is up to you.'

Moshe waved the vendor over and got two Cookielidas, vanilla ice-cream sandwiched between huge chocolate chip cookies. He handed one to Vladek, who took it tentatively, as though Moshe had just pulled the pin and it took all his resolve not to hurl it far out to sea. He took a tentative bite. A smile spread across his face like a slow sunrise. Without a word, he wolfed down the whole thing. Grinning, Moshe handed over his own, which met with a similar fate.

'Here's to love and ice-cream!'

'Love and ice-cream,' Vladek echoed, his mouth full.

Chapter 16
Al-Buraq

The helmet fitted her perfectly. Mahmoud lifted his visor, so she did the same. He swung himself up onto Buraq with practised ease. Up close, it was a hulking, metal monster. Malka refused his proffered arm and scrambled up awkwardly, only to be confronted by a new dilemma. Where should she put her hands? She could reach backwards and grab the hoop above the brake light, or hold on to Mahmoud. Holding on to the bike felt precarious. But she'd never willingly embraced a man. In the end, the bike decided for her. As the engine roared into life, she lurched forward into Mahmoud and their helmets knocked together.

'Sorry,' they both said.

Clearly, she would have to hold on to him. It was a matter of life and death. In such situations, Jewish law said that all normal rules were suspended. Not that she still believed in such things. But it was hard for her body to let go of years of training. Gingerly, she put her arms around his chest. She turned her helmeted head sideways against his back, and the scent of leather filled her nostrils.

'Not too fast,' she whispered.

'Hold tight,' he said.

Al-Buraq shot forward with a low growl, and they sped through the snarl of traffic as though they were on fast forward. Malka let out a shriek of pure joy. When they finally stopped at the lights, Mahmoud turned his head and grinned.

'Great, isn't it? Just like flying.'

'Mahmoud, it's amazing. But please slow down just a little. You always promised to show me Jaffa. I don't want it to pass by in a blur.'

'Of course! Let's visit the city behind the city.'

He gunned the engine fiercely, and they climbed uphill. The road beneath them turned to cobbles. The bike's giant springs cushioned them, and lifted her a little higher towards heaven with each bump. Malka had to fight the urge to spread her arms like wings. Next thing she knew, a floating tree hovered ahead of them in the middle of the road.

'Wait, do you see that?'

When Mahmoud screeched to a stop, she realised it was real. Someone had suspended an orange tree above the street in a huge ceramic pot. Taut wires connected it to the neighbouring buildings. Mahmoud kicked the bike onto its stand, and they walked over to a low wall near the tree and sat down. Her legs shook, the thrum of the engine still vibrating through them. She stood and shook them in turn, standing on one leg like a stork. Malka caught a faint, familiar scent. She looked up at the tree and saw that it was heavy with fruit.

'Could you get me one?'

He stood and strode towards the tree, clambering up into the pot, which swung gently, like a ship. He came back with a glowing globe in each hand. They were large, and deeply aromatic.

'Shamouti. A variety created by Arab farmers a couple of hundred years ago. The world knows them as Jaffa oranges. Very juicy.' He lifted one to his nose, and inhaled deeply.

'When I was a boy, we were not allowed ice-cream. It was considered too frivolous. So we would each get a shamouti on all the major festivals, to remind us of our heritage. I would peel mine, separate the segments and put them in a bag in the freezer, and then let them melt on my tongue.'

'So you made your own version of ice-cream. You have Jaffa in your blood. I'm still a stranger here.'

Mahmoud's face was dappled with shadows from the leaves of the tree. 'So am I, Malka. This sculpture is by an Israeli artist called Ran Morin. But when I look at this tree, I see Palestine in a jar. They keep it suspended in the air for fear it might take root.' He pounded his fist on the top of the wall. 'Sometimes I don't want to feel anything. It hurts too much.'

Malka nodded. 'I think that's why I go to the freezer so often. I don't want to feel guilty, just because I'm happy.'

Mahmoud rubbed his thumb against his fingertips, and the white scars showed vivid for a moment. 'Through all the crap choices I've made, my people's struggle has been what really mattered. At the Leviathan, I've started to let myself believe that I matter too. It feels wrong.'

'How can it be wrong?'

'To seek my own fulfilment when my people are homeless? Sheer vanity.'

'I thought you said you grew up in Jaffa?'

'I need my country to swim in, to breathe, but all around me are the ghosts of the past. Some days they crowd in so close I can't breathe. I thought if I got this bike, I could leave them behind, but they always follow.' Have you noticed that on all the road signs, it's always Tel-Aviv-Jaffa? Even though Jaffa is thousands of years older, Tel Aviv comes first.' Mahmoud waved his helmet towards the street sign and she turned to read.

'Mazal Dagim Alley.'

'This is your place, see? You're the lucky one, always rising to the surface, leaping upstream like that salmon you ruined on our first night. Me, I'm still a fish out of water.'

'I don't agree. Maybe you are an outsider-insider, like me. Rukh says that good food is all about a sense of place. That Jaffa and Tel Aviv are like two neighbours who don't speak, kept apart by that hyphen. The menu at the Leviathan is meant to get them talking again. That's why he's set us a menu challenge, to collaborate on a new dish which brings our two home cities together. But what does Jaffa have in common with Jerusalem?'

'Let's not talk about work. When you came out of the freezer, you asked me about love. You were thinking about someone in particular, right?'

Malka was glad her face was in shadow. 'I grew up believing that the right person was waiting out there for me, somewhere. I used to talk to them, at night, and feel they could hear me. But I was terrified of meeting them.'

'Me too. That's why I ran. Why do you think I've only gone for guys I know will reject me? I play it safe. Look at you, moving to a different city. It must be a big love, if you need so much space from it.'

'I'm not... I mean, I only met him once.'

'Does this heart-throb have a name?'

'Moshe. His name is Moshe.' It felt good to say his name aloud. But it made her feel so far from home. She was just like that tree, floating, rootless.

'So you like your prophets, eh? Were his lips a revelation?'

She blushed again, remembering her fear in the freezer that she would die without kissing anyone. 'Apart from my sisters, I've never kissed anyone.'

She expected more teasing, but his face was serious. 'You know, that's nothing to be ashamed of. I've kissed and been kissed plenty, but it never touched me. Love should be about risking yourself, like you just did confiding in me. You're no ice-queen. Let's drop the ice and call you Malka'

She smiled. 'I guess Buraq thawed me out. Hey, did you mean it to sound like Baraka?'

'You're right, they have the same root. Power and grace. I like to think of him as Rukh – the whole world knows him as Baraka, but only we get to call him Rukh.' He looked at his watch. 'We need to get back for our shift. We can go out on Buraq again tonight, if you like.'

She nodded, and Mahmoud grinned. 'You need to let your hair down. I know just the place.'

Mahmoud bowed with a flourish and patted Buraq's flank.

'Your majesty, your chariot awaits.'

She looked down at her faded jeans and borrowed turquoise top. Despite her name, she couldn't have felt less royal.

Mahmoud smiled at her. 'You look beautiful.'

She flushed to the roots of her hair. She had been called many things, but never beautiful. She breathed in the compliment, tasted it on her tongue. What made it so meaningful was the way he said it: without design, as if simply stating a fact, pointing out a street sign.

'So do you.'

Mahmoud was always striking, but tonight he'd turned up the volume. A long white shirt embroidered with silver shimmered when he moved, enhancing the impact of his hair. He was the beautiful one, she thought. It was a beauty all his own, wild, original and, to her, terrifying in its confidence. He'd taken what might have been a flaw, and made it his trademark. She saw that he had customised one helmet, and had painted it green, red and black. He held it up under the street light.

'The Palestinian flag. I wear the colours of a country that doesn't exist yet, like a knight carrying the favours of a lady he has only dreamed of. You know what you said about me this morning? You were right. I am as hyphenated as this city. I'm an Arab-Israeli-Palestinian. I already got stopped by the police for wearing it, but there's nothing they can do. It's still legal to carry it here, just about.'

Malka's helmet was unadorned, a blank page waiting to be written on. This time she backed up a few steps, took hold of the hoop and leapt confidently astride Al-Buraq.

They rode through the Tel Aviv traffic towards the Namal, where a fenced-off power station with a chimney like the Tower of Babel loomed. Mahmoud threaded the bike through a thicket of parked cars, down a gravel path and onto a slatted wooden footbridge, towards a huddle of low buildings which hugged the harbour wall. He cut the engine on the bridge and they climbed down and took off their helmets. Rainbows of spray glittered in the light. Malka inhaled the mingled scents of the sea and sweet river water.

Mahmoud pulled a flyer from his back pocket. '*Where salt water kisses sweet, come to drink and feel the beat.* Half price drinks with this too.'

Malka groaned. 'Enough with the kissing already.'

The club was called The Bubble. Even from the outside, it was easy to see why. The second floor was round, made entirely of curved glass. The lights swirling through it dissolved the silhouettes of dancing figures into one another, and spangled the long queue of people waiting to enter. Malka headed for the back of the line, but Mahmoud took her hand and walked nonchalantly to the front.

'ID?' The giant security guard stared at Malka. 'Do I know you from somewhere?'

She looked up at him, confused. 'I don't think so.' He reminded her a bit of Lazlo. It wasn't just his Russian accent: his smile was full of the same gold teeth.

'Come on, that line was old before I was born.' Mahmoud waved the flyer at him, took Malka's elbow and ushered her inside.

The floor inside vibrated with a bass rhythm that Malka could feel in her stomach. The ceiling was made of glass too, so the shadows of the dancers above sifted over them. It was like being underwater. The lights were shaped like jellyfish, trailing tentacles of light, deepening the illusion. Even Mahmoud was impressed.

'Just look at this place! What can I get you?' He was shouting, inches from her face.

'Whatever you're having,' she mouthed back.

She tried to match Mahmoud's swagger as he moved towards the bar, weaving adroitly through the crowd. It's just like swimming, she told herself. It's all about how you use your arms. The crowd parted for them.

The barman flashed them a wide grin, pounded mint in a pestle and mortar, strained clear alcohol through a sieve, added lime and shook the whole thing together. Malka took a long swallow, barely tasting it. She looked around over the rim of her glass. All the people talking, all the people dancing, were men. She was the only girl here.

'You never said this was a gay bar,' she hissed at Mahmoud. 'Is that a problem?'

'Well, it would be nice to be a little less... conspicuous.' Malka drained her glass in one go, and her head rang with the cold.

'I chose this place so you wouldn't have to worry about anyone hitting on you. You can be happily invisible, and dance your heart out.'

'Hitting?'

'God, it's just an expression. Do you always have to be so literal? You've got mint stuck to your teeth.' He leaned forward and she felt his thumbnail click against her tooth.

Then the whole room went silent, as though someone had pulled the plug. Everyone around them turned to face the back of the room. Mahmoud stood open-mouthed. So Malka turned too. A woman was standing on a raised platform behind a microphone. Malka knew her at once. The huge mane was gone, replaced by a cap of close-cropped white-blonde hair, but the face was unmistakable. Then she burst into song, and Malka was certain. It was Shira. Her voice was deeper and hoarser than Malka remembered, like a wounded thing seeking light and healing. Some barrier shattered inside Malka, and Safed came rushing back: the cave, Avner's looming face, the fire. She had to get outside. She turned and ran out of the bar, shouldering people aside. Mahmoud tried to follow but he was hemmed in. 'I just need some air,' she mouthed. He nodded, and turned back to Shira.

Malka rushed to the jetty railings, where the sea pounded the rocks, sending up jagged shards of spray. It would be so easy to lift herself over and let the water take her. She gripped the bars until her knuckles were white; she sagged forward, the metal cold against her forehead. She wept as though she were broken and could never be fixed. Then she doubled over and threw up her drink on the cobbles. She wiped her mouth with the back of her arm, and slowly stood up. She felt a bit better. She leaned out over the railings as far as she could, then a little further. She stretched out her arm and cupped a handful of sea-spray. She washed her face as best she could, then staggered towards the taxi rank. At the front was a beaten-up Volkswagen. It looked exactly the way she felt. She got in, and a line of figurines with multiple hands and heads nodded at her from the dashboard. Religion was everywhere. If only it would just disappear. She slammed the door, and a blaze of white surrounded the car.

The driver exclaimed. 'Hey, would you look at that? I've had trouble with the lights all week. Now they turn on before I even start the engine. Where to?'

She had no idea. Then she did: 'The Leviathan.'

He looked at her dubiously. Malka saw herself in his rear-view mirror. She looked like a melting panda. Great circles of mascara ringed her eyes, ran down her cheeks. Wordlessly, the driver handed her a box of tissues. She wiped furiously at her face, then handed the box back with a shaky smile. She found it hard to be upset with all the little deities nodding at her.

The driver set the box back amongst the figurines. 'These are from India. I went there after the army. Everyone needs something to believe in. Especially if you have to drive here.'

He edged out of the taxi rank. Malka closed her eyes and let the city lights blur over them. Thankfully, the driver said nothing more, but drove with smooth efficiency and none of the bravado she'd expected. Lucky for his upholstery. She wasn't sure her stomach could have taken it.

'Here we are.'

They pulled up outside the Leviathan service entrance. There was a faint glow from the kitchen.

'Are you sure you'll be OK here on your own? Is someone waiting for you? It's two in the morning.'

Malka just handed him a note. 'Please keep the change.'

'Look after yourself, little lady.'

The taxi beeped somewhere behind her. Mahmoud had the keys, she remembered. Fortunately, the spare was still under the vegetable crate. Her hands trembled in the lock. 'Open, please open,' she whispered. At last, the heavy door gave way and she rushed in towards the light.

Part IV
Jerusalem to Jaffa,
Earth
Nitzotzot,
Sparks

Chapter 17
Dancer for God

Malka hurried down the passage towards the glow of the kitchen, then stopped in the doorway. What she saw made no sense. She shook her head and closed her eyes. But when she opened them again, Rukh was still there.

He was in his whites, but he wasn't cooking. He was dancing, whirling, his eyes closed, his face rapt. He barely touched the ground. The hem of his jacket belled out around him like some fantastic flower. There was such concentration, such stillness in his face and upper body, it seemed as if the kitchen walls, tiles and tables all moved around him, the centre of their world. His arms reached up, up, embracing everything in the room, even her, unseen. He was spinning, faster, faster. His eyes were closed. Surely he must fall? Beads of sweat glittered on his lashes like tears.

His face expressed such naked yearning that she was embarrassed to be watching. He was leaping now, but the higher he arched, the more the ceiling above him seemed to recede. Instead of becoming dispirited, his movements became subtle. He slowed until only his hands moved, tracing out sinuous word-shapes in some divine calligraphy. Murmuring, he repeated the same words, a low hum of entreaty. *Bismillah ar-rahman ar-rahim. Bismillah ar-rahman ar-rahim.* Over and over. She knew their meaning. In the name of Allah, the Beneficent, the Merciful. With the name of Allah, the Beneficent, the Merciful. Each time Rukh said the words he seemed to reach deeper, to give them a meaning charged with unspoken feeling. They rippled against the walls, and the kitchen looked different too. Maybe it was the effect of Mahmoud's story, but Malka seemed to see a tall woman at the stove, stirring soup. A boy stood at her elbow. A tough-looking youth burst in, shouting, and she flinched. The figures faded, and there was only Rukh.

His clothing was stained with sweat, his hair curled and wild, and the shocking dishevelment of this most reserved of men brought back to her the memories of Safed that had come bursting to the surface at the Bubble. She had seen Avner's true face in the cave, and it had been ugly. Rukh's dance showed her that not all men were like him. That your body could be a tool for transcendence, not just for shame. She began to cry, quietly, for the girl she'd been in Safed, for the pure yearning she'd had then to believe, for her lost faith. Rukh's eyes opened.

'Malka.'

'I'm sorry. I couldn't keep away.'

'Me neither.'

He spoke as though it were the most natural thing in the world for a grown man to dance alone in an empty kitchen. He turned towards the larder. 'You look like you could do with some soup. I have a great Harissa recipe.' He handed her an apron, and she put it on with relief.

While Rukh made the Harissa paste, Malka chopped the vegetables he set out, enjoying the rhythm, grateful for the chance it gave for her whirling thoughts to settle. The pungent spices lifted her head from her task. Gently, Rukh took her tray of chopped vegetables and slid them into the soup with the side of his knife. He stirred in saffron, ginger, turmeric, then put the pot on low heat to simmer.

'Is this what your mother used to make?'

'Yes, this is her recipe. How did you...?'

'While you were dancing, I glimpsed a boy, standing beside a tall woman. Then an older boy disturbed them, and the picture vanished. I think that boy was you.'

He looked at her for a long moment. 'A vision indeed. She taught me so much. That was my brother Walid, come to call us to the boat. It was our last morning together.'

'Why did I see them in here?'

'I think you know the answer.'

'You used to live here.'

'Yes. You are standing in my family home. Barakas lived here for six generations.'

He lifted a chain that dangled round his neck, and showed her the curlicues of a key.

'At the height of the '48 war, Jaffa was bombed, and my whole family piled into my father's fishing boat. I refused to get on board. I didn't want to leave the only home I knew. "Someone has to keep our home ready for when you return," I shouted. In the end they left me standing on the quay. My father threw this key to me as the gap between us widened. "Look after the house," he called. When the boat reached open water, the engine caught fire. There was an explosion, and the boat was gone. I dived in and swam towards the place where it had been. There was nothing, not even bubbles. Just a pool of burning oil. I scrabbled back to shore, called their names until my voice was gone. Still the sea stayed empty. The boat and their bodies were never found. When I tried to go back home, the locks had already been changed. As Arab refugees, our property was confiscated by the new state. But I was determined to win it back one day, to give meaning to my survival. I like to think my father would understand the way I am honouring my promise, and their memory. Our home was always open to everyone, you see, irrespective of faith.'

Malka thought of her own voluntary flight from Jerusalem. Though it felt impossible that she might ever see them again, her family were still there, going about their lives. Every day Rukh worked here, he must be reminded of the family he had lost. 'How can you work in a house full of ghosts?'

They both looked at the gleaming walls, the quiet stations with ingredients already set out. Malka saw them differently now.

'Once, every breath I took in here was painful, but I have lived with it long enough to discover space within it for other feelings too. I come here early, so I can be alone with the spirits of the past, and dance with them. When I dance... I am not in Israel, I am not in Palestine. I am in God.' He stirred the soup, sniffed, tasted, and added more seasoning.

'It needs a little longer. My father's open door policy helped my dream come true. My childhood friend Aharoni, an Iraqi Jew who speaks Arabic better than I do, became my business partner. He bought the house so I could cook again in my mother's kitchen, and then stepped back to allow me to create a little bubble, free from the mistrust and suspicion I experienced as a trainee chef in Israel who happened to be an Arab. So I bring together young people from all communities who have lost their way, the broken and rejected, to fill this kitchen with their voices. Once Jews, Christians, and Muslims laughed and ate here together, just as we are about to. You and your fellow trainees showcase the possibility, the necessity, of a shared future.'

'Mahmoud never told me any of this.'

'He doesn't know. Apart from Aharoni, no one does.'

'Then why tell me?'

'You were granted a glimpse of my family. You are a child of this house, just as I am.'

He dipped a spoon in the simmering pot. 'Soup's ready.' He set down two white bowls on the counter, filled them and handed her a spoon.

Malka remembered the spoon he had given her the first time they had met. She sipped slowly. The soup was fiery and fantastic, its deep glowing red colouring her taste buds and blazing a trail to her stomach. It was so finely balanced in its ingredients, it was like a song. She hadn't said a blessing for months, but in this case it seemed sacrilegious not to.

'Blessed are you, Lord our God, King of the World, at whose Word all came to be.'

'Amen,' Rukh answered softly.

He met her startled gaze evenly.

'Every blessing needs acknowledgement. You have seen a part of me that no one else has. My dance is part of my life as a Sufi, a Muslim mystic. Like the Kabbalists in your tradition, we seek the unity that underlies the illusion of separation. Dancing helps me wipe away my *nafs*, my ego, like scrubbing this counter until it reflects the light.'

Malka recalled the legend of the thirty-six hidden righteous people who sustain the world. Could Rukh be one of them? It wouldn't surprise her. He looked at her, and she realised that tears were dripping onto the counter. Wordlessly, Rukh handed her his spotless handkerchief and she wiped her face.

'Now, can you tell me why you are crying?'

To her surprise, she found that she could. 'I thought I had run away from everything that had hurt me. Tonight, I found out that what I really ran away from are those who I hurt.'

Rukh nodded. 'Love can feel like a knife. But you can use that hurt to cut away the worst part of you, the selfish part. I've learned to open myself to the pain of others, as a flower opens its petals to the dew. For inside every pang is the possibility of a new birth. The chance to change. You showed me that too.'

'How?'

'Those fishermen you met gave you a hard time when you told them you worked for me, right?'

Malka's mouth was full of soup, so she just nodded.

'For years, I couldn't bring myself to use fish that came from that harbour, from a sea that felt tainted with so much loss. You helped me realise I was being foolish. Now they show me their catch before it goes to anyone else. More soup?'

Malka had sipped as slowly as possible, but the bowl was empty. She passed it across to Rukh, who ladled it full. 'You have a gift, Malka, perhaps several gifts. Sometimes, in the food you prepare, I can taste the past, the present, sometimes even the future.'

'Is that why you asked Mahmoud and me to create a dish linking Jaffa and Jerusalem?'

'According to my former neighbours, like Shakir, I've sold out, working with the Israelis, while many Israelis see me as an Arab who has got above his station, and long for me to fail. That's why I need you and your colleagues to prove me right, to show that a stable, shared community is possible, not despite but because of our differences. No pressure!' He grinned. 'How are you finding the recipe challenge? Challenging? It's meant to be.'

'I've no idea where to start. I'm not like you, or the others here. This was never my home.'

'I've watched you work. You are also dancing without knowing it, a dancer for God, and it is beautiful to see.'

Malka looked down at her face mirrored in the counter. Tonight, both Mahmoud and Rukh had told her she was beautiful. So why didn't she feel it? Rukh's tale reminded her of her father in his softer moments, when he had spoken to her as if to himself, of his private doubts and fears. Even of Avner, when he forgot himself in the middle of teaching. Now that she knew Shira was safe, she could allow herself to see some seed of goodness in him. So why not in herself?

From outside came the familiar call of the muezzin, and Rukh rose abruptly. 'Malka, sometimes you just need to be patient, just as this soup had to simmer for all of the ingredients to harmonise. I'm off to the mosque before the first shift. Others knowing about my true work here might complicate things. Please, keep this conversation between us.'

After he left, the kitchen filled with the shadows of a family banished from their home. Rukh's story of exile and loss resonated inside her, and shook her own past into suggestive new shapes. She thought of Moshe, still haunted by his missing sister, of Mahmoud, thrown out of his home for loving the wrong people. Her own flight to Safed, and from it. What must her family be going through, not knowing where she was, or even if she was alive? Well, they wouldn't want to know her now. Her father had probably sat shiva for her. Maybe he was right to. The Malka he knew was dead. She wept again, catching the tears until her palms brimmed. It was as if a hidden spring had been tapped inside her. Then she washed her face in the sink, and found she was hungry once more.

She finished the rest of the soup, and smiled. Through his cooking and his conversation, Rukh had shared the home he carried inside himself. Perhaps that was the only kind of home that mattered. She would cook him something in return, something that tasted both of her own home, and of her hopes of finding her place here. She began taking possible ingredients from the store-room and arranged them at her station. Just seeing them all laid out calmed her. She smiled, recalling the title of one of her father's key texts on Jewish Law, the *Shulchan Arukh*. A laid table. Maybe religion was like cooking after all, as Rukh had suggested. The challenge was to balance your ingredients. She thought she had left the Kabbalah behind her, but it had been here all along, in a different form. She would try to be a bridge, as Rukh had hinted.

Someone hammered on the back door. Mahmoud, she thought, come to shout at her for abandoning him. She couldn't face speaking to him right now. The hammering became more insistent. Malka sighed, wiped her face carefully with her apron, and went to answer. She swung the door open with a tart comment ready on her lips.

It was Shira. They stared at each other.

'So what's wrong with my singing?' She was breathing hard.

Malka shook her head. She was too shocked to speak.

'Your friend said I might find you here. Gave me a lift on his motorbike. Interesting company you keep these days.'

The silence grew thicker.

'Can I come in?' Shira asked at last.

Malka stepped back, then raced to the other side of the table. She needed space between them. Their shadows met across the surface, like a single creature with two bodies and one head. Shira edged towards her, and Malka retreated towards the freezer.

Then Shira spread her arms wide and Malka stepped in for a hug. One of Shira's arms swung back and caught her a stunning blow on the cheek. She staggered back against the table. God knew she deserved it, just not from Shira.

'What was that for?'

'I trusted you, let you close. Then you just pissed off, without a word! What did I do to deserve that?'

'It wasn't you,' Malka stammered.

'Then what was it? Why did you leave?'

'Because of Avner.'

Shira moved as if to hit her again, and Malka flinched.

'I knew it! I knew you and Avner got together. You just used me to get close to him, didn't you? Suckered him with that innocent girl act of yours, just like you suckered me. You knew I carried a torch for him, and you just didn't give a shit!'

'Shira, it wasn't like that!'

'But you know what? You deserved each other. It turns out he was a fake, just like you. What kind of idiot does that make me, for believing in both of you?' Her breath was ragged.

Malka held on to the table. She tried to keep her voice even. 'Shira, listen to me. You are not an idiot. You were a true friend. I know I let you down. But it's not what you think. Avner tried to... He tried to...'

'What? He tried to what?'

'I didn't want to. He tried... He tried...'

244

Shira looked up at her with a spark of recognition. She reached out and drew Malka close, stroking her head. Malka was crying so hard she could barely breathe. Where did all these tears come from? Was she carrying the sea inside her?

'Did he hurt you?' Shira's words were muffled, her face in Malka's hair.

Malka could only nod, banging her head on Shira's chin.

'Oh my poor baby. Did you tell anyone, go to the police?'

Malka shook her head. 'You're the first.' Shira held her tightly.

'It's OK, I'm here now. Tell me.' She made Malka sit down. She moistened a cloth under the tap and washed Malka's face, drying her gently. Then she pulled over the other stool, and took Malka's hand in both of hers.

Malka took a jagged breath. 'I went to tell him why I wanted to learn Kabbalah so badly, and he found out about my cave, and convinced me to take him there. He took off my bracelet, made me lie down. Oh Shira, I can't.'

'You can. You must.'

'He told me to close my eyes, then he lay down on top of me. He pinned down my arms. Then he started rubbing himself against me. He tried to take off my jeans, but I fought him off. I was sure he would rape me. He made out it was some Kabbalistic ritual, so I used that, told him to meet me back at the cave on Lag Ba'Omer, that it would work better then. Then there was the fire, I got scared, and ran...' The truth about the fire could wait. If she told Shira now, it might make her doubt what she was saying about Avner.

'I wondered why you didn't come to Meron. You said you were sick, but I knew something was up. Why didn't I stay with you? When we got back, the place was burned to its foundations, you were nowhere to be found, and Avner had scarpered. The police are still looking for him. They think he fled to the States. Wait. You said he *tried* to rape you. So he didn't succeed?'

'No.'

'Thank God. But why didn't you tell me? I thought we were friends.'

'I knew how much you looked up to him. I thought you wouldn't believe me. I convinced myself it was a punishment for all the people I've hurt.'

Shira lifted Malka's chin with her thumb and forefinger. Her eyes were stormy. 'Never say that. Never think it. This was not your fault.' Malka leaned her head against Shira's shoulder. 'You always spoke with such a wise tongue, I forgot how young you are. I'm sorry I hit you.'

'I'm sorry I ran out on you. What about your friend Evven? What happened to him?'

'Just promise me you won't do it again. Evven is in Tel Aviv somewhere, working as a barman. We bumped into each other once. Let's say he's trying to put the past behind him. As am I.'

'I wish I could be more like you.'

'What do you mean?'

'Tough. So nothing can hurt me.'

Shira smiled, but her eyes were sad. 'I may look tough, I may look together. But it's all an act. I trust no-one. Even when I want to. I loved you like a sister, but I still couldn't let you close. I was sure you would betray me too. I was even glad when I thought you did. It proved my fucked-up theory was right. You need to be more like yourself, that girl full of hope and wonder I knew in Safed.'

Malka shook her head. 'She's gone. I had to become someone else. Can you understand that? Can you forgive me for running out on you?'

Shira's hand tightened around hers. Malka squeezed back.

'You don't need to ask. You know, you're already stronger than me. Anyone else would have crumpled, but look at you.'

Malka laughed. 'I'm a mess.'

'One day, someone is going to see you like I do. Then you have to try to let them in. Not all men are like Avner.'

'I know that now. Actually, two men told me I was beautiful tonight.'

Shira grinned wickedly. 'Did they now? Do tell.'

Malka blushed. She looked away, and saw all the ingredients still waiting for her. 'Can I change the subject? You were always great in the kitchen. I'm supposed to be making something that links my home town with this one. Any ideas?'

'What was your favourite food as a kid?'

'Jerusalem Kugel,' Malka said without hesitation. 'I loved the contrast between sweet caramelised noodles and fiery black pepper. Everyone else bought theirs, but my mother made ours, every week. What's that got to do with it?'

'Well, kugel is the taste of home for you, isn't it? I bet no one here has ever eaten it.'

'Maybe you are right.'

'Have I ever been wrong? Don't answer that. Can I help?'

'Sure. Put this on.' Malka handed Shira an apron.

'Let's make a Jerusalem Kugel, big enough for everyone to have a piece.'

Together they carried a huge cast iron pot to the range, gathered noodles, sugar, pepper, and prepped one of the main ovens. Her mother's pot was earthenware, and the noodles were a different kind, but it would have to do.

Malka stirred the sugar on a low heat, whisking it as it turned golden, so it wouldn't burn. Then she poured it over the noodles. She measured the oil, poured it in slowly, then sifted in black pepper, shaking the pot so the noodles were evenly coated with the mixture. She looked up at Shira.

'Did you change your name back?'

Shira shook her head. 'No. I'm still Shira. It suits me. Do you still go by Malka?'

'They call me the Ice Queen.'

Shira laughed. 'Somehow, Jerusalem Kugel doesn't strike me as something an ice queen would make.'

Malka had to smile at that. But there was still something missing. Something to connect her dish to Mahmoud's home. She picked up an orange from the counter, and lifted it to her nose, inhaling deeply. She remembered his description of frozen orange melting on his tongue. She reached into the pockets of Snake's jacket, which she'd slung over a stool. The two oranges still nestled inside. 'Shira, can you get me some cream and eggs?'

'I thought you were making Jerusalem Kugel?'

'Just get them please. I can't stop stirring or the noodles will burn.' Malka nodded her head in the direction of the larder.

'I'm starting to see why they call you the Ice Queen.'

Malka tipped the ingredients Shira brought her into a blender, squeezed in the two oranges, then folded in the kugel mixture. She put the blender on a trolley, and wheeled the whole thing to the walk-in freezer. She found a socket, plugged the blender in and switched it on at the lowest setting. Shira looked at the swirling mixture.

'I've never heard of kugel being made this way. Do you really think it will work?'

Malka picked up a spoon from the counter.

'Only one way to find out. Will you taste it? As Mahmoud isn't here. He inspired this.'

'Your friend? He's just outside.'

'You mean Mahmoud has been waiting all this time?'

'I told him we needed some girl time.'

Malka opened the door. Mahmoud was blowing on his hands. He looked at her closely. 'Are you OK? You look strange. If I didn't know you better, I would say you were happy.'

She took his arm and drew him in. 'You have to taste this.'

He took the spoon she proffered. 'What is it?'

'Just taste it.'

Mahmoud closed his eyes as he rolled the noodles around his mouth. Malka watched him closely. Near and far cut against one another on his face.

'It's Shamouti and Jerusalem Kugel ice-cream. You gave me the idea. Do you hate it?'

'It's crazy, but brilliant. Just like you. Here, have some yourself.'

Malka tasted it carefully. 'Maybe some orange zest next time.'

Mahmoud took another spoon. 'Or we could caramelise the orange peel with the noodles?'

Mahmoud turned to Shira, who had been watching them with amusement. 'So did you have your chat? You two friends again? You should try some of this.'

She shook her head. 'I had a bad experience with an Italian boyfriend, and since then, me and ice-cream...'

He brandished the spoon at her. 'We won't take no for an answer. You can be our first customer.'

'OK, OK.' They both watched as she took one spoonful, then another.

'Oh. My. God. It shouldn't work, but it does. It's bitter, yet sweet and strangely comforting.' Mahmoud hugged her. 'What did I say?'

'You just gave Malka's recipe a name.'

'Our recipe, you mean. What is it?'

'Bittersweet Home.'

Chapter 18
The Voice of my Beloved Knocks

M alka stood under the shower, letting the warmth soften her aching muscles. She still couldn't believe it. Shira had been living right nearby all these months. It reminded her of something Moshe had said, on their one and only date. He had quoted the Baal Shem Tov, that there was no such thing as coincidence. At the time, she'd laughed at him. Could it be true? Look at tonight. If Mahmoud hadn't taken her to The Bubble, she and Shira might never have met. Then, if she hadn't run off, she would never have seen Rukh dance. That picture would never leave her. Then Shira had come to find her. Hadn't hated her. After all these months, she could let go of the guilt she'd been carrying.

Malka lowered her shoulders. She realised that ever since Safed, she'd been holding them close to her ears, as if to shield herself from a blow. She'd been frozen. No wonder they called her the Ice Queen. She had always taken cold showers until now – to wake herself up, she'd thought. To show no weakness, no fear. She saw now that it had been to punish herself, to deny herself the pleasure of warmth, of softness. She held up her work-callused hands and watched the water stream over her breasts. She remembered Shira admiring them. Yet no-one had ever touched them. She flushed at the thought, and switched off the water. There was a faint tapping at her door. She crossed the room, leaving wet footprints. She slipped on the towel robe that hung from the back of the door.

'Who is it?'

'It's me,' came Mahmoud's voice. 'Can I come in?'

'Give me a minute.' She looked longingly at her bed. It would have to wait. She towelled herself dry with the robe, then pulled on the clothes folded over her chair.

'Malka? Are you OK?'

She opened the door slowly. Mahmoud was still wearing his outfit from The Bubble.

'Do you need anything?'

'I'm fine.'

'Are you sure?

She looked at his concerned face, at the kindness that waited just under the surface. She was loved. She hadn't allowed herself to see it, hadn't felt she deserved it.

'Thank you,' she said quickly. It wasn't enough. She had to show him. She stood on tiptoe and kissed him on the nose. He smelt of leather and cigarettes.

He stepped back, startled. 'What was that for?'

'For being you.' She ruffled his hair so it stood up like a Hoopoe's crest.

Mahmoud grinned. 'You are full of surprises tonight. I thought you were a sheltered flower, and I was doing you a favour taking you out and showing you the world. Then it turns out you know nightclub singers, and Russian bouncers deliver secret messages for you.'

'What are you talking about? What messages?'

'Remember that doorman at the club, who said he knew you? He gave me a note when we left. Said I should deliver it straight away. In all the excitement, I forgot.'

He fished in his back pocket.

'Turns out he really did recognise you. From some photo a friend of yours showed him.'

'A friend? Who?' Apart from Shira, she didn't know anyone else in the city.

'Some guy he works with. Seems he's been looking for you for months. Talks about you all the time. Vladek, that's the bouncer, said you look different to the photo, so it took him a while to realise where he'd seen you.'

'Wait. Did you say he was Russian?' She grabbed Mahmoud's arm. 'What's the message? What did he say? Tell me!'

'Take it easy!' Mahmoud handed her a card with agonising slowness. The English text caught her eye.

Come and feel the beat, where salt water meets sweet

'That's not a message. It's just a card from The Bubble.'

'On the back, silly.'

She turned it over, and found only a scribbled address.

Mahmoud peered over her shoulder. 'Dolphin Street. That's in Ajami. Right behind my father's mosque. What are the chances of that?'

'Chance. That's it.'

'Hey, wait! Where are you going? What about your shoes?'

Malka was already racing barefoot down the stairs. Moshe. She didn't know how, but it had to be. Mahmoud caught up with her in the stairwell.

'Let me take you there.'

'No way.'

'Malka, be sensible. That part of Ajami is gang territory. Even the police won't go there.'

'I need to do this on my own.'

'God, why are you always so stubborn?' Mahmoud drew something from his waistband, and held it out to her. 'I'd feel better if you took this.' It was the silver dagger. He stepped down beside her. 'Rukh left the key in the lock. I don't know why, but I thought you might need this. Either you take it, or we're going by bike.'

'I could never use it.'

'Hopefully you won't have to. It's meant as a deterrent. Though only Rukh is faster with a knife than you.'

He held it out to her. The dagger was beautiful, chased with silver, its handle decorated with curling Arabic script.

'I take it out when I get really down, and even Al-Buraq can't lift me up. When I hold it, I feel my mother's spirit watching over me. I'd like her to watch over you tonight. Besides, this way you have to bring it back.'

Malka took it. It was warm from his body. She slipped it into the back of her belt, and ran back out into the night.

She ran as she'd never run before, the tarmac rough against her soles. Could it be Moshe? Let it be him, she prayed. She was terrified that it wouldn't be, and terrified that it would. She had no idea what she would say when she got there, only that every second it took was too long. She stopped, panting, under a streetlight on the corner of Yefet Street to get her bearings. She looked at the card crumpled in her hand. *The roof*, 7 Dolphin Street. What kind of address was that? The street sounded familiar. Of course! That great hummus place, Abu Hassan, was nearby. She took off again.

She hadn't needed Mahmoud to warn her of Ajami's fearsome reputation. She'd only been there in the daytime, and then only with the other trainees. She felt the dagger pressing against her spine. It didn't make her feel any safer.

At last, she reached Dolphin Street. She walked deliberately, trying to seem like she knew where she was going. Number 7 was a run-down apartment block. Two scorched cars sat outside, crumpled like tinfoil. The wall behind them was covered in graffiti: two giant birds locked in combat, one black, one white, arcing up towards the roof. The lift was broken, of course. As she made her way up the dank stairwell, breathing through her mouth to avoid the stench of urine, Malka remembered climbing the stairs in the old city, following Reb Zushya's cat, half a lifetime ago. A cat called Reb Moshe. Everything was a sign, if you really wanted it to be. Moshe had said that.

At last, she made it to the roof. This couldn't be right. It was bare, apart from a tin shack in the far corner, the kind of place the janitor kept his mops. She better check, just in case. Malka walked over, preparing herself for disappointment. The metal door was half open. She tried to move it, but it was rusted in place. She peered through the narrow opening. The place looked abandoned.

As her eyes adjusted to the darkness inside, she saw that someone had actually lived here. There was an unmade bed against the back wall. The room was so small, she could almost reach out and touch it from the doorway. Above the bed, a crumpled piece of paper was taped to the wall. It looked like a child's drawing. Something about it was familiar. Malka tiptoed across the room to take a closer look, her bare feet whispering on the cold tiles.

It was her own crude drawing of the tree she'd seen in Zushya's house, scribbled on the back of a sheet from one of Zushya's books. At the time she had been too afraid to put into words what she'd seen. So she had left this for Moshe, and hoped that somehow, he would understand her, and where she was going. The same tree had hung upside down over the Kinneret, then followed her to Safed, spinning off the ceiling in the Ari Synagogue, and finally blazed into life inside her the night the fire started. She hadn't seen it since. Moshe had been here, in this very room, and she'd missed him. A glimmer of blue light briefly illuminated the tree. On the opposite wall, a mirror caught the moonlight streaming through the open door and splashed it across the room. She noticed another picture, a photograph, above the mirror. Malka stepped closer, and caught her ankle bone on the iron bedpost.

'Oyy!' she cried. That really hurt. She had made enough noise to wake the dead. She hoped no one had heard her. Then she heard a sigh, and froze.

The bed wasn't unmade. Someone was sleeping in it. A thick, tanned arm was flung across the coverlet. Bent double in pain, she was so close to the sleeper that she could feel his breath on her face. How had she not seen him? She noticed dark streaks all down the wall above him, like dried blood. Had something happened to Moshe? Had someone hurt him, taken his room?

Malka reached into the back of her jeans and gripped the handle of the knife. She could hear the rush and sigh of the sea. The sleeper's chest rose and fell to the same rhythm. He had thick lashes, like a girl. She could see the life pulsing beneath them. She straightened slowly, poised to flee. Then, in a rush, he sat up and, in the same movement, threw his bedcover over her head, smothering her. Then he was on top of her, pinning her to the floor. She couldn't breathe. Instinctively, she slashed at the fabric with the knife and it exploded around her. She took a gasping breath, ready to cry out, then sneezed. The air was thick with white feathers, swirling like snow.

She pushed, hard, and the man fell off her. Malka stood over him, keeping the knife between them, its tip pointed at his chest.

He squinted up at her and spread his hands. 'I have no money. Apart from the blanket which you've just destroyed, there's nothing to steal.'

'I'm not a thief.'

'Then why are you here?'

'I thought someone I knew lived here.' It sounded crazy even to her.

'There's no one else crazy enough to live here.' He brushed at the feathers covering his face with a familiar gesture. In that moment, she recognised him.

'Moshe?'

'Who are you?'

Couldn't he tell? She looked down at her jeans, her bare arms. She'd changed too.

'God, I almost killed you! Do you always greet your guests like this?'

He squinted up at her. The moon was behind her, and her shadow splashed across the floor towards him, the knife-shadow curving across his chest.

'I don't have any guests. Apart from the occasional cat, or cat-burglar, like yourself.'

Those rolling Russian vowels. The cadences of his voice, even in Hebrew, were unmistakeable. He rose slowly, keeping his hands up.

'Let's see who you are.'

He pulled a cord. A bare bulb hanging from the roof flickered into life. His mouth hung open. He reached out to touch her, but left his hand hanging in the air between them. She took a step towards him, and winced.

'Are you hurt?'

'It's nothing. I banged my ankle on the bedstead.'

'Let me take a look.'

He lifted her foot gently in his warm palm, brushing off the feathers.

'I'll get some ice. Where are your shoes?'

'I was in too much of a hurry. I didn't want to miss you.'

She sat on the edge of his bed and watched as he bent over a fridge in the corner. The room was covered with feathers, more than the blanket could possibly have contained. It was a winter landscape, their own private weather. Moshe turned, his hands full of ice. He stood there, just looking, the ice dripping between his fingers.

He picked up a scrap of the torn blanket, and wrapped the ice in it. He bandaged her foot with surprising deftness, then moved the knife aside and sat beside her. She kept darting glances at him as he worked. Stealing glimpses, creating a patchwork portrait. Without his beard, he seemed naked. She looked away quickly, and realised what the bloodstains were. Dark blue paint made runs down the walls, as though the sky was melting.

'Did you paint your room?'

'Do you like it? I thought... I knew it was impossible you would ever come here. But if you did, I wanted you to feel at home. The colour of the sea, the colour of the sky. It's my own personal Safed. That's where I found this souvenir.' He reached across her to a wooden crate by the bed, and dropped a smooth round stone into her hand.

It wasn't possible.

'Where did you find this?'

'In this weird cave in Safed, full of Kabbalistic books. You would have loved it. This stone lay there, asking me to take it. So I did.'

'You found my cave,' Malka said slowly. Somehow, this was harder to believe than the fact that he was sitting next to her now. 'This was my meditation stone.' She smoothed it with her thumb. 'I used to think, if I listened hard enough, I would hear the voice that spoke it into existence. I used to believe that God's voice was still trapped inside, raging to be set free, like a bee in a jar. What a fool I was.'

He shook his head. Bars of red were splashed across his face. Had she cut him? No, it was the dawn, threading through the gaps in the shutters. The fingers of light thickened, branding his smooth chin, catching the feathers in his hair so they looked like flakes of fire.

He kicked at a drift of feathers with his foot. 'That blanket cost me nearly a month's pay. No heating here, you see.'

'Sorry.'

'I'm just glad it was the blanket rather than me. That's quite a knife. Can I see it?'

She slid the dagger back into its sheath, and held it out, handle-first.

He traced the words engraved there with a fingertip. 'Hebrew words, but Arabic letters. "For a sign of peace between our households."' He looked up at her, that familiar spark of curiosity dancing in his eyes. 'There's a story here. Where did you get it?'

'Since when do you read Arabic?'

'Since when do you carry a knife?'

'A girl can't be too careful.'

He tipped back his head and laughed. She glimpsed his crooked front teeth.

'What? Why are you laughing?'

'I look for you every day for months, give up, nearly drown, and then you show up in my room in the middle of the night, and trash the place. How did you find me?'

Every day. For months. She didn't trust herself to reply. She held out the card Mahmoud had given her. Moshe peered at the writing.

'So Vladek is our matchmaker? I can't believe you were at The Bubble. Who are you, and what have you done with Malka?'

He handed her back the dagger. Then he walked over to her drawing and took it down.

'Here, take this.'

'Why are you giving it back? It's yours'

'I promised myself that if I ever found you, I'd give your drawing back. I don't know why, but I feel you're meant to have it.'

Malka swung herself carefully off the bed, folded the drawing around the dagger and stuck them both into the back of her jeans.

'Can you walk OK?'

Malka limped through the feathers. Her ankle was feeling a little better.

'Good. Come outside, I want to show you something.'

She followed him. He stopped in the doorway and kissed the *mezuzah* he'd affixed there with two magnets. It was her turn to laugh.

'So you still believe in all that stuff?'

'No. But it helps me feel at home.'

She limped past him to the parapet. The view the dawn revealed was incredible. Familiar and strange at once. The sun gilded the sea mosque she knew so well.

'Beautiful, isn't it? I always wondered if you were somewhere, looking at the same thing.'

'I swim in the bay every morning. You might even have seen me.'

He looked at her. 'Malka, what happened in Safed? How did you end up here?'

He reached out and lifted a feather from her hair. She shuddered. 'What is it?'

'It's not what happened in Safed. It is what happened in Jerusalem.'

'Your mother told me about Zushya's ritual. The death of the bird has many potential meanings. Your father just chose one that fits his beliefs. Symbols are slippery things.'

'Why would my mother...? Moshe, did they send you, or are you here because you want to be?'

'Both. But I am too late.'

'What do you mean?'

'The Malka I knew is gone, and you've become someone else. Yourself, perhaps. Death is just another word for transformation. Maybe it meant the death of my duvet. Here, make a wish.'

He blew on his palm, and they watched the feather flutter away over the balcony. Malka felt her fear drift away with it.

Moshe told her how he'd knocked Vladek down when they first met, and landed his first job. Malka recalled the huge bouncer from The Bubble, and laughed. The sound lifted the corners of Moshe's mouth.

'You have a great laugh, you know.'

'I can't remember the last time I laughed.'

'Are you not happy here? What are you doing with yourself?'

'I am happy.' She realised it was true. 'I have... a sense of purpose. The visions don't bother me any more. I'm just...'

'A bit focussed? Scarily intense?'

Malka laughed again. 'They do call me the Ice Queen.'

'Who does?'

'The other trainees at the Leviathan.'

'Chef Baraka's new restaurant?' Moshe shook his head. 'You did well. Everyone at work is talking about that place. It opens soon, right? Which reminds me. I'm starving. You?'

'I'm hungry like a wolf.' She bit her lip. Around him, everything she thought came straight out of her mouth.

He pointed to the far corner of the roof. 'Let me make you my legendary shakshuka for breakfast.'

He darted back into the shack. She noticed a blue blanket and some cushions in the corner of the roof. Next to them was a railway sleeper he must have dragged up here. She knelt beside it and stroked the tiny hairline cracks in its surface. It obviously doubled as table and chopping block. There was a gas ring propped on some spare tiles, which he'd rigged up off the mains. Amazing how he'd managed to make a home for himself in such an inhospitable place.

Moshe reappeared. He looked crestfallen. 'I'm sorry. I've got no eggs, and no more smoked paprika either.'

'That's OK. My next shift is not till this afternoon. Let's go to the Shuk and get some.'

'Are you sure you are up to it? I can go on my own. You sit here. I won't be long.'

'I'm not letting you out of my sight for a moment.'

He grinned hugely. 'That's fine with me. Shall we?'

Their walk was less romantic than she'd imagined. He lent her his slippers to protect her bruised ankle. They were much too big, and she shuffled along beside him like an old lady, her stone heavy in her pocket. She was relieved when he stopped beside the tree in the jar Mahmoud had shown her.

'Whenever I pass this tree, I think of you and the drawing you gave me, the clue that started my impossible quest. At least, I thought it was impossible, till today.' He kicked off his sandals. 'Come on!'

He gripped the lip of the jar that held the tree, then swung himself up so that he stood inside it, hugging the trunk. The jar swung dangerously on its cables.

Malka burst into shocked laughter. 'What are you doing?'

She hopped closer and stood by the jar. He looked down at her through the branches, and blushed becomingly. He was very tanned, almost the same colour as the tree.

'I would feel like less of an idiot if you joined me.'

Malka stepped out of the slippers, and gripped the pot with arms sinewy from hours in the kitchen and the sea. It was warm from the sun, its coppery terracotta the same colour as her hair. Hooking her fingers over the edge, she lifted herself up. But Moshe wasn't there any more. He grinned down at her from high in the branches, daring her to follow. Just as Zushya's cat had. Perhaps it was true. Perhaps there was no such thing as coincidence. She drew herself up onto the branch where he sat swinging his legs.

'Welcome to the climbing Kabbalists club!'

The tree slowly stopped swaying.

'So what are we doing up here?'

'That picture you drew. It's Luria's tree, right? That's what you saw in Zushya's house.' She nodded, and the tree swayed. She grabbed a branch to steady herself.

'I thought that was why you ran away. So I read up on it. Luria wrote that the dream of the true Kabbalist is to climb the divine tree, to perch in its branches and try to see the world from the gaps between its leaves. So I sit up here, and try to see the world as you do. Understand you a little better.' Leaf-shadows danced across his face.

'I'm no Kabbalist, Moshe, and this is no cosmic tree. Mahmoud called it Palestine in a jar.'

'Mahmoud?'

'He's the one who gave me the knife. You'd like him.'

'If he's a friend of yours, I'm sure I will. Though tell him from me, I'm not so keen on you redecorating my room. So you ran from Moshe to Mahmoud?'

'That's what he said too.'

'You told him about me?'

Malka smiled at the lift in his voice.

'Mahmoud and I could both be right. For him, this tree represents his people, in exile in their own land. Luria called the broken connection between the Divine and the world 'the lost Shekhina'. Without her, the tree floats above us, but cannot put down any roots. We need to reconnect her to the world. I told you at Lazlo's that it might take a woman to reawaken that connection, and you laughed.'

'I thought you were crazy.'

'Oh, I didn't mean just any woman. I meant one who runs barefoot through the streets at night, and bangs her ankle on the bedposts of the world.'

Perched amongst the branches, her bare feet dangling beside Moshe's, Malka realised what she had really been running away from. It wasn't the tree she'd seen, or even her father's confession, terrifying though they had been. What had really scared her was the strength of her feelings for Moshe. She had loved him from the moment she saw him sitting on Zushya's floor in a drift of books, his face alive with wonder. At the time she'd had nowhere to put those feelings, no tools to interpret them. Now, she could allow herself to recognise those feelings. She loved him still. That knowledge gave her the courage she needed to answer his question, at least partly. She rested her palm on the branch beside his and stroked the smooth bark.

'Back on the roof, you asked me what happened in Safed. You were right. I went there to try and understand the vision of that tree, to make it safe. It burst out again when I was in danger, and almost destroyed me. It burned down the place I stayed in. So I ran again.'

He looked up quickly. 'So it was you who burned the place down? How?'

'You'd never believe me if I told you.'

'Try me. Who would believe a cat brought us together, or that I would follow you to Tel Aviv on the advice of a little boy who caught sight of you running in the night? When I saw the birds on my building, I thought it was a sign.'

Malka reached into her pocket, and took out the stone. She didn't know why, but the sight of it filled her with dread.

'You know, they never found that cult leader. I found your stone on a heap of ashes. There was a single handprint burned into the wall above it.'

They stared at one another, and a terrible certainty filled her. 'Avner was waiting there for me. Somehow, the fire I started reached him.'

'Malka, be serious.'

'I killed him.'

'You can't know that.' But his face said something else. 'Tell me exactly what happened that night.'

She told him about Avner and his own 'ritual'. This time, she didn't cry. Moshe did that for her, tears sliding down his cheeks and dripping onto the branches below. When she finished, he took her face between his hands.

'You didn't kill him. But I wish I could.'

'I was nowhere near the cave. I was in his study.' Then she remembered the rose of fire that had hurtled like a ball, out through his window. Haltingly, she described the events in Avner's study that had led to the fire.

'Malka, how can you say you are no Kabbalist? You have a power you don't understand. I'm not sure I do either. But that's no reason to keep running from it. When you were in danger, it protected you.'

'What did?'

'The power of chashmal.'

She flinched, but nothing happened.

'Something reached out through you.'

'I don't want it in me. I don't want anything to do with it. Every time that part of me awakens, people get hurt.'

'So you admit it is part of you, at least. Listen to me Malka. I believe that Avner was judged, and sentenced. Not by you. Just like Aaron's sons in the Bible, he got burned up. He got what was coming to him.'

'You don't know that.'

'I think we both do. But you are the one I care about. Let go of all that guilt. Say Kaddish for him, if you need to. Temper all that judgement and anger with something else. Something like mercy. God knows we could all do with a bit more of that.'

'You think that's what he deserves?' Malka found it hard to breathe.

'No, I think that's what *you* deserve. None of this is your fault. I see the guilt eating away at you even now.'

'That's what Shira said.'

'Well then I must be right. You see, I'm just a returner of lost things. Your drawing, your stone. You have brought me back to myself Malka. If you find your balance, you could change the world.'

'Come on, enough of this Moshe. You could talk the birds down from the skies. Let's get to the market.'

Moshe dropped out of the tree. He landed lightly. Malka climbed carefully back down, picked up the slippers where she'd left them and caught up with him. Her ankle barely protested, and the sun was warm on her back. Just as she reached him, a bird called, insistently. Moshe pulled a chirping mobile phone from his back pocket.

'Since when do you have a mobile phone?'

'This is Zechariah's actually. He gave it to me in case I found you. I used to call in every week. Then I stopped. But I keep it on me, just in case. It's never rung before.'

Zechariah. The name took her back with a jolt to all she'd left behind. The wedding she'd missed. The family she'd abandoned. Her sense of wellbeing evaporated. 'I can't believe Zechariah gave it to you.'

'Your sister can be very persuasive.'

'Estie?'

The handset stopped ringing, then started again. Moshe prised open the phone's shell.

'Hello? Estie. You are not going to believe this... What? No! When?' His face grew very still. 'One minute.' He covered the phone with his hand.

'Malka, you have to talk to her.'

'How does she know I'm here?

'She doesn't. Talk to her.'

She looked at him pleadingly.

'I can't.'

'She deserves to know that you are OK, and you need to hear this from her.'

Malka looked at the phone as though it were a snake. She took it gingerly. 'Estie?'

'Malka, is that you?'

Her sister's voice was right in her ear, and Malka almost dropped the phone.

'It's me.'

'Malka. You must come home. We need you.'

I can't, Malka wanted to say, but something in her sister's voice stopped her. 'What is it? What happened?'

'It's Devvie. There was an accident. She's in intensive care.'

Malka stared unseeingly at the wall. 'Is she...'

'She's still alive. We're in Hadassah. Get here as soon as you can.'

'I'm on my way,' Malka said, and hung up. She looked at Moshe's crestfallen face. It's not fair, she thought. We only just found each other.

'You have to go.'

'Do you have a car?'

'I have a bicycle.'

'I could cycle to the train station. No, too slow. I have a better idea. Can I use your phone?'

She dialled the only number she knew.

Chapter 19
Love is Stronger than Death

Mahmoud rode Al-Buraq like one possessed, cutting through lights, going the wrong way down side streets. He cursed fluently. Malka held on tight, willing him faster. Tel Aviv passed by in a blur of speed, then they were on the highway. It was morning now, but the sun hid its face. As they joined the motorway to Jerusalem, it started to rain, one of those rare, thunderous late-summer cloudbursts. The bike bucked and skidded like a wounded thing, grating in a low gear.

'Do you still believe in God?' Mahmoud shouted over his shoulder.

'Why?'

'Because now would be a good time to pray.'

Just ahead of them, a giant truck fishtailed and the trailer scythed towards them like a moving, metal cliff. Mahmoud twisted the handlebars with all his strength, fighting to keep the wheels under control. Malka whispered *Gam Ki Elech* under her breath. 'Though I walk in the valley of the shadow of death, I fear no evil, for You are with me.'

The truck slid past, inches from Buraq's handlebars, and slammed into the central reservation with a screech of metal. Sparks flew, and a few landed, burning, on her bare arm. But they were past.

'God, if you are still listening. Let us get to my sister safely,' she whispered. 'Let it not be too late.' She heard the wail of sirens. 'Also, let the truck driver be OK,' she added.

She wasn't dressed for rain. Mahmoud had insisted she wear his precious leather jacket, so he was already soaked to the skin. He'd smiled when she held out the knife. 'We'd better not take that with us. Ask your friend to return it to Rukh.' She'd asked him to bring her a few things, and he asked her no questions, just brought it all to her in a backpack that jounced painfully against her shoulder blades. She thought of Moshe's face as they parted. 'I will follow as soon as I can,' he'd said. For a brief moment, he had taken her hand in his. She hadn't wanted to let go. Now the memory kept her warm.

Soon they were climbing the familiar hill to Jerusalem, threading through snarled traffic. A journey that had taken her months, unmade in less than an hour. They passed the rusted carcasses of ancient vehicles lying by the roadside, relics of convoys that had been attacked on the way to Jerusalem in the forties. One truck had a pine tree growing through the cabin, a promise of hope after desolation. The verse she'd recited when she left came back to her:

'Those who sow with tears, let them reap with joy.'

All too soon, they screeched into Ein Karem and drew to a halt in the hospital forecourt. Mahmoud lifted off her helmet.

'Better go by yourself from here,' he said. 'With my Jaffa licence plate and good looks, security will hold us up for ever with questions. I will go to my cousins in East Jerusalem and wait for your call.'

She was already running before he moved off. The security guard opened her bag and looked at her strangely. She flew past him through the security gate.

'Can I help you?' the receptionist called after her.

'My sister's in intensive care.'

'*Refuah Sheleimah.* You want the eighth floor.'

Malka took the lift, counting the seconds. 'Please. Let me not be too late,' she prayed. She ran down the corridor, through two more sets of double doors. God, God, let my sister be alive. Another receptionist.

267

'Devvie Sabbatto is my sister. Where is she?'

'Room 18.'

18. *Chai*, in Hebrew. Life. She hoped this was a good sign. Malka swung the door open. At the centre of the room, Devvie lay face up on the bed, her legs raised on pulleys. One side of her face was swathed in bandages; lines ran into her arms and through her nose. Their mother slumped in an armchair beside her, asleep. Estie stooped over the bed, holding Devvie's hand. She turned as Malka opened the door. Malka was shocked, but also relieved, that their father was not there. Then she heard his voice behind her.

'Blessed is He who revives the dead.'

He was standing right by the door. The wisps of grey in his beard had spread and reduced his beard to a uniform ash. His suit hung on him.

'I'm not dead.'

'So I see. Are you wearing trousers?'

'Tateh, *shah*,' Estie whispered, cradling her stomach with an odd protective gesture. 'Malka's here, that's what matters.'

Malka was still wearing jeans and her T-shirt. There hadn't been time to change.

'I came as soon as I could.'

Estie stepped between her and her father.

'Tateh, you are tired. You were just going for a walk to clear your head. Leave us for a while. Devvie was closer to Malka than any of us, perhaps the sound of Malka's voice can bring her back.'

To Malka's surprise, her father did as he was told. He pushed through the door as though it took all his strength. Once he had gone, Malka found herself wrapped in Estie's arms.

'How I've missed you, Malkale. We all have. I hope you can forgive him. Tateh is tired. None of us have slept since last night. Should I wake Mameh? She just nodded off.'

Malka shook her head, then held her sister at arm's length, taking in the decidedly untraditional scarf she wore as a head-covering. Her face and her voice were rounded, their hard edges smoothed away.

'Who are you, and what have you done with my sister?'

Despite everything, Estie smiled. Malka finally noticed the obvious.

'Wait. Are you pregnant?'

Estie's smile widened. 'Six months, God willing.'

'I'm so sorry I missed your wedding.'

'It's been almost a year. We'd given up hope that we'd ever see you again. All of us, except Devvie.'

There would be time for apologies later. 'How is she? What happened?'

Estie took a deep breath. 'She was hit by a truck which just drove off. Her vital signs are fine, but she has internal bleeding and multiple fractures. She's in a coma and they don't know if, or when, she will wake. Even if she does, they don't know if she will ever walk again.'

Estie began to cry quietly. Malka hugged her again, gently, feeling the warm tears through her T-shirt. Estie whispered into her ear.

'Ever since you left, each Friday Devvie wanders through Jerusalem, looking for you. It fills Mameh with fear, but when they tried to forbid it she cried, hysterically, for the whole day. Yesterday, she took us by surprise. Mameh said she left very early, saying she wanted to search on the way to school. She never got there.' Estie lips twisted. 'Devvie said she had a feeling today would be the day she saw you. God knows, I wanted to see you again too, but not like this.' Estie rubbed her back. She sank slowly into an armchair beside their sleeping mother. 'Let's wake her in a minute. I want you to myself. Is that selfish of me?' She took Malka's hand and drew her closer.

'They think Devvie crossed a side street near the Mashbir without looking. The truck drove down it at speed, hit her, and just kept going. She was flung onto the roof of a parked car. Thank God, one of her classmates was there and rang us.

Do you know how many times I imagined the same thing had happened to you? Malka, why didn't you ever call us?'

'I wanted to so many times. I live in Tel Aviv now. I thought Tateh would sit shiva for me if he heard.'

'Don't blame Tateh. He's barely left his study since you disappeared. Devvie makes his meals and leaves them outside the door. It tortured us, not knowing if you were even alive. All we had to go on was the drawing you made for Moshe. After he left to look for you, Zechariah and the other students searched for days. Devvie never stopped looking. Do you really think it mattered to us where you live?'

'I thought Zechariah hated me. I thought you all did.'

'You know, after you left there was a lot of pressure on Zechariah not to marry me. If I had a *meshuggeneh* sister, it might be catching, our children might be at risk, God forbid.' She stroked her stomach. 'But he stood firm. I wasn't such a desirable catch any more but he still wanted me. Just for that, I loved him. At the same time, I worried about Devvie. I invited her for Shabbes whenever I could, but I couldn't really be there for her any more. Especially once the baby grew big. She was never close to me like she was to you. Malka, you broke her heart. At least I have Zechariah, and God willing, a new life to care for. Devvie was stuck at home with Tateh and Mameh. These days they can't speak without tearing each other apart.'

'How did you know Moshe had found me?'

'I didn't. I just said to Mameh, only you, or a miracle, can reach her now.'

Malka made herself move to the bedside. Devvie's face, always pale, was almost transparent. She took her sister's free hand in hers.

Estie leaned forward, watching Devvie's face for any change. 'Tateh begged me to stay away, said that the stress might be bad for the baby. But my baby will be part of our family too. And that means being there even when times are tough. Especially then.'

Malka stroked Devvie's fingers, the fingernails chewed to the quick. She spoke softly to Estie.

'How does it feel, knowing you will soon be a mother?'

'I'd forgotten, with you it's always questions. I haven't been able to think about it properly. It's still three months away. Tateh keeps talking about his grandson, which doesn't help. I refused to find out what the baby is, so he tried to pressure the nurse. Luckily, they need my consent. As long as it is healthy, I don't care what it is, and neither does Zechariah. Let it have a few months of peace.' She looked at Malka. 'Now I know a little how you must have felt. I was so jealous of the time Tateh spent with you. But he's always waiting for me to disappoint him.'

Malka bent down and kissed Devvie's closed lashes, pale gold half-circles. They were warm. But they stayed closed.

'Talk to her.'

'I don't know what to say.'

'I've never known you to be lost for words.'

Malka sat on the edge of the bed and whispered into her sister's ear, curled and delicate as a shell.

'Devvie, it's me. Malka. I'm so, so sorry I left you. I will try to make it up to you. I've so much to tell you, so much I want to show you. I've seen the sea, swum in it even. I've met so many different kinds of people. Some good, some not so good. You were right about Moshe all along. Don't tell anyone, but I love him. I rode here on a motorbike named Al-Buraq, after a winged horse, like a hero from one of your fairy tales, to wake my sleeping beauty with a kiss.' There was a spot of dried blood on her cheek, and Malka gently wiped it away. Then she kissed her sister's lips, trying to fill them with her own breath. They had a sour, medicinal taste. She stood, the taste of iron in her mouth. The seed of an idea grew in her mind. Estie's voice broke in on her thoughts.

'You know what I missed most? Having no one to argue with, no one to tell me how stupid I was, to share all my fears about the baby with.'

'What about Zechariah?'

Her sister smiled proudly.

'You know where he is right now? Cooking for everyone, preparing meals so Mameh and I don't have to. But even after all this time, we are still learning how to talk to each other. Think about it. I've known him for less than a year. You, I've known all your life. At least, I knew the old you.' She stood and looked Malka up and down. 'Malka, when did you get so beautiful?'

Malka looked down at her stained clothes. She hadn't had a chance to wash. But she sensed that was not what Estie was talking about. It was the fact that she was alive, that they were in the same room together, which made her beautiful. Malka knew this because, for her, Estie glowed with the same radiance.

'When did you?' she answered quietly.

Estie blushed.

'When I spoke to you on the phone, I didn't believe it was actually you. You sounded... different. You sounded... happy.'

'So do you, Estie. Despite all this.'

'I am. You should have heard Moshe at our seder. He reminded me so much of you. Crazy, but in a good way. I knew, if anyone could find you, he could. He loves you. We all do, even Tateh. Even if we don't always know how to show it.' She bent and kissed the top of Malka's head. 'I'm going home for an hour to sleep. I can't do it here, I keep waiting for Devvie to wake.' She squeezed Malka's shoulder. 'You will still be here when I get back?' There was fear in her voice.

'Can I wake Mameh? How long has she been sleeping now?'

'About an hour. I told her Devvie needs us to be strong, and for that we also need to sleep. Bless them, every few minutes the nurses switch on the lights, take another test. They will probably be in again soon. She'll want to see you, of course, but she's been living on her nerves these last few months.'

Malka, overcome, could only nod as Estie grabbed her bag and hurried out. She sat threading Devvie's breaths together, trying to plait this sign of life into a cord strong enough to pull her sister back into wakefulness. She glanced over at her mother, who had slid down in her chair. A vein pulsed in one eyelid, and her eyes moved restlessly. Malka stood, took the folded blanket that she'd been sitting on, and drew it gently over her mother. She raised the cushion that had slipped down, so that her mother's head was supported. Her mother whispered something, which she could not make out. She took her mother's hand in her own and reached back to the bed for Devvie's, so that she held hands with both her mother and sister.

'God, bring her back to us. I need to say sorry. I need her to forgive me. Please.'

Just as Estie had said, teams of nurses came and went, taking tests, blood, changing drips. Malka stood there as they wrote 'serious but stable, no change' in the chart at the foot of the bed. The bruised clouds in the window outside slowly dispersed. Then she felt fingers tighten in her own. Malka gasped for a moment, sure it had been Devvie. But it was her mother. As soon as her mother's eyes opened, she rose, one cheek still imprinted with the pattern from the cushion. She drew Malka's head to her chest, hugged her wordlessly. She stroked Malka's hair.

'It's really you. My lost bird has returned to the nest,' she crooned.

At her words, the glimmerings of Malka's idea returned.

'I want to try something to help Devvie. But I need help. I'm going to step outside a moment and call my friends.'

'No one has ever been able to stop you doing anything you set your mind to. Just promise you'll come back soon. I couldn't bear to lose you a second time.'

Malka held herself together as long as she was in the room. As she stepped through the door, before she could cry, two familiar faces greeted her. Moshe and Shira. Thank God.

'We came as soon as we could,' Moshe said.

'There was terrible traffic all the way from Tel Aviv. How is she?'

Malka shook her head. 'So you drove? Good. I need you to call Mahmoud now. Let me talk to him.'

Chapter 20
The Song in the Stone

' Salaam Aleikhum.'

'Aleikhum Salaam.' She put Mahmoud on speaker so Moshe and Shira could hear him.

'There is a famous story,' Malka said, 'about four men who enter Paradise, through a secret Kabbalistic ritual. One was a mystic, one a heretic, one a scholar, and one a lover.'

'There are four of us, too. So?' Moshe asked.

'I want to recreate their ritual. I want to use it to help my sister.'

'Avner used to tell us that story.' Shira said.

'That doesn't mean that—'

Moshe interrupted her. 'The story doesn't say what they did to get there. How will you know what to do? How will we?'

These were her own doubts. But coming from him, they felt louder.

Shira shook her head. 'Correct me if I'm wrong, but your last foray into Kabbalah didn't work out too well. Now that I recall, the four in your story came off pretty badly too. Didn't one of them die, and another lose his mind?' Shira's face was taut. 'You don't have time for this bullshit Malka. Life is no fairy tale. You should be at your sister's side.'

'Can I be the lover?' Mahmoud spoke at last. 'Or is that spot already taken?'

Thank God someone was on her side. She turned to the others.

'Please, you have to trust me. I can't do this without you. Moshe is right. There is no hint of how the rabbis got to the Pardes. I haven't forgotten that my sister hovers between this world and the next. But I have a gift. Something I've been running from ever since. Like it or not, I'm a Kabbalist.'

She heard Mahmoud breathing. She had their attention.

'What does that actually mean?' Mahmoud asked.

'Sometimes, when I say words in a certain way, they wake up and change things. There must be a reason I've been given this power. I want to use it to try and bring Devvie back to us.'

'So if you say the right word, in the right way, you think you can change things?' Mahmoud asked. 'That suggests that someone is listening. Here, in Israel, where no one listens to anyone?'

'What should we do?' Moshe said quietly. 'Just tell us.'

She should have been cheered by his inclusive language. But she still didn't know how to answer his question.

'I have no idea,' Malka admitted. 'It's like I've been given a torch that only shows me a little way ahead through the forest. As we go further in, I can see where we need to go next, and hopefully find the clearing I'm looking for. Bear with me. Why were there four? God's holiest name has four letters. As Shira said, only one of them, Akiva, survived the experience. But he left a clue, for those who know how to look.'

'Let me guess. He said you need a runaway *Charedi* girl with delusions, a gay Palestinian, a failed singer and a Russian security guard?' Shira's voice was shrill. She's afraid, Malka realised. Malka stroked her friend's forearm and, for the first time, she noticed the line of scars that rose up it, like a ruler. Was that why she always wore long sleeves? Shira leaned in to her. Malka could feel her trembling.

'There is one more piece of the story, which fewer people know. Just before they went on their journey, Akiva gave his friends a coded message.'

Moshe recited from memory. '"When you reach the marble stones, don't say water, water". No one knows what he meant, though.'

'Well, almost no-one.' Malka took a piece of paper from her pocket, and unfolded it on a chair.

'This is a drawing of the mystical tree I made for Moshe. The paper belonged to Reb Zushya, a revered Kabbalist.' There was a sharp intake of breath from Shira. 'Not like Avner. The real thing. I found the paper tucked in a book of his, which for some reason was in my father's study.'

Moshe started. 'So your father had it! I wondered what happened to it. He caught me reading it, and expelled me from his yeshiva. Why didn't he return it?'

Shira tapped the paper. 'This is all very interesting. What has it got to do with us?'

'Look at this.' Malka turned it over. The page was covered in tiny letters, marching in columns down the page. 'At first, I thought this was just a jumble of letters, a Kabbalist's mantra. Then on the way here, I realised what Zushya had written. Those two words of Akiva's, Water and Marble. *Mayim* and *Shayish*. Over and over. Look closely. What do you notice?'

Shira and Moshe bent over the crumpled paper.

'They each start and end with the same letter,' Shira said.

'They each encircle the letter Yod, the first letter of God's Holiest name.' Moshe added.

'Sounds like fun. Anything else?' Mahmoud asked.

'Yes. In repeating the words, Zushya broke them open. By lining them up above and beneath one another, he's revealed three hidden words, which repeat over and over again. *Yam. Sham. Yod Yod.*

'You lost me.' Mahmoud said. 'I'm all at sea.'

'Very funny. Yes, Yam is the sea. Sham, means there. Yod Yod is used as shorthand for God's Holiest name, the Tetragrammaton, which starts with the smallest letter, Yod. Yod's numerical value is ten. So I think the second Yod represents the ten utterances in the Torah which God used to speak the world into existence. That is the power Akiva discovered in the Pardes. The power we need to heal my sister.'

Mahmoud sighed. 'Is this really the time for Bible stories?'

'They are not just stories. If you listen to them, the words of the Torah can open inside you.' Malka held up the tree she'd drawn. 'When Adam and Eve eat from the tree of knowledge, God's voice seeks them in the garden, and asks the first question in creation. *Ayeka*, meaning, where are you? That's what I heard at Zushya's house. The question I ran away from. But I'm ready to answer it now. It's not a satnav question. God is asking us, where is your true self in this moment? If we listen carefully, we can still hear that question resonating through us. Mahmoud, what does Rukh always say?'

'Underneath the crap inside us is a diamond. We just have to find it.'

'This is the same idea. We need to dive into the sea inside us, and seek the Yod hiding there. We can use the energy of Ayeka to bring my sister back.'

'Aren't you forgetting that some of us don't even believe in God?' Shira's face was set. 'Which is kind of a problem, when we need a miracle.'

'What I always loved about the *Pardes* story was that Acher, the Other, Elisha Ben Abuya, takes part, even though he doesn't believe any more. The heretic also enters Paradise. Because doubt is part of any faith.

Moshe stepped forward. 'If there is one thing I've learned, it is to have faith in Malka, even if what she says sounds a little crazy. Especially then.'

Shira and Mahmoud murmured their assent.

'So what exactly do you need us to do?' Moshe asked again.

'According to the Zohar, when God speaks a letter, it resonates through time, through creation. I want us to try and hear the Aleph of Ayeka, within and around us. The Hebrew word Anochi, or I, also starts with Aleph. It also has four letters.

You are the other three letters that make me who I am. Shira, don't let your experiences with Avner poison you. I thought he had destroyed my faith too. What he broke was our dependence on others. Mahmoud, fixing Buraq with you helped me heal myself again a little. Moshe, if you and I finding each other again is not a miracle, I don't know what is. You've all helped me so much already, more than I can put into words. Now I need your help to heal my sister. I hope that if we can listen to the silent voice of God inside us, then maybe we can wake my sister, whose 'I' has been silenced too.'

'But how?' Shira persisted.

A gust whipped Malka's hair in her face, though the window was closed. Through it, she glimpsed a woman with flowing red hair, astride a great fish, reaching down to her. She thought of the fishermen lifting her out of the water. She thought of Rukh's dance, and of what he had told her, and she knew.

'One of the many names the Torah uses for God is Hamakom, the Place. I think it means an internal place, the broken places inside us. The ones crying out for healing. That's where I need you to go. Try to find the light hidden inside the hurt, and set it free. To help you, go to a physical place that means something to you.'

Moshe spoke first. 'I'm going to Zushya's house. It's where my journey began.'

'Well there was one time when I was a kid at the Western wall,' Shira murmured. 'I remember I cried there. But only because I knew I was meant to feel something, and I didn't.'

'Mahmoud?'

'I'm a long way from home. But I can go to Al Aqsa,' he said at last. 'My father used to make me go there with him. I hated every minute. But for you, Malka, I'd do anything.'

'Me too,' the others chorussed. 'What about you Malka? What are you going to do?'

'As Shira says, my place is here, with my mother and my sisters. I know you can't force faith. I'm not asking you to believe in anything. Well, maybe in me, a little. You have each already given me more than I ever hoped to find. The gift of belief in myself. In your different ways, you have all taught me the meaning of another four letter word. Ahava. Love also has four letters, and also starts with an Aleph. Shira, if you are going to the Wall, there is a place there I think you might like. It is a huge stone, at the right hand side of the men's section, which stretches all the way across to the women's section, mocking the flimsy barriers men have erected there. A tree grows right out of the wall just above it, its branches hanging down like a curtain. Maybe start there.'

'What should we say?' Mahmoud and Shira said together.

Malka grinned. 'I've never known either of you to be lost for words. Just go, find your place. See what comes. Whatever happens, let's meet back here in two hours.'

She waited for them to argue. Shira looked at her for a long moment. Then she turned and walked away.

'Just be careful not to slip,' Malka called after her. 'The marble by the wall is treacherous when it's wet.'

She turned to Moshe, who stood waiting beside her.

'You sound just like Akiva,' he grinned. 'You inspired them.'

Malka grinned back. 'Remember, at Lazlo's, you told me that if we can be really present in the moment, we can set a spark free, and return it to its source? I'm finally taking you up on the challenge.'

'You are going to do something dangerous, aren't you? I can see it in your face. Just promise me you will be careful. You are many things Malka, but you are also a girl.'

With that he was gone. She felt underwater, as though the whole hospital was slowly sinking. It was hard to breathe. A gurney rolled past her and its ghost twin rose briefly to meet it from the polished floor, then sank soundlessly back into the depths. Someone caught her elbow. It was Estie, dabbing at her lips with a tissue.

'Was that Moshe? Where is he going?'

'He and my friends are going to help me try to bring Devvie back to us.'

They entered room 18 together. Mameh was leaning across the bed, holding Devvie's hand. Estie went around the bed, and took Devvie's other hand. They looked up at her with a kind of hopeless hope.

'We don't have much time,' Malka said. 'Keep hold of Devvie's hands, and don't let go. I'm going to put something in each palm. However strange what I do seems, don't ask any questions.'

She opened her bag and took out a freezer bag of ice cubes. The ones Mahmoud had chosen each had a sage leaf frozen inside. She chose one surrounded by a swirl of bubbles, the frozen time she wanted to restore to Devvie. Estie's eyes widened as Malka dropped the ice cube into Devvie's palm, then folded Estie's fingers over them. Runnels of water dropped between her fingers, and dripped onto the sheet. Estie held on. Malka skirted the bed, and nestled her meditation stone in her sister's empty hand, which was so pale the stone almost disappeared. Only the swirling cloud on its surface was visible. Her mother looked alarmed – usually, you placed stones on the graves you visited. 'Mammeh, don't worry. I'm going to set free the song trapped in this stone.' Her mother's hand cradled the stone from above. Malka leaned over and kissed Devvie's eyelids, feeling the steady pulse against her lips.

Then she stepped back, cleared space for herself, and started to whirl, faster and faster, as she'd seen Rukh do. Though her eyes were closed, she glimpsed Devvie's face in the torchlight, leafing through her secret wedding book. Malka noticed that under the pictures of the brides, her sister had written a name, over and over. She couldn't quite make it out. *I love her hair. The way it curls over the back of her dress. There is soft down on her neck too. I wonder how it feels?*

Before she could hear more, Malka was borne aloft, into the Al Aqsa forecourt. An elderly attendant was sitting near the entrance of the mosque, warming his hands over a glowing brazier. Mahmoud stood before him.

'Hafez?'

'Mahmoud! Is it you?' The old man looked genuinely delighted to see him. 'I can still hear your voice, clear as a bell, calling the faithful to *Al-Bahr* when your father had fever. Allah meant for you to come today. Our muezzin has slipped and twisted his ankle. He can't make the ascent. Can you?'

'I have not made *wudu*,' Mahmoud protested. 'Not for a long time.'

But Hafez was having none of it.

'We have recordings for such situations, of course, but a living voice is so much more effective in kindling the heart to pray, don't you agree?' His voice was gently insistent.

He took Mahmoud by the arm, helped him off with his shoes, and steered him towards the muezzin's tower. As they climbed, Malka could feel Mahmoud's lungs rustle like paper, his thighs burning. She breathed deeper, sending energy to help him on his way. Mahmoud was about to protest that he could go no further, when they stepped out onto the parapet at the top of the tower. *'I will give up smoking if I ever make it back down.'* Then Malka was falling, into the branches of a great tree.

Moshe stood under the great Eucalyptus by Zushya's house. Teardrops of rain glistened on its branches and dripped from its slim leaves. In the hospital room, Malka reached towards the sky, spreading her fingers like branches. The clouds above Moshe drew apart, and for a moment, the tree caught fire in the sunlight, the rain on its branches blazing.

Coins of light and shadow from the tree's branches scattered around Moshe. He dug his fingers into the cracks in the tree's armour. A slim piece of bark came away in his hands. Malka could feel the roughness of it in her own fingers. Thoughts coursed through her like iron filings. They were Moshe's, and they hurt her. *I'm always breaking things. Why didn't I stay with Malka? What use am I to her here?* He held the sliver against the space it had left behind, and fitted it back into place. He looked up through the branches. His eyes were red and raw. When he leaned his head against the trunk, Malka could smell the wet wood. He pulled a single leaf from the tree, ran his thumb over the veins that threaded through it. He seemed to be scratching a word into the leaf with his fingernail. She concentrated, until the leaf filled her vision and she could read what he'd written. *Ayeka?*

His question carried her away from him to the Wall. From above, it was even clearer how cramped the women's side of the plaza was, how flimsy the mechitzah was that separated it from the wide area reserved for the men. Where was Shira? There. Her unmistakable blonde helmet was poised at the edge of the women's section. Why wasn't she going in?

Then Malka understood. A group of around thirty women were praying just in front of her. They wore tallitot like men, but instead of the severe black and white lines of the men's prayer shawls, theirs were bright and colourful. One near the front caught Malka's eye. It was a vivid blue. Then she saw that the woman cradled a Torah scroll in her arms, and knew there would be trouble. According to the Orthodox men who controlled this site, women were not allowed to touch the Torah, never mind read it. That's why her father had taken such a risk learning with her. In the end, his fear had been too much for him. She'd thought him weak, cowardly. Now, when she saw the reaction of the men standing on the other side of the mechitzah, she wasn't so sure. Instead of prayers, they shouted sharp, ugly words over the barrier.

'Prostitutes!'

'She-devils!'

'Reform!'

Shira sensed the danger. She tried to back away, but was hemmed in. The religious women around her, instead of protecting the prayer group, had joined in the attack, shaking their *siddurim* so the pages fluttered like flightless birds.

Soon words were not enough for the men. They began lifting themselves up onto the flimsy separation barrier, which swayed dangerously. Malka saw stones in their hands. They had come prepared. In a moment, the air was full. A chair leg glinted as it whirled past her.

Shira crouched down, and through her eyes Malka saw that one part of the mechitzah had fallen. The woman with the blue Tallit had rested the Torah on a table, and rolled it open to the day's portion. She read from it aloud, seemingly untroubled by the chaos around her. The other women in the service had linked arms, furling around her and the scroll like the petals of a flower. At this affront, the barrage increased in intensity and the women at either side of the table ducked down, but the one in the blue tallit did not move. Then a stone caught her on the temple, and her knees buckled. Her precious blue Tallit lay crumpled in the dirt. A cheer went up from the men's side. The woman held her hand to her cheek, where blood streamed from an open cut. Shira tried to work her way forward to help. Then a man climbed onto a chair behind her, a stone in his hand. He was young, with wispy side locks curled behind his ears. In a moment, he would hit Shira, and all would be lost.

Malka leapt to the bedside, and placed her hand over her mother's. 'Evven, awaken.' Malka whispered. She closed her eyes, and saw the stones of the plaza ripple like a carpet being shaken. The man tumbled to the ground.

There was a sharp sound, like a whip, and her mother drew in her breath. She beckoned silently to Malka, and showed her that the stone had split right down the middle. The glittering line had been a seam, a doorway to a hidden darkness. Inside was a hollow, like a tiny egg, the same shape as the larger stone. The stone had formed around this emptiness at its centre. One of Devvie's fingers now rested in the hollow. Malka bent and rummaged in her bag. It was time for her final ingredient, her sister's favourite spice. She crouched, and lifted a tiny twist of paper from the bottom of the bag. She poured the brown powder into one palm, then licked her other index finger. She dipped it into the cinnamon and painted it onto Devvie's lips, so it looked as if her sister was wearing brown lipstick.

When Malka stood up, instead of Devvie an old man lay on a couch beside her. Zushya. Moshe stood by the open window. Snow swirled around him, flecked his hair and coat. Zushya clutched a piece of paper in one hand, the ink on it still wet. Malka leaned over until she could see herself reflected in his eyes. She saw such yearning there. Such loneliness. Zushya gathered himself, and reached out with one arm, and pushed himself up off the sofa as if to meet her. Could he see her, suspended between her time and his? Lightly, she brushed his fingertips with her own. His hand fell back onto the blanket, and opened slowly. 'Find her,' he whispered, and was still. Moshe looked at Zushya's face and fell to his knees at his side.

Shira threaded her way between the overturned chairs and tables that now littered the plaza. She picked up a fallen prayer book and smoothed its ruffled pages. Malka remembered the same gesture back in the cave, and felt in her body the same anger. She danced it out, letting it fuel Shira on her way to the Wall. Shira moved towards the place where a large bush trailed its shaggy head down from half-way up the wall. *Roots above, branches below. That must be the one Malka meant,* she thought. Soon the Wall was all she could see. Though it was no longer raining, water from the tree dripped onto her face like tears, and ran down her chin. She wiped it away with the back of one hand, and caressed the cold stone with the other. *Help Malka to find her voice. Heal her. Then, perhaps, she can heal us.*

Malka watched as Devvie limped along the pavement. She was dragging one leg off the kerb, tapping it on the road. Why? Then, through the sole of her sister's shoe, she felt the thrum of the approaching truck. She watched her sister step into the road. The truck was thundering in her ears now. *Take my longing. Make it stop. Take me.* Before Malka could stop her, she stepped out in front of it. There was a terrible thud, and her sister flew through the air.

Moshe was running towards her along the beach, two ice-creams in his hands. He carried on past Malka, and knelt beside a little girl who stood crying at the water's edge. He handed her an ice cream, but it dropped onto the sand between them. The little girl ran into the surf. She did not stop, even when it closed over her head. Malka wanted to call out. But all she could do was watch. She waited for a head cresting a wave, for a ripple, bubbles. Nothing. A gull swept down and pecked greedily at the ice-cream puddling in the sand.

Malka looked down at the old city, melded into a whole from Mahmoud's birdlike vantage. From above, the holy places of each faith punctuated rather than punctured that harmony. Mahmoud sighed. *How can I pray if I don't believe? Whatever I do next, I will be failing someone. Failing people is my specialty.* For a moment, he glimpsed the view of the sea from the tower of his father's mosque. Endlessly rising, falling back, then gathering itself to rise again. Mahmoud straightened. Hafez motioned for him to come back into the tower, and indicated the mike.

'My voice has long since broken,' Mahmoud whispered. He thought of Nur, his sister. *You taught me that failing is better than never trying. Nur, your name means light. Help me to shine.* He took a deep breath, and the familiar words broke from him of their own volition, like trapped birds, raging to be free.

'Allah, Hu Akbar, Allah Hu Akbar...'

Malka saw her sister's body flying through the air above her. A crushing force bore down on her. She felt her knees buckle, and fought to rise. She leapt, reaching out for Estie. She missed and fell, banging her bruised ankle against the bed. She opened her eyes with a cry. Devvie's eyes were also open. She was staring straight up at the ceiling, unblinking. Estie and her mother were both weeping silently, still holding her hands, a broken stone in one, a curled green leaf in the other. The room smelt of sage and cinnamon.

'What happened?'

Devvie's head turned slowly at the sound of her voice, and her eyes widened. Malka slipped her arm gently under her sister's head and kissed her nose, her eyelids, and cheeks. Tears rolled down Devvie's cheeks. Malka wiped them gently with her thumb.

'Look at her,' Estie said. 'It's a miracle. As you danced, the air in the room grew darker, thicker. I know you told us not to let go, but I couldn't breathe. I went to open a window, and a pigeon tried to get in.'

'I'm not sure who was more scared, you or the bird.' Her mother laughed. How much Malka had missed that sound.

'When I screamed, one of the machines started beeping, and Devvie's eyelids flickered open. We pressed the alarm and the nurses came. Her eyes kept flicking over us, round and round the room. They were worried she was having a seizure, and went to get a doctor. But now I think she was just looking for you.'

'She couldn't see you because you fell to the floor when Estie let go of her hand,' her mother said.

Malka stroked Devvie's hair. Her sister's lips were still smeared with cinnamon. She leaned closer.

'I thought I saw the sea,' Devvie whispered. 'A beach with a little girl. I think she drowned.'

Malka touched her finger, still wet with Devvie's tears, to her sister's lips.

'Taste this. I brought it back for you.'

'It tastes of love. The sweetness and the hurt.'

Then Malka realised Devvie had spoken. Estie ran to get the nurse.

'What happened to me?' Devvie's eyes were wide.

'You picked a fight with a truck.'

'Who won?'

Malka looked at her sister's bruised body, and the spirit that blazed from her eyes. She whispered in her sister's ear.

'You did. You, and the love you kept hidden. That's what saved you, in the end. Don't worry, your secret is safe with me, until you feel ready to reveal it.'

Devvie struggled to rise, and then slumped back against her pillow.

'Malka, I can't feel my legs.'

'One thing at a time.'

The doctors and nurses crowded in. Malka slipped out of the room. Her friends leapt up, their faces a symphony of hope.

'Devvie's come round.'

'Oh. My. God.'

Moshe picked her up in the air and swung her around. She could smell the eucalyptus on his coat, and there was still a sprinkling of rain in his hair. A nurse tutted as she walked past. He put her down.

'So do you think your crazy plan worked?' Shira said.

Malka shrugged. 'Estie shouted, and the shock seems to have woken her.'

'How is she doing?' Mahmoud asked.

'It's too early to tell.'

'Moshe, there's one more thing I need from you.'

'Anything.'

'Kiss me,' she said.

'I thought you would never ask.'

Acknowledgements and thanks

T his novel would never have been written if not for the assistance and support of some extraordinary people.

Leone Ross and Martin Priestman shepherded an early version of this novel with energy and passion to enable me to submit it for a PhD in Creative Writing at Roehampton University. Leone went above and beyond, and helped me grow closer to the writer I wanted to be. My colleagues and students at Roehampton have been a huge part of that journey. My dad, David Kahn, pored over the final proof with his characteristic attention to detail. My mum, Leah Kahn, was there to support me when I was ready to give up.

A big shout out to Mike Morris and the team at Wowfest in Liverpool, who ran the Pulp Idol competition. It was a joy taking part in an event that celebrates new voices, and you made all of us finalists feel like winners. Thanks most of all for bringing me to the attention of Pulp Idol judge Kevin Duffy at Bluemoose, who has championed my novel ever since with wit, warmth and conviction. His eagle eyed editor, Lin Webb, has polished my prose until it gleams. Lisa White has helped it emerge blinking into the light with care and attention.

Eli Hillman, for never losing faith that this novel would see the light. Florian Kammuller, for reading innumerable drafts and drinking vast quantities of coffee to fuel our conversations and creativity. Houman Sadri for nudging the novel toward where it wanted to go, and for being a great friend and fellow traveller.

I want to express my thanks to the amazing chef and staff at Joie de Vie, who let me sit for hours fuelled by their fabulous coffee and pastries. You created a warm and welcoming environment that I've been happy to call my second home.

Everyone needs great teachers. Thank you to Ivan Marks, English teacher extraordinaire, for fostering a passionate love of literature. To Rav Aryeh Ben-David, for first introducing me to Rav Kook and the power of Ayeka. Rabbi Jonathan Wittenberg for your example of bridging the personal and the collective with an open heart, and for creating a community at New North London Synagogue that exemplifies the best in Jewish values. Raphael Zarum and all the staff and students at London School of Jewish Studies, who came to my courses on Kabbalah and helped me develop the ideas which inform this novel.

Then there are people who are no longer with us, but whose spirit nurtures me as a person and a writer. My beloved grandfather Yoel Hess, who lived such a long and fulfilled life as a questing, questioning religious feminist, inspired me to go beyond my comfort zone. My father in law Professor Shalom Applebaum, who discussed my drafts and ideas with enthusiasm and interest. I hope this work would make you proud. Dearly missed because taken so tragically young, Matt Eisenfeld, with whom I set up my first writing group, and had so many conversations about matters of the heart and the spirit. You and Sara Duker shared a passion and a profoundly ethical spiritual engagement with the world that continues to inspire me.

To my fabulous sisters, Michal, Daphna, Ayelet and Tamara, for making me a feminist. To my sons Zohar and Shachar, your love and enthusiasm keeps me growing and grounded. One person who I don't have enough words to thank is Noga Applebaum, my partner. You've inspired me to keep trying, to be and become, and supported me as we sought to balance creative practice with life as partners and parents.